ERRANT

A 12:01 Novel

ERRANT

A 12:01 Novel

Montrez

Dedicated to my grandmother,

Minnie B. Adams

CHAPTER 1

*M*y heart plummets to the bottom of my stomach as the elevator rises. I feel like I could fall through the floor at any moment. We're so high up, but we still have further to go. So I distract myself. There are ten people in the elevator, most staring expectantly at the closed doors. My cousin Angie studies her fingernails, humming a pop song. Her brother Jay stands behind her like a grim shadow, brooding about only God knows what. His dark hair falls into his eyes and hides most of his expression, but by the hunch in his shoulders and buried hands in his ripped jeans pockets, I know he's not exactly in an enthused mood. A middle-aged security guard whistles, his pitch clashing with Angie's pretty hum. He smiles at a little girl with honey colored pig tails. His teeth are crooked and yellow. The little girl holds on to her dazed mommy's leg with one hand and tightly to her oversized red balloon in another. I wonder if she's as scared as I am. We've been on this elevator for a minute.

Don't go there, I coach myself.

Three other guys, who look like they've dropped out of high school and committed to a life of crime, are huddled in a corner staring at Angie's butt. I swear they're drooling, but it's to be expected. Angie is beautiful, magnetic, and kind. She's like a princess from some fairy tale with the looks and bank account to match. She's got these luminous hazel eyes with fanning lashes that can wave at you from across the room and perfect blonde hair. She's slender and perfectly proportioned, only a few inches too short to be top model material. How is *any* girl supposed to compete with *her*? I know I can't. Not that I really want to. Sometimes I just get tired of being invisible.

The elevator lurches to a stop. My insides perform nauseating gymnastics. I feel like I'm going to vomit and pass out at the same time. Instead, I stumble out of the stuffy elevator. The early spring air hits me, but instead of feeling refreshed, I feel breathless.

People pass me like I don't exist, but I don't get mad. I'm used to it. For once, I'm happy that no one pays attention to me. I'm sure I'm close to hyperventilating. My cousins are giving me a tour of my new home, a tour that concludes at the top of one of the tallest skyscrapers in the city. Standing on the 86th floor of the Empire State Building, there's a problem. I've come to the realization I'm afraid of heights. Yeah, there's a curved fence several feet tall to keep me from accidentally tripping or being pushed off the building and going splat, but...

Scrambling for the nearest trashcan, I empty the contents of my stomach. The regurgitated strawberry smoothie and the everything bagel don't taste so good now. I wipe my mouth with the sleeve of my sweatshirt.

Everyone else seems so peaceful. Angie stands by the fence looking down at the streets below. She looks lost in thought, so I don't bother her. Jay hangs with the three guys from the elevator. They keep glancing over their shoulders. One guy with a nose and eyebrow ring hands Jay a small Ziploc bag. Jay's slender hands are visible long enough for him to snatch it before the bag and his hands disappear back into his pockets.

Maybe I can just slip away, run for the elevator and wait for my cousins on the ground-level in some small shop until it's time to go home. My legs feel like rubber-bands. Puking can take a lot out of a girl. So can terror.

I stumble towards the elevator as it opens and find myself pushing through a new crowd of people. I'm so close to making it into the haven of those doors. It's just my luck that a blond boy with a handsome face plows into me. He knocks the wind out of me, and my butt meets the concrete. I glance up in time to see the elevator doors closing when another boy bursts through. He wears a black leather jacket and his dark, shoulder-length hair is wild, getting in his eyes as he runs after the blond, nearly stepping on my hand in the process.

Curiosity suppresses the mounting panic my new phobia brings. My feet lead me clumsily back through the crowds. My eyes hunt for the blond boy and the dark-haired boy dressed in leather. I spot them just in time to see the boy in leather grab the blond by the back of his gray, long sleeved shirt. As he yanks, the blond jerks and kicks off the fence before flipping out of his grasp. The boy in leather stumbles back and bumps into the mom and the little girl with the balloon. I run to catch up with them. The tired mom turns to glare behind her but misses the boy in leather. Her gaze finds me instead.

"Excuse me," I murmur as I run past her.

I can't help wondering when the yellow-toothed security guard is going to notice the boys fighting and kick them out. As it stands, no one seems to pay any attention to them, and for the life of me I can't figure out why. It's like I'm watching an action movie. The blond kicks off the fence again and propels himself forward with his fist raised, ready to meet the dark-haired boy's face. He hits the opposite side of the fence instead and he grunts. The boy wearing the leather jacket side-steps and leaps to the other side of the fence. He climbs up the fence with the skills of someone that's been bitten by a radioactive spider. My mouth drops open and I glance at the surrounding, seemingly oblivious crowd.

If no one's paying attention it must be for a good reason, no matter how odd it seems. Maybe this is a really cool scene for a movie? Funny thing is, I don't see any directors, cameras, or famous celebrities. There are no signs. None of the security or staff make any announcements alerting the tourists and guests of anything out of the ordinary.

Stealthy climber, the boy in the leather jacket manages to climb to the top of the curved fence. As I marvel at his knack for good balance, he spreads his arms out. I see his face for the first time underneath all that hair. His eyes narrow and his mouth twists in cruel determination.

"Come on. I'll let you take the first punch!" he shouts.

The blond climbs just as nimbly as his dark-haired rival. I let out a little yelp and a few people stare at me – including the blond. He winks as he runs, just before he grabs the other boy by the leather jacket – or he tries. The dark-haired boy turns just as the blond takes his jacket, somehow undresses out of it, and grabs the blond boy in a headlock. A frustrated grunt escapes his mouth as he hurls both himself and the struggling blond off the fence and over the side of the Empire State Building's 86th floor. I scream.

Running to the fence to search for their falling bodies, I realize that way down below, there are no gathering masses around the sidewalk, no screams, and no sirens. Nothing but a sea of endless, almost mindless crowds, rushing off to continue their day. There's nothing to break the tired monotony of honking traffic agitated by the congestion. There's no sign of mangled, bloodied bodies. Nothing. It's as if I imagined it. But my senses know differently. A black leather jacket hangs off the fence like a flag. It speaks volumes.

It takes two guards to pry my fingers off the fence. They wrestle me to the ground. My cousin finds her way into the mix and gathers me protectively in her arms. I fight her, kicking and screaming. I can't comprehend what she's trying to whisper to me. All I know is what I've seen – two boys falling with purpose from the Empire State Building, a suicide and a murder.

Angie manages to help me to my feet, pushing the guards back, though they loom behind us. Jay comes at me, his face surrounded in smoke.

"What's wrong with you?"

I hear a security guard ask if I'm on drugs. Angie stutters something in my defense and cradles me in her arms again.

"Get her out of here. She's freaking people out!" a security guard snaps at another one.

A set of arms envelope me and I'm vaguely aware of Yellow Teeth. He looks grim. I don't fight him. Instead, my eyes meet the small girl with the pig tails. She hides behind her mom and her mom fishes for her hand to hold her tightly, out of my view.

"Savannah, are you okay? What's the matter?" Angie asks.

As crazy as I know it will sound, I tell her. "They jumped. They *jumped*. You didn't see? *They jumped*. See the leather jacket."

I watch as Angie cranes her head to look back at the scene. Then she turns to look at me with the most compassionate eyes.

"There's nothing there."

I want to tell Angie that she's wrong. I try to crane my head back and point at the jacket, but Yellow Teeth has a strong, commanding grip on me. I know not to make any sudden moves.

"She's nuts," Jay says.

"Miss, either she needs to calm down, or I need to ask you to leave," Yellow Teeth says. The tone in his voice matches the tenderness in Angie's eyes. It seems like a million eyes are watching me. I'm not invisible anymore and for once, I wish I was.

We load up on the elevator. When the doors close, I shut my eyes and hold my breath as we drop steadily to the main floor below. I know what I saw. I swear two boys fell off the 86th floor.

Uncle James and Aunt Vivian are waiting for us in the lobby.

Angie stiffens when she sees them and cuts a look at her brother. "You called them?"

Jay shrugs. "My video of Savannah must've gone viral."

"Your what? Jay, take it down!"

Jay rolls his eyes, but he takes his phone out. "Fine."

Aunt Vivian rushes up to Angie, breaking the two of us apart. Angie is almost identical to her mother, except Aunt Vivian's blonde hair is graying and she has lines in the corners of her eyes. She's a Grade A beauty until she opens her mouth. "We saw the video Jay posted. Why didn't you answer your phone? Are you alright?"

Uncle James is a bony man, dressed in an expensive, but wrinkled suit. His brown hair is tousled, and his hands shake as he steps away from the family to light a cigar. "Scared us half to death," he murmurs.

I struggle to find the right words to say, but Angie speaks first. "What are you even doing here? I thought you were having a lunch date with Judge Mason and his wife."

Aunt Vivian sighs. "None of that matters right now. I told you this would happen. I told you your charity case would backfire, and now we have to do damage control."

Uncle James blows out a puff of smoke in Aunt Vivian's direction. "We cancelled all our plans for the afternoon so your mother could obsess about how you were going to embarrass her. She's been tracking your phones and social media since you left the house this morning."

"Mom, that's insane, even for you," Angie says, "and Savannah's not a charity case. She's family."

Savannah's standing right here. I think to myself, tempted to wave my hand in front of their faces.

Jay winks at me. "Looks like I'm not the biggest screwup in the family now. Thanks for the show."

I can't get the image of the two boys out of my head. I'm still torn over what I saw. It was real. It had to be real. I couldn't have imagined it. Jay shows me his phone as it plays the video he hasn't erased yet. It already has a few hundred views. I try to look past the numbers, the comments people are posting, and Jay's stoned commentary. I snatch the phone from him and rewind it, desperate to prove I didn't panic over nothing. The video is a minute and some odd seconds long, complete with me wailing with snot all on my face while everyone else stands too stunned to speak. There's no sign of the two boys, but why would there be? I didn't start screaming until after they jumped.

Exiting the video, I scroll through his images, hoping to find some hint of what I saw on the observation deck. None of his other pictures have anything to do with the Empire State Building, and the more I look through his phone, the worse the images get. I throw his phone as hard as I can, only remotely satisfied when I hear the fragile screen crack. Jay scrambles to recover it. "What's wrong with you? Now I can't erase it until I get home!"

Angie inserts herself between us, shielding me from her brother's whining. "You should've never recorded it in the first place."

Jay shrugs. "I didn't think anyone would share it. It's not like it's the craziest thing I've posted."

He's right. My hands feel dirty just from touching his phone. Still, nude and drunken selfies don't compare to what I saw on the observation deck.

"That's just it, Jay. You don't think," Aunt Vivian says. She turns her gaze on me.

Wild half-breed. If eyes could talk, that's what Aunt Vivian's would say.

"Get in the car," is what she says instead, "You've caused enough trouble today."

We get in their shiny, black, luxury car that comes from somewhere overseas. Angie sits in the middle in the back seat and Jay sits on her left side. I scramble in the last seat available. Aunt Vivian watches me from the mirror over the dashboard.

"I'll have to call that mother of yours and tell her about your behavior," she says as Uncle James heads into New York traffic. He grips the steering wheel so tight the blue veins in his hand show. As rich as they are, I wonder why they don't have a driver.

"My husband isn't the one talking to you. Look at *me!*"

My attention snaps back to my aunt. Her green eyes narrow. Her red lips twist in an ugly snarl. I take a moment to ponder how Angie turned out so nice with a mother like her.

"Just what I thought. She hasn't got any manners, James. My brother and that woman didn't teach her anything," she continues.

Dad's been dead for a little over a year but hearing someone mention him, especially in Aunt Vivian's tone, can be touchy for me. My self-pity ignites into flames. I bite my lip hard enough to draw blood.

"You can talk about me like I'm not here if you want, but don't talk about my daddy *or* my black momma."

My voice comes out quiet, but I hope she can feel my anger. Maybe if she can, she'll leave me alone for the rest of the ride. Fat chance, I know, but even on the worst of worse days I can hope for one small blessing.

Aunt Vivian chuckles and pats Uncle James's leg.

"She speaks and of course she just *has* to get sassy. Just like I expected. Just like her mother. Angry, black, and bitter. I don't know how my brother got himself mixed up in something like this. I guess that's why he died so prematurely."

I'm vaguely aware of Angie's shocked, "Mom!" but it's my own reaction that's got me worried. My rational mind isn't in control. I pounce forward with hands ready to tear out as much of Aunt Vivian's silky white-blonde hair as I can. The only thing that restrains me is the stupid seatbelt, but I'm too furious to take the time to unhook it.

We're stuck in the middle of non-moving traffic. I know it's a bad place to be, but I don't care. I'm already in for it when I get home. If I'm going to be punished, I might as well be guilty for something good, feel a little bit of satisfaction in my misfortune.

I pull out a fistful of blonde hair. Aunt Vivian shrieks, more out of anger than pain, before she slaps me. My cheek stings. The vision in my left eye blackens before I see the dizzy stars. She calls me a really nasty name and threatens to take me to the police station. Her anger matches mine and I swear if her husband wasn't holding on to her shoulders and trying to calm her, she'd beat the crap out of me. She looks like a demon with all the screaming and flailing. Angie cries like a little girl. Jay laughs like someone told the funniest joke in the world. He laughs so hard he's crying, and Uncle James is so beside himself he stutters, even as his face turns tomato red.

The car ride with hateful Aunt Vivian almost seems like a picnic compared to what I know is going to happen when Mom gets ahold of me. Still, I'd rather fast forward the day to the war waiting for me at home. I unbuckle my seatbelt, open the door, jump out into New York City streets and run.

I hear Angie call out to me. Her mom snaps for her to stay in the car. She doesn't follow me. I don't know how long I run, but it feels good. A few people honk at me. I veer from the streets and bump through the crowds on the sidewalk, finding I'm breathless and shaken. What would Dad think of me now? He's probably rolling over in his grave with disappointment.

I count my sins for the day. I'm on a roll: inciting panic, tearing out my aunt's hair, plaguing New York City traffic, and wrinkling Mom's ironed out plans for our new life. My rebellious high deflates. I'm in a city of strangers filled with all kinds of chaos and I have no idea how to get home. Reaching in my pants pocket I dig out the last of my jumbled-up cash and do the only sensible, sane thing I've probably done all day. I catch a cab.

CHAPTER 2

"**Y**ou want my attention? You've got it," Mom says as soon as my feet cross the threshold of our new apartment.

She stands in the nice cherrywood foyer waiting for me.

"Savannah, aren't you going to say anything? You've got my attention."

Her relaxed, black hair curls at the edges and her makeup is smeared around the eyes. The veins in her forehead are stressed and her vibrant, brown skin takes on an angry hue.

"Savannah."

Mom isn't the type of woman who has to do a lot of talking. She just says my name and my legs start shaking like there's an earthquake under my feet.

"Mom, I didn't mean to cause problems –"

"What happened? Did you get some drugs from Jay?"

"I don't know what Aunt Vivian told you but –"

Mom crosses her arms and her stance says she's ready for war. I try to stay relaxed.

"She told me you made a scene and got kicked out of the observation deck at the Empire State Building. What's wrong with you? We can't afford for you to act this way. And don't roll your eyes at me, girl."

I'm not rolling my eyes. I'm trying not to cry. Mom is all I've got. If she won't believe me or be in my corner, I'm pretty much screwed.

"I'm sorry, Mom. Really. I didn't do it on purpose. I just… there were some boys and–"

Her dark brown eyes lose some of their fire as she interrupts me, "Did they hurt you?"

"No, but I saw something–"

"Something suspicious? You think they were terrorists?"

I shake my head. A sick feeling passes through my stomach like a thick coating of slime.

"I saw two boys jump off the Empire State Building."

There's silence. Then there's more silence. Mom chuckles and then breaks out into a full-fledged laugh. Only, she's not amused.

"Go to your room."

"But mom–"

She turns her back on me. "You heard what I said."

I reach for her and wrap my fingers around her wrist. She turns around with wide eyes. I take advantage of her surprise and start rattling off my account of the story. Miraculously, Mom does the opposite of what I think she'd do. She listens.

I close my eyes and visualize the scene, describing the blond boy to Mom, how he knocked me down and then winked at me when he climbed the fence guarding the perimeter of the observation deck. I tell her about the boy with the wild, dark hair and leather jacket who committed both murder and suicide, hoping the more detail I give the more likely she'll believe me. Lying isn't something I make a habit of doing and there really isn't a point in starting now. I tell her everything, even the bit about Jay's video.

Mom wears this tentative face, a mixture of so many emotions it's hard to tell how she's going to react. I take a deep breath and hold it, waiting for whatever happens next. I expect Mom to be stubborn. She's not going to miss a beat in telling me to go to my room and stay there until it's time to go to school in the morning. She doesn't do that. Instead, she looks at me like she's seeing me for the first time. Before, she only expressed irritation when I got into trouble or she was half-aware when I was quiet and compliant. It's as if I didn't exist to her until this moment, and the way she looks at me now isn't exactly comforting. Her brown eyes are a little larger than usual and her mouth opens and closes like a fish underwater, but she doesn't speak.

A buzzing noise interferes with our standoff. Mom's phone. She jumps back into her regular attitude as if nothing is wrong. She even smiles when she answers the phone, probably because she's talking to Tom Poindexter, her new husband.

"Come straight home. I need you," she tells him, bothering to cast me half a glance.

Mom hangs up the phone and turns her back to me.

"I'll make sure they take the video down, or your aunt will hear from my lawyer. Dinner will be ready in a few. We'll talk then."

Mom casts me a long look and then retreats into the kitchen. She doesn't cook but she's excellent at plating gourmet takeout. Dad was the chef in our house. He could make the simple comfort foods, and when he wanted to show off, he would wow us with his fine dining cuisine. Real gourmet. Not this bland, over-expensive takeout. I have a sudden taste for his french toast with cinnamon sugar and homemade butter. It used to melt in my mouth. My mouth waters and my stomach growls but I'm hyping myself up for something I'll never taste again. No one can make breakfast foods like Dad, especially not his french toast.

I walk to my room, collapse on my bed, and close my eyes, imagining the taste of Dad's french toast. Fluffy, flaky, warm sourdough bread covered in sweet cinnamon sugar, warm and tender. Tears sting my eyes. I slap at the moisture and take a deep breath.

It isn't long before Tom's voice buzzes through the walls of his luxury, New York City apartment. Mom's alto voice is hushed. I hear the clinking of silverware and smell a hint of warmed food. My stomach churns and I forget about french toast. A crisp but courteous knock on my bedroom door startles me.

"Savannah, dinner's ready."

It's Tom. For some reason, it's a relief that he's the one knocking instead of Mom. I open the door. He's a little over six feet with a slight slump in his posture. His sleek glasses are on the tip of his hawkish nose and his green eyes sparkle under the soft light in the compact hall. His slicked-back, graying sandy hair isn't as neat as usual. A few strands obstruct his clear gaze and he pushes them back.

"Feeling okay?"

I shrug, not sure I trust my voice. I know my discussion with Mom isn't over. She just wants Tom to be her support. It's impossible to compare him to Dad, but for a stepfather, he's not so bad. He doesn't ignore me any less or any more than Mom and when we do interact, he's laid back and polite. Tom balances Mom's fiery temper with patience.

He offers me a quick and comforting smile and we both head into the dining area where Mom waits for us. She's seated with her legs crossed at the ankle, twisting her six-carat diamond ring on her finger. I'm distracted by its brightness. Tom must really love her.

I collapse at the square, black cherrywood table and the smell of bland gourmet food infiltrates my nostrils. I stare at my plate to avoid Mom's steely gaze. Medium rare steak and half cooked green beans and carrots stare back at me. The mashed potatoes are lumpy with red skin and green onions, smothered with gravy that looks like thick, grayish snot.

"Savannah, you know your mother has a lot on her plate right now with relocating, starting a new job, and our recent wedding. I understand this all must be hard on you, too. It hasn't been long since your father died."

Tom doesn't ask any questions, but I know he's waiting for a response. I don't know what to say so I shove some vegetables in my mouth and chew slowly, so I don't aggravate my gag reflex. The food's already cold. I raise my eyes enough to take note of Tom's piano slender fingers intertwining with Mom's petite, well-manicured fingers.

"If you're acting out because you don't know how else to deal… we understand."

I peek at Mom's face. She's always been a vocal woman, so it's an adjustment to see Tom acting as her spokesperson. Mom stares at me. Her eyes are glassy and blank, probably because her glass of champagne is mostly empty. She blinks when she notices me assessing her and her mouth tightens. I'm not sure she agrees with everything Tom says, but we're both quiet as he continues.

"And, you know, sometimes adults don't always know how to deal with situations. We don't always have the answers to your issues–"

"Issues?"

I can't help but interrupt. The word "issues" just sounds so judgmental. I put another forkful of cold vegetables in my mouth and chew. My stomach is in knots and my throat feels tight, but I swallow and stab some more vegetables. Tom clears his throat.

"Well, we've all got issues, Savannah. I think your Aunt Vivian is an issue we can all agree on, right?"

He chuckles. Mom refills her glass and takes another drink, probably for the same reason I'm keeping my mouth stuffed. I swallow hard and interrupt Tom again.

"I'm surprised she didn't tell you when she called to complain the first time, but we got into a fight. I pulled out some of her hair."

Tom stutters on like I haven't spoken, "Yes, well, like I said, she's an issue for everyone here. We understand and if you ever want to talk–"

Mom interrupts this time.

"I'm sorry but I don't understand. I really *don't* understand. We raised her better than this and then she goes and makes a spectacle of herself in front of half of New York City?"

She's obviously not talking to me. It's almost like I'm not sitting at the table. I feel like I'm having an out-of-body experience, like Mom and her husband are just two strangers talking about a nameless, faceless child.

"Try not to blow this out of proportion, Teresa. I don't think Savannah did this on purpose. She's just dealing with some things and she needs to know she can come and talk to us. Then she won't have to act out. We can all deal with this together. We can find a professional"

"No, no, no. I don't think my daughter needs a shrink. She may have acted crazy today but she's smart enough to know she's walking on thin ice right now. If she's got issues, she better pray to God and let Him work it out. It's barely been a week since our wedding and we've still got so much to do before we're settled here. We're not even taking a honeymoon, we're so busy."

"I know and I'm sorry, but that's exactly why I think she should see someone. So someone else can guide her through the things we can't. From what you told me about today, I don't even know where to begin to deal with this. Please, just meet me halfway?"

Things they should be saying behind my back are out in the open for me to hear, and it's startling. Mom is letting Tom talk her into sending me to a therapist. I don't have the stomach to force myself to eat anymore. Reality hits home. While they're engrossed in their discussion, I assume they won't notice if I excuse myself from the table.

My chair grinds against the shiny wood floors as I push myself out my seat. I trip over my own shoestrings and escape into my room until their voices are nothing but hushed, conspiring whispers. I focus on the rain tapping at my window. Everything looks gray outside that window, reflecting the kind of depressing weather that makes me want to hibernate in between the softness of my blankets and pillows.

Collapsing on my bed, I think to do just that, at least until my stormy transition to New York living subsides. Unfortunately, I have school tomorrow. The first of many slow, torturous days of monotony and isolation. Nothing new there. I've never had any real friends; just the people who were nice enough to halfway remember my name and wave at me between classes.

Closing my eyes, I hope for refreshing, soundless sleep to meet me. Instead, all I can see are the two boys falling from the Empire State Building. My eyes snap open and drift to rain again, and I count the dreary drops falling against my window. Goosebumps spread like a rash across my arms. I shiver, crawling under the warmth of my blankets. I know what I saw and it's not going to be easy to forget.

CHAPTER 3

When I finally drift off to sleep and wake up at six in the morning, the conflicts of yesterday seem like a dark blur. I'm more concerned with getting up, getting dressed, and making sure Mom remembers to leave me cab fare. It takes me half an hour to get ready. I'm not the type to fuss at my reflection. My wardrobe is pretty much all the same: jeans, t-shirts, hoodies with a sundress or two for special occasions. My hair is an independent force of nature. I know that no matter what I do, it will do its own thing. I do what I can, gelling up the areas around my hair line and secure the frizzy curls in the confines of an orange scrunchie.

By the time I'm out of my room, Mom is just getting out of bed. Tom's in the kitchen drinking the last of his black, sugar-free coffee. He looks up from his cell phone just in time to see me. He wince. I blame the coffee for the sour face. He doesn't even blink when I wave good morning to him as I rush out the door with a steno pad under my arm and a few pencils shoved in my hoodie.

I practically have to ram my body into a cab to get a ride to school. Realizing I forgot to get cash from Mom, I'm grateful when he apologizes for almost hitting me with a free ride to school. When we pull up to St. Renoit Academy, I pause to catch my breath before getting out of the taxi. I wave to the cab driver before he speeds off, focused solely on the hazardous city roads.

"I might need to invest in a bike," I mutter to myself. I don't know how many more times I can be brave enough to thrust myself in front of raging traffic just to make it to school on time.

I don't know what it is about schools that turn me off specifically. It could be the general look of the buildings. They're massive and awkwardly shaped. They look more like prisons or factories than learning institutions. Maybe it's the way people crowd in dingy, cheap, lockered hallways like mindless herds – and I do mean *crowd*. When I'm not in the best of moods, it's irritating to have people step on the backs of my favorite sneakers and to bump into me without even the slightest glance. It can be a bit claustrophobic.

But especially irritating, is the stuff schools expect us to learn. I mean, how is dissecting a frog in biology going to help us in the "real world"? Unless I decide to be a rocket scientist or a banker, what's the point of agonizing through complicated math classes? While history is *slightly* entertaining, how do we know the textbooks we're reading are any better than modern day tabloids? Fake news can't just be a 21st century thing. What's the point? I've been asking myself that since kindergarten. I still don't get it. Here I am, though.

Taking in my new surroundings of what will be the source of my own personal purgatory, I don't notice the difference immediately. The hallways are dim, splashed with yellow light. The lockers are an unattractive bright orange. The floors are scuffed with shoe marks and the air smells like pubescent body odor, sweat, and perfume. I escape into the main office before a herd of cheerleaders can run me down. The office smells a little better, like Lysol and cherry potpourri. Strange but a definite improvement. Breathing in the sterilized, old lady scent, I march up to the front desk. The nameplate reads Ms. Linda Charles.

Linda looks like she's in her late fifties. She sits at her desk tapping her pink, manicured nails against a keyboard, squinting at the computer screen through pink rimmed bifocals. She's concentrating really hard. So hard, that she doesn't even notice I'm standing in front of her.

"Hi. Excuse me," I say, hoping to tear her eyes away from whatever important paperwork she's trying to complete. It takes a lot of effort for her gaze to slide from the screen and glance in my direction. Ms. Charles jumps. Her bifocals slide down her nose and her keyboard slams against the table as her fingers break pace.

"Didn't see you there. You shouldn't sneak up on people like that," she says.

I bite back a sarcastic comment. I don't want to make enemies on my first day. Not even with the secretary. Not that I usually make any kind of impression, at all.

"Sorry," I murmur. "But I'm new here. Savannah Scarlett?"

Ms. Charles frowns and one of her magnified eyes twitch. She looks like an unnerved owl tapping her mop of gray hair piled on top of her head. When I say my name, her gaze snaps from the computer screen. She squints in my direction. Her frown never quite turns right side up. She watches me as she blindly gathers my papers. The phone rings. She jumps again and papers go flying. I cross over to her side of the desk to help her pick them up. She's kind of plump so it takes effort for her to bend over in her chair. I have half the stack of papers in my hand before I happen to glance up at her computer screen. She's been playing solitaire.

I find my class schedule and other documents just as the bell rings. Ms. Charles doesn't jump this time. She gives me a wary glance and turns her attention towards the persistent phone. Her face is strained with irritation, but her tone is sweet and professional. Sliding the phone to her neck and covering the receiver she tells me, "I think you'd better stop staring at me and get to class. That was the late bell."

Biting my lip, I march out of the office and back into an empty hall filled with teenage funk. Wrinkling my nose, I stare at my schedule and wander around for five minutes before I find my first class – study hall.

The previous day seems like a blur as I fall into old habits. I sleep away my forty-five minutes of study hall. The bell startles me out of my sleepy stupor, preparing me to transition to the next dull period. History. Surprisingly, some of the thirty pairs of eyes watch me with mild interest as I enter the room. I give them a forced smile, but no one smiles back. They turn to each other and whisper or just stare as I take the vacant seat in the back by the window.

One thing about being in the back of a class is that no one pays attention. The guy sitting next to me smells like corn chips. His carrot colored hair looks like it hasn't been combed in days. He's totally engrossed in some game on his phone. He even has the nerve to play with the volume on. Another guy sits in front of me with his laptop and he's updating his social media. I peer over his shoulder to squint at what he's typing. I must be breathing on the back of his neck because he jerks his head back to glance at me. Then he slides his computer at an angle so I can't see the screen.

A girl sitting diagonally from me is texting furiously on her phone. She glances at me several times before asking me, "Are you related to Angie?"

If I wasn't sitting in the back of the classroom, I'd look behind me to see who she was talking to. But there's no one behind me and her blue eyes meet my gaze steadily. I nod. The girl nods back and starts texting again. I'm forgotten. I try my hardest to listen to the class discussion.

My history teacher is a stiff man in his late thirties. He wears his navy-blue, button-up shirt tucked in his khaki trousers. He has a southern twang that might prove interesting if it wasn't for the fact that he's lecturing from his notes word for word with a stutter. No wonder half the class is into their electronics. The other half of the class is wilting. I feel myself slipping back into sleep mode. Unfortunately, my phone's dead and I forgot my charger at home. So, I open my steno pad and doodle random things like hearts, stars, and stick figures dressed in boxed clothing.

The gamer beside me hisses to get my attention. "I heard you talking to Amy. You're Angie's cousin? *For real?*"

I nod again and Carrot Hair stares at me like I'm growing an extra head out the side of my neck. I still feel him staring as I shift my attention back to my pointless drawings. Carrot Hair isn't the only one staring though. Laptop Guy in front of me keeps glancing over his shoulder. At first, I assume it's because he doesn't want me to see what he's doing, but then I'm not so sure. I'm getting looks from all over the room. At least that's what it feels like. I'm beginning to wonder if maybe I *am* growing an extra head. Even my history teacher casts an uncomfortable glance in my direction.

As soon as the bell rings, I dash out the classroom and into the nearest bathroom. Is my hair drastically out of place? Do I have something stuck in my teeth? I stare in the mirror and see the same tall, gangly girl with the cacophony of auburn that gets bushy and frizzy at the slightest hint of moisture in the air. I see the pale-honey skin plagued by a confetti of freckles. The brown eyes that look ordinary at best with clumped, semi-long lashes. The hawkish nose that would look better on a boy's face and the full lips. But there is nothing stuck between my mostly white teeth. No boogers hanging out of my nose, and while my eyes do look bruised with fatigue, there isn't anything that would give anyone reason to stare. At least, nothing that I can change.

Three girls enter the bathroom giggling. Their laughter stops when they see me. I break away from the mirror, looking back at them.

"You're Angie's cousin?" the blonde girl asks.

I nod just like all the other times. The blonde girl gives her two friends a smug glance that says, "I told you so." But the tall brunette between her and a dark-haired black girl doesn't seem convinced. She gives me that "she's got two heads" stare while the other girl blurts, "You don't look a thing like her."

That's all she says, but I know what she's probably thinking. Angie and me are two different shades from two different spectrums of life. Angie is blonde and beautiful without any effort. I'm, well…me.

"I'm Sara," the blonde girl says. She introduces the brunette as Jessica and the black girl as Jeanette. I start to introduce myself, wondering, hoping I might finally make some friends. The brunette interrupts my hopes with a cold dash of reality.

"Is it true you freaked out at the Empire State Building?"

All the heat in my face drains and I feel sick. As impossible as it seems, I'd almost forgotten about yesterday. With the pressure of starting out at a new school, a private school at that, yesterday seems like a bad dream. Not anymore, thanks to Jessica. I stand under their hungry, steely gazes, completely speechless. What am I supposed to say to that? The truth? That I was the only person who saw two boys fall off the Empire State Building? If the scene wasn't replaying in my own head, I would think I was crazy, too. The protective fence that surrounded the famous building should have made it impossible for anyone to do what I saw those boys do. But it hadn't.

"I told you she was freakin' psycho," Sara says under her breath as they primp in front of the mirror.

"And she's Angie's cousin. I had to see it to believe it," Jessica murmurs back.

"All you white girls are crazy to me," Jeanette retorts, though I'm not white. She doesn't even attempt to whisper. Maybe she knows there's no point. Everything they say echoes off the bathroom walls.

"She's a nervous wreck. Look at her –"

I'm used to people pretending like I don't exist, but I'm not used to them talking about me. I stumble out the bathroom, unable to listen anymore. I manage a drink of water from the water fountain, busying myself with the class schedule. The words are a confusing mix of letters and numbers. I can't focus.

I am aware of the constant stares, the constant whispers and now I know what all the talk is about. They know. Everyone knows about my freak incident at the Empire State Building. I stumble blindly down the hall, trying not to let the liquid forming in my eyes roll down my cheeks. I run right into Angie. She lets out a small gasp as some papers slip from her hands. Her hazel eyes widen when she sees me, and her cheeks redden. I stoop down to help her pick up the papers more on instinct than courtesy. My lip quivers when I see what she dropped. It's a picture of my tear-stained face. My hair is wild, and my clothes are rumpled. Angie's in the background behind me, her face contorted in surprise. It's a still shot from Jay's video, only it's been cropped and edited, with a caption.

Angie snatches the paper away before I can read it. "Savannah, I was just – I didn't want anyone to see."

I don't wait around to hear her explain. Instead, I run back to the bathroom and hide in the biggest stall. Within a few minutes the bell rings. Geometry isn't high on my priority list right now. Aside from the very recent and painful humiliation, I just don't see the point of discussing shapes I learned about in elementary school.

Right now, I just want to fast-forward my life until everyone forgets about the Empire State Building situation. I've got to be real with myself. I can't hide in the bathroom forever. Not even all day. I've got to come out some time and when I do, I have to face the facts. I'm not invisible anymore. It's what I've always wanted but, as the old saying goes, "Be careful what you wish for."

CHAPTER 4

I spend almost an hour hovering by the stall door. I'm too afraid to sit on the toilet seat or on the floor. I may be a social reject, but public restrooms are a far cry from sanitary. So, I pace the small space pausing only as a group of girls enter the restroom. They're louder than the last trio and even gigglier. When their laughter quiets, I hear an unfamiliar voice speak, "So, did you see Angie's cousin?"

"Anna something," another girl mumbles like she's half interested.

"Savannah," another girl interjects.

I'm shocked they know my name, but I try not to get too excited. They're probably looking at the picture from Jay's video.

"Yeah, anyway," the first girl continues, "you know, this is just Tommy's way of getting back at Angie for turning him down at homecoming. Angie's brother Jay recorded Savannah freaking out at the Empire State Building. He posted it online and Tommy made a meme out of it to embarrass Angie. Did you see her snatch those copies off the lockers? I swear her face was as red as my lipstick."

One of the girl's snicker, but Red Lipstick isn't done talking, and shamefully, I'm hanging on to every word she says. Bathroom gossip gives outsiders like me the inside story.

"I swear, even when it's not about her, it's about her. I don't get what the big deal is. I mean, she's pretty but there are a lot of pretty girls here," Red Lipstick whines.

"She's got money," one of Red Lipstick's friends suggests.

"So?"

"And she's *nice*," her other friend adds.

Unlike you. I hear what's not being said.

"Being nice never gets anyone anywhere except ran over!" Red Lipstick snaps, "Serves her right. Heard Tommy posted it online, too. Her expression in that meme. She wasn't so picture perfect then."

Her comment is met with silence. I wonder if it's because her friend struck a nerve. One girl laughs. It sounds strangled. I hear the door whine and the loud, dysfunctional girls stomp out of the room like horses in heels. I count to fifteen before I step out of the stall. I'm alone and now it's quiet enough for me to think about what I've learned.

My humiliation isn't even about me. My picture was only circulated because Angie was in the background. The knowledge doesn't make me feel any better. It doesn't make me feel any worse either. At least Angie tried to trash the copies, even though the online posts are a lost cause. Whether it was for selfish reasons or not, I'm grateful. She did what she could. My chest loosens up a little and I can breathe a little easier. This is the second time my cousin has tried to help me even though the rest of her family shuns me and Mom.

I emerge from the bathroom. My goal is to survive the rest of the day and live to start tomorrow, fresh and optimistic. If I can go from being invisible to scandalous, can't I be liked, too? People still stare but now they're talking about Angie and how

Tommy, Laptop Guy from history class, is trying to make her life miserable. Angie's a saint though. She walks around like nothing's happening. She smiles and greets everyone in between classes and seems pleasantly preoccupied the rest of the time. She's into everything: student council, the school newspaper, theatre, honor's society… the list probably goes on forever. There's no escaping or outdoing her.

Maybe I can learn from her. She doesn't wear hoodies and ripped jeans. She keeps her hair neat but not boring. Today it's styled in waves. It flows down around her shoulders and illuminates her face like a halo. She smiles a lot and makes sure to speak to everyone. She's relaxed and comfortable in her own skin. I think that's what makes her the most beautiful.

After a few more trying hours, the last bell sounds. Remembering I have no cash for a taxi, I call Mom. She doesn't answer.

Angie sees me, and after a long, hesitant pause she offers me a small but warm smile. "I'm so sorry about today, but you don't have to worry about Tommy and those images. My mom threatened to sue if they weren't removed. Let me know if anyone gives you a hard time. We'll take care of them."

I shrug and watch as she effortlessly hails a cab. The first one we see stops in front of the school. Angie leans forward to slide the taxi driver some cash and looks at me expectantly. I get in.

"New York can be rough, but you'll get used to it," she tells me.

If that's supposed to be comforting, I'm not convinced. New York doesn't seem to be rough for her. I leave the door open for Angie, but she shakes her head.

"I'm tutoring French today. I'll see you tomorrow, though."

Is there anything she doesn't do?

"Thank you," I manage to stutter. She waves, and the taxi driver takes off almost before I can close my door. I'm home in barely twenty minutes. The apartment is empty. I'm all by myself.

I pass the kitchen on the way to my room. There's a note and a folded stack of money. It's my taxi fare for the week. Go figure. Mom remembered. I take the money and toss it on my nightstand. Collapsing on my bed, I let another day fade away and wake up in the morning with resolve.

No, I haven't done my homework. I haven't looked over any notes for pop quizzes. I've overslept. I barely have forty minutes to get dressed if I'm going to make it to school on time. Today will be different than yesterday or the day before. I've finally gotten people to notice me.

I take a nice, long hot shower and tame my wet, natural curly hair with leave-in conditioner, gel, and oil. The strands hang loose in bouncy tendrils around my face. I pull out my best pair of jeans from my closet and the nicest sweater I can find that fits, not wanting to wear anything baggy. I ignore the temptation to reach for a hoodie. It's not a big change on the outside but I'm feeling optimistic.

I race out of the apartment and run down a taxi. By the time I make it to school, I'm an hour late. The halls are quiet. Everyone's in second period. I slip into the main office and sign my name on the late roster. Ms. James must be playing solitaire again. She doesn't notice me. Taking a deep breath of the potpourri and Lysol scented air I head into the halls again and jog to my second period class.

I remember to hold my head up and to smile. The only response I get is a frown from my history teacher as he stutters over some Greek philosopher's name. Everyone else in class has their eyes closed or their heads buried in their arms on their desks. Even the back-row media hub looks fatigued. Carrot Hair has a hat on, covering a large portion of his face. He's slumped in his chair with his legs stretched out and he's snoring softly. Laptop Guy –Tommy – has his computer closed today. He's drooling on it. Stifling back a nervous giggle, I take my seat. Amy, the girl with the phone, glances back at me, rolls her eyes, and yawns.

"Irene, I need some gum," she whispers to a brunette with pigtails who's popping balloon sized bubbles with her gum. She slides Amy a few pieces and soon they're both blowing bubbles.

"Can I have a piece?" I dare to ask. Neither girl responds so I lean forward.

"Hey, Irene, could I have a piece of gum, too?"

I stutter over a few of my words, feeling out of my element. Irene blows another big bubble and it busts, covering the tip of her nose. She picks it off with her manicured nails.

"Who's she?" Irene asks Amy.

They stare at me.

"Savannah," I tell them, but they're already huddled together.

"Why's she talking to you?" Amy whispers, not very quietly.

"Savannah Scarlett," I try again, "I'm Angie's cousin."

It's only when I add the last part that a spark of recognition crosses their faces. It's not the look or the reaction that I've been hoping for. Their eyes get large. They look at one another and fidget as they look back at me. Irene passes Amy a piece of gum. Amy tosses it at me like I'm a zoo animal that's about to bite her. So much for a conversation starter. I pop the gum in my mouth and try to chew away my disappointment as both girls turn stiffly in their seats.

I don't get much more reaction than that. After class a wrestler shoves a band member's head into a locker and uses the opening of his trombone for a spit can. Girls bat their eyelashes at all the cute guys and giggle over gossip. Some students cram for tests and a perky red head journalist harasses students and teachers for quotes for an article on pollution contribution in New York City schools. She doesn't ask me for my opinion. She bumps right by me, too busy tapping notes into her phone to say excuse me. A boy with bifocals stops her and nods in my direction. I'm not good at reading lips but I can guess what he's saying.

There's that psycho chick, Angie's cousin.

The perky journalist pauses and turns her head half an inch to look at me out the corner of her eyes. Then she shakes her head at the boy and speed walks down the hall. Not even a journalist wants to bother with me. It's hopeless. Still, I decide to go the opposite direction just in case Perky changes her mind.

The most unsanitary place in existence is my sanctuary. Locking myself away in the biggest bathroom stall furthest from the exit, I take a deep breath. I almost gag. Whoever was in here before me didn't enjoy their breakfast. It reeks. I'm too scared to make sure they flushed the toilet. Instead, I lean my back against the stall door and close my eyes, trying to forget where I am. It's a little rough considering all the noisy traffic – girls clonking their heels against the tiles, flushing the toilets, and barely washing their hands. One girl even tries to unlock my stall. For a minute I wonder if she'll look underneath and spot me. I stand against the farthest side of the stall, hoping she can't see my big clumsy feet. Luckily, she doesn't, but I see her shoes – hot pink, ballerina style slippers. Interesting. What's not interesting are the sound effects she makes when she enters the stall adjacent to mine or the smells that drift my way.

"That's it. I'm out of here," I grumble. I can't do this. Maybe I should just fake being sick and go home. I could probably just walk out, and no one would notice.

"Not a bad idea," I mutter to myself. Ms. James is probably still playing games on her work computer. The teachers are all in their classes droning on about superficial lessons that won't really matter when we graduate. Half of us will have menial, miserable jobs even if we go to college, and we'll be working for our spoiled classmates with trust funds. School is pointless. I'm tired of being ignored, rejected, and bored out of my mind. Maybe I'm throwing a fit, but I'm done with school and I'm not coming back.

I walk into the halls and out the main entrance without a hint of problem. I don't bother to catch a taxi. I just start walking, not really knowing where I'm going. Somehow, after a few hours of walking around, studying the harried crowds, the scores of eateries and glitzy businesses, I manage to find my way back to the apartment.

As usual, I'm home alone. So, I march to my room and fall into bed. I'm flunking my junior year of high school, and my social life is dead and buried with no hope of resuscitation.

Things just can't get any worse. At least, that's what I think as I drift off into a dark sleep.

CHAPTER 5

My consciousness stirs when the sound of a long, distinctly loud honk fills my ears. My eyes open in time for me to be blinded by bright headlights. A taxi is only a breath away from hitting me. I stumble backward.

I evade one car only to hit another. Thankfully, this car is parked. I feel my way around the vehicle until I'm out of the streets and standing on the sidewalk. Unfortunately, I haven't made it out of the danger zone. My feet are bare. I don't pay much attention to the coolness of the pavement or the rough texture of it until the weight of my feet press against shards of broken glass. The glass dig into my feet, breaking through skin. I choke on a scream. Hobbling on the sides of my feet, I look for the nearest bench. People walk by with puzzled glares. A few women clutch their purses or their companions a little closer.

I pass a reflective window just before I make it to the bench, and I'm startled. My hair is a tumbleweed. I'm wearing the same clothes I must have fallen asleep in only my sweater is wrinkled and my best pair of jeans has more holes than I can recall. My fashion speaks post-apocalyptic victim.

"This can't be happening," I say to myself. The last thing I remember is falling asleep in my room. I shouldn't be here right now, in the middle of the city, after dark with tattered clothes and wild hair. It doesn't make sense. I must be dreaming.

Collapsing onto the rusted, splinter-hazard of a bench, I use my barely-there fingernails to pull out the obvious pieces of glass from my feet. It's a shame I can't dream up tweezers, painkillers, or a hospital. This dream feels so real, too real, but it's impossible. There's no way I'd be wandering the streets of New York with my eyes closed, especially in the middle of the night. But here I am, worse than pinched and still picking glass shards from a broken beer bottle out of my feet. If this wasn't a dream, I'd be scared of getting some type of infection.

"This is just a dream, Savannah," I mutter.

I know I look crazy. Especially since I'm talking to myself. It's all I can do to keep from passing out. I have no idea how I'm going to get home. Apparently, I'm not very imaginative in my dreams. Instead of my feet healing miraculously, or flying away, I sit on the rough bench like I've got nothing better to do but bleed all over the concrete.

"Lost, little girl?"

A shady looking man with a well-groomed cream suit and lime green unbuttoned dress shirt saunters up to me. He smells like cigarette smoke. It makes me sneeze. I swear I'm allergic to carcinogens. I look up at him through watery eyes, trying to blink away the tears so I don't look completely vulnerable.

"I'll take good care of you," he promises. His teeth are yellow and nasty. The teeth that don't look bad are the teeth that are missing. He's an inch too close to me, way past invading my personal space. His breath smells like a public restroom. Out of everyone walking down the diverse sidewalks of New York City why does he have to be the one to speak to me?

"No thanks," I manage to say, mustering all my strength to stand up on the sides of my feet. I waddle a few steps away from the man, but I hear his slick dress shoes clapping against the concrete.

"Come on, now. I'm not gonna hurt you."

Riiiiight is what I want to say. Instead, I take a deep breath and prepare to run, knowing it will be painful. Slickster is quick though. I barely shift my stance and he's got the back of my shirt, tugging me toward him with a rough jerk. I don't have time to scream. He's lifted me off my feet, hands around my waist, tucking me into the shadows of an alleyway. I kick my feet and throw all my weight back against him. Slickster doesn't expect me to do that and he falls backward. We both crash to the pavement. My head swims, but I take the opportunity to elbow him in the gut with as much energy as I can. He must be a little drunk or high because he jerks back and cracks his head on the pavement with a grunt and spouts off some nasty insults. Rolling over and up on my feet, I push myself to run as fast and as far as I can. I hear him call out to me, obscene things at first, but then he's yelling and screaming. I ignore the pain in my feet. I keep running and don't look back.

"This is a dream," I chant over and over to myself. My lungs burn. My feet feel like they're going to fall off, but my body is high with adrenaline. I'm still running when my sight goes dim, like a drawn curtain. My senses dampen. Enough fighting. I welcome the darkness.

✳✳✳

Pain rouses me out of a stiff, nearly comatose state. At first, I think it's because I slept too hard. I struggle to sit up, stifling a yawn as early morning light invades my small room. I squint and then give in to the tempting sheets and soft pillows. Every cell in my body screams and all I want to do is curl back into the folds of my blankets and sleep the day away.

Closing my eyes, I snuggle back into the folds of my bed. My body yells at me but I figure I can ignore it better if I'm asleep. Nothing ever goes my way, though. There's a quick, impatient knock on the door and then Mom strolls in. She's filled with nervous, excited energy. The mood looks ridiculous on her. She's always been such a stern, strong woman but right now she looks like a giddy high school girl.

"Out of bed, sweetheart. We've got a busy day. We've got to get ready for our trip."

I'm vaguely aware of some uppity shindig, something about a Poindexter family reunion at Martha's Vineyard.

"We've got our hair and nail appointment at noon and…"

Her voice trails off when she finally notices I'm not responding. I'm buried under my blankets, as if I could hide from her. She yanks my covers off, and I curl up in a ball, which really hurts. I feel like I've run a marathon, like my bones will break if I move, but Mom insists.

She stares at me like I'm a zombie waking up from the dead.

"You could really use that hair appointment and – *Savannah*, what happened to your feet?"

Though I'm not fully awake, my heart pounds against the walls of my tired chest. I fight to sit up and stare at my feet. My feet look like someone tried to dice them up. They are filthy, covered in dirt, and dried blood. Where they aren't completely black, there are pockets of red angry lines and scratches. I'm wearing the same jeans I went to school in the other day and they aren't in the best shape. My sweater is torn and covered in dirt. My arms are bruised. I look up at Mom. Her eyes are shining with fury, all butterflies and happiness gone.

"What is wrong with you? What is this?"

My head hurts trying to think up an explanation. I remember dreaming about stepping into broken glass, scuffling with a man in an alley, and running like a track star on broken feet. It had been a dream, but here I was with the scars to prove otherwise. I'm speechless and maybe in shock because all the pain I'm feeling makes sense now.

My head feels like a balloon filled with helium. I'm vaguely aware of Mom screaming for Tom. He comes running like we're in a natural disaster. I've never seen a man so suave look so clumsy. He takes one look at my feet and scoops me up in his arms. Next thing I know I'm in the hospital. They clean my feet and check for infection. Surprisingly, things look good, as good as they can look with my feet wrapped in gauze.

Mom is upset. Not because my feet are tender and swollen but because we've missed our appointments and our flight.

"Did she do this? Did she cut herself? Did she do this on *purpose*?" Mom directs her demands at the doctor.

Tom is red, probably embarrassed. The doctor looks ruffled, tired, and embarrassed for Tom.

"Well, I … it looks like glass, ma'am. Like maybe she was walking bare foot and–"

"I guess I did," I interject, and all eyes are on me like I've just stepped into the room. "I thought I was dreaming. Didn't think it was real."

Mom and Tom exchange looks with each other and then with the doctor. They all stare at me again.

"Well, sleepwalking isn't uncommon when an individual is stressed. It might explain some things here," the doctor speaks slowly. He glances at Mom, "I've seen worse than this, and even more unbelievable cases."

The red drains from Tom's face. He looks at Mom who has lost her hard, glaring edge. Her jaw is still tight, like she's biting the inner walls of her mouth.

"Sleepwalking?"

The doctor shrugs. "I'm not an expert in that area but it is a likely possibility. My suggestion is for this young lady to relax a bit and if problems persist to see a sleep specialist."

Or a shrink.

No one says the words, but I can practically read Tom's expression. I wonder if he regrets marrying Mom. Probably not. I'm not that significant in their relationship. They take one look at each other and the whole world disappears. She used to look at Dad that way. I wonder if I'll ever find someone like that, who I can share looks with, who can distract me from everything else. Probably not. I'll most likely end up living like a hermit with a dozen cats or a house full of birds.

A chuckle escapes my mouth and I startle everyone, including myself. Mom's nostrils flare.

"This isn't funny, Savannah. I don't know what you're trying to accomplish with these antics, but I'm not happy."

Tom pats her arm to pacify her. It works because she rolls her eyes at me and lays her head on his chest. He puts his arm around her and kisses the top of her head. I wonder if someone will ever hold me like that. I wish Mom would give me a hug and tell me things will be okay, even if they are far from it. How much do I have to crack before she realizes I'm about to break?

We leave the hospital and things are quiet. That's one perk to having Tom around. He keeps Mom from erupting. Dad always had the opposite effect. He could bring out the passion in her, let her self-defuse and then make her forget she was mad in the first place with a joke and a kiss.

Mom and her new husband talk in hushed voices the way adults do when they don't want little kids to overhear their discussion. I can hear all the key words and even though I don't want to, I piece the conversation together. Tom is talking Mom into sending me to a shrink. At this point I'm not mad. I'm relieved. I might have somebody to talk to that will actually listen. It's a sad state but it's reality. A shrink might be my only friend. I chuckle to myself again. Mom cuts me another glance, and she nods at Tom. Silence fills our tiny space. Tom looks satisfied. Mom looks more relaxed.

We stop at a mom and pop diner for breakfast. As much as I want some good french toast, I can't bring myself to order it. My stomach's a mess again and my feet are in pain. I order some cheese eggs, toast with grape jelly, and root beer to wash it all down. As usual, I'm forgotten as they try to decide the best way to tell his family we won't make it to his family reunion. Tom winks at me so fast that I think I'm seeing things. He smirks before distracting Mom with alternate plans for a day at the spa. I almost smile. Tom is a good guy. He doesn't try too hard, but he does try.

CHAPTER 6

When we get home, Mom retreats to her room prepping for an afternoon at the spa. I grab a bottle of water to help me swallow my horse pills the doctor prescribed. Then I wander to my room and crawl into bed. My feet are numb and my body is sluggish, but my mind rebels. I can't sleep. My thoughts wander to Tom. He hasn't been my stepdad long, but we've already had the daddy-daughter talk. He swears he isn't going to try to replace or compete with Dad. He wants to build a relationship of our own.

"I understand your dad was a phenomenal cook. I cater in. If I didn't there'd be fires in the kitchen," Tom's said. "He was a poet. Poetry is foreign language to me, but I try to quote a verse here and there to impress your mother. I'm not as eloquent as your dad was or as smart, but I'm honest and hopefully a little fun?"

"Funny," was my response and I offered him a smile even though my heart was breaking. He ruffled my hair and gave me a pat on the back.

I know his conversation was supposed to be reassuring but it made me realize the truth: Dad is really gone. This isn't a bad dream I'll wake up from. This isn't some cruel joke. It's real. It's life. I've lost my dad. From now on, everyone who talks about him will use past tense. The only time I'll see his face is in old photographs. I probably won't remember the sound of his voice in a few years, maybe even a few months and that makes me more than sad.

Mom is replacing Dad and moving on, but I don't want to. I can't forget him. I won't. Reaching in the nightstand drawer beside my bed, I take out a photo album filled with old pictures. There are several collages of Dad, Mom, and me throughout the years. I flip past my embarrassing baby photos. I glance at some of Mom's naturally stunning poses, but I linger on the pictures of Dad, pictures I haven't looked at since we've moved to New York.

There are photos of him at all the holidays, photos of him writing poetry in his journals or reading in his favorite lounge chair, slumped to the side with his reading glasses on the edge of his aquiline nose. My favorite picture is one of us together. I'm six years old with two missing front teeth. My hair is in messy, unraveled braids and I'm wearing a Big Bird pajama set. Dad is dressed in a suit with an undone tie and wrinkled shirt. His rakish auburn hair covers his smart eyes and he's reading a Dr. Seuss book like it's some academic dissertation. I'm leaning over his shoulder, hugging him tight– nearly strangling him as he reads, and I've got the most focused look on my face. Dad is smiling; crow's feet wrinkle the corner of his eyes. His cheeks are flushed, either from being camera shy or from lack of oxygen in my tight grasp. Tears blur the clarity of the photograph.

My mind finally catches up with my body as the prescription floods through my system. Dad's face and the pitter patter of rain crashing against my window are the last things I remember before I find myself somewhere else entirely.

One moment there is complete darkness. The next thing I know I'm standing on a rooftop of some random building. Scratch that. I'm on the edge of a roof top, one step away from falling a few stories and busting my body on the concrete below. Fear makes me lose my balance and I slip. My blood feels like ice, but a rush of adrenaline causes my eyes to widen and my mind to open. My reflexes kick in and instead of falling forward, I fall backwards and land on my butt with my feet dangling near the edge. I scoot backward on my bottom until I'm far from the edge, far enough to ponder where I am.

I take my surroundings in. As usual, it's cool and wet. The sun is gone leaving a faint impression of the moon shining behind thick, rain clouds. My jeans and sports hoodie keep me a little warm but my poor feet…

I'm wearing some gauze and an overstretched pair of thick socks. No shoes. The thick wrapping that encases my feet is soaked. It's only a matter of time before my feet get wet. I don't even want to think about what the rain and humidity will do to my hair. I venture close to the edge of the roof, this time, fully awake. I scan the building trying to ignore the fear that beats within the walls of my chest. How did I get up here? Where is here?

"Maybe you're dreaming again, Savannah," I tell myself.

As soon as I say the words, that cold fear invades my bloodstream again. The last time I thought I was dreaming, it felt real the way it does now. It had all been real. I have pain in my feet to prove it.

I'm on a roof top with no knowledge of how I got here or how to get down. With my arms wrapped around myself, I stare off at the surrounding rooftops. Though the streets below are bright with city lights, the heights are cold, damp, and dark. Shadows span across the empty heights and they seem to stretch toward me. A shiver runs through my body and goosebumps form on the skin of my arms underneath my hoodie.

"Please be dreaming," I plead to myself, pinching my arms. It stings enough to scare me.

I don't have my phone on me and even if I did, I wouldn't call and ask for help. Half the city already thinks I'm crazy. I scan the area again. My eyes adjust better to the darkness and I see an open dumpster a short distance down from the base of the building. It's open and overflowing with a wealth of trash. As much as the idea stinks, I realize it's my only option. I've got to jump. Of all the times I wish I could black out and be somewhere else…

I walk up to the edge of the building slowly. The dumpster is far down. Even if I jump and land on something soft or smooth, I might still break some bones.

"I can't afford anymore scars," I mutter to myself. My feet are throbbing again. There's no way I can play Spider-Man and climb down the side of the building. There's a weathered fire escape ladder a few feet down, a steep drop from the roof. It's closer to the dumpster below, but beyond the top landing of the escape, the stairs appear rusted and broken. There are too many feet between the end of the broken fire escape ladder and the dumpster for things not to go badly, but it's my only chance at getting down.

"It doesn't matter, Savannah. Do what you have to do."

Mentally crossing my fingers, I take a deep breath and lock in my trajectory. I let go of everything. Closing my eyes, I jump.

My breath hitches. My eyes snap open on impact. The rusted stairs collapse underneath me, buckling under my weight. I'm too shocked to scream as the stairs snap and I fall. My left arm smacks the side of the dumpster with a rumble and a crunch before I land on my back against, broken down cardboard boxes, an array of rotten food, and stairwell debris. What's left of the fire escape falls in hazardous heaps around me. I try to lift my arms to shield my face from impact, but my left arm feels heavy and numb. Something squirms and squeaks in the trash around me. Red eyes confirm I'm not the only one in the bin of trash. Forgetting my newest injury, I scramble to the surface and lift myself over the edge. Lowering my body down to the concrete ground I put all the pressure on my good arm flipping out of the dumpster and hobbling down the alleyway.

My eyes look up to the rooftop I just jumped from and the remains of the wrecked fire escape. Shaking off remnants of trash, my hand goes to my ruined hair. My curls are tangled and dirty. My jeans are destroyed, split halfway up to my thighs. Debris from the crash must have ripped a hole through the fabric. Scrapes and scratches litter the exposed surface of my skin, but somehow, I'm alive. I look up at the rooftop again and my mouth goes dry. There's something on the rooftop. Someone. A shadow. It crouches down and leans forward on the ledge of the building and I feel it– whoever it is, staring down at me.

"There's no one up there," I mutter to myself.

Closing my eyes, I count to five. When I look again, no one's there. Cradling my throbbing arm, I force myself to walk on my bad feet into the main street sidewalk as fast as I can.

Searching for street signs, I try to make sense of where I am and how to get home.

I don't get very far. A subtle shift in the air gives the impression of someone brushing past me.

"Wouldn't go that way," comes a voice from behind me, close enough to whisper.

I look behind me. The alleyway's clear. There's no sign of anyone with me in the alley.

"Great. Now I'm hearing voices," I mutter to myself, rubbing my temples as I stumble forward.

"I said, no!"

Fingers dig into the skin of my wrist of my bad arm, yanking me backward. I stumble and fall backward on my butt, lightheaded with pain. My eyes roam the dark alley. Nothing!

"Hello?"

I know I'm not crazy. Someone's messing with me, and I've got the irritated, possibly broken arm to prove it. Cradling my arm and rubbing at my wrist, I struggle to stand, just as a van slides up the street, blocking my exit from the alleyway. The door slides open, but I don't wait to see who's getting out. I turn the opposite direction and force myself to run out the other end of the alleyway. Unfortunately, it's another side street.

"She can't get far. Not in her condition," I hear a voice say, different than the first one, and much more substantial. The sound of heavy, persistent steps isn't far behind me. I don't know how it's possible, but someone's following me, chasing me. I amble forward, pushing myself to a clumsy sprint to find the nearest paved route of traffic and crowds. Emerging onto the main streets, my eyes adjust to the glare of the commercial signs and bright headlights of nighttime rush hour.

I look over my shoulders, into the dark alleyway. Though I can't see anyone or hear anything, I don't want to stick around. I'm on my way to the nearest, semi-populated place I can find at this late hour, when red and blue lights flash from my peripheral. At first, I ignore the cop cruiser, until it stops beside me. A light flash in my eyes and I freeze. There are two officers. The one in the passenger seat opens his door and gets out of the car. He's young, probably a rookie, with a baby face and an unsure walk. His hands are in his pockets and he looks concerned.

"You Savannah Scarlett?"

All I can do is nod. I'm too shocked and in too much pain to speak.

The young cop looks over his shoulder.

"Mitch, I got her. She matches the description. Says her name's Savannah," he informs the other cop. Then looking back at me with a slightly grimmer expression, he adds, "Your parents called us. You scared them half to death."

He helps me in the backseat of the cruiser. The bars separating me from the cops make me feel claustrophobic and… bad. All thoughts on the strange alleyway incident pale in comparison to what waits for me at home. Mom is going to murder me, but I can't help being in awe of the fact that she actually noticed I was gone.

My little warm, fuzzy moment doesn't last. When I get home, Mom answers the door on the first knock. She's gone from groomed to disheveled. Her makeup is runny. Her hair has lost some of its curl and she's got bags under her eyes. Tom is with her. His face is pale, and he looks almost sickly. He ushers me inside the apartment with Mom and steps into the hall with the cops, shutting us inside.

I am very aware of Mom's hard breathing. I brace myself for her censure, but I'm unprepared for the whimper that comes out of her mouth, the tears and the painfully tight hug.

"Savannah, where were you? What were you doing?"

Her strong hold knocks the wind out of me, robbing me of any chance at an explanation. But despite the pain I feel, I let myself rest in her arms.

Tom returns quickly, nodding at the cops before closing the door. Mom breaks away from me and collapses into him. He cradles her tenderly in his arms, consoling her as if she's the one who's been rescued.

"I'm so glad you called in that favor," Mom tells him.

Tom sighs, "It's a miracle they found her with all the things going on in this city. They said it looked like she was running away."

"No, she wasn't running away. She didn't pack anything," Mom responds. "Do you think that ER doctor was right? Sleepwalking just doesn't seem like a plausible explanation. If it were that simple, she wouldn't be in the streets. She'd be bumping around the apartment. Do you think it's drugs?"

I know Tom doesn't want to say what he's about to say because it takes him forever to respond.

"Teresa, I know we've been going in circles about whether or not she should see a professional. I think we have our answer now. Drugs, sleepwalking, whatever's going on, she needs help. Maybe more than we can give her right now. I don't know how to help her. I've never had a daughter before, let alone a teenager."

"I don't know what to do," Mom's voice comes out hushed, almost panicked.

"She needs to see someone. You want her to get better. I want her to get better. I'll make sure she gets the best of care."

Mom nods. I look away, wondering how they could have possibly forgotten about me so soon. I'm standing in the same room, staring at them while they're talking about me. I retreat to my room, knowing they won't notice me one way or another.

"Let's just get through this. I'll take care of it."

"We shouldn't have to get through things. We just got married," I hear Mom murmur. "We should be enjoying each other, making new memories."

"We'll have a lifetime of memories," Tom promises.

"Good for them," I mutter.

Frowning, I sit carefully on the side of my bed, and stare at the bottle of pills. Each capsule is half the size of my thumb, but I know I need it. My arm feels like lava filled Jell-O and my swollen feet are throbbing. The cap to my pills isn't on all the way, so I can pry it off with one hand. I'm thankful for the small mercy as I fish a pill out and take a swig of the stale water on my nightstand. Using my good arm, I struggle to pull myself into bed and crawl under my blankets. As my body numbs slowly and pleasantly, I pray I'll wake up in my own bed and not hallucinating, roaming some dangerous part of the city.

There must be a God. When I wake up, I'm in pain but I'm in my room. My vision is a little blurry and my body is in breathtaking pain but I'm home – if that's what I should call it. I struggle to turn my head and look at the clock. My neck is stiff, but I manage. It's a little after seven in the morning. I'm tired but awake. Good thing, too, because there's a knock on my door. Mom never waits for me to invite her in. She strolls into my room dressed in her white fleece bathrobe and matching house shoes. Her face is makeup free but she's still beautiful. She peers at me and nods her head.

"I just wanted to make sure you were here."

"I wasn't running away and I'm not doing drugs," I tell her. My voice sounds dry and tired, but I'm finally able to respond to the conversation she didn't realize I heard last night.

"Then why were you on the streets?" She raises her voice, but I don't take it personal.

I don't know what to tell her. I'm still trying to figure out how I ended up on the rooftop with a broken-down fire escape. Hearing voices in alleyways and running from strangers in a sketchy white van isn't something I want to talk about either. Mom misinterprets my silence and she throws her hands up.

"I don't want to argue with you. Not today. I just… if you didn't want to go to Martha's Vineyard that's all you had to say. I understand this is hard for you. Tom and I moved a little fast, but I love him, and I thought you liked him."

"I do," I interrupt, trying not to cry. I can see the love when they look at each other, but it's a struggle to hear her say it out loud. She loves – *loved* Dad.

"Sweetheart, I may not be the easiest person to talk to, but you can talk to me. I may not have all the answers and I may not always agree with you. I'm not perfect or omniscient but I *am* your mother."

I'm speechless again. I don't know if I can't talk because I'm in shock, in pain, or exhausted, but my mind is foggy. I don't know what to feel or to say.

"Okay."

That's all I manage to say but somehow, it's enough. Mom's face goes from strained with lines and darting eyes to a mix of confusion and relief. Then she does something that literally takes my breath away. She pulls me into a tight hug, kisses my forehead.

I start crying but it's not all because of our heart-to-heart.

"Mom?"

"Yes?"

"I think my arm's broken."

I close my eyes, so I don't have to see her expression.

"Okay, honey," she says.

Her voice is soft, shaken, and she doesn't fuss at me. Half an hour later I'm back at the hospital. It's the same doctor, too. He looks weary when he examines me, and he does a lot of whispering with Mom. Her forehead develops worry lines and her posture is tight and guarded. She doesn't look happy, but Tom must be wearing off on her. She doesn't go off on me or the doctor. Whatever he says to her she just nods.

Two hours later, my arm is wrapped in a sling, fractured in three different places. I must've hit that dumpster hard when the fire escape broke. Just thinking about it makes my arm hurt worse than it already does. As the emergency room doctor leaves, there's a knock on the door. Mom lets Tom in, but he isn't alone.

"Savannah, I want you to meet an old friend of the family. This is Dr. Robert Kensington," Tom introduces.

Dr. Kensington's thin lips twist in a friendly, full smile, causing wrinkles to color his face. He strides in the room, leans forward, and shakes my hand that's free of bandage wrap.

"Call me Bob. Hope you don't mind me stopping by?"

I shrug, wordlessly watching as Tom leads Mom out the door smoothly, but not so subtly.

"They make a lovely couple," Dr. Kensington marvels as he eases into one of the chairs by my hospital bed.

I grunt in response. Hearing what a beautiful couple Mom and her new husband are is not my favorite subject. Maybe my sore, stubborn body is making me cranky or maybe I'm close to snapping. It's been a long year and it isn't getting better.

"So, you're a friend of the family?" I ask. Now I'm the one who's not being so subtle.

Dr. Kensington's face flushes and he scratches his thinning, white hair, giving me another smile.

"I used to date Tom's Aunt Maggie. She was a rebel traveling all over the world, burning her knickers and fighting for equality, and, well, I was into love, peace, and... pharmaceuticals. We were horrible for each other."

I smile. "Are you still into those pharmaceuticals?"

"Not that kind. They nearly killed me. Maggie found me, rushed me to the hospital. She saved my life. I'll always be grateful for that. Got my head on straight, went to school, got a degree and earned enough to bail Maggie out of jail a few times when her protests got too wild. And, no, she doesn't burn her knickers anymore. At least, not that I'm aware of."

The sound of my own laughter makes me jump. I cover my mouth, in shock because it's been so long since I've laughed out loud. Dr. Kensington – Bob– smiles again, but not before I see the wistful gleam in his eyes.

"You should call Maggie some time. Maybe you aren't so horrible for each other now," I say.

"That ship has sailed, as they say," he says with a shrug.

"She's married?"

"No."

"You're married?"

"To my work," Dr. Kensington says with a frown. "You know; you may have a promising career in my profession. You listen, and you've got a great eye for observation."

I shrug, "It's easy to see things when you're always on the outside. So, are you a sleep specialist or...?"

"Psychiatrist."

"So, you medicate your patients?"

He smiles again. " I prescribe medication if I need to, but it's not my first course of action. A healthy mind is just as important as a healthy body. That's what I'm here for."

I wrinkle my nose, "I'm sick, mentally?"

Bob doesn't say anything.

I frown. "So, I am?"

"Do you think you're sick, mentally?"

I shrug and pain shoots through my sore joint. "I'm a mess. Just look at me."

"You lost your father recently?" he asks.

I breathe in. My chest swells, and it hurts. I don't think the pain killers working to numb the discomfort in my arm and feet can fix this pain. It's something deeper than a physical ache. I nod, not trusting my voice anymore.

"Do you think it's healthy to be a mess when you lose a loved one or to carry on like it's just a regular day?" Bob asks.

Mom acts like nothing happened, like we didn't just lose Dad, like he didn't mean anything, like he never existed.

That's what I want to say, but I can't speak. If I do, I know I'll burst into tears. Bob doesn't wait for me to answer.

"There is no one way to deal with grief or anything in life, really. Understanding who we are and what makes us act and feel the way we do is a life lesson that doesn't come with a cheat sheet," he says. "You have to live to learn and learn to live."

"And how do you do that?" I manage to say.

"Me? I try to be brave enough to get out of bed every morning and smart enough to take life one minute at a time. Most importantly, when I can't control anything else, I remember to breathe. I'm too old to take on more than that."

He clears his throat. His eyes twinkle but when he speaks again, his voice is crisp and direct.

"Frankly, I'm here because of your mother and stepfather. They love you enough to worry about you, but they don't have that cheat sheet in parenting to know how to help you."

"I don't even know what's wrong with me," I say, and with every word, the tears build up.

"Take it from your friend Bob here when I remind you that you're just learning, living, and learning to live."

I bite my lip to keep from sobbing out loud like a baby. The tears are bad enough. I don't want him to hear all the ugly sound effects.

"I think you and your mother should talk. If you need my help, Tom has my number."

He smiles at me, the kind of smile I imagine a loving grandpa might give, the kind I only see in movies and in peeks at other people's lives. He gently pats the hand on my good arm before standing.

"Be brave enough to get out of bed, smart enough to –"

"– handle life one minute at a time," I interject.

"And remember to breathe." He winks before adding, "I think you'll be just fine."

We leave the hospital quietly. In the car, Tom glances up at me through the rear-view mirror. Mom looks over her shoulder every two minutes and gives me a nervous smile each time, before working up the nerve to ask, "How did your talk go with Dr. Kensington?"

My talk with Bob sticks to me the way Dad's homemade chicken pot pie soup used to do when I was sick, but I don't tell her that. His words bring me comfort and strength, something I haven't felt in a long time.

"He thinks we should talk. I think he's right."

"I'm glad, honey. We were hoping you'd feel comfortable enough to talk to someone. From what Tom tells me, he's a really good doctor," Mom says.

"Psychiatrist," I clarify.

"He offers a lot of options for care and treatment. You'll be in good hands with him," Tom reassures me.

I ignore him, not to be rude, but because I don't know when or if I'll ever have another moment like this. I don't know when I'll be this brave or assertive again or when Mom will give me this much attention and patience. I talk over the tail end of Tom's response.

"No. You and me, Mom. He thinks we should talk, and I think he's right. Call and set up a session. Please."

Mom gets quiet and Tom looks at her in between navigating through traffic. No one says another word for the rest of our drive. When we get home, Mom retreats to her room, but the sound of her voice seeps through the thin walls.

"Dr. Kensington? It's Teresa Poindexter."

CHAPTER 7

Our session with Dr. Kensington couldn't come at a better time. Mom calls the school to excuse my absences but neither of us are prepared for what happens next. I'm shuffling cold scrambled eggs around my plate when she hangs up with the school.

"The academy's expressed some concern," she says. "While I've called in your recent absences, they still don't have documentation for some of the classes you've missed."

She doesn't ask me any questions, as if she's not surprised by my behavior anymore. Instead of lecturing me, she takes a deep breath and picks up the phone again. She turns her back to me.

"Tom, I spoke with the academy. They want to meet with us to discuss Savannah's truancy. She's been skipping some of her classes and they're concerned. They aren't going to take any action against us, but they're considering dismissing her from the school. Her scores aren't that great and she's already so far behind. They're worried she won't be able to keep up with the program."

The little bit of eggs I've eaten seem to spoil in my gut.

"Savannah, get dressed."

I abandon the bland breakfast at the table and force myself to shower. I dress comfortably in my favorite hoodie and jeans. When I get to the front door, I consider changing my clothes and wearing something that doesn't scream loner, but I don't. I'm not going to therapy to impress anybody. Mom is a different story with her tan pants suit and her hair slicked back in an elegant french roll. She frowns at my choice of clothes but sticks to the silent treatment. We take a taxi to Dr. Kensington's office, riding silently shoulder to shoulder. We haven't really talked since our car ride from the hospital the other day. I'm not sure if we ever will after we leave Dr. Kensington's. I can only hope he's as good at his job as Tom promises.

His office is in a nice area. It's a rustic, stone building decorated in climbing ivy vines. Inside, the office is modern and minimalist. The tan walls are clean and free of the stereotypical inspirational quotes. The waiting room's centerpiece is a sleek aquarium with medium sized koi fish, while a small end table carries a small spread of medical magazines. The receptionist looks like she belongs in a ballet studio. Her brown hair is styled in a flawless bun, accenting her long neck and perfect posture.

"Dr. Kensington is waiting for you, last door on the left."

She presses a button and the door beyond the waiting room opens. We follow her instructions and find Dr. Kensington stands in the doorway dressed in a dark navy suit. He smiles and ushers us in. Between him and Mom, I've never felt so underdressed. It doesn't help when Mom frowns at my clothes again.

"Mrs. Poindexter, Miss Scarlett, glad you could make it. Please sit."

He doesn't go behind his pristine desk of neatly stacked files and thick books. Instead, Dr. Kensington sits off to the side by an aquarium of more koi fish and directs us to two adjacent chairs. Mom and I glance warily at each other before sitting.

"How can I help you today?"

Mom speaks first, "Savannah's school wants to dismiss her for truancy."

I want to sink into my chair, but Dr. Kensington's response jars both me and Mom. He shakes his head.

"With all due respect, Mrs. Poindexter, I don't want to start with the problems you're facing. I want to know how I can help you today. What results would you like to see from our session today or overall?"

Mom's cheeks redden, and her jaw slackens. When she doesn't say anything, Dr. Kensington turns his clear gaze my way.

"Savannah?"

I clear my throat.

"We don't talk. So, when you suggested we talk, I thought it might be a good idea. I want to talk to her," I say and then I look at Mom, "I want to talk to you."

She tsks. "Savannah, we didn't have to come all the way here to talk. I'm your mother. We talk all the time."

It's more like she talks at me. She tells me how things are going to go, and she just expects me to fall in line. When I talk, she doesn't hear me. She doesn't have time to hear me. My voice has to compete with the rest of her world.

"Mrs. Poindexter –"

"Teresa," Mom corrects.

"Teresa," Dr. Kensington restates. "Savannah, I want you to know that this office is a safe space. What you say in here isn't to be discussed outside of these doors until we resolve it.

In my professional opinion, I believe your problems can be resolved quickly if you're both honest and respectful. I'm not here to judge you. I am here for support and guidance. Teresa, Savannah says she wants to talk to you. What do you want from this session today or overall?"

She's quiet for a moment before answering, "I don't know her anymore and I don't know what to do about it. Her father would know. She was always closer to him. I can't replace your Daddy, Savannah, but I want to know you. I want to be closer, if you'll let me in."

I stare at the aquarium, but the fish and the water are skewed by the tears in my eyes as Mom continues.

"I'm a little rough around the edges. I'm stubborn and I have a temper. I'm not perfect, but I'm your mother."

"You're the strongest person I know," I say. "I'm sorry I'm so disappointing, that I can't just get over things like you can. That I can't just move on with my life. I miss Dad. It still hurts."

"Baby, what are you talking about? How could you say that?"

My gaze flickers to Dr. Kensington, but he doesn't speak. He nods his head at me and offers me a small reassuring smile. I look back at the aquarium, watching the fish glide around in the water. I can't look at Mom or I'll lose my nerve to speak my mind.

"I know you can't replace Dad. No one can. I know he's been dead for over a year, but it feels like yesterday to me. It still hurts, and I don't know how to deal with it. How do you – how did you – deal with losing him? Because it's clear you're over him."

Mom lets out a heavy sigh and her chair groans against the sudden silence. When she speaks, her voice is hushed. I lean into the gentle sound, resting my head on the arm of the chair and closing my eyes.

"My mother always told me that still waters run deep. I didn't know what she meant until I met and fell in love with your father. He was a quiet man and he held a lot inside. Thoughts, emotions, ideas. A little bit of everything. Figuring him out was part of what made him attractive, but now that I think about it, that depth is what could've killed him. He was always so guarded. He never let anyone in. I don't want that for you," she says.

Mom's voice grows stronger, thicker even. I open my eyes and look at her. She sits beside me with her legs crossed at the ankles, while she twists her wedding rings. She casts me short sideway looks through her peripheral, otherwise staring at her hands. Knowing that she's as nervous as I am gives me the courage to keep my eyes on her, even though I can't see her clearly through my tears.

"Please, be like your father in everything else. Be Intelligent. Quirky. Compassionate. Inventive. Artistic. But when it comes to grief and pain, don't be deep. Be like me. Learn to feel it and let it run through you. Don't hold onto it. Let it go so you can feel what you want to feel."

"We left him. I can't even visit his grave," I tell her.

"Yes, you can," Mom says. "If it helps, we can go back to Georgia anytime you want to visit him."

Some of the pressure deep in my chest lifts. I blink back the tears. "Really?"

She nods.

"I loved your father and I honored my vows. But when we buried him, I had a choice. I chose to heal, to move on, and live because of you, and then later because of Tom. I won't apologize for that. What I am sorry for, more than anything, is that I wasn't there for you the way you needed me to be. Maybe we moved on too fast. I'm willing to slow down and move at your pace."

Mom looks in my direction and our eyes finally connect. She reaches to wipe my tears with her fingers, and I realize she's crying too. I grab her hand and she squeezes mine.

"We'll set up a trip to Georgia for this weekend. Just you and me, and maybe we can visit that bookstore you two used to love so much."

"Tom can come, too, if he wants," I say, and her eyes widen.

Mom smiles, but she shakes her head, "We need a girls' trip."

She runs her hand through my hair. "Can we start over? We'll work through this however we need to. Starting with finding you a new school, I guess."

I smile at her. "Sounds good. Great, actually."

Dr. Kensington clears his throat, and I swear he's blinking back tears of his own.

"Our time's up," I guess.

He nods, "Sessions like this make me feel guilty for the bill."

We stand up. He shakes Mom's hand, but she ropes him in for a hug.

"It's one of the only bills I'll be happy to pay. Thank you for this," she says.

He smiles at me, "At least, let me recommend you to one of the best pizzerias in the city."

He scribbles the name of the pizza place on a piece of prescription paper. He hands the recommendation to me. I smile at him, grateful for his kindness, but I don't have the heart to tell him Dad and I always preferred Chicago style pizza.

CHAPTER 8

By the time we get home from seeing Dr. Kensington, the combination of a good therapy session and the numbing effects of the pain killers has my eyelids heavy and my body warm and fuzzy. Mom helps me into bed, and I fall into a pleasant sleep. When I wake up a few hours later, I'm happy to be in bed and not stumbling around some random street. I count every night like this as a victory. Sitting up, I start to get out of bed, but the pain from my injuries jars me. I stop and lean against the foot of my bed to regroup.

The sound of silverware scraping against plates makes me wonder why no one woke me for lunch, but then I hear their voices.

"I'm glad the two of you talked. I think the trip to Georgia will be cathartic," Tom says, "Did you mention –"

"No," Mom says, "After what we accomplished, I didn't have the heart. Maybe things will get better from here."

Tom speaks slowly, carefully grasping for words, "I'm sure they will. I still think Dr. Kensington should know everything."

"That's not our job to tell him. It's Savannah's. I don't know enough about what's going on to tell him anything," Mom says. "And neither do you. So, drop it."

I force myself out of my bedroom, interrupting their discussion. They smile at me, though it's strained.

"Want me to warm up some lo mein for you?" Mom asks.

I wrinkle my nose.

"It's a little past noon. Now would be the perfect time to check out the pizza place Dr. Kensington recommended. Why don't you call Angie, meet up, and get some fresh air? She's been calling like crazy to check on you. I think she'd appreciate a little chat," Mom suggests.

Odd. I wonder why Angie would call Mom when my phone works just fine. Not even a text message from her, but she's blowing up Mom's phone?

"Give her a call," Mom says again.

"Sure," I say, though I'm not in the mood for pizza or fresh air. My body's a wreck. Being social is the last thing I want to do, but it's the least I can do. Angie's not my enemy. I hobble back to my room to search for my phone, hidden in the mass of sheets and blankets. I've missed three of her calls and there's an unread text message too. I lose the nerve to call her back, settling for a text instead. I give her the name of the pizza place and ask if she'd like to meet me for lunch. It doesn't take her long to respond, almost as if she was expecting me to contact her.

With less than 30 minutes to pull myself together, I throw on jeans and the best sweater I can find, shoving my painkillers in my pocket in case I need them. I do my usual: gel my edges and pull my hair back into a ponytail as tight as I can, and struggle with my shoes, all with one hand. Pretty impossible, but somehow, I manage with my arm in a cast and my feet still sore in places. Limping from my room to the front door, I'm disappointed when I find the kitchen empty. Mom and my stepdad's voices carry in gentle murmurs from their bedroom. I want to ask them for a ride, but I call a taxi instead.

It takes me longer than I anticipate to reach the pizza shop. When we get stuck in traffic, I foolishly decide to walk the rest of the way. It isn't long before I break into a cold sweat. Still, I'm convinced that hobbling through crowds is faster than sitting motionless in traffic. I don't want to keep Angie waiting. When I make it to the pizza shop, I'll enjoy a big slice of pizza with anchovies, onions, peppers, sausage, and extra cheese. My body needs fuel.

I'm twenty minutes late when I finally reach the surprisingly ordinary pizza shop. Just as I'm scanning the seats for Angie, my phone buzzes. It's her.

"Savannah, I'm so sorry. I hope you haven't been waiting on me long." she says, "I can't make it. It's Jay."

Her voice trails off, but I already have an idea of what's going on. I haven't forgotten the wild pictures on his phone or the drugs he bought from those guys. I'm not sure what he's using, but I know it can't be good. Still, Angie won't directly acknowledge what's wrong with Jay. Her silence is almost as painful as my injuries.

"Angie, it's fine. I'm just leaving the house. I was going to call you to see if we could raincheck," I lie.

"Glad I could catch you before you left. Thanks for understanding."

She hangs up and I do my best not to break down in tears in front of a diner full of strangers. Instead, I take a deep breath, blink back the tears, and plop my butt in the nearest empty seat I can find. Studying the grease-stained menu propped up on the table, I try to ignore the fatigue and bone-deep aches.

"Might as well stay and enjoy," I mutter to myself.

After fifteen minutes of staring at the menu, my eyes start to cross, and fatigue turns into agitation. No one comes to take my order, not even to offer me a glass of water. It looks like I'm back to being invisible again. The waitress in my section, Carly, if I'm reading her name tag right, flutters from one table to another and doesn't stop to get my order until I practically yell at her. Now she's got an attitude.

Glaring at me she demands to know what I want. I give her my order, amending anchovies for bacon and adding a root beer. Inhaling the scent of pizza crust, tomato sauce, and a melted mix of cheese in the air, I decide not to take Carly's attitude personal. Everything smells so good, and pizza is always better than the alternative gourmet food that's become Mom's steady diet since she met Tom.

While waiting on my pizza, I people watch to distract myself from the pain creeping up my arm.

"Hang in there," I coach myself as two boys around my age pass my table. One boy is tall with his hair spiked in a Mohawk, dyed a fluorescent orange. The other one is a little shorter than my 5'6. He wears his hair close shaven. Both boys dress in baggy, long-sleeved shirts layered with skater boy tees. Their saggy pants are filled with careless holes and shredded hems, but they have on designer sneakers. The tall, orange-haired boy has piercings in his nose, reminding me of a bull and the shorter guy has a tattoo of a dagger dripping with blood on the left side of his neck. They stomp past me and collapse at a table a few feet away, near a quiet professor-type gentleman struggling to read a newspaper with his glasses falling down his nose. The older man doesn't flinch. He clears his throat and buries his nose deeper into whatever article he's reading, leaving his apple dumpling alamode untouched.

The boys scout out the pizza place, smirking and making obnoxious jokes that I wish I could unhear. The shorter boy slides the bowl of apple dumplings and ice-cream literally from under the older man's nose. The man never looks up from his newspaper. At first, I think it's because he might be a little too intimidated by the boys to do anything, but he doesn't look nervous. He doesn't seem to show any indication at all that his food has been snatched. He's too busy separating the pages of the newspaper with saliva coated fingers. The shorter boy snickers and heads for the next table, where a trio of video game playing junior high kids talk over a spread of half eaten pepperoni and cheese pizza. The boy grabs a few slices while the taller boy with the orange mohawk mooches a milkshake from a harried businesswoman. He bumps into my waitress, who nearly drops my pizza, before collapsing back at their chosen table with his friend. Carly curses at her slightly run-over shoes, paying the boys no mind. Mohawk catches my eye and smiles before belching loudly.

I look away as Carly slams my food on the table.

"Um, Carly," I start.

"Huh?" Her response is hardly attentive.

"I think those guys are stealing food from the other customers."

I know they're stealing, and they're not even trying to be discreet. Every time Tattoo finishes shoving one piece of pizza in his mouth, he's reaching back to the table behind him to grab another one from the poor video game kids while Mohawk laughs and makes rhythms out of belches. They're disgusting.

Carly looks over to the spot where the delinquents sit and her brows crease. She rolls her eyes and approaches the table of boys playing video games. It's the wrong table but who else would she think I'd be talking about when Mohawk and Tattoo are no longer seated? Their table is empty.

"Listen, twerps. Your pizza's gone and we're going to need this space for customers to sit. Pay up and get lost," Carly says to the boys.

One kid with thick glasses sticks his tongue out at her like a four-year-old just as the other boys look down at the round cardboard carrier where their pizza should be. They automatically eye their chunkiest friend.

"Come on, Jack! Why do you have to be so greedy?"

"You ate all the pizza," whines another boy

Jack's cheeks get red, but he doesn't seem shy. He's mad.

"I didn't eat it all! I barely had a piece."

The boys continue to argue until Carly makes them hand over the money for pizza they really didn't eat and ushers them out the entrance with a shove. I hear a snicker and see Mohawk and Tattoo coming out of the bathroom doors from the back of the diner. They walk past my table and Mohawk makes a grab for my pizza. I push it out of his reach. "That's mine. You can't have it. I see what you're doing."

Mohawk's eyes narrow with a dangerous spark, but Tattoo is the muscle. He shoves Mohawk aside and strides toward me. I stand up on my shaky legs, wishing that all my limbs were working properly so I could run if I need to. Thankfully, Carly steps in between us, an irritated shield. Her lips tighten.

"What's your deal?" she asks me.

I'm shocked into speechlessness, unable to do much but let out a yelp of protest. She grabs an unused plastic container from another table and slides it to me. The customer she took it from, the man with the newspaper and slippery glasses, doesn't need it anyway. Mohawk and Tattoo ate all his food, and judging by the look on his face, he's just now noticing it.

"Just get your stuff and get out. We've had enough trouble for one day," Carly snaps.

I finally find my voice and protest, "I didn't do anything! Those boys –"

The words die on my tongue as I watch Tattoo and Mohawk stroll out of the diner. They watch me through the window, laughing. I tap Carly to get her attention motioning towards the window. Carly takes it the wrong way and shoves back at me, which looks bad on her part given that I'm half wrapped in bandages.

"Don't touch me!" Carly shrieks as her manager comes out from the kitchen.

"Carly, what's going on here?"

The customers are all watching. Everything is quiet. My stomach churns as I notice the wide eyes staring in my direction.

"Miss, I'm going to have to ask you to leave," the manager says, taking a wide stance with his hands on his hips. He looks ready for war, even though I'm a poor excuse for a threat.

"It was those boys," I start, trying to explain.

"I kicked the boys out and you started talking to yourself and freaking the other customers out." Carly argues.

Despite her frustration with me, I think she loves all the attention she's getting. It feels like the Empire State Building all over again. Great. I try to be helpful and this is what I get for not minding my own business.

"Not today," I whisper to myself.

How did I get to be the bad girl in this situation? I dig out a twenty-dollar bill and slap it on the table. I grab my pizza, taking a bite for courage before shuffling after the two boys. Following the vivid orange hair that stands out from the corporate suits and chic fashions, I break into a limping jog. My muscles and tendons groan under the sudden burst of exertion, and my feet scream every time my they hit the pavement, but the pain is worth it. I need to know what's going on. Boys jumping off buildings, disembodied voices in dark alleyways, blacking out and finding myself in strange places – it's all getting to be too much. Tattoo and Mohawk are another puzzle piece and I refuse to let them disappear.

The distance between us grows. I push myself harder, faster, weaving through the crowds as best as I can, but my resolve shrinks.

"Hey!" I call to them. Several other people turn to look at me.

"Orange hair! Tattoo on the neck!" I shout.

The two boys stop and look back at me. Their smug grins turn to wide eyed surprise, and then they're running. They're faster than me and conveniently not injured. The odds aren't in my favor, but I need answers, answers I have a feeling they can provide. It doesn't make sense that I'm the only one who saw them blatantly stealing food in the diner. People can't be that oblivious.

The boys make a sharp left turn. I pick up speed but stumble forward, nearly falling before I regain my balance.

When I look up, I'm a few feet further than I thought I'd been before. My chest burns and I'm sweating so hard it feels like someone's poured a bucket of water over my head. I lean against the nearest building, a building that faces a side street, the street the two boys went down. Only it's a dead end. There aren't any doorways or fire escapes, no dumpsters or sewers. The boys aren't anywhere in sight. I hike the next few blocks looking for any sign of orange hair or mischief, but the streets are filled with activity. My crazy, impulsive quest for answers leaves me feeling twice as lost and confused.

"I should've stayed in bed."

I sleep the rest of the day away and part of the day after that. Mom knocks on my door at dinner time, and for the first time since we've moved to New York, her bland takeout food excites my growling stomach. The dry chicken marsala, the al dente green beans, and whipped sweet potatoes are hardly my preference, but I don't regret eating until after my I've had two more servings.

The dinner table is quiet. Mom sips her wine slowly, eyeing me from over the rim of her glass.

Tom clears his throat. "I've never seen you eat like this. Is chicken marsala a favorite?"

I swallow the last of the dry chicken. "Not really."

"You aren't pregnant, are you?" Mom blurts.

I laugh, "Nope."

The idea's laughable because it's impossible. With my luck, I'm pretty sure I'll die a virgin.

"Have you been hanging out with your cousins? Did Angie bring her brother with her to the pizza place?" she asks.

"Angie didn't show up because of her brother, and no. We don't hang out."

"You did go to the pizza shop, right?"

"Yes."

We fall into uncomfortable silence again.

Tom smiles. "Don't pay attention to your mother. It's good to see you with an appetite."

We all relax, and conversation begins again. They talk about Jay's drug addiction but it isn't long before they fall into flirting. Newlyweds are so disgusting. Clearing my plate, I hope to retreat to my room before things get past PG, but Mom calls out to me.

"We've got good news. Tom got you into a nice school. You transfer on Monday. It's a slightly longer commute but it will be a good, fresh start."

I smile at them, though inside I'm screaming. Life hasn't been ideal lately, but it's been bearable without adding school into the equation. Navigating homework and fickle social circles doesn't excite me. I have half a mind to beg Mom to homeschool me, but I don't. Maybe I'm overreacting. What happened at school with Angie was a bizarre fluke. On Monday, I'll probably go back to being an average face in the crowd.

"Maybe we can take our Georgia trip this weekend before you start your first day?" Mom asks.

My throat tightens, but I force a smile. "Yeah."

The thought of going back home to visit Dad's grave doesn't engender excitement either. Seeing his headstone and putting flowers on his grave will only solidify the truth that hurts me the most. Dad is really gone. Mom thinks things are getting better, but I'm not so sure. It's all just some kind of cycle I just can't escape. I want to be happy. I want to be excited, but my heart hammers in my chest, and all I want to do is hide in my bed and sleep away all expectations and responsibilities. As much as Mom wants to support me, I don't want to disappoint her.

Heading back to my room, I decide to call Dr. Kensington in the morning. He'll know what to do. If I'm starting fresh on Monday, I don't want to be afraid. I want to be just as excited as Mom is for me. I'm going to tell him everything and maybe he'll help me find answers I can't seem to grasp on my own.

I take the last of my painkillers before curling into bed, hoping I'll be brave and strong enough to do what I need to do in the morning.

***

I wake up gasping for air, cold and drenched, neck deep in a dark body of water. My limbs are tired, and my chest feels tight. I don't even have the strength to scream for help. I don't know how long I've been in this water, but I know I won't survive if I don't get out soon. Too cold. Too tired. Water surrounds me. There's no land in sight. Just endless water.

What the-

"Stupid girl," comes a voice out of the dark.

There's a splash. Something – someone – moves in the water. I see a figure, a silhouette in the water, but I'm too tired to take in the details. I can barely keep my eyes open. Something touches my hand and my nerves flare, the last surge of feeling before the numbing cold takes over. Even with limited sensation, I'm aware of movement as wind whips across my face, but my eyes are too heavy to keep open and my mind is too tired to think.

"Wake up!"

A fresh slap burns my cheek, jolting me awake. I open my eyes. A boy stares down at me. His face is pale, his eyes are a stark gray shadowed in tired lines. Dark curls drip from underneath his wet hooded sweatshirt. I want to ask him who he is and where we are, but my body has a mind of its own. An onslaught of cold seeps into my skin and I can't stop shaking. With the shock to my system comes a brisk awareness of my surroundings, like a shot of adrenaline injected in my veins. The boy's baby face is marred by a hard frown. I hear sirens in the distance and see blue and red lights flash out of the corner of my eyes.

"Get up," he tells me, "Get up now and get out of here."

Shame I don't even know where I am to begin with.

"You hear me? Get outta here!"

He helps me off the ground, a field of damp grass, and gives me a shove. I stumble forward, still shaking, body tired and aching. I watch as cop cars drive up. The boy groans.

"Always cleaning up everyone's mess. And boy, are you a mess," he grumbles.

I frown, trying to wake my mind enough to say something smart alec, but the boy's face blurs like paint in water. His features stretch until they disappear. He grabs my arm and my body jerks forward. We move so fast my brain can't comprehend what I'm seeing. The world moves in a blur. The sound of sirens is replaced by wind whizzing in my ears. Gravity presses against me, pushing me backward while he pulls me forward until it's too much for me to take. I close my eyes and pray for the wild moment to end.

When I come to myself again, there is no gray-eyed, curly-haired boy, no water, no sirens. But my window is open, my hair is damp, and my favorite pair of shoes are destroyed.

CHAPTER 9

*I*t isn't courage that leads me to Dr. Kensington's office. It's fear. I've got so much to gain. New school, a functional relationship with Mom, a fresh start. I don't want to ruin things like I did when we first came to New York. When Dr. Kensington opens the door to his office, I barrel in blubbering in sentences I can't even comprehend. I don't know where to start or what to say. All the craziness I've seen runs through my head in jumbled flashes and fragments of emotions I can't make sense of. Dr. Kensington walks me to the nearest chair and guides me to sit.

"Savannah, remember what I told you. Breathe. Don't forget to breathe," he says.

I take a deep breath and exhale slowly, repeating the process until I stop shaking and my tears subside.

"You've been brave enough to get out of bed today. Be smart enough to take things one moment at a time. Don't forget to breathe," he says.

One moment at a time. One thing at a time. I take a breath.

"Mom got me in a new school. I start on Monday. We're on good terms, too. She's taking me to visit Dad this weekend."

"Those are good things, right?"

"So good it's scary. I don't want to sabotage it."

Dr. Kensington sits in the chair beside me.

"How would you sabotage it?"

"Did Tom tell you why they really wanted me to get help?"

"It wasn't his experience to tell. He called concerned because he and your mother didn't know what was going on in your life."

"I can't tell them. They'll think I'm crazy. *I* think I'm crazy. But maybe you can help me. Give me some kind of prescription or something."

"Savannah, one moment at a time. Don't forget to breathe."

I close my eyes and I tell him everything. When I finally stop talking, Dr. Kensington is silent for a long time, so long I'm afraid.

"You've had two instances where you've seen people no one else sees?"

I nod, knowing how bizarre it sounds.

"And when you go to sleep, you blackout and wake up in random places around the city?"

"Alleyways. Rooftops. This morning I was in water. I've got all the scars and sprains to prove it."

Dr. Kensington is silent again.

"I'm certifiable, right?"

"One moment at a time. Breathe," he reminds me.

"I can't do that. I can't take things one moment at a time. Everything's coming at me all at once. I feel like I'm drowning. I just want it to stop. Tell me how to stop it."

"Savannah, I can't promise answers in one session and I can't promise you that I'll have any answers at all. What I do know is that you can't do this alone. I will go with you as far as I can, but I think you should tell your mother the truth."

"Aren't these sessions supposed to be confidential?"

"When information you give me presents a risk to you or others, I am obligated to report that to your parents," he says.

"You're going to tell my mom?"

"If everything you've told me today is true then, yes, I am obligated to inform your mother. I can speak with her alone or I can clear some of my appointments and we can tell her together."

"She's going to hate me."

"Taking off my doctor hat for a moment, I can tell you I've met your mother and I believe she loves you very fiercely. She's strong, just like you. But you'll be stronger if you work through this together."

Dr. Kensington stands, walks to a mini fridge by his desk and hands me a cold, bottled water.

I gladly accept and take a drink before I answer. "Call her."

Mom takes the news better than I anticipate. Maybe because Dr. Kensington's so eloquent in his summary of my story. We sit in his office and he repeats what I told him. I never have to open my mouth.

Mom doesn't waste tears and she doesn't argue or hurl insults at me like I thought she would. Instead, she voices all the questions I've been thinking since the craziness started.

Am I hallucinating?

"Are the blackouts a neurological disorder?"

Is it a tumor? Cancer?

"Maybe it's just stress?"

Maybe I've snapped.

"Is it my fault? Is there anything I can do?"

Dr. Kensington can't promise any concrete answers, but he recommends testing.

"CT scans, MRIs, and an analysis of symptoms can rule out tumors or most irregularities. We can test blood work to determine any hormonal or chemical deficiencies and imbalances. I won't diagnose until we have as much information as we can get."

Mom sighs. She looks at me and squeezes my hand. "We'll figure this out together."

Soon I won't have to wonder what's wrong with me. We'll have answers, and no matter how scary those answers can be, Mom will be there with me. I'm not alone. Not anymore. Right now, I couldn't ask for more.

They schedule all the necessary testing, the blood work and all the scans as a next day priority. While we wait for the results, Tom busies himself by having cameras and an updated security system installed in the apartment. My prior blackouts never triggered the old alarm system. He hopes the new one works better.

For the first time in my life, Mom hovers. She watches my every movement. They both do, and I can tell by the bags under their eyes that they aren't getting much sleep. It makes me anxious, a feeling I'm beginning to associate with the bizarre things that've been happening to me lately.

I close my eyes and wake up on the streets again. This time it's like I've been thrust into a car chase scene in an action flick. I'm running even before I realize what I'm doing. Someone's not far behind, and instinctively I know they're after me and that they want to hurt me. Too afraid to look behind me, I force myself to move faster, pushing into the crowds, hoping whoever is after me will lose sight of me. My body's still a mess, but the adrenaline rushing through me numbs the pain.

I slow my pace, ducking through the influx of people coming out of a night club, hoping to lose whoever is after me if I take a turn down another street.

"Wouldn't do that if I were you. Dead end," A voice says.

Someone in the group of people grabs my wrist and jerks me forward. I look up at my assailant, but he moves so fast all I can see are distorted colors, almost making him translucent. His skin feels airy, but then so does mine and when I look at my arm and my clothes, my eyes struggle to adjust. I pull away from the stranger's hold, stumbling and rolling backward from the velocity of our motion. I have to curl up in a sitting fetal position to keep from being stepped on.

Scurrying off the sidewalk and back pedaling out of the line of pedestrian traffic I look around. I have no idea who was chasing me or who I was talking to, but I recognize the voice.

"At least he didn't call me a stupid girl this time," I mutter to myself as I try to make sense of my exact location.

I don't have a wallet or a phone but there's no way I'm walking anywhere else tonight, especially if whoever is chasing me is still out there. I'm not sure who they are or who the boy is that keeps coming to my rescue, but I don't think I can handle another run-in tonight. I hail a taxi, promising to pay when I get to my destination. When I tell him the area I need to get to, he relaxes a little. No way a girl from the expensive side of town would rip him off.

When we reach our destination, I walk into our apartment building, but I don't get far. Tom is in the lobby with a police officer. When he sees me, he rushes over and hugs me tight.

"I didn't have any money. There's a driver out front I need to pay."

"I'll take care of it," he says, rushing out the door with his wallet already out.

The policeman Tom was talking to gives me a long look before following Tom out the door. Mom rushes out of the elevator in her silk robe and matching pajamas by the time Tom comes back inside the lobby. She grips me tight in her arms. She doesn't say a word, but tears flow freely.

"You had us scared half to death," Tom says, gently prodding us back to the elevator. "The alarm never went off, but I happened to be awake. I checked on you and your bed was empty. I watched the video feed and I still can't make sense of it. Unless you're a genius with tech, there's no way someone could've tampered with the visuals."

"What're you talking about?"

Tom looks sick. "One minute you were standing at the front door. The next you were just gone. The door never opened. The alarm never went off. It's like you disappeared into thin air."

Tom's convinced the video footage is a glitch. He wants the security company to replace and install a new system, but I'm not sure it will help. He replays the video for me when we get to our apartment. One minute I see myself, walking with open, vacant eyes out of my room and into the entryway of our apartment. In the amount of time it takes me to blink, I've vanished from the video feed.

I replay the clip over and over until Mom shakes her head. "Stop it, Savannah. I can't take it."

She goes to her bedroom and quietly shuts the door, but Tom is just as bothered as I am. "It's got to be some kind of error. You can't just disappear like that. Nothing else makes sense."

I look down at my good arm, remembering it being a translucent distortion of colors, like diluted paint in water. A lot of things don't make sense. My stomach tightens painfully and rumbles. I salivate, not anticipating the sudden hunger.

"We have leftovers?"

Tom gives me a long look. "Some takeout. Pad thai."

At this point, I'm starting to think all the tests and examinations in the world won't be able to fix what's wrong with me. But for just one moment I'll bury the worry and enjoy the first comfort takeout meal Mom's ordered since we've come to New York. The grease, peanut, and chili pepper flavors put me in a happy place. I don't know what I'll have to face tomorrow. Tonight, I'll enjoy Thai food.

CHAPTER 10

Nothing makes sense the next day. Outside of a slightly low iron count, all my lab work and scans come back normal. While it's good news, it leaves Dr. Kensington baffled, especially when Tom shows him the camera footage.

"Even if this is a technical error, why didn't Savannah trip the alarm?" Dr. Kensington asks.

We all sit, silently stumped.

Dr. Kensington recovers first, turning to me. "Are there any symptoms you've been experiencing? Any headaches? Numbness?"

"I get hungry and thirsty. More than usual," I say.

"Have you been eating well?"

"Excessive is more like it," Mom mutters.

"Muscle aches? Fever? Nausea?"

I shake my head.

"Heart palpitations?"

I shake my head at first. Then I remember last night. "A little?"

He scribbles on his notepad and then drops the pencil, rubbing his face. "With no irregularities present in the blood work or the scans, we can rule out much of what I was previously considering. A prescription for anxiety may help since I think it's triggering these blackouts. I also recommend some modifications in diet. Limit your caffeine and highly processed foods. Try chamomile tea and lavender fragrances."

"You think it's anxiety?"

He answers slowly. "It's the most plausible explanation. Extreme and continual stress and anxiety are often culprits for physical, emotional, and mental decline. Savannah, you've experienced a lot of life changes in such a short time, and drastic changes are still ahead of you."

Anxiety. Stress. It hardly describes what happened last night. Blurring bodies moving at dizzying speeds and strangers chasing me in the dark.

"You think anxiety and stress could cause hallucinations?" Mom asks.

"A bad response to painkillers could also be to blame."

The painkillers did make me loopy, but to say they contributed to hallucinations seems off. I want to believe it's as simple as prescriptions and chamomile tea, but I can't help feeling there's another explanation. The feeling looms over my head like a dark fog. I can feel it, but I can't explain it.

Mom seems satisfied with Dr. Kensington's assessment or at least more cordial and relaxed. She thanks him with a handshake and a kiss on the cheek. Tom nods his head and gives him a tight smile.

"Thank you, Dr. Kensington. For everything," I manage to say.

He frowns.

"Don't thank me yet," he says.

Then turning to my parents, he says, "Could I have another moment with Savannah?"

Mom nods. "We'll be in the waiting room."

Dr. Kensington opens a drawer in his desk. He pulls out a newspaper and glances at the door.

"Our session is officially over, so I'm coming to you as friend of the family now. There's something I wanted you to see," he says.

He turns a few of the pages and folds the paper in half, pointing at a short article that reads, "Elusive John surrenders to police after a frightening night on the streets".

Attached to the article is a small picture with a man in handcuffs. From his side profile, I see hints of a bloody, bruised face and a wild, terrified expression. But it isn't the face I recognize as much as his clothes. Clothes that dated tend to stick out, something a guy like him shouldn't want to do. The picture triggers those frightening moments with glass in my feet.

"This is the guy that attacked me in the alley," I say, "How did you..."

"Your vivid description made him easy to identify. Witnesses said they heard screams coming from that alley. Police found him bloody and beaten. He turned himself in for trafficking. They arrested him the same night you injured your feet, the same night you remember this man trying to grab you."

"So, I wasn't hallucinating?"

Dr. Kensington grows quiet.

"Doc, I'm not sure what you're getting at. What are you trying to tell me?"

"I'm looking for answers myself, Savannah. Do you remember anything else from that night? Did this man look this bad before you got away from him?"

"There's no way I could've done that to him. I was scared. Injured. Disoriented. He was drunk so I managed to fight my way free, but I didn't do that."

I think about it. I remember running that night. I remember his expletives and drunken insults morphing into shrieks and screams. I thought it had been because he was angry I got away from him.

"Someone else got to him," I conclude. "It could've been anybody."

Dr. Kensington frowns and I know he doesn't believe that either.

"Do you think, maybe the other things I've been seeing could be real, too? The boy? The people chasing after me?"

He sighs. "I think there's more coincidences and oddities than I'm comfortable with."

"I really hope the medication helps."

I'm grasping for anything positive at this point, because the alternative is frightening. The alternative means that my problems aren't so cut and dry.

"I'm confident the prescription will help your anxiety."

I look at the newspaper. "What do you recommend for this?"

He opens his desk drawer again and hands me a brochure.

***

"Rehab?" Mom echoes for the eleventh time, "I don't know about this."

She browses through the brochure. "I don't understand. Dr. Kensington didn't mention this during your session. I leave the room for five minutes and you come out talking about rehab?"

Tom sighs. "Teresa, let Savannah talk."

"Willow Manor is supposed to be like a retreat. It's a secure facility. Our security system isn't helping. Here I'll have access to care and support 24/7."

"The prescriptions will help," Mom argues.

"So will this. The thought of going to a new school right now terrifies me. I need a break. I need some time to adjust to taking medication. It's only for a few weeks."

"It's a whole month, Savannah."

Tom touches her hand.

"What else am I supposed to do? I've been to the hospital twice because of the blackouts and the sleepwalking. I'm exhausted. You're exhausted. Can you think of anything better? Because I'm all out of ideas and I'm scared! I'm tired of being scared. I – I'm just tired. So, can we just do this? It's one month. An entire month where I won't be a problem for you."

Mom gives me the silent treatment for the rest of the day, though I hear her talking it out with Tom through the thin walls when we get back to the apartment.

"Teresa, I think we need this just as much as Savannah does. We can visit my family, take a honeymoon, get an uninterrupted night of sleep."

"She's my daughter and we're just getting to a good place again. I don't want to lose that."

"I've got one word for you. Fiji."

Mom laughs, "Tempting."

"Oh, I can be very tempting."

I cringe and cover my ears with my pillow.

"Please just say yes," I grumble.

Mom calls the school Monday morning to let them know I won't be attending until next fall. I'll be homeschooled for the remainder of my junior year. I've got a month at Willow Manor before I start rebuilding my life post-Dad. Wanting to go to Willow Manor and being at Willow Manor are two completely different things. It looked appealing on paper. It looks appealing in real life, but dread sets in the pit of my stomach.

I have my own room with cable and streaming, my own bathroom and a mini fridge. The staff even places a bouquet of daisies with a welcome card to make me feel at home, but it isn't my home.

Mom inspects my room and points out all the amenities I've already noticed. Tom smiles but his eyes look more tired than anything. "You'll do just fine here."

Mom gives me a fierce hug.

Dr. Kensington knocks on the door to my room, despite it being open. "I thought I'd come to see you before you settle in," he shrugs his shoulders and shakes his head.

"I appreciate everything," I tell him.

While I'm at Willow Manor, I'll be in the care of their physicians. Most importantly, I'll be safe. With Willow Manor's security and care, there's no way I'll be able to sleepwalk out of here.

"I have a feeling I won't be seeing too much of you after this. I don't think you'll need my kind of help. But if you remember anything about this old man, remember the three things I told you," Dr. Kensington says, "Especially when things get tough."

I want to thank him. I want to tell him I'll miss him and that he reminds me of the grandpa I never had. A lump forms in my throat and I struggle to hold in the tears. Ever perceptive, he gathers me in his arms and pats my back.

"You're the bravest, smartest, brightest person I know. I'm proud of you," he says, and then he's gone.

The staff of Willow Manor doesn't give me time alone for long. At least, not at first. Lori is an ambitious recent psychology graduate looking to further her career. Her eyes are scrutinizing and she's very proper. I can't help but feel like she's trying to figure me out and label me with some diagnosis. She's courteous but not as genuine as Robbi, a slightly older woman who looks more like a retired cheerleader than a medical professional. It's Robbi who takes the lead my tour around the facility. She shows me the dining hall, the auditorium, the spa, and the recreation area where there is a tennis court and a garden. She asks me about my hobbies and gossips about boys like we're best friends, but when I don't have much to say her chipper nature simmers to boredom until some of the other current residents of Willow Manor begin to surface.

Robbi introduces Ida.

Ida smiles at me, "Today's my birthday. I'm 74 today."

"Last year she was 82. Poor dear is so confused about her age that if we didn't have her records, we wouldn't know either. She's 97," Robbi says.

"Alzheimer's," Lori states.

Billy's a ten-year-old rebel, the kind when you tell him to sit down, he stands up just to be irritating. So Robbi tells him the opposite of what she wants him to do.

"Ignore Savannah. She's our newest guest."

He looks at me from under the rim of his Yankee's baseball cap.

"Hi," he snaps, and then runs into his room and slams the door before I can respond.

I meet a few other patients in the dining hall but they're busy playing a game of Spoons, though I'm not sure how flying spoons and cards mix. It looks fun, though.

"Best not to interrupt the Card Sharks when they're having their tournament. It can get a little wild," Robbi says.

A boy with a mass of black, thick curly hair catches my attention. He's got a thin wiry build, swallowed up with his big sweatshirt. His legs are stretched out. His shoulders are hunched. He turns his head and our eyes meet. He smiles but it looks more like a grimace. It's a look I recognize because I've felt it a thousand times.

"Let me show you the gardens next. They are gorgeous!" Robbi raves.

I don't want to see the gardens, but I follow her to be polite. Lori gives me the look again, like she's trying to diagnose me with some more disorders.

"You hungry? Our food is organic and fresh. I promise it doesn't taste like school cafeteria food," Robbi says, "You can order from your room and we'll have someone bring it to you."

We enter through the dining hall and my eyes search for the curly haired boy. He's gone. My mind wanders to the things I've seen in the past few weeks, things that've been written off as hallucinations. The newspaper Dr. Kensington showed me ruins that neat theory. If I didn't hallucinate the night from the newspaper, it's possible all of it is real.

I remember the whispering voice in the alleyway warning me, the same voice fishing me out of the water and telling me to run. We're always running, but from what? Who? I remember the fear in Dr. Kensington's eyes when he considered my hallucinations being real. He was afraid for me.

I go back to my room and call in two orders of lasagna, some garlic bread, and a brownie sundae with extra whip cream. Superbly stuffed, I fall into the deepest, most restful sleep. A quiet before the biggest storm of my life.

***

After a three weeks at Willow Manor, my injuries are almost healed completely. My cast and bandages are gone. No sleepwalking, no hallucinations. I almost question that any of my outbreaks ever happened. Willow Manor's policy for my program recommends limited interaction with the outside world, but the center encourages family support. I talk to Mom once a day and she sends me texts throughout the week. Once a week, I have individual and family sessions with my new therapist, Dr. Wilkes. He's very professional, courteous, but a little lacking in the personality department. Maybe I just miss Dr. Kensington's humor and his grandfatherly concern. Every week my results return consistent and normal, it's a win for me.

Dr. Kensington doesn't forget me. He emails me motivational quotes and links to articles on grief and anxiety. Angie remembers to check on me. I want to ask her about Jay, but I don't. Instead, I keep our conversations light, positive, and short. She doesn't need to worry about me, and I don't need to revert to those old anxieties. Tom sends me a gift a week. The first week he sends flowers. The second week I get Edible arrangements. The third week he sends the best gift – a huge stack of all the best-selling books, most signed with personal notes from the authors. Best stepdad ever. With all the amazing reads, it's difficult for me to leave the room, but my days are pleasantly filled with activity. On the days I don't have sessions or my weekly family visit, I'm busy with self-improvement classes, group sessions, and an array of fitness and artistic activities. Life is good at Willow Manor, like an extended vacation from all the craziness in life.

"Can't argue with the results," I mutter as I collapse on the stiff picnic table in the courtyard.

Billy frowns at me from underneath his Yankee's cap. He must hear me talking to myself. Wincing, I wriggle my fingers at him in a wave. He spits at me.

"Spit at me again," I snap.

"Sorry," he murmurs half-heartedly and marches on collecting rocks, probably for some prank.

Billy is a strange, troublesome kid but I kind of like him. From what Robbi says, he never apologizes to anyone for anything. Things are looking up and, if he keeps putting forth the effort to be on good behavior, he'll probably go home soon. I've got one week left before I go home. I'm afraid that if I do leave, I'll just fall back into problems. Willow Manor is a shelter. It keeps me safe from those darker, more frightening possibilities.

Pulling myself out of my thoughts, I decide I've had enough fresh air for one day, making room as the Card Sharks claim the picnic table. It's a nice out New York spring. Everyone wants to be outside. I maneuver around the Card

Sharks as they scramble to get their cards ready when I notice one of the low-key patients. I've been here for almost a month, but I still don't know his name.

It's the wiry boy with the head full of dark curly hair and the pale skin. He leans against the side of the building near the entrance. Our eyes meet, and he nods his head again, but I don't walk away this time. I don't have any other distractions. I walk towards the boy and a gentle frown causes his thin lips to droop.

"Hi, I'm Savannah."

He nods curtly and peers up at me, still frowning.

"Yeah. I know. Seen you around," the boy says, which is kind of funny because I'm not used to being talked about or remembered, and it's even funnier because I haven't seen or heard a lot about him. I find myself shuffling the weight of my body from foot to foot, giving the boy a polite space and time to introduce himself. He takes the hint, shaking my hand firmly but so fast, that I don't have time to shake his hand back.

"John."

"How'd you end up at Willow Manor?" I ask, which is probably as common a question in here as asking about the weather.

John shrugs and his eyes wander off, glancing at the Card Sharks, finally breaking the intensity of his gray eyed stare.

"The same way most people like us end up here. It just happened." He talks like it's no big deal, but his face says something different.

"Are you saying you don't know how you ended up here?"

"Not at all," John answers. He doesn't talk in an irritated tone, but I can sense that talking about himself makes him uncomfortable.

"How long have you been here?" I ask.

He shrugs, "About the same time that you came around, I suppose."

Blinking is about the only way I know to respond. We hit a dead spot in conversation, not that we really got off to such a phenomenal start.

"Sorry. I'm not used to talking about myself. Not really the interesting type, if you get my meaning," he says.

I relax. "I get it."

John's eyes narrow and he nods his head the way Dr. Wilkes does whenever I talk.

"I thought you might. You seem like a kindred spirit," he says, like he's been watching me. He stares at me, and I shuffle my feet uncomfortably. Before I can excuse myself from our conversation it takes a turn from awkward to just plain scary.

"We've got to get you out of here," he says.

My eyes veer to all the nearest exits. The door is right in front of me. Unfortunately, so is John. The Card Sharks are a few feet away, too engrossed in their game to notice us.

"Well, maybe if things turned out differently, I could agree with you, but this is the best I've felt in a while," I find myself saying.

Impatience flashes in John's gray gaze. "Listen, Savannah, I'm all for wellness but you aren't safe here. They can't protect you. You need to leave."

He steps forward and grabs my arm with surprising strength.

"There you are, Savannah!"

I jump when I hear Robbi call my name and see her wander through the doors and into the courtyard. John lets go of my arm, bumping into Robbi before retreating through the dining hall, back to wherever he normally lurks.

"I guess I'm a bit clumsy today," Robbi mutters as she approaches me.

"No. That was just rude," I mutter, thinking about John's odd behavior.

Robbi blinks, "Excuse me?"

I frown. "That kid John. He's rude."

My mouth is coated with a familiar dryness that lets me know to brace myself for disbelief and weird stares.

Robbi talks to me like I'm a babbling two-year-old. "Honey, what?"

"John, whatever his last name is. He's odd."

Robbi stares at me an entire minute. "Where is he?"

"He just bumped… Never mind."

Robbi frowns, but she doesn't push me. "You've got another gift box."

That's all she needs to say. I run to the reception desk. The receptionist gives me a half smirk, before sliding a neatly wrapped, rectangular box across her desk. "Your weekly package is here."

I mutter my thanks and race to my room to tear open the package. A note rests on top of my vintage photo album. It's from Tom.

"Savannah, we miss you and can't wait to make many more new and happy memories. Looking forward to you coming home. Love and sincerity, Tom."

I look through the old polaroid printouts of all my pictures with Mom and Dad. The quality of the photographs improves steadily to digital copies and they all make me smile, even as my eyes cloud with fresh tears. At the very back of the book is a picture of Mom, Tom, and me on their wedding day. Their eyes are light and their smiles wide, while I'm awkwardly in between them, biting my bottom lip, eyes wide like a deer in headlights. My hair is bushy, and my edges curled, while the bride and groom look like New York royalty. I look like I'm photo bombing their portrait. I'm grateful for the pictures, but all the recent images create a fresh ache in my chest.

There's a robust knock on the door.

"Come in," I say.

Robbi peaks her head in. "How are you feeling today?"

I shrug, "Okay, I guess."

She frowns, "Just okay?"

"Feeling homesick," I admit, though I'm not sure where my real home is anymore. Life with Dad in Georgia is starting to feel like a distant, almost foreign memory.

Robbi sighs and a wistful smile crosses her face. "It's your last week here."

I clear my throat, as if it will keep me from bursting into tears. "You say that like it's a good thing."

"It can be, if you're ready." she says.

I rub away my tears.

"It's about time for your weekly session."

It's my *last* session.

Robbi smiles again and turns to leave to give me privacy. When I call out to her, she stops.

I wipe my eyes again, tears wetting the back of my hands. "Thank you. For everything."

"You take care," she says, and then she's gone.

Anxiety electrifies every nerve in my body. Tears flow freely and my heart squeezes. My chest burns as I struggle to breathe, momentarily consumed with panic. Then, out of everything I've learned, I hear Dr. Kensington's voice in my head, telling me to breathe. I force myself to inhale, slowly, shakily. Then I exhale, glad I'm alone in the room and no one can hear me whimper.

You're a big girl. Pull yourself together. Breathe, girl.

My hands shake as I wipe away the last of my tears. I steady myself and take one last soothing breath before leaving my room to attend my session. If everything goes well, this will be my last week at Willow Manor. I'll return to the life I've been hiding out from, a life I'm not sure I'm ready to face.

"Get a grip," I tell myself. This is my last week. I won't sabotage it, just because I'm scared. I can't hide here forever. I pause, remembering John's warning.

You're aren't safe here. They can't protect you.

Pushing the thought aside, I move forward, ready to finish the session before I talk myself into asking for another month's stay. I'm afraid, but I miss Mom. I want to believe we can really make things work when I get home. That belief gives me the courage I need to knock on Dr. Wilke's office door. Halfway through my knock, the door opens and a man I've never seen before stares down at me. His hair is black, sleek, and glossy. His eyes are dark accompanied by an intimidating stare.

He opens the door wider and takes a seat at Dr. Wilkes's empty desk. "You must be Savannah. Come in. Have a seat."

His voice is crisp and commanding. He has a disposition I can't label. Aside from being in his early to mid-thirties, tall, and overwhelming, I'm not sure what to expect.

"Are you a doctor?" I say, secretly wondering.

"Only one of the best when it comes to cases like yours. Have a seat, Ms. Scarlett."

I inch into the room and closer to the desk where he leafs carelessly, almost impatiently through a large stack of files – files with my name on them. Cold panic washes over me and I feel my palms sweat a little. Deciding to take the doctor's advice, I sit down in the chair to the side of him, the one that's facing a hushed aquarium with tropical fish and colorful rocks. I kick my feet up and lean back. I'm grateful I don't have to look directly at this new doctor.

"Will Dr. Wilkes be here soon?"

"No," the new doctor says and before I can ask him to clarify, he says, "I instructed you to sit down, not to lounge."

For a moment I'm confused. I sit up, look around and then I notice the uncomfortable and very masculine looking chair seated directly across from him.

"Dr. Wilkes had an out of state emergency. He transferred your case to me, with recommendations for out-patient sessions as needed. I gladly accepted."

I know it's stupid, but I feel a little betrayed. "I don't understand. Out-patient sessions?"

"I am the best in the field at handling cases like yours, so naturally, I will be working with you once you are discharged from Willow Manor. That is, if you are ready to be discharged," he says.

This new doctor shuffles the stack of papers before tossing them to the side. "Any day now, Ms. Scarlett."

My cheeks flush and I scurry to the chair, feeling breathless. My lip trembles a little and my eyes start to burn. A polite knock on the door interrupts the curt tension in the room and when it opens a younger man steps in. He's tall, though not as tall as the doctor, and he's lean, wearing a pair of tan khakis and a white, crisp polo shirt. His sandy hair is loosely curled, pushed back out of his face with light gel. Where the doctor's eyes are vacuous and dark, his eyes are bright and gentle behind a pair of expensive, rectangular shaped glasses. I feel myself relax.

"My name is Doctor Raymond Santos, and this is my assistant."

The doctor carelessly introduces himself, but his voice trails off with a wave of his hand at the mention of his assistant, as if he's not important enough for him to remember his name.

"Steve," the assistant chimes in, and he shakes my hand.

Dr. Santos's posture is somehow lazy as he slouches over the desk, but his silver, glistening Rolex and finely threaded black sweater make him seem all business.

"As I have said, Dr. Wilkes is no longer in charge of your care. I am very familiar with your condition as I have worked with many patients with similar challenges."

"My previous doctor, Dr. Kensington, diagnosed me with anxiety. He was thinking the hallucinations were just a bad reaction to some painkillers I was taking, mixed with stress and bad sleep patterns," I say.

I catch Dr. Santos's gaze and it silences me. I remember my nervousness, my apprehension, and my throat goes dry again. If looks could kill I'd be on my way to the morgue.

"As I was saying, I've seen many people with your condition. I don't have to read this incessant babble to determine your case. You see, I know what you are and what your problem is, and there is only one way to handle it successfully."

Before I can ask a trail of questions, Steve clears his throat and for the first time I realize he's standing behind me, near the door.

"Forgive Dr. Santos. He believes he sees all, knows all, and is all-powerful. Most doctors like him should be labeled with a God Complex," Steve says. I can't see his face, so I don't know if he's apologizing on the doctor's behalf or teasing him. Dr. Santos leans back in his chair and the leather material groans under his weight.

"Go ahead, Ms. Scarlett. I'll humor you and let you explain yourself. Tell me what you think is going on so I can prove my assistant wrong," he says.

I've told this story too many times to want to go over it again, is what I want to say. I glance back at Steve who rolls his eyes as if to say: See, what I mean?

Fifteen minutes with Dr. Santos and I'm wondering how he has such a high success rate.

"My prior doctors' diagnosis seemed correct," I say, not really wanting to go through my embarrassing story again, especially when he blatantly doesn't want to read my file.

"Unlike you, Santos, I did read her file and not all of it is babble. It may not be what you think it is," Steve says.

Dr. Santos stops playing with a set of therapeutic marbles I'd never noticed on Dr. Wilkes' desk.

"I've been doing this longer than you, boy. It's always what I think it is."

Dr. Santos cuts his assistant a frightening look. I slump in my seat a little too afraid to interject with the deadly staring contest.

"Ms. Scarlett, my assistant and I have some things to discuss. You may be excused. For now,"

I didn't know I could move so fast. I'm up out of my seat before he can barely finish his sentence. I trip over my sneakers as I scurry to the door. Steve manages to steady me before my face meets the carpet.

Good luck, I want to say to him, but I don't say anything. I smile and just before I twist the doorknob to escape, Dr. Santos calls to me one last time.

"It was a pleasure meeting you. We will finish this soon."

That's all he says and so, before he can say more, I nod and scurry out the room, shutting the door behind me. Despite my pounding heart I lean against the door to hear what they are discussing.

"You are dismissed, Ms. Scarlett!"

I leap back from the door, wondering how he knows I'm still lingering. Maybe he is an expert after all. I take a deep breath, grateful to have made it out the office alive. Fully awake, I run down the hall and don't stop until I reach the false security of my room.

CHAPTER 11

*U*nfortunately, soon comes too soon. The day seems to fly by. I make sure to take my prescription to keep my nerves in check, but I'm too nauseated to eat so I skip lunch and dinner, picking at a piece of triple chocolate cake. Nothing beats chocolate in a stressful situation except maybe Dad's tiramisu. So, I'm quietly enjoying my dessert, when there's a knock on the door. I haven't seen anyone all day, so I figure it's Robbi coming to check on me.

"Come on in," I call out, and Steve stands in the door.

"Dr. Santos would like to see you," he says. His voice is friendly and polite, but his forehead is wrinkled with worry lines. He notices me staring at him and he smiles, all trace of grim expression gone. I don't have a good feeling about this.

"It's kind of late," I say.

Steve turns his back and steps out in the hallway. "He has his reasons."

Great. The friendly assistant is being mysterious, and not in a joking way. Something is going on, and I'm not sure I'm going to like it.

"How long have you worked with Dr. Santos?" I ask, mad at the tremor in my voice.

"A long time," Steve answers and I notice he's frowning. "Too long."

I can't help but chuckle. Steve doesn't look that old. He could still pass for a high school student, until you look at his tired eyes. He looks almost as worn as I feel.

"Is Dr. Santos that bad?" I ask.

"Worse."

I want to laugh and assume he's joking, but there's no hint of humor. I don't feel any braver or better, but I appreciate his honesty.

"Can he really help me?" I ask, hoping for some more truth.

"The only way he knows how."

"And what way is that?"

Steve stops and studies me. "You're sixteen?"

Now it's my turn to frown. He should know. He's read my file. "Yeah?"

"Unfortunate. I read about what happened to your dad in your files. I'm sorry."

We start walking again and it's only then I realize we're going in the wrong direction. Dr. Wilkes' office is the opposite direction. We're heading for the dining hall. He pushes the doors open, and we step aside as the disgruntled Card Sharks exit. They brush past us without a glance. Policy rules dictate that every patient should be in their rooms, safe and secure, by 8:30 every night. Things must have gotten rowdy if the card sharks are turning in even a few minutes early. It's not the first time that's happened and probably not the last either. Someone is always cheating.

Steve leads me through a dark and empty dining hall. My shoes squeak as I cross the floor. I feel like I'm sneaking out to somewhere I shouldn't be. I have a bad feeling.

"Where are we going?"

Instead of answering, he asks me a question, "You're afraid of heights?"

"Yeah."

"Good. Follow me."

I'm having trouble understanding why my fear of heights is a good thing. I start to ask him when I see another shadow stretching out in the courtyard. I follow the silhouette and spot a pale face frozen behind the trees. A mop of dark hair surrounds the face even underneath the telling hoodie. I start to say something, but I snap my mouth shut. No.

"Savannah?" Steve calls. I take a step to follow him but find myself looking back to the place where I saw the face behind the trees. No one's there.

"Where are we going?" I ask as we round the building. Steve unlocks a side door I never noticed before.

"Up," is all he says. 'Up' in my experience never turns out well. It usually ends with me half-awake stranded on some strange building or freaking out in front of big crowds.

"I'm afraid of heights."

"Precisely why Dr. Santos wants to have your session up here," Steve says. He climbs the isolated set of stairs and I follow against my better judgment. As I start up the stairway, I pass a door that leads back into the main hall of the rehabilitation center. Lori and Robbi are coming in and out of rooms, probably making sure everyone is settled before bed. I wonder if they've checked my room yet. I linger at the door long enough to see Robbi coming my way. She looks tired but optimistic, whistling softly. She peers through the window to the door where I am. Her eyes widen and she looks like she's coming in my direction. I whirl around to rush up the stairs and bump into Steve. He frowns but ushers me up the stairs without making a fuss. I pause when I hear knocking at the door behind us. Someone, Robbi most likely, tries the door, but it's locked.

"Are we even allowed to be here?"

"You don't want to keep Dr. Santos waiting," Steve says, prodding me forward.

As we ascend the last of the steps, Steve closes the door to the stairway, nudges me forward and leans against the door. We're on rooftop of the rehabilitation center.

 Dr. Santos waits for us and he doesn't look happy. His black, ever-bored eyes laser on Steve. "You took long enough."

His black gaze slides from his assistant to me. I have the urge to hide behind Steve's shoulder, but I don't. "What are we doing up here?"

Dr. Santos doesn't answer in words. He motions for me to step forward beside him, which happens to be near the ledge. I frown and when I don't move fast enough, Dr. Santos strides to meet me, taking me coolly by the shoulders and directing me to where he wants me to stand.

"Steve read in your file that you don't like heights," he comments, "This is correct?"

I nod and feel myself stiffen as he leads me closer and closer to the ledge. Willow Manor is not nearly as high as the Empire State Building. It's not even as high as the other building I managed to injure my arm jumping from, but it's high enough to make me nervous. Especially when Dr. Santos keeps scooting me closer to the edge of the building.

"Dr. Santos?"

He lets out a deep sigh, interrupting my whimper of a voice. "Savannah, we're simply here to enjoy the night air, to let go of pretense and discover truth."

I almost laugh but I'm shaking. Dr. Santos inhales deeply before taking a giant step forward to stand on the ledge.

"The night skyline is extraordinary from this view. Come look, Savannah."

I glance back at Steve. He doesn't offer me any reassuring smiles, but he nods curtly. I take an inch of a step forward and fold my arms across my chest, not really interested in looking at the skyline. It's not like we can see the stars. There is a dark overcast and it looks like it could rain. Something else catches my eyes, far below the skyline. Shadows are moving in the courtyard. I inhale sharply, even though I know the shadows are just trees and maybe small animals scurrying around. No one is outside, except for the three of us.

"Is everything okay, Savannah?" Dr. Santos asks, as if he can tell even the subtlest change in my mood. Weird. He's not even looking at me. He's staring off at the sky.

"I'm fine. I guess I just don't understand what we're doing here. I thought you said you could help me."

He still doesn't turn to look at me, but his jaw tightens.

"My methods are very unconventional. I am attempting patience. You can thank Steve for that. I hope to trigger the source of your problems."

"H-how do you do that?"

He looks at me then and his eyes are calm. "A few moments ago, when you gasped, what was it you saw?"

"You could tell that I – I mean, there's nothing out here. Just the three of us."

Dr. Santos shakes his head. "I need truth if I am to help you."

My eyes scan the perimeter of the courtyard again. I see a flash of clothing, a flash of shadow, and then it's gone.

"It's this kid, John. He practically ran over Robbi and she didn't even acknowledge him."

"Do you see him now?" he asks.

I bite my lip. "No. It's probably just the night playing tricks on me."

"Don't tell me what you think I want to hear. Tell me what happened. Tell me what you saw tonight."

"I think I did see a face. It looked like him, like John."

Dr. Santos nods, "John. He's a common link between most patients with your problem. I'd like to meet him."

"He's been a patient at other centers?"

Dr. Santos grimaces, "He isn't a patient."

I frown. "I'm not sure I understand."

Dr. Santos actually smiles and for some reason it's more frightening than when he glares, "Tell me, Savannah. Do you really want to do what it takes to get well?"

Steve approaches us.

"I would really like to know exactly what my issues are first. Before I commit to anything extreme," I say carefully, "What does John have to do with anything?"

Santos turns and stares down at me. "He's here to save you. You, my dear, are an Errant, an abomination to the natural order of things, a danger to yourself and everyone around you, a walking bomb without the safety, ready to explode at any moment, even in your ignorance. There are things you can do, that you have done, that defy nature itself. Things I cannot allow to continue. I will help you to the best of my ability in the only way I know how. You aren't going to like it, but the less you know, the better. You are young and as innocent as your kind can be, so I will be generous and grant you this mercy."

I try to take a step back from the ledge, but he reaches for me, his grip tight on my shoulder.

"Dr. Santos, maybe I should go back to my room and just wait – "

"We're running out of time," Steve interjects, and I hear a faint sound coming from the stairwell, "I don't think you were right about Savannah–"

"I am never wrong!" he snarls, just before he pulls out a gun. "This is my method, Savannah. Your fear will betray you. You will reveal yourself for what you really are, and I will cure you the only way you can be cured. I will end your life."

I lunge forward to knock the gun from his hand. We watch it slide across the edge of the concrete. Dr. Santos wraps a strong hand around my throat. He applies enough pressure to cause all common sense and rational thought to take flight in my mind, lifting my feet off the ground and dangling me over the edge.

"Santos, enough! She isn't one of them! Let her go! You've made a mistake. She's just a kid."

"When are you going to learn? I don't make mistakes. She's one of them. She just hasn't been trained. Best kill her now before she becomes another thorn in our side. I could just snap her neck. Tell them she jumped."

"Killing her was not the plan. We are to study her, to be sure. Santos, no!"

I can't breathe with his rough hard fingers clasped against my throat. My heart hammers against my burning chest. I can feel the rest of my body numb while my head and ears began to swell.

A cacophony of shouts rings out. Steve and Dr. Santos scream at one another, and I'm falling. Gravity refuses to support me. I stretch my arms out and scratch at the cement ledge. I catch hold of the corner of the ledge and I suck in as much air as I can. A hand reaches for mine. It's Steve!

"Your other hand," he says, and I swing it up towards him like a person being rescued from drowning. He latches on to me and pulls me to him and away from the ledge. He walks me to the stairway, but we don't get far.

"I am afraid I cannot let you go, Ms. Scarlett. Nor you, my disobedient friend."

Dr. Santos's voice comes from behind us. He sounds so calm, it's chilling. Steve and I turn around to face the doctor. He has his gun again, and he points it at me. Steve stands in front of me.

"Dr. Santos, w–why are you–"

"He's not a doctor," Steve says, just as Dr. Santos pulls the trigger.

There's no ringing in my ears, no loud sound to alarm anyone that I'm about to die. There's only a soft hiss of wind as the bullet flies. I close my eyes, but I don't feel any pain. Instead, I hear the gun click again.

Opening my eyes, I see a figure in a gray hoodie standing a few feet in front of me.

"John!" I shout.

Dr. Santos is on the ground behind him, struggling to stand to his feet.

John's pale face looks white under the night sky and his thick, untamed curls only enhance the pallor of his skin underneath his hood.

"Now!" I hear Dr. Santos hiss.

There is another click beside me this time, and I turn in time to see Steve with a gun. His face is hardened, and he doesn't seem so kind now, but he doesn't seem as quick to shoot either. John shoves me behind him and shoots Steve with Santos' gun before I can try to talk him down. A perfect round hole forms in the center of Steve's forehead. A perfect pool of blood drips down his forehead and his face. Steve's eyes go wide as he falls backward.

Before a scream can rise from the depths of my stomach and out of my mouth, John whirls us around, his arm cradling me around the waist. He aims without focus, shooting wildly at Santos. Santos isn't caught off guard but dodges with frightening expertise, almost like he can see the bullets in the dark. John unloads all the bullets and succeeds in shooting Dr. Santos once. By the way he jerks back it looks like a shoulder wound. He doesn't flinch but comes running.

John throws the gun at Dr. Santos like he's pitching rocks. Dr. Santos catches it and already has bullets in his hand to reload it. John mutters something unintelligible. It's hard to tell but before I know it, he picks me up in an awkward hold and we hurtle off the side of the building.

"Stupid girl." he says.

A scream lodges in the middle of my throat as we hit the ground a little smoother than I thought possible. We're moving so fast now, and I don't know where we're going or how. Impossibly cradled in the arms of someone shorter than me, there is an odd sense of security. I turn my face into his chest, struggling to inhale and exhale as the world around me blurs into one stream of congealed colors and finally fades away into nothingness.

CHAPTER 12

The sound of my own scream wakes me, and I jolt upright out of bed. The room is dark and foreign. Three shadows hover at the foot of my bed. One of the figures leans forward and their form takes full shape as my eyes adjust to the dark. Dark, curly hair and pale faced with gray eyes, John grabs a gentle hold on my shoulders.

"Hey now. It's okay. It's over."

"What's over?" I croak. More of the room begins to take shape. I don't recognize any of it.

"You're okay now," he says.

I must have lapsed and wandered off in my sleep.

The more John stares at me, the more I come out of my daze. I remember Dr. Santos and Steve on the rooftop of Willow Manor. I remember gun shots and blood.

"She looks like she's going to pass out again," comes another voice. There's a figure much taller and bulkier than John's scrawny form. He reminds me of a linebacker from my dad's favorite football team. He's got dark brown hair cropped close to his ears, a defiant jaw, and a dimple in his chin.

"No. She just needs a minute to let everything sink in," John observes confidently. But I'm with the other guy. My head feels like I've smashed it into concrete and my limbs are weak.

"You're in so much trouble. I can't believe you broke her out of that place," comes another voice, this time a sour, feminine tone. A lithe form appears at the foot of my bed and a girl with soft blonde hair collapses gracefully in a chair. She leans forward to stare at me.

"Who are you? Where am I?" All clichéd questions, I know, but still very important.

"That knowledge is privilege, and you're on a need-to-know basis," Linebacker says, though he sounds more amused than anything. I pinch myself and my heart flutters. This feels real, just like all the other times. Sadly, those other times I thought I was stuck in a dream were real. "You killed Steve!"

John grimaces and mutters something that sounds like, "For now."

"And Dr. Santos?"

John shakes his head and he doesn't look very happy.

"News flash, girl. They weren't real doctors. They're master manipulators, experts of infiltration and lies. They tried to kill you, and they're the type of people who won't stop until you're six feet under," the girl says.

I chuckle. This is all crazy. "Why would they want to kill me? I'm nobody."

"That remains to be seen," Linebacker says, squinting at me. Then he smiles as if he can't keep up the tough act. He turns his head and fakes a cough, but I can hear him chuckle.

My head is pounding, a feeling that only gets worse as I try to get out of bed.

John reaches to help me. "Easy there. You've had quite a ride."

I pull away from him a little too quickly. Cold sweat breaks across my skin, like a spontaneous rash and the room spins. I lose what little balance I have. My legs refuse to support my weight. I collapse back onto the bed.

"You've got to take me back. My mom will be looking for me. I promise, I won't say anything. Just take me back or let me go. I'll find my own way."

Out of all the other things that haunt my memory, I can't get the image of Steve out of my mind. The mild assistant with the soothing voice and kind smile with a bloody hole in the center of his forehead. And Dr. Santos snarling and shooting at me, dodging bullets that John fired back without hesitation. Nothing makes sense. My throat tightens, containing my overwhelming need to cry loud and ugly.

John and the other two strangers exchange a look.

"Are you sure she's not crazy?" the girl asks.

John nods, "I read her file. They did too. They've been slipping in and out of facilities for a while now."

I try to breathe, but my throat tightens even more.

John touches my arm again. "Savannah, listen to me."

I pull away, scooting back into the bed, pulling my knees up to my aching chest.

"You've got to take me back." My words are broken, nearly inaudible as I struggle to breathe. My limbs shake. Cold panic washes over me.

"I don't think she's taking this well," linebacker says.

They continue to talk and even though I can hear them, but it's getting harder to focus

"She may really be mental."

"No. Maybe she just needs a little space."

It's harder to breathe.

"You and your crazy crusades. If nothing clicks by tomorrow, I say we dump her back at that–"

"Guys, she's turning colors."

The room blurs and darkens.

***

I wake up to sunlight piercing through partially cracked blinds. The window is open and fresh air drifts in.

Linebacker greets me. "Good afternoon, Sleeping Beauty."

He looks different in the light. He could be an Olympic athlete, but he wears an infectious grin that makes me relax before I remind myself I've been kidnapped.

"Thought you were in a coma," the blonde girl grumbles. She's pretty like Angie, the type of girl that could pass for an actress, but her pinched expression is intimidating.

"What happened? Where am I?"

The pretty girl with the ugly attitude sighs dramatically. "Geezer, did you damage her short-term memory or was she this dizzy when you found her?"

The last person staring at me is the most familiar face, John. He directs his frown at the girl but somehow manages to keep his sharp gray eyes on me.

"How are you feeling?" he asks. "You've been asleep for almost two days now, off and on."

"Yeah, and apparently you talk and walk in your sleep, too," the girl snaps.

I rub my eyes and sit up. A surge of frustration stirs me out of the drowsiness.

"That's why I was at Willow Manor, dumb blonde."

I don't realize I'm talking out loud until her eyes dilate and her frown turns into a snarl. She takes a step forward, but Linebacker grabs her arm and shakes his head.

John smiles, "I think I like this girl."

"Yeah, me too," Linebacker says with a sloppy grin

"Savannah, there is a lot we've got to explain to you–" John begins.

"You bet," I say, glaring right back at Blondie. "This is kidnapping. You're going to be in a lot of trouble when the cops find you."

"Stupid girl," John says.

His words trigger a memory. I scramble out of bed only to manage getting tangled in the sheets and falling on the floor. John reaches to help me up, but I slap his hand away.

"It was you. You're the one from the alley that night I fell from the fire escape."

John's not only the voice who warned me about the guys in the van that night. He's the one who pulled me out of the water and ran with me in the streets when we were being chased. He's been with me nearly every crazy step.

John and the others watch me struggle to stand to my feet.

"Savannah, you were never hallucinating, and the blackouts aren't what you think," John says.

My limbs shake so much; I swear my body's vibrating.

"Did you beat that guy that grabbed me in the alley?"

John shrugs. "Scared him enough to keep him off your back and make him turn himself in."

This can't be happening. Things were so good at Willow Manor. I was getting better and so close to going home and starting over. I should be on a girls' trip to Georgia with my mom right now. Instead, things are spiraling out of control in the worst possible way.

Dr. Kensington's comforting voice echoes in my head. I close my eyes and try to breathe, but my panic wins. Instead of therapeutic breaths, I'm screaming at the top of my lungs, "Take me home! Take me home, now!"

"Geezer, what'd you do?"

The voice is quiet but powerful enough to cut through my hysteria. It's a brooding pitch of steeled tenor masked in silk. My eyes fly open and I find myself staring open-mouthed at the one person I thought I'd never see again, the one person this all started with. He's taller than I remember. There's no leather jacket this time. He stands in the doorway wearing a pair of dark jeans with a plain, black t-shirt. His dark eyes are sharply sculpted, the shape of slender almonds. His nose is sharply set on his angular face between high cheek bones and a chiseled jawline. His mouth is thin, and firm set in a hard line of disapproval, but I'm the one who's furious.

That familiar cold sweat breaks out on the surface of my skin and seeps through my bloodstream. My hands are cold and shaky; my legs unsteady again. "You're dead! You should be dead. I saw you!"

He frowns. "I'm very much alive."

I half-step, half-stumble closer to him. Not believing my eyes, I poke him in the chest. He grabs my finger firmly, his grip warning me not to touch him again. His hand is rough but warm and tangible.

"I can't believe this," I mutter.

Linebacker takes a half stumble, half step closer to me.

"Uh, K.O.? You know each other?"

K.O. drops my finger, but his gaze is searing. "Never seen her before."

Anger evaporates my bout of cold sweat. After everything that happened, the stress he triggered, he has the nerve to not even remember my face. He practically trampled me.

"You ruined my life!"

He takes a step closer to me, but John grabs his arm. I expect the older boy to shrug him off, but he stops and turns that glare on John.

"K.O., she saw you at the Empire State Building. That's the reason I've been watching her. They know she's one of us and tried to kill her. They read about what happened in her file."

The blonde girl with the attitude steps forward now. "Hold up a sec. What happened at the Empire State Building?"

K.O. frowns at John, "Take her back where you found her before she gets us killed."

He doesn't wait to hear John's rebuttal and he doesn't spare me any last threatening looks. He just struts right out the room like he owns the world. The impossible boy who contributed to killing my social life before it even started is somehow alive and attitudinal.

"K.O., I'm not done with you! She's more your responsibility than anyone's!" John hollers, following after K.O.

Linebacker and Blondie, stare at me with new interest. At least Linebacker is nice enough to make introductions.

"We didn't have a chance to introduce ourselves. You know Geezer from Willow Manor."

"Geezer?"

"Yup. The short, curly haired dude. Barely fourteen but acts like he's sixty?"

I smirk. John does have old eyes and he does seem to be more mature than he looks, if a little grouchy.

"I'm guessing you've met K.O., too?" Linebacker asks.

"What kind of name is K.O. anyway?" I grumble, not even bothering to answer his question.

Blondie lifts a delicate brow, "K.O. as in 'Knockout', and we're not just talking about the kind that leaves you on the floor from a good beat down. He's a *knockout*."

She repeats herself as if she can't believe I'm not drooling over him.

"The hyperventilating blonde here is Roxanne. We just call her Rox," Linebacker says, "I'm Tristan."

As friendly as Tristan is, I'm not in the mood to be cordial. "Um, Tristan, why am I here? What do you guys want from me?"

"The short story is you're one of us."

"And you are… like a fraternity or sorority or something?"

That is the most positive guess I have. Worst case scenario leads me to believe that they're some kind of gang or cult. Tristan chuckles and Rox remains tight lipped. Neither of them answers my question. I open my mouth to demand answers, but my stomach growls instead. Tristan's eyes light up.

"Just relax, Savannah. I'm going to make you the best BLT you've ever had, and then Geezer will explain everything."

He pats my hand before sprinting out the room. I'm shocked when the old wood floors don't groan under his giant footsteps.

"You know, either you're crazy or you're just plain stupid. Let me give you a nice piece of advice. Keep your mouth shut and let Geezer do the talking for you. You don't want to get on

K. O.'s bad side," Rox says and then smirking, she adds, "Oh, right. Looks like you're already there. Ta-ta, new girl."

She tosses her hand up at me and strides out the room, leaving me to figure out what I'm going to do. The no-brainer is that I need to get out of here and find my way back home. The hard work is in the details. I don't know where I am or how I'm going to get out of here. I don't even understand why I'm here. Though Tristan seems nice, I suspect that John…Geezer is my key to surviving this place. The others seem to respect his opinion enough to tolerate me. If I can figure out what Geezer wants, maybe I can talk him into sending me back to Willow Manor.

My stomach growls again and my mouth waters as I think about what Tristan promised. A bacon sandwich does sound good. Food should be the last thing on my mind. Maybe once I get some food in my system I can think more clearly. I should be figuring out a way to get out of here or at least some way to call the cops, but I find myself in a fetal position in the bed, trying to relax my pounding heart. I can't afford to lose consciousness again. I have to stay focused, calm, and alert.

Still, I manage to fall asleep and I find myself dreaming about the crazy event at the Empire State Building. K.O. and the other boy are climbing the fences and the guard rails again. But when K.O. throws both of them over the side of the building, the blond boy disappears and I'm the one he's holding. It's me he uses the wind to push down as he smiles sadistically.

My body crashes against the pavement below only for me to wake up and realize I've fallen out of bed. I'm not alone either. Tristan stands at the partially open doorway, staring at me with wide eyes. He doesn't ask me if I'm okay. I think it's obvious I'm not. I'm tangled up in the covers again, wrapped like a pig-in-the blanket on the floor. I'm drenched in sweat and my hair is pointing in every which direction but right. Thankfully Tristan snaps out of his stupor and helps me out of the knotted material. He lifts me up off the floor by my arms and wrinkles his nose.

"I know you're probably really hungry, but I think you should shower first," he says.

My cheeks feel hot, but he's right. A shower is the least of my needs right now, but it's a start.

"Kidnappers usually don't care about their captive's hygiene," I mutter.

"You're not a captive," he responds slowly, frowning at me, "Spare clothes and stuff are over there."

He gestures to the old wooden nightstand by the bed. I stumble over and find all kinds of toiletries: toothbrush, toothpaste, hairbrush, hair gel, lotions, and deodorant. My eyes trail to a duffle bag on the floor in front of the nightstand. I open it to find two pairs of jeans, a t-shirt, my favorite sweatshirt, and a plain white summer dress. It all looks hauntingly familiar.

"Geezer grabbed a couple of your things from Willow Manor. Your white sneakers are at the foot of your bed," Tristan informs me. "An extra towel and wash cloth are already in the bathroom for you."

"Thanks."

He smiles. "Just holler for me when you're ready to eat. I'll make you a fresh order of the BLT I promised you. I ate the other one."

His cheeks get a little red, but I smile back at him as he leaves.

The bathroom is plain and cramped. There are simple whitewashed walls and more old wood floors that creak underneath the weight of my clumsy feet. I brush my teeth and struggle with the faucet in the shower for a few minutes before I figure out how to turn on the water.

Ten minutes later, I'm dressed in a simple pair of jeans and an Irish green, short-sleeve tee with a fresh pair of clean white socks. I'm too hungry to bother with my half-wet hair, so I let it curl and frizz as it dries.

Wandering out of the bathroom I notice there are two other doors down the narrow hallway and a few steps away from the opposing rooms are the stairs. The stairs are narrow and steep, made of old, dull wood that groans and cracks under my feet. My legs feel like Jell-O, so I take my time going down, gripping the banister tightly to keep from falling. Once I reach the landing successfully, the smell of bacon grease greets my nostrils and my mouth waters.

I find myself in an open space with more wood floor. Only this time the wood is decorated with sleeping bags, quilts, and duffel bags. It looks like someone's interrupted slumber party. The windows are boarded up with only tiny slithers of light shining into the room. I step over the bedding and other miscellaneous items. Tripping is hard to avoid, especially when my body feels so drained. When I finally emerge into the kitchen where all the noise is coming from, a light sheen of sweat has built across my forehead.

The windows in the kitchen are boarded up like the other room with small rays of sunshine coming through. The kitchen is brighter though, thanks to mustard yellow wallpaper and a dim rectangular shaped ceiling light. The room is smoky but not uncomfortable as Tristan stands at an outdated, plain white stove with a metal spatula and a skillet handle in his hand. He whistles, lifting the skillet from the stove to spread crisp, delicious looking bacon onto fresh sourdough bread.

Rox sits idly at a round, unevenly dark colored, wooden table with four matching chairs. She examines her uneven nails with a frown while Geezer reads a newspaper. His eyes peek over the top of the newspaper to study me.

"Good to see you up and about. I thought maybe you had a concussion from our trip"

I frown.

"He's teasing," Tristan says while cutting a few slices of tomato.

My mouth waters again.

"Actually, I'm quite serious. Things were a little sticky on our way here. I was a bit reckless."

I stare at the fourteen-year-old as Tristan sets a plate with a delicious looking BLT in front of me. I don't even think about the possibility the food might be poisoned or drugged until I've devoured my first few bites, and by then I don't care. I take another bite and my taste buds explode with gratitude. I don't even realize I'm grunting until the room goes still and I notice everyone staring at me.

"Chew much?" Rox complains.

My cheeks get hot as I swallow the barely chewed hot bacon sandwich with crisp lettuce and juicy tomato.

"I'll cook for you any time, Savannah. At least I know you'll appreciate it," Tristan says.

I smile at him instead of responding because I can't stop stuffing my face, but I also can't help but address Geezer's comment with a question.

"Where is here? And what happened while I was unconscious? How is K.O. alive after making that jump?"

Geezer cuts me off. "Don't talk with your mouth full. It's rude, and I can't really understand you. Finish your food. Then we'll talk about everything."

I give him my toughest glare before forcing myself to put the last little morsel of food back on my plate. I slide the plate out of my reach and swallow the rest of the food in my mouth.

"Well?" I prompt when Geezer just blinks at me.

"Maybe you should let your food settle."

He's stalling.

"Start talking or I'll do something you'll regret."

Geezer coughs to hide a laugh, "Save your temper tantrum. You don't scare me. You're harmless. The most daring thing I've seen you consciously do is skip school for a few days and pick a fight with your aunt."

"Right. You've been stalking me."

He shrugs. "And saving your life."

"Tell me what's going on now," I demand. *"Please."*

Panic rises. Geezer grimaces and reaches across the table to pat my hand.

Rox and Tristan stare like I'm an interesting lab rat bumping around a maze searching for cheese.

Geezer turns to them. "Rox? Tristan? Give us a minute."

They don't argue, but they seem reluctant to leave. Geezer stubbornly keeps his mouth closed in a thin line until they leave the kitchen.

"If anyone should tell you, it should be me. Which makes sense, since I rescued you and–"

"And stalked me and kidnapped me," I remind him.

He clears his throat. "I know what it looks like, but I'm sure you'll thank me when you understand –"

"Enlighten me."

Geezer's eyebrow flies up, but he smiles. "You're feistier than I thought you'd be. That's good. Maybe you won't freak out."

Before I can open my mouth to urge him to get on topic, he rushes into the discussion. "You're not crazy, sick, or broken. You're just different. You're an Errant."

"What's an Errant?" I want to ask, but he interrupts me with a raise of his hand.

"This is difficult enough to explain without your interruptions," he says.

I shut my mouth. I'm trusting a 14-year-old to diagnose my case.

"This is normal," he says holding up his pointer finger. Then he stretches his arm wide and wriggles his other pointer finger. "This is you. You are an outlier. Because you're on a completely different spectrum, you don't see things like other people, and you can do some extraordinary things."

I lean forward, "Like?"

I can't help but interrupt. Getting answers out of him is like pulling teeth.

"Agility, for one. We can move so fast, the average eye can't see us, technology can't pick us up. That's why your stepdad's security system couldn't detect you."

"I can't believe I'm saying this, but that's a better explanation than anything else I can think of. What else can we do? Are we some kind of alien or something?"

He winces.

"Maybe a fairy? A vampire that sparkles in the sunlight?" I ask.

He takes a sip of his coffee. "Don't hate on the sparkly vampires. I liked those books, but no. No to all the above. You know, you're actually taking this way better than I thought you would."

"Just give it to me straight. Stalling makes me nervous," I say.

Geezer opens his mouth.

"Wait!" I say, "Did you happen to grab my prescription before you kidnapped me?"

If I'm going to survive this conversation, I need all the advantages I can get.

Before I blink, a blur of gray whizzes past me. By the time I manage to blink Geezer hands me my prescription and a bottle of water. He collapses in his chair and drinks the rest of his coffee.

"I didn't even- how did you…"

I can't put my words in logical order. Geezer motions for me to take my pill. I comply, trying to figure out how he got my pills from upstairs and a bottle of water from the fridge in the time it took me to blink.

"It's hard to define what we can do in a neat little box. Most of what I've learned is through trial, error, and accidents that didn't end in me dying. Our powers are wild, fickle, and extremely dangerous. Speed barely scratches the surface of the things we can do, but it's something we all have in common."

"What else can you do?" I ask, finally able to string a few words together coherently.

Geezer sighs again, "You ever heard of the fight or flight response? It's a little like that. Stress, adrenaline, any strong emotion can trigger it. Our abilities are like a hyperactive defense mechanism. Our body kicks into overdrive and we survive by whatever means necessary."

He reads my confusion well. "Ever heard about people who've been able to lift cars with their bare hands to save someone's life?"

"So, we have super strength, too?" I ask.

"It's another common ability, yes, but you're missing the point. There have been people all over the world who've been able to do things that shouldn't be possible, all because of that survival instinct. So, to answer your earlier question, we aren't aliens or anything else spectacular. We're human. There's nothing in us that isn't in every other person. We're just a little more sensitive. Our response to danger and other stressful situations is more… exaggerated. It can't be picked up on medical scans or any other technology unless we're having one of those moments. Is any of this making sense?"

"I think so. It's like fight or flight on steroids."

He nods. "I know this is a lot to take in. What's happening to you, happened to me when I was seven. The first thing the power does is opens your eyes. I remember waking up in the middle of the night, roaming the streets, not knowing how I got there. I saw people doing the craziest things, like they were in a circus, walking power lines like tightropes and up the sides of buildings like they had on magnetic shoes…"

His eyes gloss over, and I realize he's lost himself in his own mind.

"My dad died when I was five. I never knew my mom. I moved from home to home, so I never really had anyone to care what happened to me. One night the cops found me wandering around and before I knew it, I was back in an orphanage. No one wanted a kid like me. I had a lot of time to think, a lot of time to practice. When I had enough of being cooped up, I walked out of there, and no one even noticed."

I feel my eyes tear up. No wonder Geezer acts so old. I can't imagine being that young dealing with the confusion and fear of not being aware or in control of my body.

Geezer sighs. "Savannah, what I'm trying to say is that I understand what you're going through. The blackouts and the confusion are normal. It's not a sign that you're losing your mind. Your power will control you until you learn to harness it. I know what it's like to feel lost and alone, but you don't have to go through this alone. That much I can promise."

He grows silent, watching me, giving me time to mull over everything he's told me. A slow, deep burn ignites in my chest and my hands shake, but I breathe in deep and swallow my panic.

"I want to see more," I tell him.

Tension leaves his expression. He stands, and his eyes light up, "Speed and strength are common for us, but like I said, it's hard to put us in a box."

He walks backwards to the kitchen door and sticks his head into the other room. "Come on, you two!"

Rox and Tristan come barreling in. Tristan grins and Rox cracks her knuckles.

"Some of us have specialties. We're still learning and discovering our power. It's a lot of trial and error, and praying we don't kill ourselves in the process," he says, "I'm inclined to believe that we can do anything we can imagine, if we're brave enough."

Geezer dramatically ushers my attention to Rox. Her hair is tied out of her face in a loose braid which she casually tosses over her shoulder. She's shorter than me, petite really, but when she cracks her knuckles again, I get the impression that she's a lot tougher than she seems.

"The kitchen table," Geezer instructs, though I have no clue what he means.

Rox crosses her arms. "Really?"

He clears his throat and she sighs, but she doesn't argue anymore. She uses her slender forefinger to gently trace the edges of the kitchen table, almost like a caress. Taking a deep breath, she places one fingertip, one half bitten nail in the center of the table. Nothing happens for a minute but as she steps back, the table cracks. Then it crumbles without a sound until it's nothing but wood chips and sawdust.

"She may look delicate, but looks can be misleading," Geezer brags.

"We've all got our favorite tricks," Tristan explains with a smirk.

Rox frowns, "Now we need a new kitchen table to match the chairs."

She's just disintegrated an entire table with her fingernail, and she's worried about matching furniture?

"Tristan, as big and clumsy as he seems is very light on his feet. He moves faster than most human eyes can see. Most of us do and that's why you see things that others don't have time to comprehend," Geezer explains.

As if to demonstrate what he's talking about, my eyes wander to a trashcan that seems to disappear in thin air.

"Focus," Geezer whispers, but I can't. My body won't let me, and I don't fight it. I give into the darkness before hearing familiar voices whisper.

"She didn't handle that too well. She's weak."

"She handled it better than you, Rox."

"Please, Geezer. She's just a new project to occupy your time since you gave up trying to fix K.O. You probably won't be able to fix her either. She's not one of us."

"Maybe you're just jealous she's taking attention away from you, and you're worried about not being the only girl anymore."

"Me? Jealous of her?"

The voices escalate from whispers to shouts. It hurts my head and I try to say so, but another voice cuts through the chaos.

"Stop bickering you two. She's waking up," Tristan says.

He stoops to help me up before my eyes are even halfway open. My head is still light as he sits me up.

"How did I–"

"You passed out," Tristan says.

"Not so fast. Give her a minute," comes Geezer's voice, and then I see his shoes in front of me, an expensive, white pair of Nikes. I don't know why I stare at his shoes. Maybe because it's the only thing in the room that seems simple right now.

Who am I kidding? All I ever wanted was to fit in, to make a few friends, and feel accepted. But what Geezer is telling me is that I'm a freak of nature. Most humans don't throw themselves off buildings and not go splat on sidewalks. Most humans don't turn sturdy wood tables into sawdust with their nail tips.

Tristan helps me stand and walks me slowly back to one of the chairs.

"No way. There's no way I can do any of this. I believe you, but I don't think I'm cut out for this."

Surprisingly Rox is the one to respond. She peers at me, right before slapping me in the face so hard it feels like whiplash. "If you don't get a grip, like right now, you'll experience more pain than that. We're not messing with you. We're not joking. Though, personally I think you're a joke. You're just a whiny little brat who happened to see K.O. in some action. It's not the first time Geezer's picked up a dud."

Rox lets Tristan tug her away from me and out of my face before turning her glare on Geezer, "I'm with K.O. on this one. I think you're wrong about her," she says before storming out of the kitchen and out the front door.

"Sorry," Tristan grumbles, and then he follows Rox outside, slamming the door behind him.

Geezer peers at me with squinted focus.

"You might bruise," he says.

I cradle my cheek and the skin burns with throbbing pain I almost didn't recognize.

"Welcome to our world," he adds with a smile.

My stomach growls in response, even though I just ate barely half hour ago.

"Dinner?" Geezer asks.

CHAPTER 13

I'm three bowls of sugary cereal deep and finishing a peanut butter and jelly sandwich with the crusts cut off, when Geezer slides me two bottles of water and an apple.

"Our powers seem limitless, but they take their toll on us. It makes us hungrier, thirstier, and more fatigued than the average person. For a newbie, a trick or two a day may require eating half the food in the fridge and sleeping twelve to fifteen hours. It's exhausting being this extraordinary."

"But I didn't do anything," I say, "So why am I so hungry?"

"Your brain's working harder than normal."

I laugh but Geezer keeps a straight face.

"Right now, your power's on cruise control. You're just a puppet being jerked around. If you're stressed, furious, depressed, or even extremely happy, you're likely to blackout and find yourself in another situation. You'll be hungry, thirsty, and exhausted all the time. Once you gain some control, it won't be so bad," he continues.

"How do I do that?"

He takes an orange off the counter, peels it, and tosses it at me like a pitcher throwing a fast ball. The orange blurs. I duck, and it hits the wall with so much impact it gets stuck. The wall around the embedded orange begins to crack and split.

"Conditioning."

He peels another orange. I prepare to duck, but to my relief he juggles it from hand to hand.

"There's something else. Once you take your power off cruise control, you better commit to whatever you put yourself out there to do. You can't leap off a building and get scared at the last minute. That kind of fear short circuits your power."

Familiar panic attaches to my insides, making the walls of my chest heavy. "What happens when it short circuits?"

"The same thing that happens to anyone else. The power stops. We've lost some people that way. They wanna try something fancy and get scared at the last minute. Splat, crash, dead."

The food in my stomach churns. "How can you be sure I can do these things in the first place?"

"I've watched you do them," he says, reminding me that he's been following me way before my days at Willow Manor.

"Why didn't you tell me before now? I could've avoided a lot of trouble."

He frowns, "Kind of hard when your powers are pulling your strings. I did what I could."

"What if I can see you and the others use your power but I can't do it? What if your wrong about me?"

"You'll never really know until you test it," he says.

"But what if I test it and nothing happens? What if I end up like the people you've known that tried and didn't make it?"

His gray gaze lasers into me. "You will if you keep thinking like that. Fight, fly, or die."

It's the worst motivational tagline I've ever heard.

"Controlling your abilities isn't the only thing you need to worry about. Don't forget that we were being chased all those times I rescued you. Don't forget about Santos," Geezer warns.

I don't think I'll ever forget Santos. Those dark, focused eyes. His hands crushing my throat. Just thinking about it makes my throat burn.

"He said I was an abomination. He tried to kill me. If you hadn't been there –"

My airways constrict.

Breathe. I remind myself.

"Count yourself lucky. Santos succeeds more often than he fails," Geezer says, "But we'll deal with one problem at a time."

He sets the orange down on the counter. I breathe out slowly. The pressure in my chest eases just a little.

"He called me something else. An errand...er –"

"Errant," Geezer corrects, "It's what he calls our kind of people. Santos thinks we're the equivalent to a ticking time bomb. He's not wrong, but I'm not a fan of his solution. Killing isn't the answer. "

I shake my head. "Isn't there some way to just make it go away?"

"It won't go away. It's part of you. You have to learn to control it," he says.

Geezer picks up the orange and pitches it at me. I raise my hand instinctively to catch it, even while closing my eyes and bracing myself to get hit, but the orange is already in my hand. I'm holding on to it while still waiting to get knocked upside the head. I open my eyes, staring at the orange. My palm is sore from the impact of the catch, but nowhere near as bad as the wall behind me.

"Get some rest," Geezer says, "You'll need it."

I still have so many questions, but Geezer's right. Standing to my feet, fatigue hits me so hard, my limbs feel like lead, but one persistent thought causes me to pause.

"My mom. I need to –"

Geezer gives me a sour look, "No. No contact. Not until we figure out how to handle Santos."

"But–"

"You want to put your life in danger? You mom's life? Santos is dangerous, and he's waiting for you to make stupid choices. No contact."

I want to push the issue, but I'm too exhausted. Mom must be going out of her mind. Things were going so well at Willow Manor. When she finds out what Santos did, when they find Steve's dead body and she realizes I've been kidnapped… I can't even imagine how she'll respond. I barely know what to think or how to feel outside of the stubborn exhaustion. Somehow, I make it up the stairs and down the hall. Every cell in my body sighs in relief when I fall into the bed. I close my eyes and rehash all the craziness I've seen: K.O. diving off the Empire State Building, Rox smashing tables, Tristan moving so fast he looks like a ghost, and then I'm dreaming. I see baby-faced Geezer, pointing a gun, shooting, and killing someone without blinking. It's me. I've got a bullet in the middle of my forehead and I'm lying on a concrete rooftop decorating it with a growing pool of blood.

My eyes snap open. I'm no longer in bed. I'm no longer dreaming. A bitter night wind slaps against my wet, tear-stained cheeks. It's not the first time I've cried in my sleep. It's also not the first time I've woken up to find myself somewhere other than in bed. It's just that this time tops the charts for worst case scenario.

I'm not in an alleyway being chased by drunks, and I'm not barefoot stepping in broken glass. While nearly drowning in some unidentified body of water was bad, the current situation ties for the worst blackout ever. I'm up high, only I'm not on a rooftop. I'm standing flatfooted on a ledge, sharing space with a creepy looking stone gargoyle. My heart pounds like it's beating through my ears. I struggle to breathe as I force my eyes shut, praying that I'm just dreaming, though I know when I open my eyes I'll still be on this ledge. Cold sweat saturates the surface of my face.

"Don't panic."

I jump at the sound of a calm voice. My foot slips but I catch myself just in time to crouch on the glaring gargoyle and cling to the sides of its stony frame. Eyes wide open, I scan the darkness, coaching myself not to look down. My own breath comes out like hiccups. Elegant, dark brown eyes peer at me from over the top of the gargoyle. K.O. kneels at an impossible angle, on the slanted rooftop above me. Looking up at him makes me dizzy.

"How did I get up here?" I ask, my voice reduced to a shaky whisper. In the back of my mind I'm praying this is some bizarre nightmare. But the way the wind stings my cheeks with intense cold, and the way the chill of the concrete seeps under the fabric of my sock-covered feet, I know I'm not dreaming.

"Geezer said he explained things," K.O. says.

"Just get me down!"

"Ok."

It's just that simple. Before I can prepare myself or change my mind, I feel his hand wrap around my waist. The wind rushes around me before my eyes can take in the change of my surroundings, but I know I'm falling. Only, I'm not alone. K.O. holds me tight to him as gravity pulls us quickly towards the ground. I can't scream for choking on air. I might die of suffocation before I splatter on the ground below. Or maybe I'll die of a heart attack. My heart feels like it's going to fly out of my mouth.

K.O. presses me closer to him suddenly, using one hand to cradle my head and the other to secure me around the waist. We're still falling but it suddenly feels like we're falling in slow motion. Time feels like it's slowing down, like it's allowing me to experience my last few moments in all its horrifying detail. So, I surrender, soaking it all in.

My face presses against K. O.'s neck. The warmth of his skin defies the cool air surrounding us. I feel the strength of his hold, and in my last few moments, it comforts me. I hold onto those sensations and let the darkness behind my eyelids swallow me as I wait for the grand finale of my life.

I expect every bone in my body to break. I expect every nerve in my body to scream so hard and loud that my heart slams one last beat. But it doesn't. Instead, I'm weightless. The air around me becomes a pillow holding me up and the only weight on me comes from K.O. I've never felt so afraid or so free. I don't even realize that we're on the ground again until I hear another familiar voice.

"It's a good thing we followed you."

My eyes open instinctively when I hear Geezer.

I'm standing on solid ground. K.O. has me by the waist, holding me tightly in his arms. My cheeks heat up and I push him away. Big mistake. My legs wobble, unable to support my weight. My head feels like a hot air balloon and I stagger for a solid anchor. K.O. crosses his arms. Geezer offers me a hand and drapes my arm around his shoulder.

"What happened?" I ask.

Geezer's look mirrors K.O.'s. "You blacked out again and nearly got yourself killed."

I look up at the building I stood on. It's a large gothic, gray cathedral with slanted rooftops. My stomach erupts, and I vomit on the dirty, cracked sidewalk. Taking in quick, deep breaths, I try to calm my nerves. K.O. stares at me with his narrowed gaze again and that disapproving crease of his mouth doesn't budge.

"Thanks," I say, wiping my mouth with the back of my sleeve.

We stare at each other for a few painful heartbeats. He breaks the eye contact first, shoving past me and Geezer without looking back. A lump forms in my throat as Geezer looks between the two of us. Maybe accusing him of ruining my life was a little harsh. He saved my life tonight, but it doesn't undo what I saw at the Empire State Building. It's what started me on my downward spiral.

"K.O. may be silent, but he's not all deadly," Geezer says.

"You weren't there when he fought that guy. K.O. tried to kill him."

K.O.'s altercation with the blond boy gave me nightmares even after I was convinced it was a hallucination.

He motions between us, "You ever think the guy he was fighting could be one of us?"

No. I didn't think about that, but instead of admitting it, I say, "There is no us. This is crazy. I may be able to see you guys do what you do, and you may *think* you saw me do something, but I'm not like you."

I don't care about the details of what happened between K.O. and the blond boy. All I care about is the fact that I can't seem to control myself, that I keep putting myself in these crazy situations. Things are getting scarier by the minute. Especially the way I'm thinking and feeling and reacting. For a second, I thought I could be one of them, like maybe, just maybe, I was safe with them, with K.O.

"I've got to get out of here."

I turn away from Geezer breathing in and exhaling slowly. And then I run as fast as my legs will carry me. I don't know where I'm going or if I'll even get anywhere at all. The further away I am from Geezer and his friends, the better. My barely covered feet hit the sidewalk with painful force. My heart beats so fast and so hard that the inner walls of my chest feel like they're caving in. My lungs expand to the point of breathlessness. I feel like I'm on fire as my muscles protest the strenuous movement. I have to push. I have to try.

"K.O., she's panicking!" I hear Geezer screech close behind me. I can't stop running. I need to push harder, run faster. I've seen what they can do. I need to go home. I need to see my mom, to throw my arms around her. More than anything I need Dad. I need to feel his strength, to hear his deep voice spout off something wise and thoughtful. He would know what to do right now. He would be here for me. Of course, he isn't here when I need him the most. He's dead.

I don't realize I'm crying until I'm gasping for air and everything in front of me blurs like an unfocused picture. All I see are a whirl of colors contrasting in the dark. I hear the pounding of my feet against pavement. I feel like I've been running forever, but I don't stop. I can't see Geezer or K.O. anymore but I know they're right on my heels. I can feel it. If I can make it to a crowd of people and scream at the top of my lungs, either I'll have help or people will think I'm crazy again.

I trip just as I emerge onto one of the main New York City streets. City light explodes into my tear-stained vision, nearly blinding me. I don't see the oncoming car until it's too late. I stagger backward and close my eyes, bracing myself for sure impact.

There is no collision. Instead, an unnatural wind whips across my face. I inhale sharply and swallow my exhale when a pair of hands close roughly around my waist and yank me upward so fast I feel like I'm on a roller coaster. My eyes fly open and a high yelp escapes my lips. I reach out for something, anything solid, and realize quickly that I've got my arms wrapped around K.O.'s neck. His eyes glare into mine and he chews his bottom lip determinedly before shoving me out of his arms and onto a crowded sidewalk. I look around and realize quickly that we're in the middle of Time Square.

Just as I adjust to being on my own two feet again, instead of whizzing through the air, K.O. grabs my arm and jerks me into the flow of pedestrian traffic. His calloused hand feels rough and hot on my goose-bump pricked skin. My heart flutters and feels light, but it's not the anxious kind of flutter I'm used to.

Maybe K.O. isn't so bad, I tell myself.

Then I remember he's the whole reason I'm in this mess. I jerk my arm out of his grip, but he moves fast and grabs me by the wrist. I pull away again, but he pulls me closer. I try to punch him, but he catches my fist easily in his other hand. He adjusts to hold both of my wrists together in one hand, wrapping his other hand around my waist to keep my struggling to a minimum. I stomp on his foot as hard as I can, but without shoes on, it doesn't make much impact. I elbow him in the stomach, but he pulls back enough to evade me.

"Stop fighting! Both of you!" comes Geezer's winded voice.

He herds both of us into the nearest alley where it's darker and isolated. It isn't until then I realize people were starting to stare at us.

"Tell him not to touch me!" I tell Geezer.

"Kinda hard to save you when I can't touch you," K.O. says.

"Don't talk to me either."

My voice is hysterical and squawky while his is calm, almost bored and very irritating. I want to wipe that blank expression off his face and when I see him gnaw on his bottom lip again, I know I have. He cuts his eyes at Geezer, "Geezer…"

His tone is still low but there's a hint of an edge. I notice his shoulders rise and fall almost as fast as Geezer's, though not quite as exaggerated. I'm breathing hard too, though it makes more sense for me to feel tired.

I sniff, "What do you want with me, and what's wrong with you? Why are you breathing hard? It's not like I was hard for you to corner."

Geezer's eyes widen, and he exhales, running a shaky hand through his messy curled hair and chuckles. "You're kidding, right?"

One look at my face tells him I'm not because he continues, "Savannah, you're faster than you think. *Very* fast."

Now it's my turn to laugh, "It's easy to run fast when you're afraid."

My legs are long, so my stride is fairly easy, even without shoes. In school, I always enjoyed running in gym class. I wasn't the star runner, but I never got left behind either. I almost joined the track team at my last school, but then Dad died, I got distracted, and we moved.

"I don't think you get what I'm saying," Geezer says. "You run like one of us. You move like us, but you're letting your fear control you."

His eyes dart back and forth, searching my face for answers to a question he hasn't asked.

I blink back at him. "You're crazy."

"You're in denial," he snaps back, "and it's going to get you killed. Our abilities come with a lot of untapped potential, like a can of shaken soda. Once the cap gets loose…"

He makes a gesture with his hands, mocking an explosion.

"When we move at high velocities, the average person can't see us. All those times you felt invisible, you were most likely moving faster than you realized. We call it road-running."

"Cute," I say, "You named your superpowers after a Looney Tune character."

Geezer frowns, "Don't talk about the Looney Tunes and don't let the name fool you. Your ability is controlling you and that's dangerous. That car K.O. saved you from would've hit you before the driver even realized you were there. You need to learn how to control your road-running. That means learning how to navigate around everyone and everything else. If you don't, you'll get hurt or someone else will."

"You're wrong. There's nothing special about me, and even if there is, I don't want to learn to control it. I just want it to go away."

My heart drums in my ears again. Bile rises in the back of my throat. I take short, sharp breaths to keep from vomiting again.

"Savannah, your ability is a very unstable defense mechanism and with your level of anxiety, it will kill you if you don't learn to control it. There's no off button once it's been activated. You have to manage it."

"I don't want to jump from any more buildings," I say.

Geezer lifts his hands up to calm me, "And you don't have to… yet."

"Yet?"

"We can take this one step at a time," he coaxes.

"Enough," comes K.O.'s voice. He was pacing before. Now he's filling the space between me and Geezer. His eyes have a shine to them like a knife glinting under the right light. I take a few steps back because he's in my personal space. He grabs for my wrist again and I manage to swat his hand. K.O. huffs at me and then motions behind me. Broken shards of glass wink at me, barely illuminated by the night lights. So, he's saved me from having another foot injury. Big deal.

"You're coming with me."

"No," I tell him.

"I wasn't asking you a question. We've wasted enough time with you. Come with me or go on and get yourself killed. But if you walk away, you won't be able to blame anyone but yourself for what happens."

I can feel his breath on my face. He's still breathing hard. So am I. He extends his hand. My mouth goes dry as that fickle flutter returns to my chest. Geezer makes a small sound like he wants to protest but his mouth tightens, and he doesn't speak.

"Last chance," K.O. says.

I can do the smart thing, or I can do the crazy thing. The trouble is, I don't know which is which. So I do the first thing that comes to mind. K.O. drops his hand and turns his back to me just as I reach out. My fingers graze his until our hands intertwine. His warm, rough hand squeezes my cold one.

"Hold on tight," he says, guiding my arms around his neck. I open my mouth to ask, "Why?" but it's too late. K.O. takes off, pulling me along for the ride. I hold on tight, but we move so fast I feel like I'm still falling. Night wind whips against my face leaving me too breathless to scream. I can barely breathe. I *can't* breathe! I close my eyes, praying silently for this all to end.

"Weak," I hear K.O. say.

"She's stronger than she thinks," Geezer says. "She just needs someone to believe in her."

"She needs to believe in *herself.*"

CHAPTER 14

I don't realize that I've fainted again until I find myself waking up in a bed that I don't remember getting in. My body is stiff and every nerve ending screams for me to lay still and not breathe so much. I feel like I've been run over by a train. It's even worse when I open my eyes. K.O. stands at the foot of the bed.

"You slept so hard I thought you might be dead," he says.

"I'm sure you'd like that," I snap out of agitation. My voice comes out as a hoarse whisper.

A smile actually flickers across K.O.'s face, but it's gone before I can confirm it.

"You have no idea," he mutters.

I glare at him, "Why didn't you just push me off the side of that building if that's the way you feel?"

I instantly regret my words. He takes a step closer to me, coming around the left side of the bed. A disheveled looking Geezer comes into the room, interrupting his stride.

"You're awake. Recovery time is improving."

"How long was I out?" I ask.

Geezer peers at me with eyes underlined in bags and rings, "The first time it took you a few days to recover. You were in and out of consciousness. This time, it's been about four hours. It's almost five in the morning."

Geezer yawns without covering his mouth and scratches at his curly mop of unkempt hair.

"It's time for us to go," K.O. interrupts before Geezer can babble some more.

"Sounds good. Good night," I say, thinking to close my eyes again and pretend like everything is fine for at least a few more hours.

"No," K.O. says, "You. Me. Now."

"What is he? A caveman?" I try to imitate his narrow gaze of steel, but my eyes sting. All I want to do is sleep.

"Get up. Get dressed and meet me downstairs."

I sit up with a groan and force myself out of the bed. My limbs feel like lead. I'm still wearing the jeans and t-shirt from the day before. With the mood K.O. is in, I know I don't have the time to be hygienically correct. No shower, no brushing my teeth, no primping in the mirror… not that I need to. It's not like I want to impress K.O. I don't think I like him very much. Maybe I can torment him with my morning breath.

He raises an eyebrow at me, which seems more on impulse than on purpose. I try not to look as stiff and sore as I feel. Instead I stand tall and face him with crossed arms. "What?"

"Shoes," he says.

"Right."

My eyes hunt around the plain room searching for shoes. Geezer finds them at the foot of the bed, half covered by the disheveled bedspread.

"Where are we going? What are we doing?" Geezer asks.

"What's going on?" Rox asks, materializing in the doorway. She looks tired, a different sort of tired than Geezer, like she's been out partying all night. Her fair hair is tied up tight in a high ponytail, but a few strands rebel, brushing across her forehead. Her eyes are smudged with thick mascara.

Tristan stumbles in behind Rox. His dark brown hair is tousled and shades his bright, friendly eyes. His jeans and shirt are just as windswept as his hair. "What's going on?"

"Apparently, K.O.'s taking our little friend out," Rox explains.

"On a date?" Tristan asks.

"No!" K.O. and I snap at the same time.

Tristan's eyes widen but his shock is quickly swallowed in humor. He gives me one of those sloppy grins.

"I'm not explaining myself," K.O. says to no one in particular. Then he lasers his gaze on me, "If you want to stay here, you're coming with me now. I don't make a habit of repeating myself."

In my opinion, he doesn't make a habit of much outside of frowning and being vague. I don't want to go with him. I'm not sure I still want to stay with him and his friends. The smarter part of my brain screams for me to walk away and not fall any deeper into whatever weird world they exist in. Unfortunately, the inquisitive part of me is stronger. We watch K.O. stalk out of the room and then all eyes are on me. I only hesitate for a moment and then curiosity urges me to follow him. The others trickle out of the room after me, until we're moving in a quiet line of anticipation.

K.O. stands at the bottom of the steps.

"Just you," he says, looking at me.

"Nice knowing you," Rox murmurs under her breath.

"Rox!" Tristan hisses.

She shrugs, "You've seen them together. It's going to end in a fight and K.O. is going to smash her six feet under."

"See you when you get back, Savannah" Tristan says. He cuts his eyes at K.O. before winking at me.

Rox whines that she's hungry and that seems to be all it takes to distract Tristan. His baby blue eyes light up and he rambles about a deconstructed vegetarian omelet. It sounds delicious but my stomach protests. I'm not going to be here for omelets. I'm leaving with K.O., but it's business as usual for everyone else. Tristan and Rox flirt over cooking as they follow us downstairs, but I'm forgotten.

I force myself to look at K.O. who's already at the door, dressed and ready in black t-shirt, jeans, and black hiking boots. His black leather jacket is loosely draped over his shoulder and his black hair hangs slightly damp, slicked back behind his ears and tied with a band at his nape. He looks good. Well, good enough for me to second guess my decision to just jump up and go somewhere without fussing at my reflection in the mirror.

My clothes are bed-wrinkled, and I feel a morning film of plaque on my teeth as I run my tongue uncomfortably over them. I don't even want to think about how my breath must smell. It *feels* hot. My hair is dry, frizzy, and big. I do the only thing I can think of and maneuver around Tristan and Rox to the kitchen sink. I turn on the water and, though it's cold and I'm embarrassed, I dunk my head underneath the stream of water and wring it out gently. I tease it and shake it out a little and the frizzy spirals seem to shrink and re-curl. I know it's only a temporary solution. The fierce lion mane will frizz back as soon as it dries. Everyone stares as water drips from my hair, down my shirt and onto the floor.

"K.O., give us a minute, please," Rox huffs, tearing her hair tie out of her hair and shoving it at me. Her hair spills out and tumbles over her shoulders like a golden curtain. Her eyes shine with irritation as she shoves me out of the kitchen and into the room covered with sleeping bags and duffel bags.

"What are you thinking? You're about to go out with the hottest guy in existence and you throw water on your hair? For what!" she growls.

I open my mouth to speak but she interrupts me, "Don't waste air with your excuses. Let's just fix this."

She gathers my hair in her hands without asking for permission and uses her hair tie to tame it in a high ponytail, teasing and fluffing it for what seems like forever. Then she stares.

"Rox, it isn't like that. This isn't a date."

Rox ignores me. "You can't go anywhere looking like a zombie bag lady. I don't care who you're with."

She winces at me before digging in her pocket to hand me two sticks of gum.

"Surprisingly, you smell tolerable. Your clothes are..." she shakes her head, "Never mind. Just don't embarrass me."

Me? Embarrass her? We aren't even friends. She doesn't even like me. Before I can respond to her, she's shoving me back into the kitchen. I trip and nearly hit the floor, but I catch myself and straighten quickly.

K.O. stands in the doorway. When he sees me, his eyes widen just an inch and then go back to glaring. I stick a piece of gum in my mouth and follow him out the door.

It's quiet, so quiet that I jump when the door slams behind me. The early morning air is cool. Chill bumps rise on my uncovered arms almost immediately. I'm grateful when Geezer appears beside me, offering me a black pullover hoodie.

"I'm coming with you," he says.

"Thank you," I whisper, putting the hoodie on quickly.

Geezer wears his usual gray pullover hoodie which seems to work with his personal style. Mine swallows me, making me feel like an amorphous blob. I'd rather be warm than cute, though.

"Where are we going?" I ask. Geezer ushers me into a light jog so we can catch up with K.O., who looks just as intimidating from behind as he does face to face. I watch as he shrugs his leather jacket on while managing to keep up his jungle cat stride. He's taller than me by a head or two, easily a few inches over six feet with his thick black boots on. Both of his hands are clenched in fists like he could spontaneously punch someone for the slightest offense and keep moving. He doesn't look like he's in the mood for conversation but I'm the idiot that repeats my question, "Where are we going?" I ask, louder this time in case he really didn't hear me the first time. Still, K.O. doesn't answer. I settle into silence and jog a few paces behind him.

Geezer's steps synch with K.O.'s even though he's much shorter than the both of us. He looks like he's working hard to keep up while K.O. moves effortlessly. It would be funny if I didn't realize he was voicing my concerns.

"What are you thinking?" Geezer demands.

K.O. answers him in one word, "Initiation."

"Why don't I like the sound of that?" Geezer snaps.

"She's in denial and she'll get us all killed. This'll take care of that."

Our stroll ends at the local subway station. K.O. leads us down the stairs and through a crowded plaza. New York City really doesn't sleep. We weave in and out of the congestion and slide past the ticket booth without much effort. The bored clerk with graying blonde hair stares right in our direction but he doesn't even say anything as we hop over the bars blocking our entry to the trains.

"Was that guy asleep with his eyes open or something?" I murmur.

"Or something," K.O. mutters back, taking my hand to pull me along.

"Road-running," Geezer reminds me.

I follow them onto the train, and we sit in the back. I hope K.O.'s idea of initiation isn't some sort of hazing ritual. My only comfort is in knowing Geezer's got my back. I sleep while I can, gathering my strength for whatever I'm going to face. It seems like no sooner than my eyes close, the curly headed teen is nudging me awake. K.O. is already off the train, moving quickly towards the stairs and the exit. I follow him, walking along side Geezer. A yawn escapes me and my eyes water a little, but I try to shake off the fatigue. We emerge from the subway station and back into the early morning streets of New York. As crowded and lively as the city is, I wonder if this is as silent and still as it gets. There are pockets of crowds and isolated corners.

It's not long before we stop again, this time for good. I can't help but feel the irony of the situation. It's the place where my normal, sane, and invisible existence died.

"The Empire State Building? Really?" I mutter to myself.

The massive height is intimidating in the daytime. At this hour, ten times the horror.

"Let's go," K.O. says.

I'm not looking forward to the long elevator ride again, but I force myself forward, making my way towards the entrance until I feel Geezer tugging on my arm.

"This way."

"How're we supposed to–"

My words are drowned out as I swallow a mouthful of cool air. My head jerks back as I'm propelled upwards against gravity. My stomach lurches. I reach out for anything solid, wrapping my arms around Geezer's neck, probably smothering his smaller frame. Before I can work up a scream, I find myself stumbling on the concrete of the colossal building's rooftop. A sputtering Geezer falls beside me.

"You almost strangled me!" he screeches.

"What'd you expect? You can't just do something like that without warning me," I say.

I gag a little, but there's not much for me to throw up. I don't even know how to describe what just happened. I'm not the rollercoaster type but I imagine what Geezer did is something like that. I pat at my hair, knowing I look crazy. My eyes are probably rolling around in my head because I feel lightheaded even though my heart is pumping like I've ran a marathon. I guess leaping up eighty-six floors in a manner of seconds is the equivalent to a marathon.

"This is initiation," K.O. announces taking my focus off of my frazzled nerves, "Fight, fly, or die."

I groan internally at the rhyming slogan, though coming from K.O. the words don't sound corny at all.

"What happens if I don't participate?" I ask, surprised at how strong and defiant I sound.

"Then we'll take you back to Willow Manor and we won't bother you anymore," Geezer says with a shrug. He smiles, and an impish light strikes his gray irises, "You've got this, Scarlett."

My heart jerks and the fear starts up again, "So, what am I supposed to do?"

K.O. sprints, jumps, and sails upwards until he lands like a nimble cat on the tall curved fence guarding the roof. I know I've seen him do this before, but my jaw still drops.

"Jump," he says.

He leans forward and dives off without hesitation. I choke back the urge to scream and panic, reminding myself that he's not a normal person. Jumping off the Empire State Building isn't going to kill him.

"You ready?" Geezer asks.

I shake my head, "I can't get up that fence. How do you expect me"?

Geezer runs toward me, wrapping an arm around my waist, and propels us upward to stand on the railing. The movement is unexpected. I struggle to keep my balance on the slippery slope of the fence. At what feels like thousands of miles up in the air, it's a daunting task when there's nothing to catch me if I fall. I can hardly breathe as I stand there, legs shaking while trying not to look down.

"You can do this," Geezer coaches, walking the slippery railing like he's not standing eighty-six stories up.

"Geezer, I can't. Take me back down," I say.

"Only one way down."

The tone in his voice brings up a memory I've been trying hard to forget. The force of the memory makes my knees buckle and I slide off. Somehow, I manage to grip the slippery railing. I pray the fence will hold as my legs dangle, frighteningly free. A quiet, paralyzing fear takes hold of me. I feel heavy like stone. I know I am powerless in this situation, but I refuse to beg. If Geezer really wanted to help me, he wouldn't do this to me, he wouldn't let me fall.

"You're just like Dr. Santos. You're crazy and you're going to get me killed," I say, and my shaky whisper of a voice comes out almost like a holler in the quiet morning hours. The passionate light in Geezer's eyes goes from fear and concern to a steely gray, something much more frightening and deadlier than anything I've seen in K.O. But his eyes soften, and he reaches for my hand. Instinctively, I reach out to take it. Tense as I feel, I relax as his hand latches on to mine, but something's wrong. Instead of pulling me up, he dives off the fence railing and pulls me with him.

We slide off, falling into the open air. His mouth moves but I can't hear anything but the wind rushing through my ears, so fast that I'm deaf and breathless all at once. Squinting, I'm too afraid to close my eyes.

"Just let go!" Geezer finally screams, and I feel him pulling away from me. I scratch at him, knowing that as long as I'm connected to him, I can't die. He floats upward while gravity takes over, pulling me down like a magnet towards the ground.

I close my eyes, trying to make fast peace with my inevitable end. The morbid part of me wonders if maybe this is all for the best. The impact of my fall will grant me a quick death. My throat swells with a surprising sob. I don't really want to die. I want to live. I don't know where the realization comes from – maybe the pain, maybe the steady stream of memories that creep into my frenzied conscious, like a last attempt to convince me to live when death is about to be a fact and not a theory.

I hear Geezer's last words in my head. I open my eyes and see him propelling, hurtling purposefully beside me, "Just let go."

I smack into the pavement. My back connects with hard concrete. My vision explodes, from black to neon stars as my head thuds against the hardness of the ground. I wait. Then I wait some more. I'm not sure what I'm waiting for, but I don't expect to feel the burn in my back or tenderness on my head. I manage to open my eyes; eyes I didn't know I was squeezing so tightly closed. My hands are scraped from the rough concrete. I'm sure I have a few other knots and scratches, but I'm alive. As if one death defying moment isn't enough, I realize that I didn't really hit the ground as hard as I should have. It was more like I lost balance and fell backward instead of falling from a skyscraper.

K.O.'s face appears over mine. He has something like a smile on his face. He offers me a hand, peeling me off the ground without a word. Geezer stands a few feet away with his hands in the pockets of his hoodie. His head is down, and his curly mop of hair covers his expression, but I hear the smile in his voice, "Welcome to the team. Questions? Comments?"

"What else can we do?" I ask.

"Anything you're brave enough to try," Geezer says.

My stomach takes the wrong moment to growl.

"Right on time. Let's get back home. I'm sure Tristan's whipping up something in the kitchen to celebrate," Geezer says.

"Celebrate what?" I ask.

"You," K.O. answers, and for once his tone is light.

For the first time in a long time, I exhale and relax.

CHAPTER 15

"*W*anna go again?" Geezer asks me.

I stare back up at the Empire State Building. The look on my face must say enough because Geezer laughs and pats me on the back. K.O. stands in front of me.

"Hold on tight," he says, moving to carry me onto his back. I don't move.

"Let me try on my own," I say, anxious to test the abilities I didn't think I had. It seems surreal and exhilarating. I'm still juiced up on adrenaline. I may not want to dive off more buildings, but I do want to explore the new world I've been introduced to.

"No," K.O. says.

Geezer clarifies the situation, "One step at a time, Scarlett. You need food and rest. Plus, you're a little banged up."

Right on cue, the adrenaline plunges, and I start to feel the burn of my scrapes, scratches, and bruises. My head hurts, too. Sighing, I climb awkwardly onto K.O.'s back and tighten my arms around his neck and my feet around his waist. He lifts me up like I'm a pound of sugar, his hands firmly gripping my lower thighs right above the knees. I'm glad he can't see me blush.

"Close your eyes," he says.

"You might get sick if you don't," Geezer explains, before I can protest.

Exhaustion sets in, only dulled in comparison to hunger. Closing my eyes, I feel the rush of air almost immediately. Cold air fills my nostrils to the point where it's hard to breathe. I bury my face into K.O.'s shoulder, preferring to smell the biting remnant of his leather jacket to suffocating on fresh, cool morning air. Even though my arms are tight around his neck, I feel myself relax. My breathing steadies and my mind goes blank to the point where it doesn't even feel like I'm moving anymore. Maybe I'm feeling that way because we really aren't moving anymore. I must have dozed off.

K.O. shakes me off his back and I almost collapse.

"You snore," he says.

There's no judgement in his tone, no irritation, just a simple observation. I feel my cheeks heat up again.

Hope I didn't drool on him.

I rub sleep out of my eyes and struggle not to yawn. Geezer raps on the front door like he's talking in Morse code. It automatically swings open and a bright-eyed Tristan is there. His gaze finds me, and he smiles wide.

"There's our girl. Get in here!"

He guides me in the house and wraps an arm around my shoulder, attempting to ruffle my wild hair.

Rox's eyes are wide with interest, "Details, Geeze. I want details! Did she cry like a little baby? Scream like a girl–"

"I am a girl," I interject, "And I'm standing right here."

She ignores me, "Where did you take her? Is she a natural like you thought she'd be or was it disappointing?"

Geezer shrugs and opens his mouth to hopefully defend me in between Rox's never ending interrogation. K.O. surprises me by speaking up, "She passed initiation just like you did. That's all you need to know."

The scowl I thought he reserved for me pierces through Rox and he folds his arms in that "don't mess with me or else" way. Rox blinks, shocked. Everyone stares at K.O. and Rox. She opens her mouth, closes it, and her cheeks redden as she stumbles for words. I'm in awe that anybody can shut her down, even though it doesn't last long.

"You don't have to get all defensive. It's not like she's your girlfriend or anything," she says.

K.O.'s jaw tightens and so does his posture. Rox notices it too because she's smart enough to shut her mouth. K.O. cuts her a deadly look before dismissing everyone with his turned back. He stalks somewhere upstairs and doesn't come back.

Geezer sighs, "Welcome to our band of extraordinary brains, brutes and bit–"

He cuts off his last word, but by the way he's scowling at Rox, I get the message, "If you'll excuse me, I'm pooped."

His voice is distant and all business, lacking the quirky tone I'm used to. I don't know Geezer well but the way he drags himself out the room makes it seem like he's more than a little tired. I can't help thinking his lackluster attitude is partially my fault.

"Way to go, Rox, you little mood killer. Now no one wants to celebrate," Tristan groans.

Rox rolls her eyes, "I'm sorry everyone's so sensitive nowadays," she snaps. Then turning to me, she plasters a sweet smile on her face. "Look. I'm sorry if I ruined your little cake and ice cream party. Maybe I'm just a little tired, too. I'm sure you'll be thanking me later when you see what I got you, though."

She pecks Tristan on the cheek before she enters the sleeping bag room.

"Well, I still feel like celebrating if you do," Tristan says defensively and just like Rox said, he's got a store-bought sheet cake and Neapolitan ice cream. I take half a second to wonder when he bought it and how he could have known I'd make it back from the initiation in one piece. He reads my look well.

"Some of us were rooting for you," he says.

I have no problem figuring out who doesn't want me to be here and that makes me second guess my choice. I can jump off skyscrapers like I'm bungee jumping without the rope and survive. Still, I'm not sure I'm safe. The changing moods in this house alone could kill a person.

"Chocolate cake with whipped icing," Tristan announces, cutting a quarter of the cake for a single slice.

He gestures toward the ice cream, "Pick your poison."

When it comes to cake, I love chocolate with any kind of frosting. When it comes to ice cream, I don't discriminate either. I love all flavors. Chocolate cake with a large scoop of chocolate-vanilla-strawberry sounds mouth-wateringly delicious.

As much as I want to say yes, there are a few things nagging me. I've got this nasty taste in my mouth and I think it has something to do with my gut instinct. I won't be able to enjoy cake and ice cream if I don't make sure everything is okay with the people I owe my life to.

As much as I hate to admit it, Rox is right. I was terrible to K.O., and even though I still can't say I'm over the fact that he's partially to blame for my traumatic introduction to their world, I need to admit I'm somewhat wrong about him. He's saved my life on multiple occasions just in the past few days alone.

Then there's Geezer. He's had my back from the beginning. He's been my guardian angel right from the start. The kid has been nothing but welcoming and supportive. As scared as I was back at initiation, he doesn't deserve the things I said to him.

"You okay?" Tristan asks, waving a hand in front of my face. I almost forget he's talking and what exactly he's talking about until I see the piece of cake in his hand.

"Later?" I ask, even as my stomach grumbles.

Tristan smiles, "I'm confident it won't be too much later."

I have a feeling that if I have any more excitement right now, even in the form of chocolate, I might die. Not that death by chocolate is a bad way to go. A hot bath just sounds better right now and some rubbing alcohol. I feel like I've had a ten-hour workout. My body is crashing from my adrenaline high with a vengeance and I'm not completely sure sugar is the best solution.

"Oh, you've only dived eighty-six floors off a skyscraper," I mutter under my breath.

I offer Tristan one last polite smile before backing out of the kitchen and carefully past Rox in the next room strewn with sleeping bags and excess baggage.

"Get some rest," Tristan calls from the kitchen.

I give him a noncommittal grunt before treading lightly up the stairs. Immediately, I'm confronted with two opposing doors. The one on the left is closed. The one on the right is cracked open. Taking a deep breath, I peek inside. Geezer sits slouched on the side of a neatly made bed, staring out a window. He stares at the city skyline with his back to me. I watch the sky, too, momentarily distracted by how beautiful the sunrise is. The sun colors the sky a kaleidoscope of orange, pink, violet, and blue.

"You should be resting," Geezer says.

I guess I wasn't that quiet coming up the stairs.

"How'd you hear me?"

"I see your reflection in the window," he explains, still staring out the window.

I nudge the door open wider just enough for me to slip inside.

"I thought you'd be sleep," I start awkwardly.

I do a lot of people watching but I don't have much experience making and keeping friends. My skills are limited to introductions, hellos, goodbyes, and "remember me?". I'm not exactly memorable enough to get practice in conflict resolution. I don't even know if I have the patience for it. But I've had good home training to know that the nagging in the pit of my stomach won't go away until I make things right with Geezer. He may not admit it, but I think I hurt his feelings. He won't even look at me.

"Sleep isn't always the remedy for rest," Geezer grumbles, sounding like an old man, "Is everything okay? Rox giving you a hard time?"

Of course, she's giving me a hard time, I want to admit but instead I shrug and say, "Everything's okay. Well, no. It's not. I'm sorry. So sorry."

My sentences come out broken as I stumble through my apology. Geezer turns to look at me. His gray eyes are shadowed with fatigue and so round and wide they look like they hurt.

"I shouldn't have said those things earlier. You're nothing like Santos," I say, choking on a lump forming in my throat. Thinking about Santos takes me to a frightening place in my mind I'd rather not remember. He tried to kill me. He would have succeeded if it hadn't been for Geezer getting me out of there. I owe Geezer my life.

"I was scared. I didn't think I could– All I could think about was…" I pause to gather my thoughts and to keep myself from crying before trying to speak again, "There's really no excuse for what I said to you earlier. I'm sorry."

Geezer stares at me. I start to worry that he didn't hear me at all, but his long stare ends in a smile. "You've got some grit, girl. You'll need it. Get some sleep."

I find myself smiling back, "Thanks, Geezer."

It feels weird calling someone so young and boyish a "geezer" but then his smile wilts and he's staring at me with the haunted look of a much older person. "Don't thank me yet," he says softly.

He turns back to the window where the sun is high and bright. I give him one last look before stifling a yawn and backing out of his room, feeling a little more at peace. The feeling doesn't last long. When I turn around K.O. is standing in the opposite doorway studying me. My smile drops. My relief crumbles. I stumble at an awkward pause, suddenly exhausted. Staring into his eyes, I know I'm not ready to have a heart to heart with him. He doesn't blink, and it's unnerving. If this counts as a staring contest, he wins hands down. I look away from him and force myself to keep walking to my room. I know his eyes are on me. I feel them on my back, but I try to ignore him.

If I stand too much longer, I may fall apart, and it's not just because I'm exhausted. My brain turns to mush when K.O.'s around. Seeing him was the beginning of all my trouble. I know blaming him for everything isn't fair, but it's easier than acknowledging that uncomfortable flutter I get when he's around. I tell myself that fickle feeling is just gratefulness. He's saved my life.

Then why don't you feel that way when Geezer's around?

I shake my head, dismissing the thought. Sleep. I need sleep. My eyes burn, my joints ache, and my thoughts are taking a drastic turn I don't want to deal with. I have every intention of going to sleep but the new clothes laid out on the bed stir my curiosity. This must be Rox's present to me. Taking an assessment of what's in front of me, I find myself conflicted. There's a pair of black denim, skinny jeans and a black tee with white lettering and a red heart that reads "I Love NYC". Next to the abominable shirt is a feminine, black leather jacket that is waist length with a matching belt. A pair of black, knee high leather boots are at the foot of the bed with horrifyingly high heels.

The outfit is stylish, but it's not me. I'm a sweatshirt, sneakers, cropped jeans type of a girl. This outfit screams Rox. I'll look foolish. The leather jacket is my favorite piece of clothing out of the entire ensemble, though I'd never admit it. I wouldn't want K.O. thinking I like his style. Still, I try the jacket. It soothes me like a security blanket.

Rox's gifts don't stop there. My eyes wander to the nightstand. There's a note, written in pretty penmanship complete with all the right loops and swoops.

Anyone who can stand up to K.O. deserves the leather and the boots. Stand tall and strut your stuff. You've gotta be stylish if you expect to hang with me.

- Rox

P.S.

No more hoodies or sweatshirts!

Behind the note are dozens of lotions and perfumes. She was even thoughtful enough to get makeup, not that green eye shadow and plum frosted lip gloss is my style. Yawning, I crawl into bed, still wrapped up in the nice leather jacket. I fall asleep as soon as my head touches the pillow.

***

A loud knock and a crash jolt me out of a blissful sleep. The door to my room is no longer attached to the hinges in the doorway. It collapses on the wooden floor with a whooshing thud while Rox stands in the doorway red-faced with her hands on her hips.

"Forgot my strength," she says.

I shoot her my meanest glare, but she rolls her eyes and strolls into my room like she owns it.

"You don't have to be a bully. You could've knocked," I tell her.

Rox folds her arms across her chest, "I did. You didn't answer. We thought maybe you choked on your drool while you were sleeping or something else damsel-in-distress like."

You almost gave me a heart attack. I want to retort.

Instead I state the obvious, "I was sleep."

Tristan peeks from around Rox and walks on top of the door into the bedroom.

"I'll fix your door," he offers and then he throws Rox a reprimanding glare, "That was a little uncalled for."

"It's not like it matters. We aren't staying here. I'm *not* sleeping on the floor again. I need my privacy and beauty sleep if you expect me to behave. I'm not sharing a room or a bed either," she snaps.

I'm so tempted to lie back down and cover my ears between the pillows, especially when Rox keeps venting.

"Why can't *she* sleep on the floor? It's not like she's even grateful," Rox whines, then her eyes burn into me, "I got you new clothes, perfumes, makeup, and accessories and you can't even say thank you!"

Not wanting to end up like the bedroom door or the kitchen table, I choose my words carefully. "Is there a reason you're here?"

I'm not used to being yelled at when I first wake up or having people kick or punch in my doors. I regret turning down the cake earlier this morning, because I'm hungry, too.

"It's almost 7:00. You missed dinner. We wanted to make sure you were alive. Geezer said you hit your head pretty hard this morning during your initiation," Tristan admits.

And I thought the headache was Rox's fault.

"I don't have a concussion, do I?"

Tristan shrugs, "Probably not. You're not dead and I've heard concussions can kill you if you go to sleep."

"I'm kind of hungry," I admit, though 'kind of' is an understatement. Rox tosses me some daggers with her eyes but I give her my sweetest smile as Tristan dashes down the stairs to prep ice cream and cake.

"Thanks for the clothes, Rox," I concede.

"You're welcome," she says before following Tristan downstairs. She's out of my hair for the minute.

I slide out of bed and decide to get dressed. I take a brisk shower to wake myself up and toss on the jeans and tee Rox brought me, hoping it will appease her enough to keep her from whining. The pants feel tight and awkward, almost like a second skin. I pull at the form-fitting tee. I'm used to wearing big, baggy, warm clothes here in New York City. It's always seems cool and wet.

"I really don't like New York City," I mutter at the thin shirt. At least she didn't get a shirt with a ridiculous self-compliment like "Juicy" or "Too hot to handle". That would've been really mean, because anyone can look at me and know those words are a joke. My gangly form is far from juicy. I don't bother with the boots, because, let's face it, I'd just be setting myself up for disaster. Instead, I put on a pair of black socks and slip on my basic white sneakers. I quickly brush my teeth, rinse my mouth out, and leave my hair wet and wild to air dry in a spiral, curly frizz.

Going back into the bedroom I turn my attention to the perfumes and makeup Rox attempted to pick out for me. I have to admit her lotion and shower gel choices aren't bad. Compliments of Rox, I smell like black cherry vanilla. Her perfumes are a different story. I pick up a pink, cat shaped perfume bottle and spray. The air smells like powder and butt-crack. I'm afraid to play with the makeup mostly because I'm afraid my face will look like a toddler drew on it.

Leaving the makeup and perfume on the nightstand, I put on the leather jacket, hoping it will keep me warm and make up for my lack of curves and my bubble butt. I stumble downstairs into the kitchen. Rox and Tristan have already helped themselves to large chunks of cake and full bowls piled with ice cream. Tristan's eyes brighten when he sees me, and he plates another mammoth slice, a whole quarter size of the cake.

"You clean up well," he says.

Rox's eyes rake me with approval until she gets to my feet. Thankfully, she doesn't ask me about the boots.

Tristan asks what kind of ice cream I want. I ask for all three. He rakes the spoon heavily over the dairy goodness and scoops a serving as large as my cake slice into a bowl before handing it to me. I stare at it as I retreat to one of the chairs lined up against the wall. We haven't had a kitchen table since Rox destroyed it.

"Trust me. It's not too much," Tristan says. I'm too hungry to comment so I dig in, holding my cake carefully over my lap to keep from spilling one speck of food onto the floor.

"Where's Geezer?" I ask, swallowing my first bite of delicious cake. My taste buds rejoice, and I eagerly devour more.

"Cake with vanilla and strawberry ice cream," Geezer says, sauntering into the kitchen with a grumble.

He's got on another hoodie, this one a thin Irish green, "Cup of coffee, black," he adds before plopping in the chair beside me.

K.O. steps in half a second later. My stomach sours when I see him, though I can't blame his presence completely. I've eaten an insane amount of cake and ice cream. Tristan hands Geezer the last piece of cake.

"We're out of cake," I say to K.O.

He doesn't look at me. He doesn't even answer. Geezer seems to be his mouthpiece because he answers me with a mouth full of cake, "He doesn't like cake."

I try again. "There's still ice cream."

I wonder what type of ice cream he'd ask for. He doesn't look like a strawberry kind of person or vanilla for that matter. Chocolate, maybe.

Tristan pours another cup of coffee and passes it to K.O. without cream or sugar. K.O.'s dark eyes flicker in my direction before he stalks out of the room. Rox rolls her eyes at me, "I guess he's too cool for ice cream, but I think he liked your jacket." she says. My face gets hot, and Rox laughs. The room falls into silence apart from Geezer slurping his coffee down and Tristan washing dishes.

"Well isn't this a celebration!" Rox observes.

She drips with sarcasm but she's right. For a crew as lively as this bunch, cake and ice cream seem so anticlimactic. K.O. steps back into the room, shrugging on his leather jacket. His hair is slicked back out of his face though a few renegade strands trouble his dark eyes. He's got on his black boots to match the rest of his black attire. All he needs is a comb for his hair and a soulful pout. His modern-day James Dean rebel look would be complete, only K.O. doesn't pout. He glares. K.O. slides his coffee mug to Tristan and makes his way through the kitchen to the front door.

Rox perks up. "I'm bored. Please say you're going somewhere fun."

"Subway," Geezer informs her, slurping up the last bit of his coffee.

Rox scrambles up, sliding a hair tie off her wrist and tying her hair up in a high ponytail.

"I'm in," she says.

Luckily for her, she doesn't have to do much to get ready. She's already dressed in a pair of hip hugger jeans, a pale green, spaghetti strap top, a denim jacket that matches the color of her jeans, and ankle high boots with wedges. Tristan drops the dishes into the sink. They make an annoying clinking sound.

"I'm in, too. Wait for me!" Tristan exclaims. K.O. sighs but he doesn't leave.

"What happens at the Subway?" I ask Geezer.

He laughs. "Nothing you'll enjoy. You can stay here with me and"

"It's only one of the coolest way to kill time!" Tristan interrupts, "We play chicken. Only it's with trains. Geezer and K.O. came up with it. You should come with us."

K.O. doesn't voice his opinion. He doesn't seem to care one way or another. He's just ready to go. As excited as everyone is, I can't help but be curious.

Stay safe, my mind whispers while my heart thumps wildly, screaming, *Live a little!*

I just jumped off a skyscraper and survived. I'm curious to see what else I can do. Maybe I'm not ready to play chicken with trains but I can at least watch and learn.

"Geezer, you said I need to learn how to control myself. I can't do that if I stay locked in here," I tell him.

He grimaces, stuffing his hands in the pockets of his hoodie, "Yeah, but it isn't exactly a hobby for beginners."

Being pushed off skyscrapers isn't exactly safe for a beginner either. My mind is made up. I look at Tristan, "I'm in."

That seems to be all K.O. needs to hear before he opens the door, takes one step, and disappears into the night.

"Keep up if you want to hang," Rox challenges and then she's gone just as fast as K.O.

"She's your responsibility tonight, Tristan," Geezer lectures before following after Rox and K.O.

I start to wonder if I've made the right decision. I can't run like them. I know for sure I won't be able to keep up.

Tristan winks at me, "You'll keep up."

His eyes have a mischievous sparkle as he nears me. Before I know it, he's hoisting me on his back.

"Hold on tight."

As soon as I lock my arms around his neck, my vision blurs and wind rushes, beating against our skin as we push forward.

"Breathe!" Tristan shouts over the sound of the wind in my ears. I manage half a breath, overwhelmed by the force of the cool air that's gusting up my nostrils.

"Relax. Your choking me," he groans, but I'm too scared. If I relax my grip, I'll slip and fall off. There's no way Tristan can hold onto me at this speed.

"Can't breathe," he warns. I can't breathe either. My head feels light. Trying to breathe is more like gasping for breath. I thought K.O. was fast, but compared to Tristan, maybe he'd been jogging.

Or taking it easy on you. The thought crosses my mind.

My nostrils burn and my head pounds and feels like it's going to explode. Just when I think I can't take anymore, we stop. Tristan trips, almost falling down the steps of the subway station. Once he balances himself, he lets go of me and I manage to slump down without hurting myself.

"First one here, as always," Tristan brags.

I'm more concerned about not vomiting up the delicious cake and ice cream from earlier. Thick bile rises in my throat before I erupt into gags. I'm vaguely aware of Geezer fussing at Tristan.

"This is exactly why she shouldn't be here. Your competitive streak could've killed her!" Geezer shrieks.

No one notices him yelling. As people pass us, they're staring at me, frowning and wincing in disgust. Tristan makes a guilty effort to brush my hair out of my face while I begrudgingly empty my stomach of all its precious contents. When I'm finally finished, I straighten my posture and try to look stronger than I feel.

"You alright, Scarlett?" Tristan asks.

I nod as he slides me some napkins and a small bottle of milk. I don't ask where it came from. This crowd travels so fast things might as well pop out of thin air.

"I can take you back," Tristan offers, but I shake my head.

"What's the milk for?" I ask.

"It's the drink of champions!" he says, and then with a wince adds, "It coats your stomach."

Pepto-Bismol does that, too, but I don't tell him that. Instead I chug down the milk to help mask the icky taste in my mouth. Tristan watches me wearily.

"You sure you don't wanna go back?" he asks.

Milk must really be the drink of champions because, as my stomach settles, I feel better and braver. "No way. Where is everyone?" I ask.

"Already on the tracks," Tristan says. I catch a hint of disappointment in his tone of voice. It's easy to guess that Geezer made him look after me while everyone else is busy having all the fun.

"Well, let's go!" I say.

Tristan eyes me again. I'm almost afraid he's going to tell me no and take me back to the house.

"Okay," he says, "But you can only watch. Geezer will kill me if you jump on the tracks."

He takes my hand and promises not to run as fast as he did before. It's still too fast. The speed is jarring. I barely have time to inhale before the world around me whirls and comes to an abrupt, dizzying halt.

"How can you move so fast without running into stuff?" I wonder.

Tristan shrugs and offers me one of his boyish grins, "Practice."

We both turn our attention to our surroundings. We're on a dark set of narrow train tracks with molded, cracked brick walls on either side. It's full of dust and from the scurrying sound not too far from the track we're walking on, I'm sure there are rats down here. I shiver, telling myself that I won't get squeamish unless the rats try to attack me. Dim lights hang on the brick side walls. Some lights flicker. Some lights shine a sickly yellow, casting an eerie shadow, while other lights are completely busted. We walk in patches of light and dark. It smells musty and moldy giving me the eerie feeling of a graveyard or some scene from a scary movie.

Tristan is tall. Even when he walks, it's like he's running. From all the earlier trauma, the disgusting smelling air, and the fatigue settling in my chest, I'm practically wheezing.

"I told you to stay home if you couldn't keep up," comes Rox's arrogant voice echoing from a distance. She stands in the center of the tracks with her arms crossed in front of her chest, looking as smug as ever. I try to steady my breathing just as I realize something wet running down my nose. I wipe at it subconsciously and stare at my fingers. Blood. I wipe at my nose again, but my fingers are empty. No one seems to notice.

Hands clasp my shoulders from behind and before I can turn around, I find myself on the narrow strip of ground between the decrepit wall and the tracks far ahead of where Tristan and Rox are. Geezer stands in front of me, giving me his squinting rendition of stern attitude, as if daring me to move.

"Stay," he says, reinforcing his parental look with the command fit for a dog. I'm too curious to be offended. I watch as they stand apart from each other. Further ahead of Rox and Tristan, K.O. is ready, flexing his fists and cracking his knuckles. I feel Geezer watching me absorb the scene.

"Since you're so eager to learn, here's a quick lesson. We hop on the tracks and run in and out of the computer operated train. The person who gets the most runs, wins."

I feel my eyes go big. "You run across the tracks while the train is coming?"

Geezer nods solemnly.

"But can't people see you?"

Geezer shakes his head. "We move too fast, even for a camera to see. We have to or –"

Tristan shouts at Rox, and Rox turns to look at Geezer. Her cat eyes are wide and wild. "It'll be here in five!"

Geezer sighs and stares at me. "I really wish you stayed back. Even standing on the sidelines could get dangerous," he warns, and I agree. They're getting ready to play chicken with a train. They're not even going to try to outrun it. They're going to run through it, repeatedly.

"How does it work?" I ask.

"Well, naturally our bodies are made of atomic particles that are tightly packed together to…" Geezer pauses, reading my face and simplifies his lecture in a single sentence, "We *ghost*."

The idea sounds amazingly impossible and frightening.

"It takes a lot of guts and a lot of practice," Geezer continues, "One shred of doubt or hesitation can get you killed. If you can't handle running, you definitely can't handle this."

My cheeks heat up. I get it. One wrong move and my guts could be splattered all over the train and the rusted tracks. His little lecture should dissuade me but telling me I can't do this really makes me want to try. I conquered my fear on the Empire State Building. It doesn't matter that Geezer had to push me and that I'd nearly died from fear on my way down. I survived. I can survive this, too. I think.

I don't have a lot of time. That makes me nervous, but I don't really care. I've never belonged anywhere. With Geezer and the others, I finally have a chance and not just any chance – the chance of a *lifetime*. It's not that I've ever wanted to be super or extraordinary, but the rush of it all makes me feel more alive, more vibrant. It almost feels like I didn't start breathing until last night.

Geezer and Santos think fear ignites my abilities. Right now, even though I can't hear, feel, or see it, I know the train is coming. My palms sweat. My heart races. Strange as it sounds, these signs of fear encourage me. I can do this.

Geezer is still talking, deep in his lecture, when I make a dash towards the tracks. I stand on the tracks, listening, trying to pay close attention to any sound or feeling to signal the train is close.

"Savannah, no!" Geezer screeches, and I feel all eyes on me.

"Don't worry," I say.

I just want to practice running. I'm nervous, anxious even, and just sitting on the sidelines is going to drive me crazy.

Taking a deep breath, I run to the other side of the tracks opposite of Geezer. I'm fast but not as fast as I should be. Tristan takes notice. He and Rox inch closer to us, grinning at me.

"Relax. Breathe!" Tristan says.

I can't relax but I can embrace my fear. I take a couple breaths and exhale in one long steady stream before running again. I'm still too slow. Geezer shakes his head, but Tristan coaches me, "Again!"

I run back to the other side and this time I don't stop. I run back and forth breathing in and out. Exhaling. Inhaling.

Exhaling… Before I realize it, I propel forward, nearly slamming into Geezer before smacking into the nearest wall. My head hits the wall and the brick forms a venous crack. My hand goes to my head. I feel along my hairline. Thank God, there's no blood but I already feel a mean headache coming on.

"Stay focused, Scarlett. Don't run with your head down!" Tristan says.

"Unless you've got a hard head like Tristan," Rox teases.

"Try running along the side. Stay off the tracks. The train *is* coming, after all," Geezer suggests grumpily.

He isn't enthused at my efforts like Tristan is, but he's not mocking me like Rox. His baby face is pinched. He's curious and he's testing me.

I'm a bottle of nerves and I use it to my advantage. I breathe deeply once, then twice. I close my eyes. Inhale. Take a step forward. Exhale. I take off and find myself running at normal speed. Pushing myself, I run so fast my lungs burn, but I'm not fast enough. My heart beats against my chest and I push myself, begging my body to go the impossible speed it had gone just a moment ago. I run the narrow strip of ground, lungs burning, my chest an inferno, eyes watering, and I try not to cry. I feel myself slowing down even though I want to move faster with everything that's in me. I've done it once. So why can't I do it again?

K.O. stands on the tracks ahead of me. Even though I refuse to look at him directly, I feel his eyes watching me, like a laser burning into my skin. I blink hard, willing the onslaught of tears away. I don't want to pass by him blubbering like a baby. I don't even want him to see the tear stains on my cheeks.

I know K.O. doesn't think I belong with them, but he can choke on the dust my shoes are about to stir up.

"I can fit in. I belong here," I tell myself, even as I pass K.O. jogging like I'm in gym class. I look over at him, even though I try not to. He isn't the type of guy you can really ignore. His body faces the tracks, but his eyes slide to meet my unwilling gaze. My heart slams in my chest and deflates.

Despite all the pep talks to myself, I'm a failure. I'm a loser, a disappointment. The accusation is clear in his dark gaze. I close my eyes to hide from his stare and nearly lose consciousness. The world around me moves so quickly, I feel like I'm going to be ripped from my own skin. Stumbling and tripping, I land on my hands and knees against the rusted tracks as I try to catch myself from falling. I feel like I've run a marathon.

"Go figure, Savannah. Maybe you have," I mutter breathlessly to myself.

I crouch on the tracks, catching my breath when I feel that familiar burning stare. I crane my neck to peer behind me. K.O. is at least 100 feet behind me. Just a few seconds ago, we were only a few inches away from one another. He's not facing the tracks looking for the train anymore. Instead, he stares at me, and he doesn't seem as careless and mocking as I expect. Geezer's instructions scream at me.

"Try running along the side. Stay off the tracks. The train is coming, after all..."

There's one slight problem. I'm on the tracks, and the train really *is* coming. I hear the engines, the tires grind as the headlights of the train light up the dreary tracks, illuminating Tristan, Rox, and Geezer moving in beautiful choreography.

They run back and forth in ecstasy, laughing, shouting, and dancing. The train is here. It seems to move in slow motion while the trio runs a frenzied tempo. The train approaches Tristan first. He runs back and forth, back and forth from side to side until he runs right into the train. My breath hitches as the train pushes through him like he's nothing but air. Tristan appears on the opposite side of the tracks, flowing like a current of water until he's whole again.

Rox and Geezer run back and forth across the tracks. K.O. is the only one standing still and he's the closest one to me. I stand up, suddenly realizing my predicament. I can run like the others, but I can't control it. My ability only seems to kick in when I'm not thinking about it, but there's no way I'm willing to test that theory when a train is heading my way.

Rox passes through the train, ghosting her way to the other side. Geezer stops running and like K.O. stands flat footed, head up, and arms relaxed at his side in the middle of the tracks. I stand, too, but I can't move like I need to. My shoestring is tangled and stuck to some rusted broken off part of the track.

I struggle to untie my shoestring to dislodge it from the rusted piece of track it's stuck to. The strings are all knotted up. I try to jerk the shoestring out of the rusted hold. It only makes the shoestring knot up more. In hindsight I could have tried to slide my foot out of my shoe altogether, but it's hard to think when a train is heading my way, sure to be the death of me. The train comes and K.O. ghosts through it and bursts ahead of the train, like a ghost reborn into solid, live form. He collides into me, coolly assessing my situation. He bends to help me remove my shoe but stops. Instead, he stares at me, eyes wide for a moment in what seems to mirror my own panic. His smooth, flawless forehead wrinkles with tension but his face quickly becomes unreadable. The familiar stoic expression blankets his face and his dark eyes go cold.

"Are you afraid?"

His voice sounds like a whisper compared to the loud chaos of the oncoming train. I stare at him, my answer delayed because I can't believe he has the nerve to ask me a question like that. I almost expect him to tell me this is all a prank and that we're not going to get smashed by a train.

"Yes!" I scream at him.

"Terrified?"

"Yes."

The train is coming fast while we're standing idle on the tracks. We're both going to die because when Mr. Silent Deadly Eyes finally decides to talk, he's asking me stupid questions. All I can do is cry like a baby.

"Good," he says.

His voice is sharp and quick, containing no fear and no sympathy. I'm afraid he's going to step back, maybe ghost through the train and leave me to die. Instead, he steps forward. Instinctively, I put my hands up to push him away, but he puts his hands on mine and closes the space between us. K.O. breathes deep and closes his eyes. His face goes first, from solid, stoic frowns and glares to something I can only think of as a static color TV. His face is blurry, fuzzy and then the static spreads to his clothes, his arms, and even the hands that are holding mine. His hands feel like fog – cold and damp but there is no moisture. His hands are electric mist and his condition begins to overtake me.

"Relax," I hear him say, though his voice sounds hollow, almost disjointed. I'm nowhere near relaxed. The train is coming. It passes through K.O. I expect to feel bones break and other unimaginable pain. Instead my whole body goes numb and fuzzy. My head tingles almost like butterflies kissing my skin. I try to breathe. The air is hot and cold all at once. I take in air almost like it's part of me. I get the strange sensation of being blinded by color nearly as radiant as the sun, unable to blink or close my eyes. But then I do blink and the radiant, dancing light becomes skin, smooth, honey-cream colored skin. The feeling of mist dissolves and strong hands are holding my shaking ones as my cheek rests on a shoulder covered in black leather. My trembling lips are barely an inch away from kissing the groove of K.O.'s neck. I pull away only slightly, still close enough to see a thin trail of blood drip from his nose. He lets go of my hands and steps away from me, wiping his nose clean with the sleeve of his jacket.

The train is behind us. I hear it whisper, a shushed sound of marching wheels and whining rails. The train is gone. We're alive.

CHAPTER 16

Now that the crisis is over, I'm amazed at how easy it is to take off my shoe, even with the shoestrings tangled in the tracks. I know I panicked and that I wasn't thinking. Everyone cheers me on. Even Rox seems impressed, but K.O. is quiet and pale. Geezer follows my gaze before I can look away, and he frowns.

"Let's eat!" Tristan roars victoriously.

K.O.'s eyes find mine and his glare lets me know there's unfinished business between us. Before I can thank him for saving my life again, he takes off road-running. Rox follows him. I hesitate, afraid to even try.

"Don't worry. We'll work on your running. You'll be a pro before the end of the week," Tristan says, stooping down so I can climb on his back. I latch on to his neck and wrap my foot around, so grateful I almost cry.

"Great job tonight. You'll never hear me say what you can't do again," Geezer promises with a slight smirk.

That one looks and the tone in his voice lets me know that he won't go easy on me in the training to come. Before I can deny the natural talents they think I have, I'm blinded by dizzying speed as Tristan takes off. All I manage to do is hold on tight to Tristan and try my hardest not to choke on my own spit.

Before I know it, we're back at the house. K.O. and Rox have five fresh boxes of pizza with the works. I salivate at first smell. Between the five of us, we devour all the doughy, saucy goodness. After eating an entire box full of pizza, I can't say I'm anywhere near full, and I'm far from content. I'm a fraud. I didn't ghost through that train, at least, not on my own.

I cut a glance at K.O. He stands in the doorway, leaning against the wooden frame with his arms crossed. Our eyes meet. I redirect my gaze to my mauled, dingy white shoestrings. My eyes wander across the floor in time to see K. O.'s black boots stride out of the room. I grit my teeth and push myself up out of my chair.

Geezer looks up at me. "Get some rest. It'll be busy for you from now on."

"From now on?" I echo.

"Yeah, you're one of us now. We've got to get you in shape."

An unexpected lump forms in my throat. "That sounds kind of permanent. I thought…"

Geezer sighs. "You can't go back home. Not now."

"I get that, but at least I can call my mom and let her know I'm okay."

I can only imagine what she's thinking right now. After everything I've put her through and after how much progress we've made, I'm breaking her heart all over again.

"I just want to hear her voice."

He fishes in his pocket and pulls out a flip phone. "Call her."

He hands me the phone. My hands shake so bad I almost drop it.

"It's a burner phone. Keep your call short and when you're done, give it to Rox. She'll get rid of it," he says.

A few stray tears roll down my cheeks. "Thank you."

I turn my back to Geezer and my hands shake as I push the buttons. I struggle to dial her number. There's a tap on my shoulder.

Tristan holds out his hand, "What's her number?"

I hand him the phone, and he calls her. Rox sits grim-faced, only offering me a smile when our eyes meet. Geezer remains sullen. "Remember to keep it short," he says.

I nod, taking the phone from Tristan. They hover over me as the phone rings.

Mom answers on the second ring. "Hello?"

An onslaught of tears interrupts any words I might say. I cover my mouth and try to swallow the lump in my throat. Mom sounds strong, but there's strain in her voice, enough for me to know she's worried and tired.

I hear Tom in the background. "Is it her?"

"H-hello?" Mom tries again.

"Mom."

"Savannah, baby, is that you? Where are you?"

I fight the tears, wiping at my eyes and trying to steady my own voice."Mom, I love you. I'm okay."

"Savannah, where are you?" she asks.

I look at Geezer. He reaches for the phone. I pull away from him. "I don't know. I–"

"Baby, you've got to give me something to go on. I need to know where you are. What's going on?"

Geezer snatches the phone and tosses it to Rox.

"I love you! I'm okay!" I scream, hoping she can hear me.

Rox smashes the phone in her hands until it's dust. She steps over the scattered remnants of the phone and throws her arms around me.

"So sorry," she says, and I realize she's crying too.

Tristan joins in, silently offering his strength and warmth. Only Geezer remains detached. "You lucky girl, you've got a lot to lose."

CHAPTER 17

I cry until my eyes are dried out and swollen while Tristan cleans up the phone debris. Geezer disappears to his room and Rox leaves, promising to return with some clothes to cheer me up, even though I haven't worn everything from her last splurge. I finally feel like I belong somewhere, like I have friends, but the cost of their acceptance is so high, too high.

Climbing the stairs to regroup in my room, I'm unprepared for K.O. He stands in his doorway, staring at me with his arms folded. He's been waiting for me. I stop and face him as I weigh my options. I can say what I need to say through the doorway. It's as simple as thank you and goodnight. Of course, K.O. isn't a simple kind of guy.

K.O. doesn't invite me into his room but he doesn't slam the door in my face either. He takes a few steps back. I take a step forward, hovering at the open door. We get into a staring match again, until I lower my eyes and stare at his black boots.

His silence forces me to speak first.

"Thank you," I choke. "F-for saving my life."

We both know I wouldn't have made it if he didn't ghost us both through the train. I lift my eyes to sneak a glance at his face. He's not glaring at me. His brows are furrowed. He opens his mouth, fishing for words. He catches me looking at him and his glare returns.

"You were an idiot to be on the tracks," he says.

I expect the criticism.

"My shoestring got caught on the tracks."

I know I sound stupid.

"You weren't supposed to come at all," he continues.

"I got distracted," I say, ignoring his last comment.

He pauses before asking, "And how is that not your fault?"

My eyes have the nerve to sting with tears which only makes me mad. I've cried enough tonight."I came in here to thank you for saving my life, not to be criticized."

"I didn't."

We've been talking in hushed conspiring whispers, almost like two snakes, hissing at one another. He glares at me.

 I glare at him. "Wait. What?"

Maybe I didn't hear him right. I couldn't have heard him right because my ears are drumming, and anger pumps through my veins. He doesn't repeat himself but breaks eye contact to stare at a wall while I struggle to piece our broken dialogue together. The rushing blood in my veins mellows with confusion.

"I didn't– *couldn't* ghost us both," he admits, and for once the usual stoic voice is thick with emotion I can't decipher. He's so cryptic even when he's being straightforward.

K.O.'s dark eyes wander back to my face and his mouth tightens as he searches my face. He lets his words sink in as I frantically try to piece them together.

"You mean you…" I don't know how to voice what I think he's trying to tell me.

"You may just be a natural after all," he says.

I'm too shocked to be flattered. K.O. tried to save me, but he hadn't been strong enough. If my own abilities hadn't kicked in, I'd be dead right now.

"You tried to save me. You could've died."

"Never gonna happen," he responds.

"Don't worry. I won't tell the others," I say, and watch with guilty satisfaction when he turns slightly to regard me, "I won't tell them you're not invincible."

The corner of his mouth seems to spasm, flirting with a smile before setting in a wicked frown.

"Don't expect me to keep saving you," he says, turning his back on me in a wordless dismissal, "I *won't*."

I'm not sure if he's trying to convince me or himself.

"You *didn't* save me tonight. Thanks for the clarification and thanks for trying," I say.

I genuinely mean what I say, but I don't want him to know. So, I put a little stank in my tone and roll my eyes. When he doesn't respond, I turn my back to him and exit the room. I don't look back and he doesn't stop me.

Glad to make it to my room alive, I collapse on the bed. I just survived an actual conversation with K.O. Now if only I can survive everything else. I close my eyes thinking I can let all my worries melt away with oblivious sleep. Instead I'm haunted by memories, memories that morph into nightmares.

I find myself at Dad's funeral. It's a day I'll never forget as long as I'm alive. The moment is so real I almost forget I'm dreaming. I can feel the humid Georgia heat suffocating me even through blasts of air conditioning. My hands are especially clammy and hot as I bunch up the fabric of my black maxi dress with my fingers. As if that will keep me from crying. Tears sting my tired eyes and as the minister officiates, all sound is like static in my drumming ears.

Mom sits beside me dressed in a lovely black pants suit. A black lace short veil covers her face, but I can see her tear stained cheeks through the thin, delicate mask.

"Savannah, say goodbye to your father," she says.

A coffin made of expensive cherrywood looms before me and my heart lurches.

No, *I think, but I never open my mouth to speak. I stand to my feet as Mom opens the coffin. She bends down to kiss Dad's lifeless form. Then she motions me forward.*

In real life, I remember getting out of my seat and running to the bathroom where I vomited repeatedly and lost myself in hysterical tears. No one came after me. Not my mother, not even the polite and professional funeral director I bumped into on my way out the doors. I remember thinking that I didn't want to say goodbye and that Dad wasn't really gone. I remember thinking I was just dreaming and hitting my fist against the bathroom stall hard enough to confirm that I wasn't. The funeral continued without me and I never said goodbye. I never looked at his pale, lifeless body lying in that confined box, dressed in that stiff black suit he hated wearing. It wasn't him. He was a jeans and button-up, casual shirt kind of guy.

Now here I am, stuck in the nightmare, facing what I escaped in real life. My feet move against my will. Mom steps back, smiling at me. Her smile frightens me more than it brings comfort. Approaching the coffin, I see Dad lying there. He's not dressed in the black suit I remember Mom fussing about. Instead he's wearing black khaki pants and an expensive black sweater. A sparkling silver Rolex decorates his left wrist. Odd, he hated watches.

My eyes dare a painful glimpse at his face. Instead of the dull, graying skin I expected, his complexion is the familiar ruddy tan of a man who liked to be out in the sun. Not only that, he's breathing. His eyes are open, staring at me.

194

"Dad-Daddy?"

I know this isn't real. Dad is dead. I may not have personally seen his corpse in the casket, but I was very aware of the lifeless body during my short time at the funeral service. I remember them closing the casket and burying him in the ground. This is a dream. His eyes aren't really open. He isn't really breathing.

"Savannah."

His dead but very live looking lips move, and he speaks in that cool rich tenor. I've almost forgotten what his voice sounds like. Taking sharp, shallow breaths, I struggle not to cry. Even though I know I'm dreaming, I can't stop the tears from flowing.

"Daddy."

I want to tell him I'm sorry. There's a long list of things I'm sorry for like not saying goodbye to him for the last time, for all the times I'd been a brat, for forgetting him in even the smallest capacity, for not being as strong as I should be, for all the times I disappointed him, and being mad at him for dying…

"Dad."

I don't get to apologize for anything. No sooner do I call his name, his loving face twists into a harsh snarl I never thought his face could make. He sits up. Dad's hand reaches out, lightning fast and clasps my throat tight. He squeezes with one hand, sitting up and kicking himself out of the coffin in one fluid motion. He stands and lifts me off the ground. My feet dangle wildly in the air.

"You, my dear, are an abomination," he snarls.

Only his voice doesn't belong to him. It belongs to someone else and so does his face. My dad isn't the one strangling me anymore. Dr. Raymond Santos stands in his place.

"I will cure you the only way you can be cured. I will end your life," he says.

I wake up screaming, drenched in sweat.

"Nightmares, huh?" Geezer guesses.

His pale face appears from out of the darkness. He sits on the edge of my bed with a sullen stare. "Get up. Get dressed. Your training starts now."

I know I'm awake, but my neck hurts like something from my nightmare carried over. I might as well get up. Maybe staying busy will drown out the lingering terrors.

Geezer doesn't say much else after he barks his orders for me to get ready. Instead he slides out of my room, sauntering off to God knows where. I take a shower, wet and tie up my hair. I dress in the clothes Geezer left behind: a pair of black leggings and a long black, sleeveless muscle shirt that's two sizes too big. I feel like I'm wearing pajamas until I see the massive combat boots. The shoes make me nervous.

By the time I get downstairs, the kitchen counters are set up like a buffet. There are platters stacked with meat– bacon, sausage, bratwursts, and chicken wings. Fruit platters are lined with apples, oranges, bananas, grapes, and strawberries. Yogurt of various flavors are stacked next to a large bowl of hard-boiled eggs. The healthy content stops there. Boxes of pizza, bags of chips, and a large bag of king-sized chocolate bars are intermingled with the standard breakfast food. Pop and alcohol are mixed in the beverage line up with a variety of juices and water bottles.

Geezer drags into the room drinking from a silver thermos. Steam rises from the drink, swirling around his face. His eyes are red-rimmed with bags underneath. He looks like he hasn't slept in a few days. "Eat. You'll need your strength."

"You okay?" I ask.

He cuts his gray eyes at me over the rim of his thermos. "No. None of us are. This is all fun and games until you remember there's someone out there trying to kill you. Several someones, actually. And while I'm happy I saved your life, I need you to wake up and smell the coffee–"

"No one says that anymore," I mutter a little too loudly.

"Focus. Things are about to get serious! Between Santos and the Fleet–"

"Fleet?" I ask, which earns me another growl.

"No more questions until I actually start teaching you something. My point is that from now on, you're going to lead a dangerous life simply because of who and what you are. Don't get any bright ideas about going back to mommy and trying to be normal. Won't happen. If you don't learn to discipline your gifts you die. If you don't kill yourself from ignorance, there are plenty of people standing in line, waiting for an opportunity."

He gestures towards the food, "Eat."

He seems grumpier than usual. Maybe I missed something. Lately I sleep like I'm in a coma.

"Eat," Geezer responds more firmly, before taking a long sip of his hot drink.

He doesn't have to tell me a third time. Just because I can, I pile slices of supreme pizza and a bag of chips onto a plate. I grab a blueberry yogurt as a guilty afterthought. At first, I'm reluctant to eat much, but once I swallow the first few bites of food, it's not long before my plate is clean. Odd thing is, I want more. I'm not full at all. Before I can go back for seconds, Geezer signals for me to follow him. I snatch one last slice of pizza and scurry out after him.

He leads me outside. It's early morning. The sun's not even up. Traffic sounds in the distance with horns blowing and tires screeching. The air is cool but not biting.

"Where are we going?" I ask.

"Up," comes Geezer with another one-word answer.

I assume he's going to leap in the air and over the side of the roof like I've seen him do before. Instead, he leads me to a fire escape that runs up the side of our current home. This is the first time I've been able to take in our surroundings. It looks like we're in an industrial area or some abandoned ghetto. Unlike other New York areas, the streets are nearly abandoned. There's graffiti sprinkled on random walls, litter aimlessly blowing down the sidewalks, and not much else.

"The city's in the process of remodeling these parts. The other side of the tracks is pretty impressive. These parts are so rough not even criminals like to come here. At least, that's what we push for," Geezer explains.

He winks at me and I see a glimpse of the kid I'm used to dealing with. Then he scrunches his face up again.

"Up the fire escape," he barks.

I've got this crazy feeling of deja vu. Last time someone offered to help me like this was at Willow Manor. My recent nightmare flashes at the forefront of my mind, accompanied by the memory of the night Geezer abducted me from Willow Manor. I hesitate.

I force myself to shake off past events. Geezer isn't going to kill me. He's as close to a friend as I've ever had. I run after Geezer and up the fire escape as fast as possible. My heart races. I ignore it. I won't freak out. Even as I tell myself that, the food I scarfed down begins to sour in my stomach.

We reach the rooftop and we're not alone. K.O. waits for us, standing at the opposite end of the roof. As always, he's dressed in the infamous leather jacket. His hair is pulled back at the nape. Rox is on the opposite end, dressed in a denim jacket, jeans, and boots like mine. As usual, her hair ispulled up and out of her face. Her wrists are wrapped in tan cloth like she's prepared for a fight.

"Where's Tristan?" I ask.

He's the only one not around. In fact, he's usually the first person I see in the kitchen.

"Exactly where you'll end up if you don't shut up and learn something," Rox says.

Her words are the equivalent to being doused with a bucket of ice water.

"Tristan's…"

I can't say the word.

"On the mend," Geezer says, choosing his words carefully.

"Hopefully," Rox grumbles.

I want to relax but I can't. "Was it Santos? Did he–"

Rox lets out an exasperated sigh. "You two deal with her. I'm out!"

She casually jumps off the side of the building. Out of natural reflex, I run to look below, picturing her body as a blood splattered corpse on the sidewalk. The sidewalks are clean. She's already halfway down the street by the time I calm down and focus long enough to spot her.

Geezer clears his throat. "We don't have all day, Savannah."

Whatever happened to Tristan is a sore spot for everyone. I force myself to be content knowing he's alive. Looking at the intensity in both Geezer and K.O.'s stance, I choose to focus on the here and now, so I can survive training.

I try to relax, even though my nerves scream at me. "Should I stretch or something?"

K.O. shakes his head.

"When you get in a sticky situation, there are two major skills you need. Master them and you should be able to take care of yourself," Geezer says. "Running and diving. Normally, Tristan would train you in our running tactics but he's out of commission and we're running out of time. I won't lie to you. It's going to be rough and dangerous. Tears won't move us either."

K.O. cracks his knuckles. "Geezer."

Geezer nods. "Run laps around the perimeter of the roof until you pick up speed. Once you do, control it. If you can't, you'll end up over the side of the roof. If that happens, well then, baby bird, it's time to flap those wings and fly."

They both stare at me expectantly but I'm still processing his instructions. "You want me to run?"

"Run laps, yes," Geezer answers.

"And try not to lose control?"

Geezer laughs but there is no trace of humor. "You don't have any control. You'll find some today."

Maybe if I pretend like I'm in gym class this won't seem so bad. The roof is just a scenic gymnasium. Geezer is just a baby-faced PE teacher. I jog a lap and then another, safely avoiding close corners.

"Faster!" Geezer commands.

I gradually pick up speed with each lap until my lungs burn and my head is light. Cool New York air invades my nostrils and whips at my skin, somehow energizing me. Despite the heaviness of my boots, my feet feel light. My body melts into the wind and I feel like I'm floating. The speed gives me a high so delicious I close my eyes, growing accustomed to the adrenaline rush. My heavy lungs lift, and it almost feels like I don't need to breathe. I'm somewhere between breathless and breathing in excess. I should be panting for air. My chest should feel heavy. It doesn't. I throw my hands up as my legs move faster than they should.

"Open your eyes!"

My eyes snap open at the sound of K.O.'s voice. I can barely hear him over the wind in my ears, but his voice snaps me out of the dreamy rush. I'm no longer running. I'm falling but I never hit the ground. Geezer catches me, runs us up the side of the building's brick wall like he's running on the sidewalk, and tosses me back into the center of the rooftop.

"Try again," he says.

I shake my head to clear it from panic. I just fell off the side of a building. I should've died or been seriously injured, but here I am as if nothing happened. This isn't normal, but then, neither am I. I take a deep breath and start running again. It takes me a minute to pick my momentum back up, but once I start, the familiar rush takes over. I fall again and again Geezer is there to catch me.

"Focus!" he warns.

He thinks I'm not trying to focus? Even with the reassurance that someone is there to catch me, I'm not happy about falling from a rooftop.

"Focus, Savannah," I repeat to myself.

It's getting easy for me to pick up speed after so many starts and stops. I welcome the rush, the wind in my hair and on my face. I welcome the feeling of near intangibility as my skin vibrates with speed. I just can't get distracted. I reach the first corner of the roof and turn successfully. Then another. I nearly miss the next corner of the building, but I kick my feet off the ledge and realign myself on the right track.

"Good!" Geezer says.

Not good. His compliment is all it takes for me to get distracted. I turn my head to wink at him and find that I'm no longer running. Instead, I'm dangling head first from the balcony. A hand wraps around my ankle, the only thing preventing me from falling. My eyes stare at the distant sidewalk as my body sways at a dangerous angle. Blood rushes to my head and my throat constricts.

"Pull me up," I say. My voice is a strangled whisper as my head grows light with fear and pressure. "Don't let go!"

The firm hand that holds me suspended loosens its grip. They let go.

CHAPTER 18

I fall. No one calls out to me or tries to rescue me. This is it. Sink or swim. Fly or die. I close my eyes and try to tap into the power within me, but all I can feel is fear. The wind fills my ears and my nostrils. My blood goes cold.

"Just let go," I remember Geezer saying to me. But my body is heavy as granite, heavy with the realization I have no control. I'm going to crash and get hurt. I may even die. I am going to –

My thoughts are jarred by a sudden sensation of whiplash. My head spins and my neck snaps back. I land with my back cracking against the cool concrete sidewalks. My eyes burn, heavy with tears from the pain of my fall. It should have turned out so much worse. Something – someone interrupted the impact of my fall. I sit up. Geezer and K.O. tower over me with arms crossed and eyes narrowed.

"Did you even *try* to break your fall?" Geezer shrills.

His voice cracks in the pubescent way that reminds me he's 14 and not 60. I glare up at them, struggling to stand to my feet. I think I hurt more than my pride. My shoulders, back, and butt are screaming.

"Which one of you dropped me?"

K.O. makes a sound in his throat that sounds suspiciously like laughter. Of course, I'm probably imagining it.

"What would you do if I said it was me?" he asks.

"Was it you?"

He shrugs and takes a large intrusive step forward, purposefully invading my personal space. I feel my body stiffen.

"It's not like you could do anything about it, if I did," he continues. His voice is low and chilling. Literally. The tiny hairs on my arm stand on end.

"Wanna bet?" I say, taking a step forward to reclaim my space and invade his. My heart pounds.

"Guys, training isn't over," Geezer warns.

K.O. studies me, "You're all talk."

I don't back down. "I may surprise you."

He smirks. "Haven't so far."

Those words are the match that sets my temper off. I lunge at him, but he backs up, evading my attack. I stumble forward. Before I know it, he's behind me.

"Weak!" he accuses.

"I'm not weak!" I say, swinging at him.

My fist meets air. K.O.'s standing a foot from where he was just seconds ago.

"Dead meat!" he goads.

"I'm not!"

Running forward, I'm astonished when he takes one step and ends up further down the street as fast as it takes me to blink.

"Show me!" he yells.

I run after him with Geezer right behind me.

"Guys! This isn't the plan!"

K.O. slows down to a regular run, but he's still faster than me. I push myself to pick up speed. He accelerates effortlessly, maintaining an impressive distance. It only fuels my frustration. Taking a deep breath, I push through the burn in my lungs and the pain from my earlier fall.

I've got to go faster. I embrace the pain and let my mind go on autopilot. Soon Geezer's grouchy lectures are lost with the wind in my ears. I push myself faster until I'm no longer staring at K.O.'s back. We're side by side. As my body adjusts to the speed, K.O. veers to the left. Before I know it, he's climbing up a random building like a burglar wearing sticky gloves. I hesitate, placing one hand on the side of the building. Shaking my head, I run to see where K.O. will jump from. Only he doesn't. He hops from building to building with me running below him on the streets.

"Show off !" I call to him.

In all our running, we find our way back to the hideout. Geezer is already there, waiting for us. Surprisingly he doesn't look as angry as I thought he would. He looks relieved.

"Good. You two didn't kill each other."

I try to catch my breath to respond. It's funny how all the activity catches up with me now that I'm standing still. All I can manage is a gasping smile, a smile mirrored on K.O.'s face, until he meets my gaze. His smile fades just as quick as it came, and it takes my smile with it.

"Like I said, you're all talk," he says, pushing past me to enter our makeshift home.

Geezer grins. "Not bad, but tomorrow I expect even better."

As we walk into the house, I make my way to the stairs, looking forward to twelve hours of deep sleep. I'm aching all the way down to my bones, but my stomach growls. I think I'm dangerously beyond hunger, but I don't know which is more important at this point: sleep or food. I'm in the valley of decision when Geezer dictates a plan of action I can't refuse.

"Shower. Eat. We're going to see Tristan."

Curiosity and concern are all that keeps me standing. After a quick scrub in the shower I pick through bags of clothing. The results of Rox's latest shopping spree are in. The bags contain clothes with tags on them, tags she's labeled for me by style and event appropriateness, as if I'm fashion challenged. I put on a pair of faded denim jeans labeled casual in bubbly script, and hunt for a comfortable top. I bypass a ruffled white tee and a black tube top (one reads "date" and the other reads "party").

"Like I'll ever go on a date," I say to myself.

It's not like I know a lot of people that pay me attention. There's really no one I'm interested in either.

K.O., my mind whispers.

That prickly feeling in my chest stirs, but I squash it. K.O. isn't bad looking. Okay, he's smoking hot. But there's no way he'd ever look at me that way. I'm not his type. He's probably into biker girls with wild hair, piercings, tattoos, and attitudes as terrible as his.

Geezer clears his throat, turns his back, and averts his eyes. I appreciate the manners, especially since I'm only wearing a pair of jeans and my bra. My room still doesn't have a door thanks to Rox.

"We've got places to go, people to see, and things to do," he reminds me, "I'll be waiting for you in the kitchen."

With a sigh, I stop inspecting clothes and throw on the first non-frilly top I can find, a plain white tee, with my leather jacket. I bind my wild mane with a thick hair tie and splash on some random perfume before rushing down the stairs. The food from this morning is still sitting on the counter. Geezer notices my hungry gaze and frowns.

"That's one test you failed."

"Huh?"

"Food is fuel. We need premium fuel if we're going to keep up our strength."

I'm not a fan of metaphors. I hate pop quizzes and surprise tests too – which is apparently what breakfast was. I raise an eyebrow and stare at Geezer. He sighs.

"Healthy food like fruits and vegetables literally gives us more energy. Fats, starches, and sugars spike our energy for a while but, like anyone, they'll make us crash. When we crash, we crash hard. The wrong food will slow you down and get you killed."

I frown. "So the nasty stuff keeps us going?"

"The healthy stuff, yes."

"Well that's disappointing."

Feeling somewhat deflated, I ask if we can take a taxi to see Tristan.

"Just this once," Geezer says and tosses me an apple, "No more midday naps. You've got to learn to function on our schedule."

I'm too grateful to argue. We run far enough to get to civilization and hail a cab. I turn my face to the window and manage to close my eyes for a few content minutes. Geezer lets me sleep, though I'm sure he wants to complain.

After half an hour of napping while we're stuck in a traffic jam, I'm feeling refreshed and Geezer is cranky.

"We could've been to Chinatown in fifteen minutes' tops. Don't ask for another handout. We don't have time for this."

He's probably right. Running is much faster than New York traffic, but I'm not sure I'd be conscious afterward.

When we reach Chinatown, we leave the taxi and dissolve into the crowds faster than the driver can request his payment. I feel a twinge of guilt. My parents didn't raise me to be a thief, but I don't have any money. I shouldn't have asked for the ride.

Geezer navigates through the crowded streets like a contortionist, untouched and able to maneuver without much fuss. Me? It's like I'm invisible again. People bump into me left and right. I should be used to it. The streets are jammed with tourists and locals alike, but my nerves are grating. I grit my teeth.

"Geeze, wait up!"

He glances back at me but keeps moving. I'm losing him. I try to maneuver again to avoid the thick crowd. By the time I'm able to reach Geezer I'm exhausted again. He pauses long enough for me to catch up before continuing his harried pace.

Taking a deep breath, I hurry after him, wondering if he's being so difficult because he's teaching me another lesson. It wouldn't surprise me. I'm finding out that I secretly like to be challenged. I focus, breathe deeply, and press forward, bumping right into Geezer's back. He lets out a surprised grunt just before he falls face first onto the sidewalk, barely catching himself. He doesn't bother to turn around, but straightens himself, dusting his clothes off.

"About time," he grumbles.

"You were testing me!"

"I knew you weren't as slow as Rox says."

I roll my eyes. "How far away is Tristan?"

"Not far."

Geezer jogs down a set of descending stairs hidden between large green bushes in gray pots. A red valance hangs but there's no store sign along the busy neighboring buildings. I follow Geezer down hesitantly and watch as he rings the doorbell to a barred, steel door.

"Let's go," Geezer says, turning to acknowledge me directly for the first time since we left.

His expression is cautious, but his eyes are bright. I don't have time to question him. I get as far as opening my mouth when the floor beneath me opens. The drop isn't far, but I land in a clumsy heap. My flesh bruises against what feels like concrete. Wherever we are, it's dark, cool, and smells faintly of antiseptics, like a hospital. Standing, I call for Geezer. There's a clicking noise and bright lights explode from the ceiling, nearly blinding me. Blinking, I see Geezer standing in front of me. I punch him in the shoulder.

"You scared me!"

He frowns, nurturing his shoulder, "I want you to meet someone."

He leads me down a narrow passage surrounded by cobwebs and metal shelving stocked with dusty old boxes.

"Where are we? What's in those boxes?"

He doesn't answer but continues down the narrow hallway to a larger, gray carpeted hall.

"Doc? You in? How's the patient?" Geezer calls.

There are four doors lined up along the hall. The one to the farthest right opens an inch.

"Come in," comes a deep and warm voice.

Geezer smiles at me. "I brought her with me, too. I think you'll like her."

"I trust your judgement completely."

I can't tell if the faceless voice is being serious or sarcastic. I bite back laughter, partially because I'm nervous. Geezer leads me through the door. The room is compact but set up much like a hospital room with monitors and gadgets surrounding a hospital bed. Tristan sits up with his leg propped and wrapped in a cast. He grins when he sees me and all the tension in my tired body subsides.

"Good. You're not dying," I say.

"Nope," he says, but his eyes lose a little spark.

"It was a close call," the adult voice amends and I turn to look at the only person in the room I don't recognize. He's a middle-aged man of medium build with salt and pepper hair and reddish, brown skin. He's got a strong, wide nose, a slightly wrinkled face along the contours of his mouth and the corners of his friendly dark eyes. His beard is thick but neatly trimmed. He's dressed in a white button up shirt with his sleeves rolled up to his elbows and a pair of crisply ironed denim jeans. He smiles at me and his eyes scrunch up.

"You must be Savannah. You can call me Doc. Everyone does."

He shakes my hand firmly swallowing my hand in his larger calloused hand. It isn't the kind of hand I picture belonging to a doctor.

His dark eyes regard my face, and he shrugs. "I'm not your typical doctor. Life has taught me more than any medical school."

His eyes go distant for a moment and I wonder what he's thinking about.

"You're right. I think I like her," Doc says to Geezer. "She's observant, this one. Even though she's an open book."

My cheeks heat up. Nothing escapes Doc. He smiles. "Who says open books are always dull?"

Everyone settles in a serious mood, all frowns and business.

"Though there was a lot of blood, his injury was not as severe as I anticipated. Nothing's broken. Just a slight sprain, bruising, and a new scar to show off to Rox. Girls love scars," Doc says with a wink at Tristan.

"He'll need to stay off his feet until the swelling and tenderness goes down. I've packed him some pain killers and extra bandages in case the stitches for the entry wound reopens."

Tristan smiles but it's not the lightbulb bright smile I'm used to. "Lucky it wasn't a break, I guess."

I want to ask how he got injured. If we can ghost through solid trains, run so fast we're invisible, jump and dive from skyscrapers, and break wooden dinner tables down to dust with a finger nail, we should have thicker skin and stronger bones.

"We aren't invincible," Geezer says. I feel like he's reading my mind. But then Doc did say I'm an open book.

Doc continues the explanation. "Our gifts are extraordinary, but our body has limits just like everyone else.

We don't have long life expectancies. Either our powers will get us killed or men like Santos will. We're tough, but

Santos has some tricks of his own. Train hard, Savannah, and maybe you'll live long enough to get a few gray hairs like me."

Instinctively I look up at his salt and pepper hair. Doc gives me a knowing look.

"Hope I won't be seeing you any time soon," he says before turning his back to wash his hands. He doesn't turn back around, and he doesn't say anything else. I guess that's the way this bunch says goodbye.

Geezer helps Tristan off the bed and carefully to his feet. Tristan places one arm around Geezer's shoulder and I offer my shoulder for balance, too.

"I heard you rocked at training this morning. Sorry I missed it," Tristan says as we help him out the room.

"You just missed me falling off the roof."

"I missed you running like a goddess, you mean."

I blush. "I've still got a lot to learn."

"Well, I can't train you, but I'll cheer you on," Tristan says before he ruffles my hair.

We take a cab to our side of town. No one really speaks, even though I'm burning with unanswered questions. My mind wanders to all the times I've done something extraordinary. I've walked with swollen, throbbing, glass punctured feet, a broken arm, scratches, bruises, whiplash. Maybe we aren't quite invincible. Still, my wounds were mostly due to inexperience and clumsiness. How could anyone catch Tristan long enough to hurt him?

The unknown possibilities frighten me, but the known threat is even worse. My thoughts venture to that terrifying moment on Willow Manor's rooftop. I almost died that night.

Unconsciously, my hands go to my neck as I remember my nightmare about Dad and Santos trying to kill me.

"It was Santos. He found us, but we ran. At least, I would have but before I could start, he aimed for my legs and then at my head," Tristan confesses out of nowhere. His voice sounds as haunted as I feel, and he refuses to look me in the eye.

"We can't stay in New York long," Geezer says. "It's not safe anymore."

My heart aches because I know what he's trying to say. If I really want to stay with them and survive, I'll have to leave New York. I'll have to leave Mom.

Geezer locks my gaze. "We'll teach you the basics of survival and then you'll need to make a choice. You can come with us, or you can go back with your mom. We can lead Santos away from here and you can be safe. No one else has that choice. No one else has family."

His offer should make me happy but instead I feel even worse. I'll have to choose between a family I love who might never understand what I really am and a group of loveable misfits who finally make me feel like I belong. They've saved my life and they're still giving me more than I can ever repay them for – a chance to live up to potential I never knew I had.

We all ride in silence until we're on our side of town again. Rox meets us a few miles from our hideout. Fierce yet daintily beautiful, she offers Tristan a dazzling smile.

"You need a lift?"

Tristan doesn't answer her. He just grins in that "I love you and you're amazing" kind of way. Rox effortlessly hoists him on her back and takes off running. I guess I shouldn't be so amazed. The girl can break down tables with her fingertips.

Why shouldn't she be able to run while giving a 200-pound hottie a piggyback ride? I chuckle to myself, still in awe of my new circumstances. Who knows what I'll be able to do in a few weeks?

"Let's get back to training," Geezer says right before he takes off running. It takes me a minute to get my speed up but, before I know it, I match his pace like I've been running this fast all my life.

CHAPTER 19

From sunup to sundown Geezer holds me hostage to training. If I do any more running, I swear my legs are going to fall off. My entire body feels so sore that it even hurts to rest. That's the only reason I haven't called it quits yet.

The more time I spend with Geezer, the more I understand his nickname. He's like a militant grandpa. To keep from crying, I try joking to lighten the mood, but he's a stubborn little task master. My humor sours when he tells me to do pushups with my index fingers. Thankfully Tristan is home to save me. Somehow, he makes it up to the roof with no crutches or assistance. He's pale and sweaty, but he offers us a smile.

"Let's go out. I'm starved, and it looks like you could use a break."

"Yes!" I exclaim at the same time Geezer says, "No."

Tristan looks from Geezer to me. I'm sure he can see me salivating at the sudden thought of food. I'm not sure when I last ate, but it's been long enough.

"Come on, Geeze. Let the girl refill her tank before you kill her."

Geezer frowns. "Well, I guess we could go to that vegan gluten-free place."

My heart collapses. Those words don't exist on any menu I'd eat. At least not if I have my way. Give me the grease. Give me the meat. I won't go back to bland takeout food! As hard as I've been working, my taste buds deserve to splurge.

"I was thinking more like our favorite greasy spoon. Not really feeling healthy food tonight. I want my big double decker supreme BELT on rye with loaded fries and a root beer float with some pecan pie," Tristan says.

I'm beyond salivating. I'm practically melting from hunger. Geezer's frown deepens.

"I know. Good tasting food is bad for the body but, hey, I almost died, and I could really use some comfort food to celebrate the fact that I'm still alive. I'd really love the company, too," Tristan argues, "Besides, you could always get your Tex-Mex guacamole burger."

The frown on Geezer's face goes slack and his old eyes brighten. "There is another important lesson we should teach her."

Tristan blinks but his eyes flare with recognition. "See. It won't be a total waste of time."

He winks at me.

"You're right!" Geezer says suddenly very excited. So excited I'm nervous.

Our group gathers quickly, but Rox doesn't seem too content to be going anywhere right away. She takes one look at my sweaty work out gear and refuses to budge from the kitchen until I'm properly clean and dressed.

"Put that speed to use and hurry up!" Geezer calls as I race up the stairs to freshen up and change clothes. I take Geezer's advice, but it doesn't go as smoothly as I hope. I survive a shower but getting dressed is another story. After getting all tied up in fabric, with a few bruises and head bumps later I nearly tumble down the stairs.

"Sounded like a war up there," Tristan teases.

"It was," comes a voice behind me. K.O. strides into the room. He keeps to himself so much I almost forget he's part of our group.

"We're headed to our favorite greasy spoon. You in?" Tristan says.

Everyone stares at K.O. and he stares back at everyone. His eyes linger on me last. His face is unreadable, but his tone is odd. "She going?"

"We all are," Tristan says.

K.O. looks at me again. "Okay."

"We're going to put her up to the Tab Test," Geezer says.

"What's the Tab Test?" I ask.

"Just keep up, Scarlett!" Tristan says as everyone takes off out the door running. He's got some nerve considering Rox is carrying him again.

Twenty minutes later we're all sitting at a hole in the wall in a neighborhood I don't remember from the tour Angie and Jay gave me all those weeks ago. We would have been to the diner sooner, but I fell behind and took a few wrong turns. Exhaustion and hunger will mess with anybody's performance. Geezer waits until we're all seated in a corner booth before he explains the Tab Test. It boils down to eating, walking out without paying, and not getting caught. Dine and dash. It sounds simple. People do it all the time. Not that it's legal or right. If one of us gets caught, we have to pay the tab for everyone.

"Uh, no money here," I say.

"None of us do," Geezer says with a shrug. "We have to be resourceful and use what we've got. It's a little hard to get a steady job when you're being hunted."

"You're used to being invisible right? Just be your usual self and you'll do fine," Rox says.

Tristan cuts Rox a look but she just shrugs. Geezer flags down a waitress. I ignore Rox's comment and study the menu. When it's time to order, I have no clue what I want. Tristan gets his BELT, a bacon, lettuce, and tomato sandwich with a fried egg. Geezer gets his guacamole burger. Rox orders a sirloin steak, cheese fries, a strawberry shortcake, and a diet coke. K.O.'s order is the most simplistic, a bacon cheeseburger with fries and a root beer float. I open my mouth to mimic his order, but the waitress closes her notepad and turns to walk away.

"Hey!" I call out and the waitress jumps.

"Sorry, didn't see you there," the waitress says and even though she's talking to me, her gaze glosses over me with boredom.

Embarrassed I spout off my order. "I'll have the bacon cheeseburger & fries. But I'll take it with a chocolate shake."

She scribbles it down, batting her eyes at K.O. before bouncing off to the next table.

"See," Rox says, "Just be yourself."

Our food comes out fast. With a little ketchup and mustard, I'm ready to dig in. I stuff my face like I haven't eaten in days. Thankfully Rox sits on the same side as me and Geezer is in between us. She can't comment on how desperate I eat. Since K.O. sits across from me, he notices. I notice something, too, and it makes me laugh so hard I almost choke on my food. K.O.

has neatly finished off his burger and fries, but he doesn't get so lucky with his root beer float.

"You've got stuff on your face," Geezer says, noticing the way K.O. frowns at me. I laugh harder.

K. O.'s face tightens, and his eyes narrow in that glacial stare. I try to quiet my chuckles, sipping on my shake carefully. I slide him a few napkins. He snatches them and taking the entire bundle, rubs his face clean. He tosses the napkins on his plate and gets up from the table without a word, walking out the door. No one stops him. No one follows him or seems to notice he's gone at all.

Tristan clears his throat and I realize he, Geezer, and Rox are all staring at me like I've ghosted through a train again.

"No one's ever laughed at K.O. before," Tristan says.

"Like, *ever*," Rox echoes.

"I think you made him mad," Geezer observes.

My cheeks heat up, but I shrug. "I… he just caught me off guard. I didn't expect–"

Rox rolls her eyes, "You're hopeless. I'm out of here."

We all get up from the table, ready to walk out.

"Hey, wait! Wait a sec'!"

My hand is on the exit door when the waitress grips my arm. I turn to her, panic rising, when my eyes find a television out of the corner of my vision. Some people are watching the news. Most of them are looking at me. And why wouldn't they? My school picture flashes on the screen. The one with my same big hair, my plain white t-shirt and awkward smile. I remember when I took it, wondering if I should smile with my mouth closed or flash some teeth. I ended up giving something between a grimace and a wince. Mom hated it. Dad loved it. He knew I didn't like pictures. He probably knew cameras didn't like me either.

Now, almost two years later my picture circulates the state, "Local Teen Missing".

"You're her!" Mia, our waitress says, as if I'm some kind of celebrity, "Savannah Scarlett."

I'm in shock. This is much worse than not passing the Tab Test.

"Vince, it's her!" Mia calls to someone behind the counter. I'm frozen. My feet are stubbornly planted to the sticky tile floors. My mouth dries. I can't speak, even if I wanted to.

"You wait right there, hon. Lots of people are worried about you," the manager says. The man goes to a phone. Some of the customers are already on their phones. Geezer stands outside the diner. He's the only one from our group that hasn't abandoned me, and hr gives me a frantic wave, mouthing something to me. I've never been good at reading lips though.

Annoyance seems to be my saving grace. My limbs unfreeze, and I pry myself out of the waitress's grip. My situation is clear. With my face all over the news, I'm in real danger. Not only are Mom and Willow Manor looking for me, but so are the police, and worst of all, Santos. I wouldn't be shocked if he's the one who filed the missing person's report.

My heavily paralyzed feet are suddenly attached to feather light legs. I know one thing for certain. I can't just stand here and wait for the cops or anyone else who's looking for me. I've got to get out of here. I run for the door, throw it open, and take off running so fast I almost crash into oncoming traffic.

Navigating blindly for the sidewalks, there's even more risk of hitting pedestrians crowding the pavement. I move faster than cars stuck in traffic, a streak of hair and white fabric that barely registers to the average eye. But no matter how fast I run I don't feel safe. Santos is looking for me and he's got the entire city helping him. I don't stop running until I run into something, rather someone.

Tristan grimaces from the impact but manages to brace both of us from falling. He holds me as steady as he can. Sirens sound in the distance. The police are probably heading to the diner. Tristan jerks me into the nearest side street. He stumbles on his bad leg and nearly crashes to the ground but Rox steps out of the shadows to prevent him from falling.

"Slow down and watch your leg. Do you want to tear your stitches?" she says.

Tristan winces as he leans into her. "You know I'm not used to moving so slow."

"Better to move slow than not at all," she says.

I hear their conversation but right now I can't comprehend. I can barely breathe. "I– I'm on the news!"

"Yeah, we saw," Rox says.

A hand touches my shoulder from behind and I almost take off running again. The hand on my shoulder tightens.

"Relax, Savannah. Calm down," comes Geezer's voice behind me.

I turn to look at him, still shaking, unable to stop. "They're looking for me!"

Geezer sighs and assumes his old man attitude. "Yes. They are. They probably won't stop until they find you, either. Welcome to the life."

"But, I'm on the news!"

"Well, you passed the Tab Test, but you're far from invisible," Geezer says.

"No kidding. So, what do I do? Do I have to leave town now?"

Geezer looks past me and nods at Rox.

"You'll be fine. I'll take care of this. Rox, you know what to do," he says, "I've got Tiny Tim, here."

I've never seen the blonde look so genuinely excited about anything. Her eyes practically sparkle. She takes one look at me and smiles. The upturned mouth looks so weird on her it's almost scary.

"Don't look so nervous. We're just going to have a girl's night," she murmurs.

Her idea of a girl's night doesn't sound fun.

Rox rolls her eyes. "Stop looking so clueless. I'm giving you a makeover. It's okay. You don't have to thank me. My work will speak for itself."

Thank her? The thought doesn't cross my mind at all. Forget having a girl's night. I don't know who's scarier: Santos or Rox.

CHAPTER 20

*N*ew York will be looking for a bushy haired, bi-racial girl in jeans, a t-shirt, and a hoodie. That girl has to change if I'm going to stay under the radar of cops and the media.

"Okay hon, you ready for this?" Rox asks.

We're in front of the bathroom mirror. Rox wears latex gloves dipping a small, generic white brush into a relaxer kit. I bite my lip at her comment and cringe as she moves the brush towards my vulnerable head.

"Do you know what you're doing? Do you really need to put that stuff in my hair?"

I've had my hair relaxed. Well, once. It was easy to manage, but the burn didn't seem worth it.

Rox pauses. "Old Savannah's got to go on hiatus if you want to stay under the radar."

"Can't I just wear a wig?"

"That's no fun," she says, setting the relaxer kit down, but she nods, "Fine. No relaxer. But we've got to do something with all this hair."

Rummaging through a duffle bag at her feet, she pulls out deep conditioner, detangler spray, mousse and two boxes of hair color. I squint to figure out the color. She quickly sets them down out of my view. She reaches for me but freezes, "Can I touch your hair now?"

Changing my hair is like changing the one thing that makes me feel most like myself. It's all I have. Funny, I didn't realize that until I'm threatened with changing it.

"What are you going to do? Are you sure you know what you're doing?"

"I know a thing or two," Rox says.

I wipe my sweaty hands on the legs of my jeans. She hasn't botched my hair yet. There's still time for me to run.

A soft smile touches the corners of Rox's mouth. "Before I knew I was an Errant, I wanted to be a celebrity stylist. Since your lovely face is on the news, I guess I'm finally living the dream."

"Not helping," I grumble.

She leans in and whispers like we're the best of friends. "I used to do hair for the kids in my group home. No one wanted us, but I made sure we didn't look the part. You're in good hands. Let's make it fun."

Fun didn't involve a burning scalp. "Fine. But I mean it. No relaxers," I repeat.

"Great! You're going to look amazing. But first…" She shows me the two boxes of color. "Mahogany or scarlet?"

I open my mouth to reject both colors, but she squeals and randomly tosses one of the boxes over her shoulder. I've never seen her so excited. I take a deep breath, and for once, my heart races from something other than fear. "Do your thing."

By the time she's done with my hair, I'm too tired to care about what it looks like. My head hurts, I can barely keep my eyes open, and the muscles in my jaw hurt from yawning. Rox, on the other hand, is just revving up.

"Don't look at your hair, and don't mess with it either." she snaps, when my eyes wander to the mirror for the hundredth time. "I want you to get the full picture when we're finished."

I can barely keep my eyes open. "It's been hours. You're not done yet."

She gives me a once over. "Stop whining. Your hair is perfection. Your clothes? Not so much. We're going shopping."

Without looking, I toss my sweatshirt hoodie up and we head out. As tired as I am, my body sparks into motion, pulsing with life as we race through the streets, side by side. The speed is easy now. It's funny how quickly I've adapted.

Hanging with Rox isn't nearly as bad as I thought it would be. She's gorgeous and acts confident, but she's just as awkward as the rest of us. She has a habit of putting her foot in her mouth. She's got no filter and says whatever pops into her head without apology. She loves fashion and talks about it like its art and science. Like it's life.

"High ponytails and buns, form-fitting jeans and dresses, one-piece pants suits, jumpsuits, and boots, knee high and up are part of my signature style. As much as I'm sure you'd like to, you can't have *my* style. You need to find your own," she says.

"Fine by me," I mutter.

We raid closed stores and walk out of changing stations without paying in the open stores. Dad's probably rolling over in his grave right now, and if Mom could see me, she'd be furious. I look at the tags on the clothes.

"What are you doing?" Rox asks.

"Adding up the cost of all these clothes."

She frowns. "Why?"

"We're stealing! Doesn't that bother you?"

Rox rolls her eyes. "What are we supposed to do?"

"Clothing drives?"

Rox shakes her head. "It's how I cope, okay? Tristan cooks. Geezer parents. K.O. goes on his angsty, hermit sabbaticals, and I shop…lift. If it makes you feel better, I'll donate the clothes to a shelter when I'm done."

We fall into an awkward silence. I push through a rack of clothes, struggling to find something to say to lighten things between us, but Rox, speaks first and the tense moment between us slowly dissolves.

"We travel light. At least we get to shop often," she explains as she inspects another stack of clothes.

Light to her and light to me are two different things. I end up with seven new outfits to satisfy my shopping itch. Rox looks over my outfits with approval. "Not bad, hon."

She hefts the previous bags of clothes she got me on her shoulders and sighs. "I'll drop these off at the women's shelter. Since you didn't appreciate these, I'm sure someone else will. Get some shut eye. Beauty sleep is the final key to an amazing makeover."

With a wink, she blurs out of the room before I can open my mouth to tell her thank you. Beauty sleep sounds good. Rox may just be as awesome of a stylist as she thinks she is.

***

"Sleep well?"

Geezer's voice is the first thing I hear when I emerge from a long, satisfying rest.

"It was epic," I mumble.

My face is smashed against my pillows and all my nerve endings sigh with relief.

"Yeah, figures. It's going on 10 pm," Geezer grumbles.

I sit up and stretch.

"You've been sleep for –"

His voice trails off and his eyes go bigger than I've ever seen. His shocked expression draws attention to the heavy shadows under his eyes. He could probably benefit from some beauty sleep, too. I smirk at that, trying to imagine how Geezer would behave for one of Rox's makeovers.

"Your hair…"

My hands fly to my hair. "What?"

Geezer stares. "Nothing."

The way he speaks sounds more mystifying than insulting.

"What's up?" I ask, getting more nervous the longer he stares.

"Get dressed. We're going out tonight for some fun. We'll sprinkle in some training while we're at it."

He backs out of my room, still staring at my hair. I haven't looked at myself since the makeover started and now I'm not sure if I want to.

"Stop being a baby," I tell myself.

I shower and dress. Then I look at my reflection. My face is still the same. Not much has changed, but something in my expression has. I look a little less lost.

My eyes slide over the rest of my profile only to find my natural auburn hair has been colored a deep, vivid red. Scarlet red. Old Savannah would've freaked out at the color. The bold and rich color against the freckled, pale honey of my skin gives me a sun-kissed glow. My hair hangs in my face and down my shoulders in loosely curled tendrils. I miss the ferocity of my full independent mane, but the tamed, polished look is refreshing, if not just a little frizzy.

The pile of new clothes, on the other hand, has me second guessing everything. I grab the first outfit at my fingertips, a fitted black lace baby doll dress, and try not to talk myself out of wearing it even as I put it on. The sleeves are a lace pattern with intricate flower designs. The high-low hem flares at the bottom of my thighs in the front and touches the crease in the back of my knees. I complete the look with a thin pair of black socks and tie up ankle boots and add a touch of frosted lip gloss.

I pace the narrow hall for a few agonizing moments before grabbing a black knit cap, shoving it over my curls. Racing down the stairs and into the kitchen, three sets of wide eyes study me with gaping mouths. Of course, K.O. is the exception. He doesn't even glance in my direction. He's more interested in the chipped paint outlining the front door.

"We ready?" Geezer squeaks.

"Just about," Rox says, frowning at my cap covered head.

Geezer is in a button down, checkered green and white shirt with baggy jeans and tennis shoes. Tristan wears a tight navy-blue shirt to show off his chiseled pecs with dark denim jeans. His brown hair is spiked with combed sideburns. A gold chain dangles around his neck and beneath his shirt. He looks like a model.

K.O., as always, wears his signature black leather jacket with a black tee, jeans, and boots to match. I wonder if he has any clothes in other colors or if he dresses in black 24/7 on purpose. Rox sports a fitted red jumpsuit with her off the shoulder sleeves and a golden belt around her waist. Her hair is pulled back in a high ponytail. Her ears are decorated with gold, glistening, cross-shaped earrings. Her face is outlined in bold mascara and smoky eye shadow, and glittered highlights above her eyes. Her lips are a deep red. She looks like she belongs in a fashion magazine right next to Tristan.

"No, no, no," Rox says.

She frowns at me, sizes me up, and snatches the cap off my head. My hands belatedly try to grip the cap but all I feel are smooth, curled tendrils.

"Now we're ready," she says, slapping my hands down.

Tristan whistles, "Lookin' good, Scarlett."

Rox shoves my hat in the trashcan before I can snatch it back.

"The goal was for Savannah not to draw attention and–" Geezer begins.

"No," Rox interrupts. "The goal was for Savannah not to look like that girl on New York's most wanted list. Problem solved. Let's go."

Geezer seems satisfied with her answer. He doesn't ask any more questions. I keep my eyes on Tristan and follow him as we take off. Even though he's still moving faster than the average person, his run is more like a limping jog. Poor guy.

The wind feels good in my hair as we speed down the crowded streets, weaving in and out of the herding sidewalks and heavy street traffic. I almost don't realize when we've reached our destination, but a strong hand grips my arm and jerks me to an abrupt stop. I swallow a big gasp of air in time to compute the fact that K.O.'s fingers are digging into the skin of my arm. He still has the audacity to avoid looking at me. I snatch my arm away just as he drops it and I almost trip in my boots. He steadies me and then let's go so fast I almost fall again.

"Hey!"

He grabs for me, but quickly lets me go, as if he just remembered I have cooties. He watches me trip again, this time up the two stairs in front of me and into Geezer's back. Geezer frowns at us. "Can you two behave?"

I draw in a breath as K.O. invades my personal space to whisper a warning. "Watch yourself," he says, before walking away from me.

Rox shakes her head and hooks her arm undermine, leading me into the pulsing, loud club in front of us.

I don't manage to catch the name of the club before I'm sucked into the atmosphere. I've never been in a club. I've never had anyone to go with. Rox leads me straight to the dance floor. If I could, I'd shrink back to the sidelines and people watch, because I really can't dance. Rox makes it look easy, though. Not too far away Geezer break dances like a pro. Other dancers form a small circle around him, cheering him on and blocking him from our view. I know dancing is the last thing I should be worried about but, for a minute, I forget about our powers and the problems that come with it.

"Just sway side to side," I tell myself, but my feet won't move. They're glued to the ground and all I can do is stare at Rox like an idiot before retreating. I run over someone else's feet and I whirl around to apologize. Tristan winces.

"Sorry. I – Why are you up? Shouldn't you be taking it easy?"

Tristan winks, "Yeah, when it comes to work, but I play hard. Plus, I'm still light on my toes."

He doesn't look light on his toes. Despite the smile on his face, he looks miserable. His tall body is hunched. Under the scarce light his skin looks pale and clammy.

"You should've stayed home," I yell over the music.

Tristan shrugs, "Couldn't miss your makeover celebration."

I frown. "Did I look that bad before?"

He shrugs, "Not to me, but it seemed like a fun excuse to party."

His eyes twinkle despite the obvious pain he's in. "You've gotta give K.O. a break," he says, "Seriously, Scarlett, the guy's saved your life at least a dozen times. That's gotta mean something."

My cheeks get hot.

"Look, I don't know what choice you're going to make, but if you stick with us that means you're sticking with all of us. K.O.'s my boy and he'd do anything for his friends, no matter how rough around the edges he is."

Rox dances her way over to us and smiles at Tristan. "Dance with me?"

She doesn't give him a chance to answer but pulls him into the middle of the congested dance floor and they disappear in the crowds. Standing on the sideline I let the music beat through me. For a moment I feel invisible again, like I have for most of my life. Tonight that's okay, but alone time in a noisy club is unrealistic.

"Whoa there, Red," comes a gruff voice.

The voice matches the appearance. What's worst, I recognize the face. Or rather the tattoo. The guy is shorter than me but thicker. The tattoo, a dagger on his neck drips inky blood. It's one of the terrible guys from the pizza shop.

"You look kinda familiar," Tattoo says, reaching for a strand of my hair, "A cute face like yours would be hard to forget, though."

I sat at his hand. He doesn't reach out again. "What's your name?"

An arm slips around my waist and jerks me tight. I look up to see K.O. giving Tattoo the most frightening stare I've ever seen. His voice is stiff and deadly. "She's with me."

K.O. doesn't wait for Tattoo to react. His fingers tap into my back, prodding me to follow him across the dance floor. Saved again.

"You know that guy?" I ask at the same time that K.O. says, "Stay away from him."

"Why'd you say I was with you? Like…"

Like we're together, *together*, I want to say.

He just stares at me as if I should already know the answer. Maybe I should. Maybe I'm overthinking. There's no way… No. Just, *no*. Like Tristan said, K.O. does what it takes to keep his friends safe.

Are we friends? I wonder.

K.O. pulls me in closer to him and his lips lower to my ear. "Dance with me?"

His breath tickles the skin of my ear and the fine hairs on the back of my neck raise.

"Why?" I blurt. "No one's going to believe that you and me – "

He pulls me in close and leads me in a small circle, matching the slow song playing with the deep, throbbing beat. My palms sweat – sweaty hands that K.O. grabs, placing them around his neck. I step on his foot. K.O. stumbles and our legs tangle. We nearly topple to the floor but K.O. catches me in an almost dramatic dip. He sweeps me upright so fast my head swims and I tighten my hold around his neck.

Geezer steps in between us and he doesn't look so happy. "Fighting on the dance floor?"

"Trying to keep this one out of trouble," K.O. says.

"Yeah, well, trouble seems unavoidable," Geezer says.

Both K.O. and I follow his grim gaze across the club.

"Great," I mutter as my eyes land on Mohawk. Tattoo's tall, rooster shaped friend has already spotted us. Both he and Tattoo glare at us from the wall closest to the club exit. Tattoo smiles at me from across the room. He doesn't look quite as nervous now that he's with his pal. I feel the animosity brewing and I know something bad is about to happen. Tattoo's smile says it all.

"Geezer, get the others and get her out of here," K.O. says.

I pull away from Geezer before he can grab me. "I know you're tough, but those guys are trouble."

"Exactly," K.O. says.

Geezer places a tentative grip on my shoulder, but I shrug him off.

"We outnumber them if we stick together," I say.

K.O. doesn't bother responding. Geezer grips me firmly this time. "Trust me, they're not alone," he warns me, nodding his head off to the side.

I follow his gaze along the other side of the club walls. Another menacing pair stare at us. I don't know how I missed seeing them. One guy is basketball tall, all legs but from the way he balls up his fists, he looks like he could pack a bruising punch more than he could shoot hoops. Next to him is a much shorter guy with a hunched posture and so many facial piercings he looks like that horror movie.

"Maybe we should just all leave," I say.

Of course, K.O. doesn't move. I plant my feet just as solid as his. I won't leave until he does.

"Where is he?" a voice demands from behind us.

I turn to see a boy two heads taller than me with dark eyes outlined in mascara. His white-powdered face is prettier than mine and his build is willowy, almost graceful. But there's something lethal under all that mascara and litheness, something predatory. My gaze slides to K.O. and I'm impressed. He holds Mascara's gaze with no problem.

"What did you do? Where is he?" Mascara asks again, this time emphasizing each syllable with painful precision.

"I don't know what you're talking about," K.O. says.

Mascara takes an aggressive step forward. I fight the urge to step back even though his dark gaze isn't directed at me.

"Max. What'd you do with him?" the boy asks.

Geezer inserts himself between K.O. and Mascara while I'm frozen, a helpless liability. Before Geezer can open his mouth to say something mature, Mascara side-steps him and whispers something to K.O. I can't hear what he says but it causes K.O.'s jaw to tighten. His nostrils flare and he reaches up, grabbing Mascara by the collar of his black shirt. I can't hear K.O.'s response over the music but it doesn't take a rocket scientist to realize he's threatening the guy. Mascara's already pale skin goes an impossible shade lighter.

Out of the corner of my eyes I see Needle Face and Tall Fists work their way through the unsuspecting clubbers. On the other side of the club, Mohawk and Tattoo are only a few feet away. They're surrounding us, or at least they try but we're equal in number. Tristan and Rox shadow Tall Fists and Needle Face. Geezer and I stand tall facing Mohawk and Tattoo. They don't look as scared as they do smug. I've never been in a fight before, but I've seen enough kids get beat up to recognize the wild aggression charging the air just before a fight.

Mascara's eyes darken but shine in the center, a look I've only seen before in K.O. He's like a cobra, postured, waiting to make the killing strike. "We want Max."

"Can't help you," K.O. responds.

The music in the background changes pace, quickens and pulses. A knife shines under the erratic strobe lights. I scream and dive to stop Mascara from slicing K.O., but he maneuvers around me and swings for K.O. The world fast forwards around me and I'm not sure what's happening. My vision's delayed. My eyes see too slow. I will myself to focus, knowing this could be a life and death situation. Mascara moves just like a snake, striking quick but K.O. is fluid as water, evading his sharp attacks with almost a lazy, but precise resistance. Their movements are double time in comparison to the frenzied rock/electronica music blasting through the club. K.O. manages to grab Mascara by the wrist and snaps it backward. I don't have to hear the crunch of bones to know something's broken. His venomous face twists in agony and he screams, but it doesn't stop him from retaliating. The pain and rage in his eyes make me inadvertently take a few steps back, forgetting about my little stand-off with Tattoo and Mohawk- until I bump right into them.

"Where're you going, Red?"

Tattoo wraps his arm around my neck, holding me in the crushing headlock. I literally feel the walls of my throat painfully caving in under the pressure of his grip. My feet kick wildly at the floor as he drags me backward. Then something – no – someone blurs between us, hits us so hard that I'm separated from his hold. I fall to the ground as he slides across the floor from the impact. It hurts to breathe, and my throat is on fire like I have the worst case of strep throat. The guy who'd been checking me out barely fifteen minutes ago just tried to kill me.

CHAPTER 21

"*I*'m not finished with you, Red."

Tattoo's voice snaps me straight into panic mode. My throat is too raw and swollen for me to scream the way my nerves want me to. Tattoo grabs my wrist. My free arm flails, blindly aiming at my attacker. He spins me further, throwing me into another pile of unsuspecting bystanders. I manage not to land on my butt again but have the displeasure of watching the big bully charge towards me.

"Should've picked our side over those losers," Tattoo says.

"Funny. I never got an invitation," I say, despite the raw ache in my throat.

"You'd never make it anyway. You're weak!" Tattoo snarls, giving me an unadmiring full body inspection. I couldn't agree with him more. If the two of us go toe to toe, I'm a goner for sure. I look around for friendly, familiar faces but I don't see any sign of the people who are supposed to have my back. They've left me.

I back up, trying to get lost in the crowds but Tattoo sticks out like a sore thumb, staring at me like some demonic serial killer from one of those cheesy slasher flicks from the 80's. It doesn't seem so cheesy now. I feel like the bimbo who always trips and falls before meeting a bloody demise. My clumsy backtrack turns into a full-fledged run, though in a room packed like sardines in a can, that doesn't accomplish much.

Tattoo's pal Mohawk blocks me from trying to run.

"Well, well. Just can't stay away, huh?" He cracks his knuckles.

I back up right into Tattoo. They sandwich me between them and, at first, I'm deathly afraid. I don't want to die.

Then, in the brief seconds I have to think, I realize these guys are lazy cowards. Why single me out? Why not pick a fair fight? I'm outnumbered. Fear transforms into hot, trembling rage. If these guys are going to bully and hurt me, they may win, but I won't make it easy. Tears well up in my eyes. I ball up my fists. "You like hurting helpless girls?"

"It's your fault you're helpless. You're playing for the wrong team," Mohawk snaps.

"Wrong team," Tattoo echoes.

Mohawk nods his head at Tattoo. I know I'm running out of time. Desperate, I wrap my arms around Mohawk's neck, close enough to distract him before bringing my knee up hard and fast to his groin. His eyes cross and he doubles down. I duck and slip between him and his buddy just in time as Tattoo charges forward. He stumbles, nearly trampling Mohawk. Before I can gain ground, a rough hand grips my hair and yanks me backward. I use the momentum, turning into my attacker and swinging my fist as hard as I can. Tattoo catches my fist and twists my arm until there's a crunch. A hoarse scream escapes my lips and I bear down on the pain.

Dark spots float in and out of my line of vision before I see a blur. My eyes are working too slow, again. I'm in too much pain to concentrate. Tattoo's hold on me is abruptly disconnected and my eyes focus long enough to see Rox fighting Tattoo. She's got him in the same hold he had me in, only he's on his knees and screaming at an octave I never thought a big guy like him could reach. Mohawk tries to sneak up behind her, but Tristan is there. He restrains Mohawk in a bear hug before tackling him to the ground.

"What's the first rule? The first thing I taught you?" Geezer yells over the music, his arm sliding around my waist to help balance me. Grateful for the support, I lean down against his shoulder.

"Run," I croak.

I don't argue that I tried. I really did but running hadn't been my first instinct.

"That's always been your problem," Mascara's voice comes from behind us.

Geezer stiffens. "We don't want any trouble, Emery."

Mascara, or Emery, as Geezer calls him, turns his dark, creepy gaze on me. "Stick with them and you're dead, girlie. Running never solved nothing."

His eyes cut back to Geezer and he opens his mouth to speak. I don't know what he says because my senses dull. Sound becomes muffled and the black float in and out of my vision. I blink darkness away long enough to see a pair of dark, finely sculpted eyes staring into mine. It's K.O. I feel his arms envelope me before we propel into whirlwind speed and I give into the dark, lulled into unconsciousness.

***

"Dislocated shoulder, bruised ribs, swollen larynx and trachea, bruises galore, bumps and scrapes a million... Honestly, we're lucky she won't suffer permanent damage."

"Lucky she's alive," comes another voice, this one more recognizable even though it's hardly over a whisper. I'd know that voice anywhere. For a while it haunted my dreams. Now, it merely agitates me. My eyes find the will to open. My lids are about all I can move.

"Hello again, Savannah. I thought I told you I didn't want to see you back here any time soon."

When I see Doc's face, I realize where I am – Chinatown at his medical hideout. My eyes drift around plain, sterile room before landing on Geezer and the gang, huddling and bunched up by the doorway. When I lock gazes with each of them, everyone but K.O. looks away. He holds my gaze with arms folded and we lock in our staring game until I find my nerve to talk.

"What. Happened?"

I want to scream at them. Everyone shuffles, fidgeting with clothes and hair, not knowing what to do with their limbs. Even Doc looks a little nervous.

"You're alive."

I'm not surprised that K.O. is the first to answer. His steely posture and unwavering gaze unnerve me, only adding to my frustration. Why does he look so offended? I'm the only one who's injured and laid up in a makeshift hospital bed. Everyone else just looks like they've been for a jog around the block or to a great party. They're clean, bruise-free faces remind me of my inadequacies. I'm the only train wreck.

K.O. flings his jacket over his shoulder and turns his back to leave the room.

"Don't just walk out. You don't get to do that!" I want to scream at K.O. but my raspy voice cracks.

He doesn't give me the slightest consideration. In one fluid motion his jacket's on and he's walking away. Everyone else just stands and stares, silent spectators. My face heats up, and even though it hurts, I find the nearest thing in the room to throw at K.O. A glass of cool ice water flies in his direction. Not even looking, K.O. dodges it with a slight turn of his shoulder. The glass shatters against the door and water splashes everywhere. Ice slides and splatters loudly against the gray cement floors. K.O. walks out dry and silent but the way he slams the door lets me know I've succeeded in getting under his skin the way he's gotten under mine.

Everyone turns to stare at me. No one says a word. The tension in the room multiplies but I don't offer any apologies. I'm not sorry I threw the glass. Not that it matters. Guys like K.O. are like cockroaches. He thrives when chaos is killing everyone else.

He's way more appealing than a cockroach, some tiny part of my brain whispers.

I bite my tongue in disagreement, startled at the thought.

"You have every right to be upset," Geezer says. I almost hug him for pulling my mind out of the dangerous detour it was taking, but I remind myself I'm still mad at him, too.

"If it helps, we made sure the other guys looked much worse than you," Rox offers.

It does help a little.

"Maybe you should come back later," Doc says, "Savannah needs her rest if she's going to heal properly."

"I need *painkillers* and answers," I manage to argue, though with every other word my voice fades in and out.

"Don't talk anymore," Doc snaps.

He shoos Geezer, Tristan, and Rox out of the room before I can object. They each give him a grateful and knowing look. I watch as the trio rush out the doorway without so much as a goodbye. They're happy to leave and I'm glad to see them go. I almost felt like I belonged. Almost. But being alone in the fight of my life without anyone to count on for those few moments leaves me feeling more alone than ever. I realize I'm still alone no matter how many people swear they want to help me. People only let me down. My so-called friends ushered me onto a battleground I didn't even know existed.

Doc shuts the door calmly. He gives me the kind of look Dad used to make when he was disappointed in me. Like Dad, Doc doesn't address my behavior in words. His expression is chastisement enough. He fiddles in some drawers and pulls out a small, clear bag with two large white pills.

"I've got pain killers and something for anxiety. I've got your answers too," he says.

Thousands of questions cross my mind, but I don't know where to start. Thankfully, Doc keeps talking.

"The group you met tonight were from Max's gang. Max has some history with your friends. He used to be part of the group, part of the family. He was Oliver's brother."

"Oliver?"

Doc's eyes flicker and he visibly winces. "K.O."

He doesn't wait for me to digest the new information, but rushes on. "It started in Kansas, a small town far from all the crowds. It was a quiet life and for a while. Things were safe, nice even. Then the hunters found them. People died. K.O. and Max changed."

Doc frowns. "Max became wild and reckless. He wanted revenge for the people they lost at the expense of the survivors. It was a suicide mission. K.O. did what he had to do to protect the majority. He left his brother for dead, so he could save the others. I don't think K.O.'s ever forgiven himself. Everyone thought Max was dead. Apparently, Max has done quite well for himself. Not only did he survive but he's amassed quite a following."

"They said he's missing," I croak, recalling Emery's accusation of K.O.

Doc hands me the pain killers, but I don't take them. The pills are too big to swallow dry and my glass of water is dripping off the doorway and all over the floor. Doc notices and frowns again, just like Dad would.

"Do you think K.O. is responsible for Max's disappearance? Do you think he knows where he is?" I ask.

Doc stoops to pick up the biggest pieces of broken glass. "K.O. loved his brother."

He doesn't answer my question.

"I'll be back with another glass of water," Doc says.

He hesitates at the door. I've never seen a grown man look so uncertain. "If K.O. had something to do with it, he had good reason."

CHAPTER 22

I exist in a blissful, drugged stupor, free of bodily pain for the next few days. In my delirious state, I might as well be facing a brush with death because my entire life seems to flash before my eyes. I dream about my childhood, growing up in the humid Georgia climate. Where my childhood was pleasantly dull in real life, it's precious in my dreams. I think of the long, lazy summer days I spent reading under the shade of my favorite tree in our backyard hammock. I would drink strong, sweet tea and munch on fresh strawberries from Mrs. Landry's garden next door. When I wasn't snacking or reading, I was hunting bugs, playing in the mud, or helping Mom plant flowers. I loved being outdoors.

When I wasn't outside, I was Dad's constant shadow. I cleaned while he cooked and half paid attention while he taught me his secret recipes. When he played handyman around the house, I was his assistant, in charge of handing him all the tools he needed. When my nose wasn't stuck in a book, he was reading bedtime stories to me. He was my best friend. Now he's gone and I'm far from the home I knew and loved. Somewhere between dreaming and waking, I think of the last time I saw Dad alive. He'd given me that crushing look of disappointment I'd seen in Doc's eyes.

"What's wrong?" I asked.

He had folded up my latest report card and shook his head.

"Savvy you're much better than a C average," he'd told me.

I didn't think so and I wasn't interested in trying harder. School was boring. School was a waste of time. It's not like I wanted to go to college. College was for doctors and scientists. I didn't know what I wanted to do with my life, but I knew it wouldn't be something that required more school. I hated school.

I remember him ruffling my hair.

"You just have to conquer your perspective. Then you can conquer this," he said, tossing my report card in the trash can, "I won't tell your mom, this time, but you've got to promise me you'll find the wonder in you that I see."

"School isn't for everyone," I argued stubbornly, "And grades only matter if you're going to college. I'm not going."

Dad didn't say anything else, but his eyes twinkled, and he smiled at me. I knew he was talking about much more than school. He knew I was aware of it, too.

"I promise," I'd finally said, though back then, I only said it to get him off my back.

With Dad gone, I'm barely surviving. I may not be as average as I thought, but I'm far from being a wonder. If anything, I'm underwhelming. Here in New York, I've learned that some nightmares are real. Being anything but average is terrifying. I've almost been killed because of something I didn't ask for and something I can't control. What's even scarier is the fact that I have to rely on strangers.

They promised to help keep me safe and to teach me to control my abilities. While I've learned a lot from them, I don't know if I can put my life in their hands. I don't know if I want to make their battles my own. There's still so much I don't know about them. I appreciate Doc for explaining why I took a beating for the team, but it's only left me with more questions and reservations.

I can't get K.O. out of my mind. Knowing his real name and hearing about his past gives me an entirely different perspective of him. It's like I'm dealing with two different people. There's the K.O. I know who's stoic, lethal, and withdrawn, the one who answers to no one. Then there's Oliver. Doc painted Oliver as someone heroic, caring, and self-sacrificing. He puts the lives of others before his pride and even his family. I try to put myself in his shoes. Could I have done the same thing? Could I have left my family if it meant saving the lives of others? I don't have any siblings, but I imagine, if I did, we might be close. K.O. and Max were close. He loved his brother. Had he exhausted all his options before leaving Max behind?

I don't ask Doc these questions. K.O. is the only one who can answer them, though it's hard enough getting him to talk in complete sentences. The guy just isn't very social.

"He's really from Kansas?"

Even though the thoughts in my head are much more serious, some of the smaller details of K.O.'s life still bug me enough to make me ask uncensored questions aloud between medications. Doc laughs at me but answers honestly.

"His family is originally from South Korea, but yes. Kansas was his childhood home."

"Oliver's his real name? He doesn't look much like an Oliver."

"What does he look like, Savannah?"

I giggle, "K.O."

"Hence the nickname."

"Who gave him that name?"

"One of his friends who–"

"Passed away?" I finish.

Doc pauses. "Yes."

"Was it a girl?" I ask.

"I think so," he says carefully.

"Did he like her?"

He doesn't answer.

"Why doesn't he like me?" I ask.

"Do you like him?"

I don't answer. Instead, I ask another question. "If he's so heroic, why's he so scary?"

"Ignorance breeds fear, Savannah."

"You calling me ignorant?"

"When it comes to K.O., yes."

Doc is brutally honest. I like that about him.

"Maybe you should get to know K.O. for yourself," Doc suggests.

I shake my head and fight a wave of dizziness. These pain killers really messing with my head.

"Not going to happen. We're like fire and gunpowder or a gun with bullets. Gas with matches. We shouldn't be anywhere near each other. Too dangerous. Explosive."

Every time we're alone in the same room and, even when we're not, we always end up fighting. I never thought I was much of a fighter. I still don't. Up against K.O. I'll probably always lose, but it's like he brings the fight out of me. I always thought I was a relaxed person, complacent even.

"Interesting comparisons we can analyze when you're a little more aware of what you're saying," Doc murmurs.

He pats my hand and starts to leave the room.

"Doc, was K.O. the one who brought me here after the fight?"

"Yes. Now get some rest. Tomorrow you're back to your old routine."

I give my eyes and voice a break, not that it helps much. I'm restless. My body is only half as sore as it was. I manage to push myself to sit up in bed. I notice a tray of cold cuts, a bottled water, and written instructions from Doc telling me I smell, and I need to shower. Apparently Rox dropped off more new clothes. I take the folded items out of their bag and hold them in front of me. It's a pair of black skinny jeans, a long burgundy colored tee and five pounds of accessories from purses, necklaces, bracelets, and rings. Beside the bed are my black, combat boots. My leather jacket is draped across the boots.

The shower isn't too hard to find. It's around the corner from my room though it's one of those gym group showers that self-conscious people like me avoid. Thankfully, the shower locks from the inside. I shower quickly under cold water to shock myself into alertness and then in steaming water to ease my aching joints. I'm still all scratched and bruised up but I'm healing. I'm alive. I dress quickly, carrying my boots and leaving all the accessories. I'm feeling the best I've felt in days until I see who's waiting for me back in my room.

"K.O."

I have the urge to flee the room and hide in the bathroom until he leaves, but thanks to my own big mouth that won't be possible. He turns around slowly as if he heard me coming long before I blurted his name. His hair is pulled back today.

Without his hair in his face, I'm drawn to the delicate upward curve of his dark eyes and the sharp strong tilt of his nose. His jaw seems extra stubborn which, in contrast, makes his lips look extra soft.

His lips part as he assesses me from the top of my wild hair to the bottom of my bare chicken feet. I'm painfully aware that I'm gangly and that there are a confetti of bruises and scrapes across my arms and my face. I wish he would stop staring at me, but then, I'm staring at him, too.

"What are you doing here?"

His finally looks away from me. "Let's go."

He doesn't move automatically. It's like he expects me to argue. I want to fight him. I really do. He hasn't answered my question. Instead, I throw on my boots, bite down on my tongue and take the initial step out the door. For once K.O. follows instead of rushing ahead of me. It's an uncomfortable feeling, especially with how quiet he is. I stop until we're walking side by side. It's even weirder. I can feel heat radiating from him. I inhale. He smells like leather and peppermint.

He gives me a long sideway look.

Really, Savannah? You're sniffing him now?

We emerge from Doc's makeshift clinic and into colorful Chinatown. The streets are crowded with vendors and seasoned tourist haggling for the best deals. First-time tourists walk around like they're at one of the Seven Wonders of the World. I take in a deep breath, enjoying the feel of fresh-ish air. It feels good to be outside.

"Thank you."

The words slip out before I can think about it.

"For saving me." I clarify.

Though the streets are crowded and chaotic, my words seem to echo.

"Repeatedly," I add.

"What?" K.O. stops walking so I stop too and turn to face him.

I'm not about to repeat myself. I roll my eyes and open my mouth to tell him so, but he does something unexpected that almost makes my eyes get stuck mid-roll.

"No threats? No fighting? N-no accusations?" he stutters. His face gets red. His voice isn't the quiet, ominous whisper of doom I'm used to hearing. It's colored with emotion. His nostrils flare and his eyes widen. This wasn't the reaction I was expecting.

"I just said thank you. Why are you yelling?"

My voice comes out like a frog croaking.

"You. *Hate*. Me."

He emphasizes each word and with each syllable invades a little more of my personal space. He's so close I can see the tiny beauty mark above the crest of his upper lip and the slight swell of his lower lip that looks like it's healing from the impact of someone's fist. There's a slight yellowed discoloration of his jaw and around his right eye.

"I thought *you* hated *me*," I admit.

He laughs but there's no humor. "I know you blame me for getting you into this mess, but I've gone out of my way to make you feel comfortable. I treat you just like I do anyone else. Training and saving you, protecting you, fighting for you, but it's still not enough."

"All you do is glare at me. You hardly ever talk. I didn't think you wanted me around," I say, my eyes stinging with unwanted tears.

"Every time I do talk, you get upset. Just being in the same room with me gets you riled up. So, I shut my mouth and disappear. For you."

"I don't want you to disappear," I say.

He sighs. "Then what do you want? Because I'm sick of trying to figure you out."

"Figure *me* out?" I'm the open book. He's the complicated one.

This is ridiculous. We're arguing in the middle of Chinatown's streets like we're the only two people in the world and there's not a group of crazy hunters trying to kill us or a rival gang that wants to fight us. I don't want to fight him, not anymore, but I don't want to face him either. I take a step back and then another until I'm running through the crowds.

"Savannah, wait!"

He's yelling, and by the sound of his voice, he's close behind me. I try to pick up speed, but he catches me, whirling me around to face him. His fingers dig into the flesh of my healing arm and I flinch. He releases me immediately and the red rage drains from his face. Tears brim at the corners of my eyes, hot and stinging as pain awakens from my healing injuries.

"When I saw you on the Empire State Building that day, it changed my life and not for the better. I had nightmares for weeks, picturing you and that boy splattered on the sidewalks. I couldn't get you out of my head. It frightened me. Everyone around me thought that I was crazy. I had no one to turn to or talk to."

Even though I'm trying to be reasonable, we're fighting one another with our eyes. I look at his eyes and he looks down. He sneaks a flicker of a gaze and it's gone before I can lock into it. I push past the resistance and take an uncomfortable step forward.

"My opinion of you might not be fair, but you've got to admit that wasn't the best first impression. You threw a guy off the Empire State Building."

Our eyes meet and our gazes lock.

"I didn't see you," he admits.

The blond boy saw me. I remember him winking at me when they nearly trampled over me, before K.O. threw him over the side of the building. I try not to think about it.

"Did you kill him?" I squeak, not expecting him to answer.

"No."

I can't tell if he's disappointed that I asked or disappointed that he didn't kill the blond.

"Look, I'm sorry. Point is, it's not my place to assume. I didn't know anything about you, but Doc told me–"

"What did he tell you?" his voice takes on that low, dangerous tone again. The hairs on the edge of my nape bristle.

"He told me about Kansas. He told me what happened with you and your brother Max. I–"

"So now you're feeling sorry for me? You think you know me?"

"I didn't say that," I fire back.

He rakes a hand through his hair. "I can't keep saving you. I told you that. So, if you're counting on me to show up every time you get into trouble, you'll be disappointed. I told you to run the other night, but you didn't listen."

"I didn't want to leave you by yourself," I say.

"And what could you have possibly done to help *me*?"

He's right. I'm a liability They were doing fine until I came along. I've been blaming him for turning my life upside down. I never stopped to think of the crazy impact I've had on K.O. and the others.

"You're right. There's absolutely nothing I can do to help, except leave."

I turn my back on him, fully intending to walk home or anywhere as long as I'm away from him, but K.O. grabs my wrist. Before I know it, he's throwing me over his shoulder, running in that world-whirring kind of way. I beat at his back and call him names I normally wouldn't dare let pass my mouth until he stops and tosses me carelessly off his shoulder like I'm a bag of groceries, right in front of our cozy little hideout. I land on my feet, though not prettily.

I try to walk past him. "I'm not staying where I'm not wanted."

He blocks me. "Go inside."

I attempt to side-step him. "Get out of my way."

He's back in my face again. Only this time his face isn't flushed or flustered. He's not stuttering or yelling. His eyes lock into mine, immobilizing me. "You need rest. You need more training."

"I need you, but you obviously don't need me," I tell him.

His jaw tightens, but he doesn't deny it.

I nod. "When training is over, I'm gone. Then you won't have to be bothered with me. You can go back to sulking or whatever you do best."

I don't want him to see the tears welling up in my eyes. I can't control them, and I can't stop them from running down my hot cheeks. I race into the house. The last thing I want is for him to have the satisfaction of seeing me cry. I tell myself these are tears of rage, but as I'm met with three sets of eyes staring at me, I can't be so sure. K.O. doesn't follow me inside. I take a deep breath to gain my composure. It comes out shaky and hitched until I completely fall apart. It's the ugly type of breakdown with the runny nose and the slobbering twisted lip. It's not your Hollywood cry.

Rox surprises me. Her eyes soften when she meets my gaze, and she wraps her arms around me. Though we couldn't be more different in personality and appearance, in that moment I feel that she's the closest thing I'll ever have to a sister.

"What happened?" Rox asks.

"It must've been pretty bad," Tristan grumbles.

Geezer doesn't respond but walks out of the room, grim-faced without so much as looking at me. He doesn't want to choose sides. He and K.O. are close or as close as K.O. will allow anyone to be. Tristan follows Geezer out the door until it's just me and Rox.

"Why's K.O. like that? Why does he have to be so frustrating?" I ask her.

Rox isn't usually in such an understanding mood. She pulls away from me and shrugs her shoulders.

"Why are any of us the way we are? We just are," she says. Her eyes narrow and the sympathetic look fades. "Maybe you're the frustrating one."

I start to argue with her, but she talks over me. "You had us worried back at the club. We thought we lost you. I've never seen K.O. so scared before. So, maybe he's like 'that' because he cares about you. We all do."

Leftover tears from my earlier meltdown roll down my cheeks. I swat at them. "You don't need me, though. K.O. made that pretty clear."

She shrugs. "You *are* a handful."

I turn from her, but she shoves at my shoulder until I look at her, "But, we *do* like you and want you around."

I wipe my eyes. "Not K.O."

Rox groans. "Especially K.O. Have you ever thought that maybe the real reason you two can't get along is because you actually really like each other?"

"I'm not listening to this right now. There's no way," I say, and throwing up my hands, I race up the stairs. I don't have a door to slam, so I bury my face in my pillows and let out a muffled scream.

"No. No way," I mutter, curling into a fetal position. I'm exhausted, but Rox's words nag me.

I can admit that I don't hate K.O. and that I don't *not* like him. On some levels I might even I admire him. But like him? I can't admit that. The thought of K.O. liking me is even more ridiculous. It's laughable. I'm a pest to K.O., a huge inconvenience. There's no way. We're just not compatible. End of story.

Only it's not the end of it. My stubborn mind continues to mull over Rox's words. My heart drums through my ears. My pulse is off the charts, making me feel flushed and furious. I think about the things he said to me before I completely set him off. He avoided me because he thought it was what I wanted. But every time I needed someone, every time that really mattered, he was there, even though he thought I hated him.

"You know, it's rude to run off when someone's talking to you," Rox says, striding into my room uninvited.

Rox stomps her heel so hard into the floors it makes a thunderous BOOM and our hideout shakes. She pulls her heel out of the hole the impact creates and stalks over to me like nothing happened.

"I've tried to be patient with you since you're new and all, but I'm really getting tired of your water works and all your meltdowns. I don't hang out with crybabies."

So much for the sisterly bond. Rox gets into my personal space, waving her lethal finger in my face. I scoot back in bed, closer to the headboard.

"I didn't ask you to hang out with me," I mutter.

"No, you just sulk around like a little whiner with bad hair," she snaps. "You're such a disappointment."

"You're really gonna talk about my hair? Get out!" I yell before I can think about it.

I have a deadly finger inches away from my face. I don't think she's one for murdering, but I've seen what she's capable of. I brace myself, but I don't back down.

"That's more like it," Rox says, "Now, get up. It's time to shape up."

CHAPTER 23

The next few days are all about beauty sleep.

"When you're injured or overworked, you'll need as much rest as you can get. Sleep is healing. Literally. The more you sleep, the faster you heal," Rox tells me, and she's right. Injuries that should take weeks to completely heal disappear in record time. In less than a week, all my bruises and scars have faded. It's not automatic, but it's still nothing short of miraculous.

When I'm all healed up, the real work begins. Rox and Tristan have me up before the sun rises. We go out for morning runs all over the city, and Tristan teaches me to dodge traffic without slowing down. In a place like New York, avoiding traffic while running at an insane speed is near impossible, no matter how effortless he makes it seem. I almost get hit by a taxi seven times our first day. More times than that I feel like a bowling ball plummeting into harried crowds of people on their way to work. The bruises from the club fight haven't been gone long but my skin is already plagued with a new rash of injuries.

Rox has no mercy. After three hours of daily runs, we stop long enough for her to check me for breaks and sprains. Then we're scaling skyscrapers, running up the sides of the slick, glass walls. Up. Over. Down. Repeat. She alternates our building runs with sparring. Heights still get to me, but slowly I'm getting better at maneuvering.

We only take breaks long enough to refuel. It's all vegetables and good carbs, lean meats, and low fat. Soda and sweets are restricted while we're training. I stock up on colorful, organic foods like my life depends on it. Sometimes I eat so fast and so much I vomit in the middle of our trainings. Rox looks at my eating habits as training too.

"You have to learn balance and discipline in everything you do. Pigging out can cost you your life, but not eating enough can get you killed, too," she tells me.

By day five of our training, I can't get out of bed by myself. I feel like refried roadkill. My body hurts so bad I can't decide if it hurts worse to move or be still.

"We don't have a lot of time, Scarlett. If you want to survive, you have to push yourself," Rox says.

Geezer's ultimatum still stands. They're going to train me to survive on my own. After that, they're leaving the state. I can either leave with them or choose to stay behind with my family. I'm grateful for the training, no matter how brutal it seems. The pain of training takes my mind off everything else. I don't have to think about what I'm going to do when Geezer and the gang are ready to leave New York.

I crawl out of bed until I can pull myself up, ignoring the pain and preparing for another day of training. I don't have to think about how I'm going to deal with the fallout surrounding my abrupt departure from Willow Manor or the fact that the cops and the rest of the city are looking for me. I don't even have to think about Santos hunting me. Geezer and the others are going to take care of that.

Unfortunately, my thoughts of K.O. are persistent, a constant ache that can't be soothed by rest of workouts. It's been nearly a week since I've last seen him. After our argument he took off and hasn't been back. If he thought I hated him before, there's no doubt in his mind, now I don't like how we left things. What if he doesn't come back? I hate how much the idea of never seeing him again scares me.

I shake myself out of my weary thoughts, just in time to dodge a fast and forceful punch from Rox. She's been teaching me to block and evade attacks. It's been a hard lesson that's left my nerves a little frayed around the edges, but it's worth it. My muscles ache and my clothes are soaked in sweat. My body is exhausted, but I feel fresh, vibrant, and alive.

I used to feel this way when I ran track in gym class back in Georgia, but this is even better than a runner's high. I feel like I can do anything, at least I do until Rox's fist almost catches me in my left eye. Her reddened knuckles are barely a hair away from my face. I take a step backwards and trip over my feet, catching myself just in time to dodge another punch.

"How do you feel?" she asks.

"Alive," I say, though what I really mean is that I'm happy to be alive. If Rox had punched me, I'd probably be dead right now. She tosses her golden hair over her shoulder and the wild braid swings like a whip. She could probably use her hair as a weapon if she wanted.

"Good. Let's take a break."

By break I think she means our usual injury check and lunch. Instead, she leads me back to our hideout. We race through the streets, scaling building tops. I almost beat her to our destination, but I get slowed down by another taxi.

Thankfully my training with Rox pays off. I effortlessly leap into the air, flip over the vehicle, and land on my feet on the sidewalk. The driver skids after the fact and stops, not even knowing what almost hit hm. At the speed I was going, both the taxi driver and I would have both been wrecked. We make it to the hideout in record time, but I'm so tired I feel like I could kiss the floor with relief.

"Shower and get dressed," Rox commands.

I'm a little disappointed that I can't shower and go to bed, but I don't argue. I'm too busy wondering what the next test or challenge will be. I start for the stairs but Rox grabs me firmly by the arm.

"I know being an Errant isn't easy. We live short, fast lives, so you don't have time to waste. Stay out of that bed and live your life while you can."

She releases my arm and gives me a curt nod. I gape at her. "Who are you and when did you become a motivational speaker?"

Though I'm teasing, her words resonate. She's right. I can't sleep away my problems, even if I have reason to be exhausted. I've got to start living. The scary part is learning how to do just that. I think of Dr. Kensington. He would tell me something similar. Get out of bed, take one moment at a time, and breathe.

"Hey, could you teach me to french braid my hair?" I ask Rox before she disappears down the stairs.

Her eyes widen, but she nods. "You know your hair's amazing, right?"

"I know," I tell her.

After Rox helps me with my hair, I shower and dress quickly in a thin, loose fitting black shirt that hangs off one shoulder, a red and black plaid skirt, and a pair of black leggings with my black, tie-up boots.

Rox has taught me that accessories are beneficial in a fight, but they can also be used as a weapon against me if I'm not careful. I put on a pair of thick, black wrist cuffs with silver spikes and a long silver chain around my neck, hiding it under my shirt. I consider changing my shoes to a pair of heeled boots. Heels can be used to stab someone's feet but walking and running are a better use for these feet. There's no way I'd be able to move in heels without hurting myself, especially not at high speeds.

I grab my leather jacket as afterthought and race down the stairs, nearly tripping over a lazily tied boot string. I know Rox is probably timing me or testing me in some way but when I get downstairs, she's relaxed, leaning against the kitchen wall laughing with Tristan. When they see me Rox straightens and Tristan offers me a warm smile.

"Still conscious after that workout?"

"Tougher than I look, I guess."

Rox rolls her eyes, "You've earned some downtime."

She wants to take me out for some music and dancing. Her favorite band is playing at some local spot. I guess she didn't get the hint from our first night out that I'm not much of a dancer.

"Geezer's got some errands to run so he won't be able to join us tonight," Rox announces.

I nod but my eyes unintentionally slide back towards the stairs.

"Don't worry. K.O. won't be joining us either. He usually disappears for a while when he goes off the deep end," Tristan informs me.

I wonder if he's prone to going off the deep end once a month. I chuckle to myself, but the laughter dies quickly as I find myself wondering more about him. Where does he disappear to? What does he do when he's not with the others? My mind migrates to the first time I saw him, and I shudder.

"Stop thinking about him," Rox snaps.

"I'm not," I snap back, even though I am.

Tristan winces at Rox and she nods. They don't say a word to one another, but I know they're talking about me.

"Keep up," Rox orders, and then they both take off.

No longer afraid of my road-running ability, I follow them without hesitation. I don't have to know where we're going to get there. I tunnel my vision enough to keep Rox in sight, but my eyes scan through my peripheral to ensure I don't hit any oncoming vehicles or pedestrians.

Rox's choice of destination is a place called Shax, an underground club located right under the feet of Manhattan's elite. Where the streets above are polished with expensive retail and luxurious hotels, Shax is dark and gritty. The brick walls are black and grimy. The floors are made of dirt and the smells… well, by the smell of things, I'm sure Shax is a place where anything goes.

I can't believe a girl that spends so much time fussing over fashion and appearances would find this place sanitary enough to step her delicate heels into. Then again, Rox may be a beautiful face with a petite form, but where she's concerned, appearances are deceiving. There's more edge to her than just her punch.

Rox's eyes brighten as we descend the uneven stairs and emerge into the dark abyss of moving shadows and pulsating music.

"They're playing now! I don't wanna miss this," Rox says, pressing into the crowds.

I watch as Tristan joins her. The two dance with confidence and passion, so in sync with the beat of the music. I shrink to the backdrop, my eyes drifting from my friends to watch strangers. Most people are on the dance floor. There are no shy people there. I feel like I'm the only wallflower. Everyone else is fully engaged in something or someone.

"I wish I'd bought a book with me," I grumble. It's been a while since I've cracked a fresh read open, maybe because my life's been crazier than fiction for once.

At one of the corner tables to my left, a group of people are tattooing each other's skin underneath dim, yellow lights. There's a hookah off to my right, crowded with vapor and subdued bodies, right next to a vibrant, nearly violent game of cards with people yelling and shoving. I can't make out their conversation over the music.

Everywhere there's a dark, shadowy corner, couples are making out like they need to share oxygen to live. I get the feeling that the music playing isn't the only thing that charges the atmosphere of this place. Anyone could be performing. Any kind of music could be playing. What really makes Shax appealing is the location, a shrouded oasis where anything is possible. If a person wanted to lead a double life or just get away from everyday doldrums, Shax is the place to go – a mini slice of rebellious fun.

Musicians can play without worry because no matter how crappy they sound; the dance floor will never be empty. People are too drunk, too high, too numb, or too full of life to care about opinions. In a large room full of people from all walks of life, I still feel isolated somehow. I'm not confident enough to be on the dance floor with or without a dance partner, and Rox has drilled me so much about eating healthy that I've lost my nerve for drinking anything outside of water and Gatorade.

I find one of the few tables that haven't been populated with some extreme or illegal activity and collapse into a chair that doesn't have any random stains or liquid on it. I guess this is exciting to some people, to be in a place that feels forbidden and free, but I'm bored and claustrophobic. The room is packed, and the dank smells are getting to me. The bass shakes through the room making me feel like my ears are bleeding.

"You look like you could use a friend," a voice whispers in my ear, "and a drink."

Flinching, I whip my gaze around, finding myself staring at a face I'd rather forget. Emery offers me a smile that doesn't quite translate to his deadpan eyes. The tangy bite of alcohol on his breath makes my nostrils sting. He's so close to me, too close. I stand up and ball my fists, scanning the room in search of the rest of his crew. I spot Rox and Tristan working their way quickly through the crowd, heading in my direction.

"Relax, girl," he says, "I didn't come to fight you. Neither one of us is going to find what we're looking for tonight."

"What's that?" I ask, instinctively curious.

His black eyes beat into my gaze.

"Answers," he says, slamming a drink on the table in front of me.

Mystery liquid splashes out of the glass and onto the table, while the bottom of the glass cracks in a webbed pattern, but it doesn't break.

"You tell your boy K.O. something for me. Until we find Max, we'll be looking for him."

Emery doesn't give me enough time to respond. He's gone before Rox and Tristan can reach us.

"What did he want?" Tristan asks me over the music.

"You said K.O. usually takes off for a few days. How many days exactly?" I ask, because now I'm worried.

"K.O.'s the best of us. He's fine," Tristan says, but he doesn't sound so sure.

Max's crew obviously doesn't know where he is if they're asking me to give messages to him. Why would they come to me? Maybe seeing Emery at Shax is just a bad coincidence. All this week I've been training I've felt so invincible, so empowered. Now? My mind migrates to last week when all the bruises, scrapes, and wounds were fresh and painful, when I was helpless.

Feelings like this should inspire trembling and gratitude towards Rox and Tristan for attempting to come to my rescue. Instead, I'm angry again. If Emery wanted to hurt me, he could have. They wouldn't be fast enough to stop someone who can move just as fast as them. As much as I've improved in my skills, I feel like I'll always be a step behind. I won't ever really belong.

I'm hit with a wave of homesickness. I'm not homesick for Georgia or even for Dad. I don't miss our New York apartment.

I just want to see Mom. I don't care if she argues with me, punishes me, or even looks right through me and ignores me completely. I miss her. I need her. I need her strength. I remember being afraid that she might try to hurt herself when Dad first died. She cried so hard and so long, nearly starved herself for those first few days, and went to bed without sleeping. She'd been in a waking coma. But by the time we closed his casket, she put on a brave face and her big girl shoes.

Mom is the face of resilience, strength much different than Dad's sturdy and reliable resolve. She runs hot where he was warm. She's passionate where he was compassionate and sometimes volatile where he was calm. She can lose her temper quickly, pout when things don't go her way, but when the going gets tough, so does she. In a world of danger and instability, I need her grit. I need her no-nonsense, tough love.

I know I can't see Mom. Things are too wild, too crazy. The very reasons I should stay away from her are the reasons I need her the most. I know she wouldn't believe me if I told her what was really going on, but I don't need her to believe me. I just need her.

"I need some air," I tell Rox and Tristan.

They respect my demands, probably too aware of the negative shift in my mood. I don't try to hide my frustration. Instead, I project it and surprisingly the overcrowded wave of dancers, smokers, and couples part, giving me space to exit the dark atmosphere. Without hesitation, I race up the stairs, letting go of all restraint and submitting to the wild pleasure of running. I run so fast I feel like my feet don't even touch the ground. For all I know, maybe they don't. I don't know where I'm going, and I don't care. I just need this freedom, this feeling of power and some element of control in something. I can do the impossible. I can do whatever I put my mind to. I am invincible.

I tell myself this lie, and I believe it until my bones begin to ache and my stomach twists with hunger. Skidding to a stop, I almost stumble headfirst into a closed vendor's shop. I lean against the contraption and take in a deep breath before nearly collapsing. Running like this is addictive. But the high it gives me is only a temporary solution to alleviating my insecurities, and now I'm hungry.

Ironically, I find myself at the pizza shop where I first encountered Mohawk and Tattoo. Without a wallet or any loose cash or credit cards, I'll have to resort to what I saw them do that day. My eyes inspect strangers' plates but then I see something even better. A full box of pizza sits at the front counter of the diner, calling my name while its true owner, a mother of two bratty pre-teens, fusses and snaps at her children. I take a deep breath and steady myself. In such a small space, I'll have to time it just right.

Inhaling then exhaling, I prepare to snatch the pizza and snap back out the door and into the streets, but I falter. My ears catch the sound of her voice before my eyes confirm it. A small television sits at the front counter. Mom's voice echoes from its speakers. Patrons pause, looking at the screen as the breaking news plays. A small hush minimizes the sound in the immediate vicinity of the television as Mom makes her plea.

"My name is Teresa Poindexter, and this is my daughter, Savannah Scarlett."

One of my school pictures flashes across the screen. It's my freshman portrait, the best one I've taken outside of the rare natural moments my parents managed to capture on film when I wasn't looking. My wild hair is pulled out of my face with a red headband. Though the portrait is only a headshot, I recognize the red and orange, geometric patterned sundress I'm wearing by the spaghetti straps. My smile is more of a cringing lip-bite and my eyes are watery like I'm getting ready to cry. I was a blinker and the camera flash had gotten the better of me. The photographer had to take my picture three times just to get the mediocre shot.

"Please help me find my daughter," Mom says. Her voice shakes and there are tears in her eyes, but she still radiates that resilience I envy so much. Her black hair is relaxed and curls softly at her shoulders. Her deep brown skin is free of blemish and her eyes, though tired, hold deep-rooted strength. She dares a small smile.

"Savannah, baby, I love you very much. If you can hear me, come home," she says, staring directly into the camera.

Her voice is firm, but there's love in her tone. I almost laugh, but the longing chokes out the humor and a small sob escapes my mouth. I can count on one hand how many times she's called me baby, and almost as rare, how many times she's told me she loves me. I've always believed she loved me but hearing it is another kind of confirmation that's hard to ignore. Just as the news station transitions to another story, my eyes recognize a familiar face in the background of Mom's public address. Too polished for a police uniform, Santos's face leaps out at me. First, he poses as a therapist. Now he's a cop. Not only has he infiltrated the police force but he's with my mom. He could –

"No. You're seeing things. He wouldn't dare," I tell myself.

I look away from the television as the reporter recounts the facts surrounding my disappearance. Tears sting my eyes and the burning hunger in my gut transforms into a heavy weight of guilt. Mom wants me to come home. I want to go home more than anything, but I can't.

Instead of pizza, I set my sights on the fussing mom's unattended phone. I know I shouldn't, but I need to do something. I need to warn her about Santos. If nothing else, I should at least let her know I'm okay. I have to hear her voice. I dial Mom's cell number. It rings. Once. Twice. On the third ring, there's some static, some rustling and then she answers.

"H-hello?"

I cover my mouth to keep from crying out loud.

"Savannah, baby is it you?"

My lips quiver. I want to answer her so bad but if I do I'm scared the tears will explode. What if I make things worse? What if she talks me into coming home? They'll easily be able to track my phone call but for all she knows this is just a random butt dial from a stranger. That's all I can afford for her to think. The less she knows the better. I hang up the phone, slide it back down the counter before busting out of the pizza shop and back into the streets, unseen and unheard.

CHAPTER 24

I'm not a good liar and I'm a terrible actor. Everyone knows I'm not in the best of moods. They just have the reason all wrong. This has nothing to do with K.O. or the incident with Emery. Though I'm worried about K.O., I have confidence he'll be okay. If he can survive an angry mob of hunters, run through trains like a ghost, scale rooftops in one super leap, and save girls like me on a regular basis, he's capable of just about anything.

The others try to cheer me up, but my problems can't be solved with avoidance. I push Rox to train me more, to push me until I'm almost broken from the pressure and intensity. I want to be stronger. I want to be my best no matter how far behind that is from everyone else's capabilities. Rox refuses. She claims my head's not in it and that too much of a good thing is just as bad as not enough.

Another week passes and once again, I end up stuck on the sidelines, a wallflower at another club watching the rest of the world dance around me. Rox and the others think partying the night away will bring us closer together. They don't realize I'm feeling even more isolated. Give me some good music and a good book and let me shut myself up in my room. Let me watch a movie curled up on the couch with some buttered popcorn drizzled with melted chocolate and I'll show you a real smile. Right now, I'm feeling claustrophobic and paranoid.

What if I run into Emery again? What if, despite my makeover, someone recognizes me from the news and calls the cops, cops that Santos may have infiltrated?

Am I strong enough to hold my own right now? What if K.O. comes back? I don't know how to deal with him, but I'm worried about him too.

I'm tempted to borrow another stranger's phone to call Mom again. I just want to hear her voice. I resist the urge and try my best to fake being happy.

"You sure you don't want to dance?" Geezer asks me for the twentieth time. He does some goofy shuffle I'm sure was popular in the seventies. Even if I was in a dancing mood, I'd still do him a favor and refuse to dance with him. I'm saving his feet from some serious pain.

"You don't have to be a loner with us," he tells me, getting that serious, old man look in his eyes.

I don't know how to be anything else or even if there's anything wrong with the way I am. I'm quiet. I'm aloof. Now I'm quiet, aloof, and New York's most wanted teen.

"Live a little, Savannah," Geezer says lightly, though his eyes say something different.

I look away.

"Have you been thinking about our proposition?" he asks, and I automatically know what he's referring to. It's pretty much all I've been thinking about since getting beat up by Max's gang. Do I run with them or cut them loose and cling to an illusion of normalcy?

"Yeah," I admit.

"I hope your relationship with K.O. doesn't affect your decision," he says.

As if I needed reminding. I can't help thinking I scared him away, that he won't come back until I'm gone.

Geezer raises his hands and backs up a few steps. "Don't look at me that way. We'll revisit this later. Just try to relax tonight?"

When I nod, Geezer melts into the crowd, reappearing next to a dazzling Rox. The two dance playfully, even making faces at one another. I've never seen her look so silly or so happy. Tristan, obviously not part of the fun, sits next to me. For a long moment we don't speak, even after losing interest in watching the others on the dance floor. He drinks shots and I watch, counting them as he slides the empty glasses across the counter. He gets up and stumbles around every so often to collect drinks from unsuspecting people. I guess tonight I'm not the only grumpy one. He belches loudly and collapses in the chair beside me, clumsily nursing a handful of drinks. I intercept shot glasses, taking them out of his hands and set them on the counter, out of his reach.

"What's wrong with you?" I finally ask him.

"I needed those drinks," Tristan grumbles.

"I think you need to sober up."

Rox trained me well. Being drunk won't help Tristan get around tonight and God help us if we run into trouble. He'll be a sitting duck or a dead one.

Tristan frowns. "Thought you'd be more fun."

"You're not the only one," I mutter.

Tristan tries to reach across the counter for a drink, but I slap his hand and pull him up from his seat. He's a tall, sturdy guy so I have to pull on my ability to force him to stand. Strength doesn't come as easily as running, but I manage.

Draping Tristan's arm around my shoulder I drag him out of the club for some fresh air. By the time we're outdoors, I'm out of breath and Tristan looks like he's about two seconds from passing out. I pat his face to keep him conscious.

"You pass out and I'm not carrying you," I warn.

"Rox would make you and call it part of your training."

He laughs but I don't see the humor in it. He's right She'd probably make me do laps around the city with him strapped to my back. I'm surprised she hasn't tried that while he's sober. I shudder.

"Cold?" he asks, and I'm amazed. As drunk as he is, he's still concerned about me. They all are. I might not have their history or their experience, but even with all their own drama, they still seem to care about me. Well, most of them do. No one's heard from K.O., so it doesn't look like I'll be delivering Emery's message any time soon.

Tristan looks ready to offer me his disheveled jacket, even though I'm already wearing my leather, but he wobbles on his feet and nearly falls forward. I make a grab for him and we both topple toward the sidewalk. I balance myself midway and recover into a sitting position on the pavement, pulling Tristan with me. He can't fall if he's already sitting down.

Sitting in silence, shoulder to shoulder, it isn't long before Tristan takes me by surprise again. He sniffles and clears his throat. When I turn to look at him, I realize he's crying. He's the kind of dream guy I've heard so many girls say they want. He's strong, loyal, and not afraid to show emotion. He's living proof that the perfect guy does exist. Rox is so lucky to have him, though if I'm honest with myself, all I can see him as is the annoying big brother I never had. He doesn't make my heart do cartwheels or my hands sweat from nerves. I'm comfortable with him.

I lean my head onto his shoulder for support. When Dad died, I learned that sometimes words are the worst thing a person can use to comfort someone else. Sometimes they just need someone to be there for them, not to speak encouragement or show tough love, but to simply be present with them in the moment. I'd needed that, though I didn't have anyone at the time to lean on. Mom had already moved on with military fortitude. I had no friends, no other family, and the only one who really got me was gone. It's not like that anymore.

My eyes water but I force the tears away. I owe Tristan a moment of strength. He and the others have done so much for me. For all their faults, I owe them my life.

Tristan puts an arm around me and rests his chin on top of my head.

"I don't deserve her," he says. "I may look like I'm strong but she's stronger, you know?"

I stay quiet, giving him a chance to talk, to be heard.

"When the hunters came after us, we were all fighting for our lives. We ran. Rox was stubborn, tried to injure one of them. I-I almost didn't go back for her, but when I did–I only put her in more danger. I got hurt and she had to carry *me*."

I feel my mouth gape open despite wanting to keep a good poker face."That's how your leg was injured?"

He nods. I don't know what else to say, so I let him continue.

"I love her. I love Rox. And for a fraction of a second, I thought about leaving her to fend for herself. She never hesitated when I needed her. I'm ashamed I even needed rescuing."

He sighs, "I really needed those drinks."

I chuckle, not because of what he's said but because a random thought just crossed my mind that Tristan is the only one without a nickname. John is Geezer. Oliver is K.O. Roxanne is Rox. Tristan is Tristan. Maybe he doesn't need some codename because what you see with him is what you get. He's a light-hearted open book that's loyal to a fault. I respect him even more for his confession, for his honesty, and for his heart. He may have thought about leaving Rox, but he didn't. He was there when she needed him. That's what mattered. I want to tell him that, but Tristan's silence turns into easy rhythmic breathing and his posture relaxes into a heavy slouch. He's asleep.

"Tristan? Savannah?"

It's Rox. I'm on my feet before I can think about it and poor Tristan crashes into the sidewalk with a firm thud, still snoring.

"Rox, it isn't what you think it is," I say, mentally kicking myself for sounding so cliché.

She looks me straight in the eye. Her mouth tightens and her eyebrow twitches. "Just what do you think I thought it was?"

I shrug, not trying to offer any suggestions that might make the situation worse. "He's drunk."

"I know," she says, "I was just coming out to check on you two."

"Tristan is a great guy and he really loves you," I say. "I wish I had someone like that. Not exactly like that, I mean, but you know."

I eye Rox nervously. She rolls her eyes.

"You do," she says, giving me a pointed look. "And don't say I'm lucky. I'm not. If anyone should be jealous here, it's me. It's the rest of us."

She nods her head in the distance and I turn to see Geezer dragging a half-conscious Tristan back into the club. It would be something I found funny if I wasn't so distracted by what Rox says.

"We should be jealous of you. I know I am. You might not be on the best of terms right now but you've gotta know your mom loves you. At least you have a mom. At least you had a dad. I never knew my dad. He could be anyone, anywhere."

Rox frowns. "My mom was practically a kid herself when she had me. You know what I remember most about her, other than starving and living on the streets while she begged strangers for booze and heroin? My happiest memory is when she left me with my grandma and never came back.

"Not that Nana was any better. I thought she was crazy. She could never remember my name. She forgot I existed half the time. She forgot a lot of things. When she started having her fits I thought it was because she hated me, because I looked so much like my screw-up of a mom. I didn't know she was suffering from dementia until the social workers took me away. One of our neighbors tipped them off. It was foster care from there. I'm sure you've heard horror stories about that.

"So, you see, you're the lucky one. Yeah, the guys are my family. You have the guys, you have me, but you also have a mom who's worried sick about you. And yeah, your dad's dead but at least you knew he loved you. Scarlett, you've got the best of both worlds. You have a *choice*."

I don't respond to her. I can't. All I can do is stare at her hardened, angry face and admit she's right. I do have a choice. I do have the best of both worlds. That's what makes things so hard.

"The angst is so heavy here. I feel like I could cut it with a butter knife," Geezer interrupts. "We should go home and watch *The Breakfast Club.* Seems appropriate enough. Anyone up for a good ol' John Hughes' film?"

Rox and I look away from each other.

"We gotta steal a new TV first," Tristan slurs.

"I'll do the heavy lifting, boys. I'll get the TV if you rig us some internet and cable," Rox volunteers. She's acting like nothing happened, like she didn't just drop the bombshell of her life story.

"So is internet wiring one of our skills, too?" I ask.

"Not at all," Geezer says, "Living on the run you pick up a few things here and there."

We leave the club, smiling and joking and teasing one another but I can't forget everything Rox said. Geezer's ultimatum looms. Ordinary sounds so tempting. It also sounds very wrong.

Tonight, I've learned a lot about the new people in my life, about their histories and their faults. It's not the past that concerns me, though. The future is the problem. I have two homes. I have two choices, and no one is forcing me into anything. With eyes wide open I realize that whatever I decide to do, if I choose wrong, I'll only have myself to blame.

CHAPTER 25

I don't want to think about training, dangerous hunters, worried mothers, and I really don't want to think about K.O. I can't afford to worry about where he is, if he's safe, or in serious trouble. It's too much. I have to worry about myself. I'm too exhausted to get out of bed and commit to any more training. If the hunters found us right now, I'd be dead-meat and I wouldn't care.

Sleep comes easy, though it doesn't last. It isn't long before I feel cool air on my face. By the time I'm fully awake, I realize that I'm no longer in bed. My entire body is cold and wet. I'm drenched in water, literally sopping from head to foot. My jeans cling heavy to my thighs and my hair is loose and drips all over my already wet shirt.

"What the…"

It's been a while, but I recognize the signs of another blackout. Cold sweat breaks out across my face and I feel faint. I thought I had control over my abilities, at least enough control to not sleepwalk anymore. It's going to be hard to get home, since I don't even recognize where I am.

"You don't even know where home is. That's part of the problem," I grumble to myself.

I'm standing in front of an old brick house with a long, park sized lawn that's damp with early morning dew. In the middle of the lawn is a fountain encased in light stone with water gushing out in a light arching spray. It looks like a plantation home straight from the set of some period piece film. I half expect to see girls dressed in petticoats fluttering around with dainty fans. It doesn't look much like the New York I'm used to seeing, but it looks vaguely familiar.

Unconsciously, I've isolated myself from everyone I know. I'm far from Mom and from my friends, at least I think I am. I've never seen so much green in New York before. I miss greenery. I miss the clean fresh feeling of being in the company of trees, soil, and pollen-covered flowers. I'm reminded of the large trees and plush lawns in Georgia. I miss the south, which makes me wonder if I should make another choice no one's considered. Maybe I don't leave with Geezer and the others or stay with Mom. Maybe I should go my own way and start a new life completely.

"Savannah? Is that you?" I stop pacing when I hear the familiar voice.

"Angie?"

My cousin's blonde hair is almost like a sun-kissed nightlight in the dark. It's the first thing I see when I turn to stare at her. She stands in the lawn dressed in black ballerina slippers, black pants with white stripes and a white fitted t-shirt. It's weird seeing her in something so casual when she usually looks like she's stepped out of the house to attend some red-carpet event. Even her Brazilian blown hair is plain, tied in a flipped-up ponytail. Her eyes are wide in the dark. I know she's probably seen the reports on the news. My current appearance doesn't help either.

Rather than run from me like I thought she might, Angie runs to throw her arms around me. She leads me to the porch and inside her fancy house. So much has happened since I first came to New York. Maybe that's why I couldn't recognize my cousin's house in the dark. I've only been here once, when we first moved to New York, and it's not my fondest memory.

"Let's get you warmed up," Angie says, leading me from the grand foyer into the front sitting room. The foyer was as far as I'd been the day they'd taken me for a tour. I take in everything.

All the stiff furniture is carefully placed. The only sign of life in the house is the impressive fireplace where flames dance, warming up the otherwise stiff and chilly front room.

Angie runs up the rich, wooden spiral staircase to get a towel and a fresh pair of clothes for me to wear. She shows me to the main floor restroom past the glamourous open floor kitchen. It looks like a chef's kitchen. Dad would've loved it. The bathroom is fancy, too, with golden hooks and handles and fancy hanging white towels with M's embroidered in the plush fabric. A golden rimmed mirror hangs suspended over an elegantly sloped, spotless sink. I avoid looking directly at my reflection though it's hard to ignore the mangled hair and wild eyes. Stripping quickly, I peel off my wet clothing and pat myself dry with the towel. Then I put on Angie's clothes. Since I'm much taller than her, the pink jogging suit only covers three-fourths of my limbs, leaving my shins and lower arms exposed.

I don't want to come out of the bathroom, but I know I can't stay in here forever. I'm on borrowed time. Angie isn't the only one awake. The house comes alive with the muffled sound of heavy bass vibrating from one of the upstairs rooms and strained voices echoing from another room. I need to leave. I force myself out of the bathroom where Angie's waiting on me.

"My parents are fighting again," Angie explains.

I try to ignore the thumps and shattering glass from upstairs, responding only by thanking her for the clothes and temporary shelter.

"What are you doing here, anyway? What's going on with you?" she asks.

"You've seen the news?" I ask instead.

She frowns. "I don't believe everything the media says."

I want to tell her everything that's happened, but I know she won't believe me. Separated from all the chaos, I barely believe myself.

"You're shaking," she notes and pulls a decorative throw from the loveseat and wraps it around my shoulders. "Did someone hurt you?"

Santos is out there, scouring the city looking to kill me but … I shake my head. No one's hurt me in the way she must be thinking.

"How'd you get here?" she asks.

"I don't know," I say. It's mostly true, sense I wasn't consciously trying to come here. Of all the places, why would my powers bring me here? I shake my head and thank her for the clothes again.

I give Angie the throw blanket, but she takes it reluctantly. "Your mom's really worried about you. I am too," Angie says.

I can tell she wants to talk some more but I can't afford that. The commotion from the second floor has gone still and eerily quiet.

"I better go."

I make my way back to the foyer. My aunt stands at the front door, blocking my exit. She's wearing a white silk robe and fuzzy white slippers that look a little mediocre to be on such snobbish feet. Her graying gold hair is covered with a plush white towel and she's wearing an avocado mask.

"Yes, I think it's time for you to go," she says, only her voice doesn't have the same spit I'm used to. She sounds eerily composed, but I'm not fooled. The woman's a snake.

"Your ride is waiting," she says, opening the door slowly.

The cop sirens are muted but their red and blue lights shine bright in the dim early morning. Police officers are already on the porch.

I raise my hands in the air immediately. "Please."

I start to beg them not to hurt me and not to arrest me, but then I remember who and what I am. I make a run for the back door. I know it's stupid to turn my back to them, but I have the element of surprise on my side. I find the back door to the patio easily through the kitchen and burst outside, past the grill, and into the open backyard. The cool air hits me, along with a painful amount of electrical force. Before I can even lock into my gifts and kick my speed into overdrive, I collapse on the wet grass. My body convulses uncontrollably and for a minute, the pain is so great I can't breathe. My heart palpitates so wildly I can't even gasp or scream despite the fiery pain of what must be active tasers. Even after the electric charge stops coursing through me, my body struggles to recover. By the time the tremors stop, I don't have the strength or energy to move. I lay helpless in the grass, my heart pounding as footsteps sound behind me. An officer stoops down. He takes his hat off and looks me right in the face with black eyes I'll never be able to forget.

"We've got you," Santos says.

No one can help me now. This isn't how I expected things to turn out but maybe the hunters are doing everyone else a favor. No need to rack my brain over the choices I have to make.

"Just get it over with," I tell him.

Santos takes the thick black club and swings it up before whipping it down. My eyes are closed long before I lose consciousness from his burning strike.

I imagine I'll be dead before I regain consciousness and so I let myself slip away into dark oblivion, praying it will all end quickly.

CHAPTER 26

I open my eyes and my head burns with frenzied pain. A harsh light hangs overhead. My arms feel like they could fall out of their sockets. My hands are tied tightly at the wrists, merged with one thick, intricately tied rope with handcuffs intermingled through the threaded weave. I can't move much. I'm helpless, lying on cold cement floors splattered in dirt and what looks like old blood stains. Is it my blood?

Aside from the light flickering above me, there isn't much else. There's no bed, no windows. I'm surrounded by unfinished walls of dirt and rock. Panic runs through me as sudden as the taser's electricity. My mouth opens and a shrill scream escapes, piercing the eerie silence. I push up into a sitting position. I try to muster more strength, to break the rope around my wrists but it's tight and the more I struggle, the tighter it cuts into my skin. I push myself up again, this time to stand and take in my surroundings from a new perspective.

I realize there is no door to my prison. It's more like a zoo cage made of thick glass. Aside from the disadvantage of zero privacy and what I'm sure is a camera watching me from the right, front corner of my prison, its transparency has benefits. Others can see in, but I can see outside, too. The ground outside of my prison is made of dirt, like I'm in some sort of burrowed tunnel or hole. I'm underground, which means if anyone is looking for me, they'll have twice the challenge.

If they're looking at all.

Aunt Vivian sold me out to who she thought were the police. Santos must've intercepted her call. Just like he had at Willow Manor.

But why am I still alive?

Santos wouldn't take the time to cage me if he was just going to kill me. It'll be nothing short of a miracle if I survive whatever he has planned.

"Just breathe, Savannah," I tell myself.

At least I'm not completely alone. Across the tunneled corridor is another cell identical to my own. I peer into the short spanning distance to make out my captured companion. I see disheveled locks of fair hair and tattered clothes, but not much else. It doesn't really matter who's across from me. The fact that I'm not the only person here makes me feel comforted in some small way.

I turn sideways and ram the wall with my shoulder. The backlash from the impact makes me feel like I've hit a brick wall.

"I wonder if I can ghost through the wall."

I'm not so eager to try. My life may depend on it but if I make a mistake…

I shake my head, attempting to free myself of the bloody image of being sliced in half by thick, likely bullet-proof glass. I hesitate, but only for a moment. Taking a deep breath, I make up in my mind to run full speed toward the wall. I just have to believe in myself. Closing my eyes, I remember what ghosting felt like in the subway station. I remember feeling light, fuzzy, and pleasantly numb. I remember -

"Open your eyes Ms. Scarlett. You are not dreaming."

My eyes snap open. Santos stands in front of me as the barrier to my open cage electronically and silently lowers. My stomach sours. If I hadn't hesitated, if I hadn't closed my eyes, I could be free by now.

Could've. Should've. Most definitely would've. It's too late to do anything now except face him with as much dignity as I can. If I have to die today, at least I can do it courageously.

And hopefully quickly, my mind adds.

Who am I kidding? I can't even breathe. My mind immediately takes me back to the most traumatic night of my life, which is saying something since I've had a lot of those lately. Nothing is quite as bad as someone trying to kill you and almost succeeding.

Santos stands relaxed and nonplussed, like a jungle cat that's only slightly hungry, one who's entertaining the idea of catching an easy prey. He's dressed in what seems to be the usual business casual clothing: charcoal colored suit pants, a gray button-up shirt with sleeves neatly rolled up to his elbows, and a loosened collar. His Rolex glistens even in the dim light and his dark hair is pulled back at the nape of his neck. The only thing he's missing is a tie and a suit jacket.

"Do you normally wear nice clothes when you're about to kill someone?"

I don't know how I find my voice to speak. There is no tremor in my tone and my voice carries more confidently than what I feel. Santos's eyes widen a tiny fraction and he laughs.

It's a deep, rich laughter that causes all the nerves in my body to constrict.

"Savannah, for you I will provide a courtesy that I have not afforded to anyone. I will listen to my constituent. Show us what you really are. I promise it will all be over quickly."

He tosses a smooth but dismissive nod over his shoulder and only then am I aware that someone else is in the room. Steve. He's got the same careful, kind eyes that seem gentle at first but upon closer inspection are professionally detached. He has the same reserved posture, the same sandy hair.

"You -you're dead!" I shriek. There's no way he can be alive. I saw him get shot. But here he is with not even a hint of injury, not even a scratch or scar. He seems just as healthy as when we first met.

"She still doesn't know," Steve says to Santos, his calm voice sounding just as I remember it.

"I assure you, she knows enough," Santos replies.

Steve steps forward to study me. There's no trace of trauma, no telling scars. He should be dead, but he's alive and he's staring me straight in the face.

Steve shakes his head. "She's just a girl. She's not like the others. She isn't one of them."

Santos looks bored. "We will put her to the test."

He lifts a hand and the glass barrier rises until the doorway is completely open. I search for the trigger they use to control the barrier. There's nothing on their hands, no keys jingling from their sides, or high-tech gadgets within view. This means that someone is controlling the barrier remotely and that they're watching everything that's going on.

Santos and Steve are all that stand between me and freedom, but they are formidable roadblocks.

"You may leave."

I stare at Santos. Something's off.

"You'd let me just walk out of here?"

"I want you to run. After all, that is what they teach you, isn't it?" Santos says.

I could blur pass them at the speed of light but for some reason, I can't move. It's as if my body is trying to tell me something my brain can't understand.

"What are you doing?" Steve whispers, though his voice is urgent as he questions Santos.

Santos remains unconcerned, confident he can predict my attitude and my choices. I refuse to play his game. Running won't help me. Even if I get out of the cell, I don't know where to go next. I don't even know where I am. Nothing Geezer or Rox taught me can get me out of this. I can't run if I don't know where I'm going. I can't scale rooftops if I'm underground. I'm no match for Santos.

My pouncing heart calms to an eerily slow rate and my breathing levels out in a way I never thought it could when I'm angry or afraid. I stay focused. I won't let him provoke me into doing something stupid.

"I'm not running," I say.

Santos doesn't look surprised. He doesn't look pleased either. "No?"

"No," I repeat.

He takes a slow step toward me. As much as I want to back up, I plant my feet firmly in the ground.

He frowns. "I will kindly give you two choices, Ms. Scarlett. Either reveal yourself for what you really are, or be assured, you will never see the light of day again."

I flinch at his threat, praying he doesn't notice my reaction. Of course, he does. He smiles.

"If you are not one of those abominations then we have no use for you. It is not our code to kill those we protect, but we can't let you walk freely now that you know we exist."

Santos' face twists and he lunges forward. I freeze and this time I close my eyes. I know what he's doing. He's trying to trigger my abilities. I choose to cling onto defiance and stand my ground waiting for pain to erupt.

Nothing happens.

"You have made your choice," he says.

I open my eyes to see the monster of a man put his mask of cool civility back on. "Call Willow Manor. Tell them you found her. I'll make recommendations they send her to a more secure location equip to handle her condition."

I shake my head. "My mom won't let you do that."

Santos looks bored again. "I am a very convincing man."

"Call them and see if my friends don't break me out again." I say.

There are times when bravado is good. Then there are times like this when it's better to stay silent. I've already set this man off today. He looks levelly in my eyes and asks, "And just where are your *friends* now?"

"They'll find me," I say, though I don't know if I believe it.

"Let them know we recommend she receive the highest dose of medical treatment. She is a danger to herself and others," he instructs Steve.

"You're not a real doctor," I say. "They won't believe you."
I hope.

A muscle jumps in Steve's jaw, a tick of irritation. He hates this man as much as I do. Why isn't he doing anything? Why doesn't he speak up?

"You can't do this!" I scream.

Santos turns his back on me. "You've done this to yourself, Ms. Scarlett."

He walks through the open entrance to the cell, pauses to observe the prisoner across from me and then disappears down the tunnel with a self-satisfied smirk. Steve turns to leave and then stops. He looks at me and then looks away.

"How are you even alive?" I ask, hoping he hears how disgusted I am with him, "I watched you die. I saw the bullet – the blood."

He meets my gaze then and I'm astonished by the familiar haunted look. If he wasn't on the wrong team, I'd think he was one of us.

"In your wildest dreams you cannot imagine," he says. "I know you're scared, Savannah. I'm sorry it had to turn out this way but –"

"But it's for the best? Yeah, well, at least I have my dignity which is more than I can say for you. Why not just kill me?"

He frowns. "We don't kill humans."

"Errants *are* humans."

He levels his gaze and once again I'm surprised by the cool calculation and detachment in his expression. Santos' hatred I get, but Steve's mercurial apathy? He is worse than Santos.

"Savannah, you're on the wrong side of things. We're not the bad guys."

He still believes I'm an ordinary girl caught in some dangerous misunderstanding. I shake my head. "You're crazy."

"And you're a fool."

"Coward!" I yell since we're on a name calling basis.

His jaw ticks again. "I've got to go now. I'm sure the doctors will be happy to know you're safe and secure, though not quite as sound."

He turns to leave but I call him back.

"Santos thinks I'm one of them. You don't. What if I was?"

"If you had run, he'd have killed you."

"And if I run now?"

"I'll kill you."

I believe him.

Steve turns his back on me again, signaling for the door to open. I watch as he leaves, and the door starts to close. Nervous energy surges through my body. Before I know what I'm doing, I'm running full speed. I slam into Steve with everything I've got. He inhales sharply before he falls and slides across the hard ground. Unable to stop the rush of momentum, I burst through the locked barrier of the captive across from my own cell. Instead of making impact with the barrier, I ghost through it. My ropes and cuffs fall off while my body transitions from mist back to solid. Unfortunately, my unstable talents give me a clumsy finish. I trip over the immobile body lying in the middle of the cell and fall on my face, scraping my chin.

Scrambling to my feet, I glance over my shoulder. Steve is slumped on the ground in the hall with his head at an odd angle. Panic rises and I resist the urge to check to see if he's alive. An alarm blares suddenly and very loudly, snapping me back into a frenzied focus. Steve is not my priority. I've escaped one cage but I'm in another one, and now I'm not alone. I draw my attention back to the body I've probably added injury to.

"I'm going to get us out of here," I say, trying to debate if it would be best to drag the guy or toss him over my shoulder and use strength I haven't quite tapped into.

"Don't bother."

My eyes lock in on a pale, ashen face. A blond-haired boy grimaces. His eyes are closed so I can't determine their color, but none of those details matter. I don't attempt to assess his condition. I'm just happy I'm not alone. I can take him to Doc later to get him patched up, but first things first – we've got to get out of here.

"No time for a pity party. You can't give up. Come on," I say, trying to rouse him into action. I don't know how long he's been here, but I need this guy, whoever he is, to be positive. I don't think I can make it out of this place alone but, if I have help, if we can work together, we might have a shot. Worst case scenario, at least we don't have to die alone. I tell myself that no matter what happens, I won't leave this guy. I wouldn't want anyone to leave me behind. I wonder if there are others. I scream at the top of my lungs for any other signs of life.

"Everyone else is dead," my newest companion informs me.

"Then we'd better get out of here."

Only one blue eye opens. The other is swollen shut and his face is decorated in a myriad of bruises and bloody scrapes. Beneath all the injuries, there's something familiar about his face. The one open eye jars my memory back to the Empire State Building, back to the guy I saw K.O. fighting. He's the blond boy who winked at me before K.O. threw him over the side of the skyscraper.

"You."

He smiles and despite his injuries, the smile is a charming one. "You. I thought you might be one of us."

He sits up, cradling one arm before standing slowly and yawning. "What's your name, Red?"

"Savannah."

His open eye takes in my hair. "I think I'm going to call you Red."

"My last name's Scarlett," I offer, recalling how the others call me by my last name.

"Yeah, Red, sit tight. You didn't trip the alarm. My boys are coming to get me and you're coming with us."

I feel my jittery nerves still and for the umpteenth time I'm in shock as his words settle into my brain. Everything makes sense now. He's injured but he's not worrying himself about much. When he was lying immobile on the ground it wasn't because he was unconscious or hopeless. He was resting, waiting.

Commotion sounds down the tunnel. Gunshots pop and spray, sounding like rain during a thunderstorm. People are screaming in pain. It's a warzone. I stare at the blond and he smiles at me with his bruised chin tilted up.

"Who are you?" I ask, though I'm beginning to think I already know.

He doesn't answer, his attention drawn to what waits outside of the cell. My ears perk too as smoke rushes down the tunnel towards us. I move towards the door just as a figure smashes against the barrier, breaks apart into a mist of particles and materializes into the cell as a familiar face emerges into solid, human form.

"Max!" Tattoo yells, "We gotta move quick."

CHAPTER 27

*L*ife is one big ironic mess where dead enemies come back to life and I just happen to end up trying to rescue my friends' fiercest rival.

Tattoo notices me. "What's she doing here?"

I back up.

He's wearing enough ammo to take out a military compound all by himself, and he's pointing a gun in my direction. My body stiffens but I try to keep my composure. This guy and his friends beat me up some days ago. I've healed up nicely and I've learned a few things. He won't beat me again.

"You better point that gun somewhere else," I tell him.

Max laughs. "She's coming with us."

Tattoo looks like he wants to argue but he keeps his mouth shut. I frown, grateful that Max is willing to include me in the rescue mission, but from what I've experienced, his crew isn't something I want to be associated with. If Santos and Steve's people don't kill me, I'm sure Max's guys will try. Besides, I don't think the others will appreciate me hanging around with people they don't get along with – and that's an understatement. I wonder if Max would still mind me coming with him if he knew who I'd been running the streets with before I ended up in this place.

Max ghosts through the barrier as easy as normal people walk through doors. He doesn't have to work up momentum. He doesn't have to rev himself up. He just walks through the barrier. Tattoo shoulders his way through, less graceful, definitely not as skilled.

"A little help?" I ask. I've ghosted twice but both times have been by accident.

"Pull your own weight, princess," Tattoo spits before stepping over Steve's body and taking off after Max.

Panic sets in like someone's thrown a bucket of ice-cold water on me, but I steel myself. I've got to practice saving myself.

I touch the barrier tentatively with my fingers, wondering if I can just walk through it as simply as Max. I close my eyes and imagine that I can. I imagine my fingers sliding through the barrier like I'm dipping them into water. The barrier that's holding me isn't solid. It's malleable, a portal to another world. As I feel the hard-resistant surface begin to yield, my mind throws a curve ball. I see myself being cut in half by its now solid substance. I visualize my body splitting down the middle into two bloody heaps. I move to yank my hand out of the pooling barrier before it hardens, but a calloused hand grips mine and pulls me through.

The feeling of breathing but not breathing is scary as it is exhilarating. It's as if I'm over-breathing. All of my cells are bouncing off of one another, so hyper and alive, composed of nothing but air and vapor. Then, I'm falling on top of Mohawk. I land on my knees, right on his chest. We stare at each other in surprise and once recognition sets in our surprise mutates into hostility. He pushes me off him. He looks like he's ready to attack me, but an authoritative voice cuts the tension.

"Quit flirting and come on!" Max yells from somewhere down the long tunnel. Mohawk looks startled again but recovers, giving me the evil eye before hopping to his feet and breaking into a sprint. Reluctantly, I follow him.

I try to block out the scene of broken bodies sprayed in blood and bullets. Though their faces are masked, and their bodies are armored in black uniforms and ammo, they're still people. Or they were. The angle of some heads and necks makes it obvious they're not sleeping. They're dead. Max's gang did this. They killed these people. But they aren't the only ones guilty of violence. I think about Steve. His posture was all wrong, awkward and grotesque. When I ran into him, the impact must've been too great for his body to withstand. He's dead. I killed him.

I tell myself I did what I had to do to escape, but what I did wasn't out of necessity. It was out of anger, a response to the threats Steve and Santos made. I could've just run past him and escaped.

I swallow hard, suppressing tears and self-hatred. Rather than feel dirty and inhuman, I stop internalizing and push everything but thoughts of survival out of my head. That's the only way to make it through all this chaos. Taking a deep breath, I forget about everything but the wind in my hair. I deafen my ears to everything, and when I can't block out the noise, I stop trying to make sense of it.

Though my eyes are wide open, I narrow my focus to my current allies as we race out of the underground labyrinth of intricate tunnels and traps. I let go of worry and fear. I let go of self-loathing and the feeling of inferiority and shame. I stop thinking and let my body take control. I let my instincts take over, and for a moment I don't exist. Darkness takes over my line of vision even though my eyes are wide open. I have to die to the world around me if I'm going to survive. I won't let my awareness be revived until I'm free of the constricting air filled with the aroma of death, blood, and violence. I am senseless. I am nothing. I am…

"Red, hey! Wake up."

A voice penetrates what must be a true unconscious moment. My eyes are closed. I don't have the strength to open them. I feel so heavy, so sluggish, so painfully numb. I can't move.

"They call her Scarlett," I hear a voice say.

"She's with K.O.," someone else adds.

All these voices sound familiar, but my mind is too tired to make sense of them.

"Leave her," one voice says.

There is more muffled talk, unintelligible to my ears. Then one voice rises above the rest, causing the protests to stop.

"Bring her."

Those two words and the fresh, startling air jar me into full consciousness. I inhale. My eyes snap open. Someone is carrying me, tucked under their arm like I'm a sack of vegetables. My arms and legs dangle helplessly, and all the blood rushes to the top of my head. I can barely breathe as my nostrils fill with blasts of cool air.

No! I want to say, but no sound comes out.

The air chokes out my voice. It suffocates me.

I can't help wishing it was K.O. that found me. I've taken him for granted. This time, he isn't here. This time, it's Max. The sense of irony is almost amusing. Before I met K.O. and Max, I was just an awkward, lonely girl grieving for her dead dad. Now? I'm a vessel filled with unlimited potential. But all the potential in the world doesn't matter if I don't know how to use it. I live in a very dangerous world. I know I'm far from safe, and I still can't save myself. If Max is anything like the company he keeps, I'm in way over my head. I've escaped one danger only to leap right into another.

CHAPTER 28

I sleep free of dreaming, but all good things come to an end. The serenity of my silent, dark rest ends abruptly with what feels like a torrent of ice-cold water smacking against my skin, aggravating my exhausted body. I sit up, inhaling sharply, too cold and stunned to scream. My tired, stinging eyes search around the dark as my fingers feel at my surroundings.

I'm sitting on a stiff mattress that has the consistency of cardboard. Thin blankets cover my legs with paper-thin sheets beneath me. The generic bed, my clothes, and skin are soaked with ice and water. I shiver, cold rather than afraid. My body feels the aches, the pain, and the cold but mentally and emotionally I'm numb. I know I should be afraid. I should be worried and maybe even begging for my life. Max's crew is radical. They're dangerous and they're also very aware that I hang out with people they don't get along with. A boy grabs me roughly by the arm and forces me up.

As my eyes adjust to the dark, I busy myself, taking in my surroundings. I ignore the way his short, jagged nails dig into my skin and the way he purposefully walks faster than he thinks I can keep up. He half drags, half pulls me along, but I don't fight or protest. Our footsteps make a muted thud that echoes off the silence of the building, but New York traffic is ever present in the background. There are honks, screeching tires, vibrating music, the steady whirring of cars whizzing by and sirens loudly announcing another emergency. There is even the distant murmur of voices beyond these plastered, aged walls.

From the holes in the walls, the unfinished wood and exposed installation, I'm guessing we're in an abandoned building. There is a slightly moldy smell coming from dripping cracks in the ceilings. Rusted pipes smell like copper pennies and sewer water. Faded, half-broken lockers line portions of the halls and several average sized rooms with wooden doors and small windows reveal chalkboards and desks. We pass a gymnasium and cut across what looks to be a wrecked entrance. I notice an empty glass showcase and offices. This is a school building or at least it used to be.

For once I'm led down a flight of stairs instead of up to a rooftop. As we descend, I expect the smell of rust, stale water, and mold to grow stronger. I'm surprised when the smell disappears altogether, and the halls are lit, the cement floors are clean. Things look Spartan but sanitary. The lower level is much different than the main floor. Music welcomes my ears with a thrumming bass, steadying the last of my uncooperative nerves with its pulsing beat. I wonder if I'm being led to an execution or some sort of interrogation where they're going to torture me until I spill secrets I don't really know about K.O. and the others.

We stop at a plain gray, steel door at the end of the hall. I study the guy who's been leading me through the maze. It's Tattoo. He notices me staring at him and he growls. Half out of my mind from stress and fatigue, I growl back. His eyes widen. He opens the door and quickly shoves me inside. The door slams behind me. Still dripping wet, clothes clinging to my torso and limbs, I find Emery sitting calmly at a plain white, plastic table with a computer on it. His black cobra eyes study me top to bottom. I stare back at him, wishing my gaze could laser a hole through his forehead.

"You look a lot better than I thought you would. Thought you'd be dead by now," he comments.

I could respond a million different ways, but I keep my head up and my mouth shut.

"Did they cut your tongue out? You were mouthy last time we met."

"Yeah and you had a bloody face," I snap.

His deadened eyes light up and he offers me a chilling smile. "There's that fire. It's what saved you, you know."

When I don't respond he adds, "You impressed Max."

Oh joy. Some militant extremist thinks I'm cool enough to join his band of violent crazies. Am I supposed to do cartwheels? I feel a little insulted that he thinks I'm impressive.

"It's shocking, really, since I remember you being weak and pathetic. K.O.'s not here to save you, so you may wanna be careful around these parts."

"K.O.'s got nothing to do with this."

He laughs again but this time it's more like I expect, an unamused half chuckle that doesn't quite reach his cold eyes.

"We've got ears and eyes everywhere. Everyone knows about the girl who drives K.O. wild. Literally! You should see him now. He's been running the streets looking for you."

Some of the numbness melts away and my heart flutters. *Stupid heart.*

"Don't get excited. He won't find you. Like I told you before, you're on the wrong team. If you only had those screw-ups to rely on, you'd be dead by now. You're lucky we were watching you."

With the numbness melting away, fear becomes a reality again. The hope I felt knowing K.O. was looking for me dims in comparison to violation of knowing Max's crew has been spying on me, probably on all of us.

"We started tailing you in Chinatown the day you and K.O. were having your couple's feud. It was entertaining stuff."

Invasion of privacy aside, if he's telling the truth that meant his guys were at my aunt's house when Santos abducted me. They didn't lift a finger to help me.

"Santos could've killed me."

Emery shrugs, his eyes glazing over with boredom, like he's been waiting for me to piece everything together.

"We had to find Max some way. You were the logical bait. Your family's so dysfunctional. That aunt of yours is a piece of work. Your cousin's hot though."

I take a step forward, blood suddenly hot, rushing, and roaring in my ears. I leap into the air, land on the table and slide across the slick surface on my knees. My fists fly, hitting Emery's pale, pristine face a few times before he recovers enough from the shock of my attack to deflect and hit me back. He uses an open palm instead of a fist, but it still feels like a brutal whip. The force is enough to turn my head and cause a temporary loss of breath. I blink back blind spots just as another figure grabs me by the waist and tosses me back. I stumble but land on my feet.

Max stands between us. Emery cools down first, spitting and smiling with bloody teeth. "She's savage. She'll fit right in."

"I don't want to fit in. I want to smash your face!"

Santos could've killed me, and they would've just watched. To think, they call Geezer and the others cowards.

"Cool it, Red. You don't want to make enemies of the people who just saved your life," Max says.

"You know, you could offer me some food and a nice hot shower before we continue with whatever we're doing. It's the least you could do after using me as bait," I say.

"Red, once you see this, you may wanna make yourself at home," Max says, tapping the laptop in front of him.

The horrible feeling in my stomach grows exponentially worse. I try to stay calm and not wring my hair out, but my brain starts creating scenarios.

"Never gonna happen," I say.

Max seems more confident in his opinion than I do mine. He smiles at me and then gestures for Emery to turn the computer around. I almost turn my head away and refuse to look, but the screen automatically catches my eye. The computer shows an image of my cell at Santos's underground compound. From the angle of the camera, I can see Steve's body slumped against the wall in the dirt hall against Max's cell. His eyes are wide open, glassy, and vacant. His skin is pale and waxy. His neck is craned a little too far to the right. The reality of the situation slams into me with such force my throat constricts. The sound that comes out of my mouth is a mix of screaming, sobbing, and dry heaving. I didn't look at Dad at his funeral, and I really don't want to look at the body of the person I murdered.

"Settle down, Red," Max says, "Watch what happens."

I close my eyes, refusing to look at the video. I don't care if they see me fall apart anymore. Forget bravado. I'm a murderer. Max and Emery can't torture me anymore than I'll torture myself. I'll never get the image out of my head.

Tears pour out of my eyes. My nose runs and I'm a shaking, blubbering mess. All these months of feeling depressed, isolated, and afraid suddenly stir and burst within me, brought to a head by something much worse: a guilt that I won't ever be able to get rid of. I'm a murderer.

"Red, listen to me and listen to me carefully," comes Max's level voice. He's not yelling at me and his voice is close enough to make me open my eyes. He motions for Emery to give me his chair and helps me sit. He sits on the table in front of me, blocking the computer screen. " I need you to watch the surveillance feed. There's something you need to see."

I don't answer him.

"Please," he adds.

I can't stop crying, but I don't close my eyes again.

"We retrieved some of their surveillance feed. Most of it is much worse than what you're about to see but..." Emery's voice trails off with a shrug. He avoids my gaze, his eyes going back and forth from Max to the computer.

I glare at him and Max laughs at me. "I see why Oliver likes you," he says. "Sweet and sassy."

"He doesn't like me."

"A girl that doesn't know she's attractive," he mutters, rolling his eyes.

"He hates me," I admit, though I'm not quite so sure anymore.

"Then you're my new best friend," he says.

"I don't want to be your friend."

As bad as I thought K.O. was, Max is a thousand times worse. He pretends to be charming but he's really a manipulative bully with a pretty face.

"Once you watch this, you'll realize we're your only friends. Ollie can't help you. He can't save you. He'll get you killed if you trust him."

He talks with such conviction and his speech sounds eerily familiar. K.O. said almost those exact words. If Doc hadn't told me about their history, I might almost believe Max.

"Watch," he growls.

He stands up and moves to stand behind me, so I have a clear, unobstructed view of the computer screen. He hovers over me to ensure I comply. Emery casts one last look at Max. His eyes skip over me and he resumes the video. I hold my breath as I watch the feed. I don't look at Steve's eyes or his frozen face. Instead, I focus on the blood-stained cement. Emery's words replay in my head.

"We retrieved some of their surveillance feed. Most of it is much worse than what you're about to see but..."

What could possibly be worse than watching the body of the man I killed broken and abandoned? Then I remember. Max and I weren't the only ones Santos and his men captured. We were just the lucky two who made it out alive. I shiver. Max leans closer to me to make sure I'm watching, but he doesn't have to worry about me. I can't tear my eyes away from the computer screen now if I wanted to.

The longer I stare at Steve's lifeless body, the more I'm reminded of who he really was. He was like Max. On the outside, he was handsome and friendly, the yin to Santos' crazy, dark yang. The good cop to his bad cop. But he was just another face with the same values Santos upheld. Both times I had the misfortune of being at their mercy he hadn't argued that it wasn't right to kill. He just wanted to be sure he was killing the right type of person. He was a serial killer, just like Santos, who justified the taking of lives by associating being different with being evil. The shock and some of the guilt I feel slowly subsides. My hands might be dirty now, but at least it was worth it. I've taken a monster off the streets. No one like me will have to worry about Steve again.

"Santos, what happened to him? Did anyone –" I start.

"Watch," Max interrupts, silencing my question.

Gripping the sides of my chair, I stare at the screen. I see our escape from the camera's perspective: a confident Max biding his time, unworried by the sudden chaos blooming outside his cell, and me, a wide-eyed, skittish mess of a girl who looks like she's on the verge of another breakdown. Looking at myself from the camera's perspective is different than living in my shoes and looking at my face in the mirror. I'd told myself I was brave in that cell, that I was strong and defiant. I was far from strong and everyone knew it.

You were strong enough to kill Steve, some part of my mind argues.

It was an accident; I tell to myself.

Shaking my head, I refocus my attention on the screen. I'm a murderer and I'm arguing with myself. Can it get any worse?

It can always get worse; my mind reminds me.

The camera feed remains on Steve, and for a while nothing happens. All the chaos subsides, and things are eerily still. My focus retreats, sliding to other thoughts and concerns like sleep and food, when my eyes zoom back in at the sight of movement. I blink a few times. This can't be real.

Steve's ragdoll corpse twitches. It happens in small ways at first, a finger, then a foot. Then his entire body begins to convulse. I've heard somewhere, probably from a movie, that dead bodies can move and even make sounds. It has something to do with the releasing of gas and bodily fluids or something like that. Somehow this is different. This is something more, something unnatural.

Steve's twisted neck unwinds. It cracks and pops, reshaping into its proper alignment. His broken, awkwardly angled legs snap back into place. I can practically see the blood refilling his empty veins. The pallid complexion of his skin flushes with color, transforming from an off white to an even, unblemished, golden tan. His skin becomes supple and his muscles well defined in his arms, rather than saggy. Steve's mouth opens wide as he takes in a sharp, painful breath. He sounds like he's recovering from attempted strangulation. Ironically, I'm having a hard time breathing. My chest and lungs feel like they're on fire. This can't be happening. It can't be real.

But I continue to watch as the vacant, glassy film of death clears from Steve's eyes. He stretches his neck muscles from side to side, his body snapping and cracking as if he's only recovering from the stiffness of sitting in one place too long. His hands ball into fists and a frown contorts his mouth as he rises to his feet and strides out of the room like he's just had the most refreshing nap.

Emery disconnects the video and snaps the computer closed as Max moves from behind me to sit on the table again. They stare at me and I stare dumbly back at them. Max and Emery give me time to make sense of what I've seen. I don't know if I really want to make sense of it. Unable to take the prolonging silence, I state the obvious.

"He was dead."

My voices come out low and raspy. My throat is dry. I clear my throat, really wishing I had some water. My hands shake and, as much as I try to still them, I can't.

"I killed him," I say aloud.

Max nods.

Cold sweat forms around the edges of my hairline.

"But he-he just…"

Max's bruised jaw tightens.

"Yes, you killed him. He was dead. Now he's alive and very, very angry."

As bizarre as it sounds, things make more sense. This isn't the first time I thought Steve died. I remember very clearly how Geezer shot him. I remember the vacant gaze and all the blood. While I'd been distraught, Geezer and the others hardly batted a lash.

"Ollie and Geeze must've forgotten to mention the lethal hunters who want to murder us are immortal," Max says.

They weren't the only ones. Rox and Tristan never told me either. Max pats my shaking hand and offers me an electric smile.

"You're welcome to leave and go back to my brother. But, if you want to live, training starts tomorrow, 5:00 AM sharp. Welcome to the Fleet."

CHAPTER 29

*M*ax hops off the table and struts out the room looking way happier than when he first walked in. I hear him whistling out the door and down the hall, leaving me to stare stupidly at Emery, who's still avoiding eye contact.

"I'll show you to your room," Emery says, moving to the door. I'm in too much shock to point out that I haven't made my decision yet. The answer seems obvious, I guess. If I leave, I might not even make it back to the others. Santos and Steve are looking for me, and now I'm sure they'll kill me on sight. There's no more guessing what I am.

Then there's the fact that no one thought to tell me that Santos and the other hunters are *immortal*. While it's bad enough having someone try to kill me, it's even more disturbing knowing that my enemy can't die. How are we supposed to beat people like that? Why even try? Maybe the others were doing me a favor by keeping that major detail a secret. Maybe they were going to tell me after they felt more confident in my training or maybe they didn't think they would have to. If I chose to stay in New York and return to live with Mom and Tom, they were going to lead Santos out of the city and away from me. They had my back, didn't they?

Things just keep getting more complicated. As if it isn't hard enough to choose between a normal-ish life with Mom or a new start with K.O. and the others. Now I have another choice. I can stay with Max and his Fleet, who were able to find me and Max, defend themselves against an entire compound of armed guards and lethal immortals, and successfully get us out of that death trap. They don't seem to shy away from combat. They revel in the challenge and danger of the fight.

I tell myself I won't make a choice now. There's too much running through my mind, too much chaos going on around me, and there's too much at stake. If I make a decision out of fear and pressure, it could cost me my life. I don't speak to Emery. Instead, I let him lead me through a maze of hallways, the sound of thrumming music growing in the background. The longer we walk the louder the music gets until Emery ushers me through a set of steel double doors. Darkness surrounds us immediately, highlighted by strobe lights flickering through crowds of sweating, dancing bodies. We're in Stax. No wonder Emery was able to find us the night he gave me the threatening message for K.O. Their hideout is connected to Stax.

"We own Stax," Emery says, pride practically dripping with every word. The place looks like a walking health hazard, but based on the crowds, I'm sure they make a nice number of dollars, dollars they probably don't pay taxes on, but who am I to judge? For the last few weeks, I've been eating and wearing stolen goods and house squatting.

"Everything we make here funds our weapons and resources. We work shifts to pay for our own individual expenses," he explains.

For a bunch of militant radicals, they sure are organized. They aren't just some kids running the streets doing whatever they want. They all answer to Max and Max seems to execute everything like a seasoned entrepreneur. Unlike the others, Max's crew is stationary. Their compound stretches through the city's underground into an intricate network of tunnels and sewer lines. They're currently living in an abandoned charter school. They could easily move to one of their other locations throughout the city and no hunter, civilian, or unaffiliated Errant would ever know.

As we maneuver through Stax to the bar, I feel like everyone in the room is staring in our direction. As versatile as the crowds are, I must stick out with wild hair, ripped, dirty clothes, and grimy skin. I haven't showered or brushed my teeth in two days. As many times as I've been unconscious in the past few hours, I haven't had a good night's rest either. I probably look like a zombie.

"Let's get you to your room," Emery says. "Then you can shower before you go to bed."

"What time is it?" I wonder.

"Almost 9:00 pm."

"Who says I want to go to bed?" I snap, though the nearest bed is exactly what I want. I'm finding out I just don't like being told what to do by people who, only days ago, tried to kill me.

"Trust me, if you knew what was coming you would eat, drink, and sleep while you can," Emery says.

My stomach growls and he gives me one of those slow, snaky smirks just as a girl with a pink mohawk, Hello Kitty earrings, and a glittery face slides two boxes of pizza across the counter. She winks at him.

"Here ya go, Emery. Tell Max I said hey," she says, smiling at him while managing to cut me an evil eye.

"Best pizza in the city," he brags.

"That's not saying much," I mutter, though the smell of cheese, tomato paste, and garlic wafting from the hot boxes makes my mouth water. Emery doesn't hear me. He's focused on Glitter Girl. He shoves me the pizza boxes.

"Eat," he says, then slinks back to the bar to chat with the girl. "Sheila, take a break with me."

I retreat to one of the only open tables in the nearest corner of the hot, smelly, crowded space. I'm barely sitting down before I've opened one of the boxes and I'm tearing into a slice hot pizza. It's greasy and messy but Emery's right. It's the best in the city. It has the perfect blend of spices, the right amount of cheese, and it's not stolen. My stomach sours a little on that last thought, or maybe it's the familiar face standing over me that makes me lose my appetite.

Geezer is dressed in a baggy black hoodie that swallows his curly hair, youthful face, and slight build, but I'd recognize those old soul eyes anywhere. He turns his back to the bar and drops his head, further obscuring his face.

"You're playing a dangerous game. You know that, right?" he asks.

"They rescued me," I snap.

"K.O. looked for you. We all did," he says. "I'm glad you're alright."

There's an awkward moment of silence as he looks over his shoulder at the bar. My eyes follow his and I see Emery still at the bar flirting. I'm grateful he's distracted. Another fight might erupt if he sees Geezer.

"You shouldn't be here," I tell Geezer.

His face and voice harden. "Neither should you, but I need you to stay."

I open my mouth to argue but he sits down across from me, shushes me, and continues. "I followed you the night you blacked out, thinking I'd get you out of any tight spots, if you needed me."

"You let Santos capture me!"

He shushes me again, "I saw Emery and the others tailing you, too. I got a little distracted. By the time I was focused again, Santos had you. I knew Emery's boys would follow you and find out where you were. They have eyes everywhere."

"I could be dead right now!"

Geezer glares at me, urging me to be quiet.

"No. If Santos wanted to kill you, he would've done it already. You've seen the news. People resist arrest and get shot all the time."

I take a deep breath. "They used me as bait to find Max,"

He doesn't look surprised, but he doesn't look happy about it either. "As much as I'd like to get you out of this mess, I can't. You wouldn't be safe with us right now. I think everything that's happened proves that."

"I'm safe here?"

"For now, but I've got a feeling none of us will be safe for long. We're never really safe."

Geezer opens the second box of pizza and takes out a bacon, pepperoni, and sausage slice. He takes a big bite, and after he's quickly devoured the slice, he leans in closer. His baby face is still in old man mode, and his tired eyes are as serious as ever.

"I need you to watch Max. He's up to something, and if I know him like I think I do, that something'll get us all killed," Geezer explains.

"What makes you think I can do this?"

It's not that I don't want to help. I owe Geezer my life. If it wasn't for him, I'd be dead right now and what's more, I trust him more than anybody. Not only has he proven he's the smartest Errant around, but he's the one who's always believed in me and looked out for me. If I can help him in any way, I will. Realistically, I just don't know if I can. Max is ruthless. People don't just respect him. They're afraid of him. He gives off the vibe of a crime boss straight out of a mafia movie. As cold as Emery is, when it comes to Max barking orders, he moves like a scared little puppy. Emery is smart and sneaky. If Max wasn't smarter or stronger, I'm sure Emery would try to run things.

I'm not like them. I'm the amateur screw-up.

"Max isn't stupid, but he is arrogant. He knows how K.O. feels about you–"

"Why does everyone keep saying that? K.O. hates me and–"

"–And so, Max will want you on his team just to spite him. He'll give you royal treatment just to prove he's better than his brother," Geezer continues as if I never interrupted him.

My mind strays a little and I interrupt him again, "They aren't really brothers, are they? Max is white and K.O. is–"

"They kind of adopted each other," Geezer answers, "Now, please focus. I don't have a lot of time."

We both look back at the bar. Emery turns his head when Sheila turns his head back in her direction and leans further over the counter. She winks at us.

"She's distracting him," I say.

"Sheila owes me one, so yeah. You're observant. That's why you're perfect for the job. Watch Max. Play on his arrogance. Gather all the information you can and report to us at Doc's as often as you can."

The chance of getting caught is extremely high for the simple fact that I'm me. I sleepwalk into trouble. I have a bad feeling this isn't going to turn out well. There's no way Max's crew will let me out of their sight, especially since they know about my connections to Geezer and the others.

"Play dumb but be smart," Geezer advises and if I didn't feel a little anxious already, he adds, "We're counting on you."

"Hey!"

I jump when Emery approaches the table. My eyes automatically go to Geezer, thinking he's found us out, but Geezer's gone and Emery's eyeing the Meat lover's pizza.

"You weren't supposed to eat that one," he grumbles.

"It was just a slice."

"This was Max's pizza," he explains, as if that should mean something significant.

"What? Max doesn't know how to share?"

Emery glares at me, "Watch it."

Then in a flash, he's back at the bar ordering another pizza and flirting with Sheila. Geezer's seat remains empty, but I look around Stax just in time to see a hooded figure slide out of the main entrance.

While I wait on Emery, I eat the rest of the meaty pizza for spite. Why let it go to waste? When he returns with a new pizza, I'm so full that the fresh, hot aroma of the new meaty pie makes me nauseated. I expect him to lead me back through the hidden entrance through the tunnels and back to the school. Instead, he takes me through the kitchen and through another set of steel doors. These doors lead to another set of tunnels.

Max has a good reason to be arrogant. These tunnel systems are elaborate. If Emery wasn't guiding me, I'd be lost. It's hard to say which tunnels lead to what, but Emery is a pro at navigating. After what seems like an hour of random turns, we stop in front of what looks like a large bank vault. I hesitate.

"Where are you taking me? I thought everyone stays at the old school.

Emery frowns, "You deaf or something? We move around. Besides the school's not the best of our locations. The city's looking to demolish the building since it caught fire a few months ago. They're gonna build these luxury apartments instead. We prefer the tunnels anyway."

That makes sense. New York doesn't have much vacant real estate. There's no way this city would let old buildings just sit when they could be renting overpriced space and justifying it by tacking the word "luxury" onto it.

I can see why Emery's so proud of the tunnel system. It's an intricate web of transit with a unique design of wood, cement, and dirt flooring and walls. All the doors are made of strong metals and there is a sophisticated network connecting all the utilities. It's a city beneath a city.

Emery opens the vault and the massive door swings open slowly and silently. Hushed air escapes and dust stirs up off the dirt path. Emery steps into the dark opening and I follow him reluctantly. He clicks a single light overhead and the pale light illuminates the surrounding walls of knives, staffs, guns, grenades, military gear and other things I can't really identify. I've never seen so many weapons before.

"This is one of our armories," he says.

"There's more than one?"

He doesn't answer me, but I watch as he feels under one of the shelves and presses a hidden button. One of the caged and locked walls of weapons lifts to reveal a hidden path, leading through another system of tunnels.

"Really? I'm never going to remember how to get where I need to go."

"No need," Emery says, "We won't let you wander around by yourself."

Translation: They'll be watching me.

CHAPTER 30

"Welcome to the dorms," Emery says.

The tunnels look more like caverns with low, smooth sculpted rock walls and ceilings. The floors are made of dirt and very little light shines. I feel like I'm in a coal mine. The dorms are a lot more rustic than everything else I've seen so far. Each room is literally a hole in the wall covered only by different patterned sheets and curtains. The small spaces look uncomfortable with low hard rock ceilings, leaving only enough room to squat, sit, or crawl. There isn't much room for personal belongings either. There's only space for a sleeping bag and a few other knickknacks at best. The dorms look like a crypt. All they need are skeletons and skulls and the dorms could be a smaller replica of Rome's famous catacombs.

"The dorms are for resting and recovery," Emery says quietly. "We purposefully designed them to be uncomfortable. Life is short. We'll sleep when we die."

"With your shield or on it," I mutter, quoting one of Dad's favorite macho movies.

Emery actually laughs, though it sounds hollow.

"You could say that. If we've gotta go down, might as well die fighting."

We walk on for a somber moment and I try to estimate the number of dorms, placing the total somewhere around thirty to fifty. Each curtain covering the room entrances are decorated differently, reminding me of flags. Even the rock above each dorm is unique with chiseled names and slogans.

"Which one's yours?" I ask.

Emery grunts, "Depends. You wanna keep me warm tonight or are you gonna try to kill me in my sleep?"

I stop walking. "Are you going to kill me in *my* sleep?"

Even when he's making passes at me, I know the flirting's not genuine. He's only making lewd comments to make me feel uncomfortable and unsafe.

"We don't kill our own," he says, though by the tone of his voice and the cold look in his eyes, I imagine that doesn't include everyone.

"It's getting late," he says, "Let me show you where you'll be staying. For now."

He keeps walking and I have no choice but to follow him. I'm dreading what little hole he'll assign me to, when we stop in front of a space that could fit an entire wall of sleep dorms. It's at the end of the tunnel and it's covered by a sturdy wooden door instead of a curtain. The wood has several detailed carvings around its perimeter and in the middle of the door, in bold etched letters it reads: MAX.

"There's no way–"

I turn around, convinced I sort of know how to get out of these creepy sleeping quarters, but Emery grabs me firmly by the shoulders.

"Relax, Red. No one will bother you here."

"Except Max," I counter.

"It is his room," he points out.

"I'm not that kind of girl," I retort.

"Your definitely not his kind of girl," he says, not missing a beat.

I pull out of his grip, fold my arms, and plant my feet firmly in the dirt path.

"I'm not staying in there."

"No, you're not. 5:00 AM you'll be up and out. Rest up, Red. Tomorrow we'll see what you're made of."

He doesn't stick around to argue. Instead, he road-runs out of the dreary tunnels, leaving me stranded, contemplating what to do with myself. I can try to navigate my way back through the tunnels to Stax or to the school and find my own place to sleep, or I can find my way out of this place completely. I can be on my own again, free of everyone around me. I can leave New York by myself.

"That didn't go over too well last time you thought about it," I mumble to myself. On my own, I'm an easy target. I won't last a day.

I could get out of here and go back to Geezer and the others. The idea sounds like a winner until I remember what Geezer said. He doesn't think I'll be safe with them. He actually thinks I'll be safer here. Then there's the fact that he wants me to spy on Max. What better place to spy than the blond tyrant's room?

I open Max's door, holding my breath, not knowing what to expect. I'm relieved to see something that resembles a real bedroom. His ceilings are high enough for me to walk through the room comfortably. More light comes from the chandelier in the center of the room and standing floor lamps plugged up sporadically around the rest of the room's perimeter. Underneath the chandelier is a mahogany wood desk with a sleek laptop and printer. The desk chair is black, plush, and professional. Behind the desk is a ceiling to floor bookcase embedded in the wall, covered with books, weapon displays, rolled up maps, and stacks of files. Facing the desk is an impressive electric fireplace. In the left corner of the room is a king-sized bed neatly made with a plush black and white checkered comforter set and pillows galore. It looks so inviting but at the same time I can't help but wonder how clean his sheets are.

Off to the right of the room is a small enclosed area with a separate doorway. It's a bathroom complete with a shower and bathtub and a sparkling toilet. Next to the bathroom along the adjacent wall is a built-in clothing rack and a dresser. The room literally has everything. I might as well be staying at a hotel. His room is tidy and cozy, drastically different from what's on the other side of the door. I yawn, and my eyes go back to the bed. I look over my shoulder, back at the door. I'm relieved to know that it locks from the inside, and I rush to do so before collapsing on top of the comforters and pillows in the bed.

The blankets and pillows have little aroma other than a hint of detergent and fabric softener. There's no lingering cologne smell or body odor. There are no visible stains in the sheets. The bed is clean.

Somehow, I manage to close my eyes. My body relaxes into the nest of pillows and for what seems like a short few moments of bliss, I settle into sleep. I tell myself I'll only sleep for a little while and then I'll get up and see what I can get my hands on. I need to learn more about Max and whatever he's planning. Unfortunately, by the time I open my eyes, I realize I'm not alone.

Classical music blares from speakers above the door, something I hadn't noticed last night. The music is so loud I cover my ears to keep my eardrums from busting. The sound of the music nearly drowns out a small alarm clock on the desk. Its thick red digital numbers read 4:15 AM. I frown. Training starts in less than an hour. Black leggings and a spaghetti strap tank hang above a pair of black sneakers. In a pile on the edge of the bed is a bag of unopened underwear and socks. Everything looks about my size. Someone must have brought the fresh clothes in while I was sleeping.

"Kinda creepy having a guy buy my underwear," I mutter to myself.

Grateful for the bathroom two feet away, I quickly shower under nice hot water and linger in the resulting steam until it clears. Reluctantly, I get out of the shower and dress as fast as I can. I open the door to Max's room. Max is standing on the other side of the door looking dressed and fresh himself, like it's the afternoon and not dawn. He offers me a wide smile.

"Morning, Red."

Before I can respond, two blurred figures streak against the melancholy backdrop of the catacomb dorms. My vision goes dark as a thick sheet is forced over my head and then we're taking off at break-neck speed. I let them carry me without resisting, saving my energy for whatever is to come. I keep my breathing as easy as possible though the air feels thick and hot underneath the head covering.

When the running stops, I'm dropped to the ground and I land hard on my butt. Pain is not my first concern though. My hands are still free, so I snatch the covering off my head. The silence in the room is so intense I don't expect to see an arena filled with people. As I stand, I look around at an open ring while at least thirty sets of eyes stare me down. I feel like I'm on a reality show, the one girl act for a deadly competition, as Max and a few other familiar faces surround me.

The audience around us shouts and cheers as a set of bright halogen lights illuminate the dirt encased arena. If the ceilings weren't so high, I'd feel claustrophobic. I've never seen so much dirt in my life.

Max's crew take me by surprise, leaping from a balcony high above the perimeter of where I stand below. They land in waves, all on their feet. My mouth drops open as they close in on me, forming a rowdy circle of spectators. Max holds up a fist and the crowd gets louder, shouting like they're in an army preparing for battle. I stare out at the roaring faces, not surprised to see that they are bruised, broken, and scarred. Some are even missing a few limbs while others are shaped like Olympic athletes and sports models. I can count the number of girls amongst their testosterone strong numbers on one hand.

"I like your fire, Red, but it's not enough. If you want to be part of our team, you've got to prove yourself," Max says, "and we don't discriminate here."

A few guys, all taller and older than me, step forward, cracking their knuckles and flexing their muscles. They look like the type who wear their scars like badges. One guy's eye has cut coming through his brow and down through his milk colored eye, cutting across his cheek and wrapping around the side of his face. He has a few more scratches on his rugged face but he's shaped like a bodybuilder. Another guy is shorter than Mr. Muscles, but he looks like he's just stepped out of a bloody hockey game with a broken nose and a well sculpted body. Next to Hockey is a guy with bright red hair that looks like he should be dominating WWE. These guys are nightmares. They're all in their late teens, early twenties with the bodies of well-seasoned sports pros.

"Choose your opponent."

I look at Max and then I look at the three burly man-boys I'm supposed to pick a fight with. Max explains initiation as a system of ranking. The fight will determine where I rank in the crew and can change with every challenge or fight.

If I beat my opponent, knocking him unconscious, I take their rank and they are ranked below me.

If I get knocked out, my opponent keeps their rank and I am ranked below them. They will train and supervise me until I challenge and beat them or someone else of higher rank.

In a fight, there are no rules.

"You're joking, right? Is this some initiation prank?"

No one laughs. In fact, the cheers have died down with Max's challenge. Everyone watches me. I look at the three guys, studying each of them, praying that while I stall my decision some small miracle will get me out of what's sure to be another beat down. Why didn't I run when I had the chance?

"I'll take her on," comes a soft-spoken voice.

The crowd parts and the three man-boys take a step back. A little girl steps up just a few feet in front of me. She stares up at me, managing to look confident even though she's less than five feet. She's got a baby face with big eyes and a button nose. I'm not so confident in my skills but to pick a fight with Baby Doll seems wrong.

"No. I'm not going to fight her," I tell Max.

He smiles but Baby Doll speaks, "What? You afraid? You should be."

"I don't want to hurt you."

"You won't," she says, dropping down into a fighting stance. She balls up her small fists and her mouth tightens with determination. Her eyes, the largest feature on her face, are unflinching in their focus.

"Chloe has volunteered to challenge you. Do you accept?"

"I'm not a fighter," I blurt.

"You will be if you want to survive," Max warns.

I stare at Chloe. She juts her chin out.

"Fight! Fight! Fight!" the others chant.

"How old are you, anyway?" I ask over all the noise.

"Doesn't matter," she yells back at me

There's no way I can do this. I can't fight a little girl. Even if I beat her, what does that make me look like?

"I'll fight you," I say, turning to face Max.

All cheers and chants cease immediately but my mind screams at me for making such a stupid decision. I stand firm crossing my arms and stare him in the face. If I have to get hurt, I might as well contend with the boss of the system. Even if I lose, his rules will give me the access I need to compile good information for Geezer.

Max's eyes widen a fraction and then narrow. That charming, dumb grin disappears, and his face hardens. I've caught him by surprise, put him on the spot and changed the stakes in the game. We both know there's no way I'll beat him in a fight, especially a game with no rules, but I refuse to look like a coward and to be intimidated.

"Play dumb. Be smart."

I recall Geezer's advice, wondering what he'd think of my impulsive decision. To Max, fighting me would look as bad as me fighting Chloe. If by some miracle I win, then he and all his minions have to do what I say. If he crushes me like everyone knows he can, I still win. He'll be my personal mentor.

"You can't–" Emery starts, but Max holds up a hand to silence him.

"It wouldn't be much of a fight," he warns me.

"You told me to choose."

"From the selected opponents."

"You didn't specify."

"Even if this is a battle of wits, you've got nothing on me," he says.

He gestures to everyone standing behind me.

"You fight me, you fight *them*."

Like an idiot I turn to stare at all the other members of his so-called Fleet. They look ready and willing to fight me if I so much as blink the wrong way in Max's direction. They circle in tightly around me while Max stands on the outside looking in. In a game with no rules, he could just order everyone to fight me. He wouldn't have to lift a finger.

"Coward!" I yell.

Everyone freezes. All eyes go back to Max, but he becomes a blur, reappearing in front of me almost as fast as I spat out my accusation. His nostrils flare and his eyes are wild, but he does a good job of still looking in control. "Spunky, but not too bright are you, Red. You're not good enough to challenge me," he says. "But you will be."

He motions for Chloe.

"Until then, you fight her."

We're back to square one only I'm twice as humiliated, in deeper trouble, and I've apparently lost my right to choose my opponent. Still, I can't bring myself to do it. I open my mouth to refuse but the words don't even escape my lips before the little girl strikes. Her fist connects with my face. I fall to the ground, my heading bumping into the hard floor before I slide against the concrete. Somehow, I manage to sit up, but I have problems focusing. Everything is blurry. Everyone has a twin. Two Chloes come stalking toward me.

"Don't worry. We'll get you into shape," she promises sweetly, right before she delivers the knockout punch.

CHAPTER 31

When I regain consciousness, it takes me a moment to realize where I am. Hard earth surrounds me from above, along the sides, and underneath me. The air is dusty and stale. There's barely room for me to sit up. I'm in the dorms.

Sitting up, I almost hit my head on the wall. I expect to face a circular entrance covered only by a thin sheet and dim light. Instead I face an opening that extends into cool, vast darkness.

"H-hello?"

"It's about time you woke up," comes a small voice.

My eyes are slow to adjust but I'm able to see Chloe lounging a few feet away from me. It feels so small and stuffy in this tunnel, but Chloe is nestled comfortably. I try to level my breathing to keep myself from freaking out as I realize heights aren't my only fear. Claustrophobia threatens to strangle me when I notice that beyond Chloe is more darkness with no end in sight.

Chloe sits up and her large brown eyes study me.

"Sorry I punched you," she says.

I almost forgot that she's the reason my face hurts. I've been beaten by a pre-teen.

"I may have a concussion, but it could always be worse," I say.

"From what I hear, Emery and the others really took a chance on rescuing you," she says. "You could be dead."

I laugh. That's an understatement. After everything that's happened, it's a miracle I'm alive. Chloe misunderstands my laughter and rolls her eyes.

"You are crazy," she grumbles.

"Everyone down here is crazy," I say.

She stares at me for a long moment.

"I guess you're right. We've gotta be a little crazy if we're going to survive, but I think you're crazier than the rest of us."

"Why? Because of what they're saying on the news?" I grumble.

She looks confused. "Wait. What?"

Her large eyes double in size.

"Never mind," I say.

She blinks. "I think you're crazy 'cause you challenged Max when you've clearly got *no* skills."

I shrug off her comment trying not to think of the fact that we're underground in this tight little tunnel.

"Well, I didn't want to fight those man-boys and I didn't want to fight you–"

"Just because I'm a kid doesn't mean I can't take care of myself!" she erupts. Her voice echoes along the pathway in front of us.

"Just how old are you? Twelve?"

"Ten," she snaps. "Almost eleven."

"Even better," I mutter to myself. I got knocked out by an *almost* eleven-year-old.

"I can beat anyone. Max made sure of that."

"So, he does have a heart," I mutter.

Chloe frowns at my sarcasm and rushes at me with lightning speed. Her honey brown hair falls into her face making her eyes look wild.

"Of course, he has a heart! If he didn't none of us would be here."

I hold up my hands in surrender. The space we're sharing isn't big enough for us to break out in a fight, and even if it was, I don't want to get punched out by an almost eleven-year-old again.

"Speaking of here, where are we exactly?"

Chloe blows the hair out of her face with a frustrated huff, but she retreats, scooting backward and lounging along the dirt wall with her feet crossed and her hands behind her head. She looks completely at home underground.

"The dorms of course. Each room is a tunnel that leads out to another exit if our base is ever compromised. I like sleeping near the exit route. The boys are loud sleepers and…" she hesitates, looking a little sheepish.

"What?" I press.

"Well, there aren't many girls or kids my age."

"I get it," I tell her.

"I like it here, too," she continues.

"Well, I don't. How do I get out of here?"

I've been trying to ignore the fact that I'm below ground, holed up in a space the size of a grave plot, but it's starting to get to me.

"You don't," she says.

My skin is clammy, dusty, and I swear something is crawling on me. I try to even my breathing but all I can think about is how stale the air is and how confined I am.

"What?"

Chloe remains calm. Her eyes are closed, and she looks half asleep. "I said, you don't."

"I thought you said this leads to an exit."

"It does, but you're not going. I knocked you out at your initiation so now you have to do what I say until you can beat me. It's the rules," she says, and I can't help but think she feels pretty satisfied with herself.

"I don't care about your rules right now. Get me out of here!"

The air is thick. My throat tightens, and my mouth is dry. Chloe sits up, watching me quietly. "Do you know how long it took me to drag you here? We aren't going anywhere."

My eyes adjust more in the dark and I see the outline of Chloe's face enough to pick up on her surly frown. "I can't just sit here."

She shrugs, "Well, I've got time."

I try to control my breathing but instead of breathing I feel like I'm gasping. The more I try to control it, the more erratic it becomes.

She sighs, "Oh, alright."

She lunges at me in the middle of my panic attack. I see her fist coming at my face and barely manage to evade her, slamming hard against the wall to my right. With perfect control, Chloe stops momentum and remains on her knees with her fist frozen where my head had been only seconds before.

"If you want out of here, you've got to go through me, and the only way you can do that is if you beat me."

She cracks her knuckles, one at a time. She stretches her neck and her shoulders pop when she rolls them. Being shorter than me, she has the advantage in such a tight space. She has more room to maneuver. She moves behind me, pulls me backward by the shirt and propels us into the dark opening.

I would scream but all I can manage is a mouthful of air as we fall into cold water. No longer in her grasp, I scramble to my feet, pushing my hair out of my face as my eyes struggle to adjust to a new degree of darkness. I've barely found my footing when Chloe comes at me again. By the time I make out her slim, small frame, she's diving at me, headfirst. She slams into my abdomen with such force that on impact I'm flying through the air. I crash into a hard rock wall. My vision sparks with a fuzzy collage of lights. I shake my head to clear my sight in time to see Chloe's fists coming at me. I dodge. She moves faster. Before I know it, I'm caught in a whirlwind of non-stop assault. I'm her punching bag, and there's nothing I can do about it. I'm getting beat by a child and there's no one around to make her stop. No one but me. I have to stop her.

The little girl might be better in a fight thanks to her training with Max. She might even be stronger, but I can be smarter. With her next few punches, I let myself fall to the ground, submerging myself in water that covers everything but my face. Maybe if I stop trying to avoid her hits, she'll stop hurting me. Maybe if I pretend to be unconscious, she'll take a break. A swift, hard kick to the side of my abdomen shocks my nervous system as water splashes up my nose and mouth, muting my cry of pain.

"The Immortals won't stop attacking you because you're down!" she screams, "They want to kill you."

She kicks me again. "You just going to lay there and take it? Come on!"

She kicks again. "You've got all that power inside you and this is what you're going to do with it?"

She kicks me so hard I curl up on my hands and knees, coughing uncontrollably. I'm pretty sure the thick wet stuff spewing out of my mouth is blood.

"Still think you can hurt me? Get up and fight! Get up!"

Maybe playing possum isn't the best solution. If she keeps hitting me, I won't be able to think straight for much longer, and if I can't think straight, I won't be able to defend myself. I won't be able to get out of here. Panic stirs within me but so does anger. I take in my surroundings. Chloe is right. I've got all this potential. It's time to use it.

"Get up," she says.

Chloe's foot seems to push through the water in slow motion. I hear the water splash and flow around the force of her movement. I know if I don't do something now, this is it. I scramble to the nearest wall, stealing a moment to recover and center my mind. Anxiety transforms into adrenaline. My body goes numb to pain, replaced with an electric strength I've never consciously felt before. Chloe lunges forward, fists ready. She is wild, quick, and the force behind her oncoming punch promises unconsciousness if she hits me. I feel the air around us, like static, charged with power and force. The closer she gets, the heavier the feeling becomes.

Her knuckles graze my cheek, but I dodge just in time to miss the full brunt of her punch. With her back to me, I'm at an advantage. I use her momentum against her, pushing my elbow into her back. She slams face-first into the wall and falls back into the water.

With the air still charged with power and adrenaline still running through my veins, I lift Chloe's light, unconscious form and take to the tunnels and back to the dorms before I burn out and collapse.

CHAPTER 32

"What happened?"

Someone shakes me out of a delirious haze. I bite back tears as awareness takes hold and pain courses through my battered body. My clothes are soaked, stained, and ripped. I can't stop shaking. I don't know if I'm coming down with some kind of virus or if I'm in shock, but all I want to do is curl up in a ball and rock myself into deep unconsciousness. For a moment I forget where I am, what I've endured, and what I've done.

"What happened?" I blink, opening my eyes, feeling like my head could split in half at any moment. After battling a ten-year-old, I'm covered in bruises, blood, cuts, and scrapes.

"Stop shaking me," I slur.

I'm not mad at Chloe. As ruthless as she seems, she's still a little girl. This is someone else's fault. My eyes focus. Max stoops over me, his fingers digging into my shoulders as I try to collect myself off the dusty dorm ground. He's shadowed by his entourage of tough guys who are all familiar to me now: Emery, Tattoo, and Mohawk. Behind those haters are at least five other guys.

"I won't ask again," Max says.

We lock gazes. His eyes blaze with promise of violence if he doesn't get his way.

"You did this. You put her up to this," I say.

Seeing that I'm fully conscious, Max pushes me away from him and stands at his full height. I manage to keep from cracking my head by catching myself, using my elbows to steady me, before standing slowly to my unsteady feet.

"What did you do?" Max demands.

"You told her to attack me."

His eyes widen and his nostrils flare. "She's a kid. If you hurt her, I swear I'll–"

"I played by your rules. She knocked me out. I knocked her out. We're even. Now her rank is *mine*."

He takes a step toward me. I brace myself.

"Max!"

I recognize Chloe, only because her soggy form is the one pulling Max back.

"Max, I'm okay," Chloe says, staring at him with a wide-eyed vulnerability that I hadn't seen in the cave.

Max's back is turned to me. I can't see his facial expression, but I can read his body language. His rigid stance relaxes and his shoulders hunch as he bends down to inspect the drenched and muddy girl. She looks her age when she's with him, not at all like the hardened, little old soul I faced.

"I'm okay, really," She repeats and then looks over his shoulder in my direction. "How are you, Red? I beat you pretty bad."

All eyes are on me now, but the lethal looks are replaced with marbles for eyes. Looks like I'm not the only one confused.

"I almost killed her before she fought back but you should've seen her, Max!"

She almost beat me unconscious but to say she nearly killed me is an exaggeration.

Max looks at us. "Is it true? Did she knock you out?"

Chloe's eyes widen to an impossible size, making her look even more vulnerable, but she seems more mystified than ashamed.

"I kinda knocked myself out, but you should've seen her!"

She recounts the whole encounter as if it was some exciting sports play. When she's done, mystified expressions spread. Only Max seems unimpressed. Despite the grandiose descriptions of the events, I'm left feeling a little ashamed.

"I came at her with a strong punch. You should've seen her face. She just got real calm and dodged me, smacked me right into the wall. I hit face first. I blacked out – just for a minute but–she's amazing."

Max's face tightens again. Chloe notices it too, and stammers on, "I mean, she's not as amazing as you are. Not even close. She's okay for a newbie."

Max glares at me. "You've got Chloe's rank now. We'll see just how amazing you are."

I look at Chloe. Her hair shrouds her face, so I can't read her expression. Still, I offer her my best smile. My lip is split so my smile quickly becomes a wince.

"I'm definitely not as amazing as you," I whisper to her.

Chloe lifts her head enough for me to see her eyes brighten. It's the last thing I see before someone puts a hood over my head. They still don't trust me enough to let me see their compound. I don't waste what little is left of my energy fighting or demanding answers on what they're going to do with me. I'll figure it out sooner or later. I just need to be prepared. I need to save up my energy for what really matters. Geezer's advice becomes my mantra.

Play dumb but be smart.

I can't beat them using my strength or skill. If I'm going to survive their training and get information, I need to be much smarter than they think I am. I'm amazed that Max and his crew aren't road-running, though it's not long before we stop moving. Someone removes my head covering and tosses me off their shoulder. I land on my tired feet and squint at my surroundings. To be underground, the room we're in is bright and large. Outside of the dirt floors and rock walls, the room is a well-constructed gymnasium. There are all types of exercise machines lining the perimeter of the room from exercise bikes, treadmills, weights, punching bags, and even a much larger basketball court. My guess is that we aren't here to work on my cardio or strength.

Max leads everyone towards the center of the room, to the boxing ring. Reluctantly I let them prod me along. Max climbs into the ring with one graceful motion and smiles down at me. I'm not fooled by his pearly whites. His eyes are fueled with vindication.

"You used a few parlor tricks on a kid, and you think that makes you tough now?"

I wince. That sounds just as bad as I was afraid it would.

"You've got Chloe's rank now. It's top level stuff, but everyone knows not to mess with her."

I know for a fact that Chloe's a tough girl, but I doubt her skills are the only reason people don't mess with her.

"I think the bruises and blood on my body speak for themselves, but I had no intention of fighting her," I say.

It's not like I'm proud I won a fight against a ten-year-old.

Max ignores me. "Step into the ring."

I look around the room at the dozens of guys of various size and strength. Are we really about to do this? Mohawk shoves me forward.

"Move," he snarls.

I stumble forward, tossing him a glare as I awkwardly crawl underneath the ropes and struggle to pull myself up. Someone snickers. My face flushes, but I ignore them.

"As I said before, we don't discriminate. You beat Chloe fair and square–"

"You know that fight never would've happened if you hadn't encouraged it," I interrupt.

My words echo in the silence of the crowd. Max's blue eyes dilate into something far from charming. He blinks away the violent look and charisma spews out of his mouth once again.

"Seeing that your new rank is a pretty high position, I'm afraid we have a problem," he says. "They want what you've got."

He points in the direction of five guys standing apart from the rest of the crowd. They each give their threatening peacock stances, but I've seen so much lately I'm underwhelmed.

"You know, if a ten-year-old is your best fighter, these guys must be a bunch of punks."

Max's eyes light up, but he plays off his surprise, shaking his head. "You really are crazy, Red."

Maybe I am. When I turn my attention back to my competitors, they've already entered the ring. They circle around me, cracking their knuckles and putting on a show of just how tough they are. I put on a show of my own, bouncing on my feet, jabbing at the air. With each motion my body screams for me to stop, but I ignore it, learning to embrace the pain. I have a feeling it's going to be a lot worse from here, but I'd rather get it over with than stand around worrying.

"Who's first?" I challenge.

Max grunts and his eyes get that surge of brightness, that spark of crazy glee that lets me know he enjoys this more than anyone else here. "All of them."

I'm not expecting that. When they all charge at me, coming from all sides, it's hard for me to gain focus. My mind is overwhelmed. All I can do is cringe and curl up in a standing fetal position, squeezing my eyes shut and preparing for pain.

Nothing happens.

I open my eyes to find my five challengers standing around me like sentinels, barricading me in place. Each of them have their arms crossed, glaring at me, but no one throws a punch. I punch at the guy closest to me and kick him in the shin. While my foot meets some resistance as it collides with well-toned, muscular flesh, my too slow punch doesn't reach its target. The guy catches my fist, swallowing it with one meaty hand. I swing my other fist. He catches it easily in his other hand. While I'm impressed with his reflexes, the feeling is definitely not mutual. He seems bored with my lack of skill. He's big in a steroid, body builder kind of way, so I can see his angry veins ticking when he frowns at me. He looks back to Max, wordlessly begging to end me like we both know he can. Max shakes his head, so Steroids lets me go. All five challengers take a step back from me as Max steps forward.

"Let this be a lesson. When you're in a real fight, you don't have time for tricks. Your real training starts tomorrow morning. Until then, rest, heal, and watch your back."

Max takes off and so do the others, but they don't leave me behind. A blur of a figure snatches me up and speeds back to the dorms, leaving me behind in a whirlwind of dust at the door to Max's room. I stumble inside feeling shell-shocked. Shaking my head, the stupor lifts enough to allow me to move to the bed before I collapse into the fold of plush cushions and blankets. Barely a breath away from falling into sweet sleep, my eyes go wide. As much as I want to, I can't go to sleep. I could've easily avoided all this torture and drama. Max gave me an out, but Geezer's insane request is why I'm here. For once, I can be useful instead of being the girl who always needs saving.

"You've got a job to do," I mutter to myself.

While everyone else is out doing whatever it is they do, I pick myself out of bed, as painful as it is, and search Max's suite. I don't know what I'm looking for, but I figure if it's something important it will catch my attention.

"Please let me find *something*," I say.

I scan his desk and my fingers dance across random items, tentatively feeling around for anything that might be of use. I wish I knew how to hack into electronics but since I don't, I leave the computer alone. There's a daunting stack of papers piled on Max's desk. I give them a noncommittal once over. They look like printouts of financial records and my eyes widen when is see all the zeroes attached to the number at the beginning of the account. It looks like Shax really brings in some money.

"Don't get distracted," I tell myself, pulling away from the records and going to another pile of papers.

The next stack is a collection of newspaper clips and internet article printouts. I pick up a handful and scan through them. They range from random murders, odd incidents from freak acts of nature, to freaky people doing crazy things. The articles that catch my eye are all the ones on Houdini – his exploits and accomplishments, and information about his tragic death. While all the printouts look recent, some of the content is photocopied from older sources. Maybe these articles have some degree of relevance? The thought gets solidified when I see some items are highlighted and underlined. Max has been studying Houdini. I take a few articles and set them to the side. Maybe Geezer can make sense of it.

I scan the desk for anything else but decide that if he's creating some nefarious plan, all the information will be on his computer, locked away from prying eyes like mine. There's a switch blade open and gleaming underneath the chandelier light. I take that too, hoping I won't have to use it, but grateful I have something to defend myself with if I need to.

I look around the entire room again. Maybe there's a safe or a secret passageway. Everyone else has an escape route attached to their sleeping space. It would be inconvenient if Max didn't have one too. I eye his bookshelf, feeling around the books for a secret trigger or button. From what I've seen of Max, I understand he's arrogant for a good reason. The guy is calculative and smart. He's turned a seedy club into a million-dollar business and owns pretty much all of New York City's underground, not to mention a huge following of loyal, highly trained spies and fighters at his beck and call.

What's Max up to?

"Looking for a good book to pass the time?"

I jump when I hear his voice, and a few books on the shelf topple to the floor, revealing a plain wooden shelf. I turn around and offer Max a shrug.

"I was just looking for a secret passageway to your evil lair," I say.

I've never been a good liar, so I tell the truth with all the humor I can muster.

A slow smile spreads across Max's lips. "Don't worry. I didn't expect you to mind your own business. Though I'm sure you know what happens to curious girls, don't you?"

I turn my head back to the bookshelves pretending to study what he likes to read.

"I've heard of curious cats," I offer as some of the books catch my attention.

Machiavelli's *The Prince*, Thomas Paine's *Commonsense*. Sun Tzu's *Art of War*. *Mien Kampf by* Hitler. These books are mostly required texts for high school and college. There are no Sports Illustrated magazines, no comic books, graphic novels, or any light reading whatsoever. Most of the reading material on his shelf is authored by dead guys.

"Julius Caesar!" I exclaim.

I pick it off the shelf and study the fancy cover design.

"A personal favorite?" Max wonders.

"Shakespeare's okay."

He watches me for a second before striding up to me, taking the book out of my hand and returning it to its proper space on the shelf. "I read it to remind myself that the people closest to me are my greatest threat."

Barely an inch away from me, he stares into my eyes. I can't help wondering if he's keeping me close because he knows why I'm really here.

"Keep your friends close and your enemies closer, huh?" I say.

"Sometimes the people you call friends and brothers are your greatest enemies."

I relax a little. Max isn't talking about me. He's thinking about K.O. and how he left him to die in Kansas. I'm just a pawn that Max mistakenly believes K.O. wants.

"Oh, here's another one I recognize," I say, reaching to pull *Lord of the Flies* from the shelf. Max puts his hand on top of mine to prevent me from removing the book. He slides the text back on the shelf.

"Forget the books. Do you want to see my secret lair or not?"

My mouth drops open, but I recover fast, "It wouldn't be a secret if you showed me."

"Consider it a privilege of rank," he says.

I don't respond but I store that fact in my mind. High ranking teammates get more intel and privileges within the organization. That means Chloe and Emery are at least two people who know more about things than others.

"Well? Do you want to see it?"

I nod, not able to trust my voice.

His hand slides off mine and back across the line of books, stopping at Machiavelli's *The Prince*. He pushes the book inward until there is a distinct clicking noise. The bookcase pushes back on smooth gears to reveal a descending set of stairs.

"Ladies first," he says.

Fearing he might try to push me down the stairs or lock me in some underground dungeon, I shake my head. "Lead the way."

Max chuckles before jogging down the stairs. Reluctantly, I follow him.

The room automatically lights up thanks to motion detecting electronic lights along the wood planked walls. Plush burgundy carpet lines the floors. Televisions cover the entire left and right walls revealing real-time camera feed. In the center of the room is a fancy black leather recliner. On the thick, fluffy arms of the chair are a panel of buttons. Beyond the high-tech gadgets and comfort is nothing but black expanse.

"If you take the tunnel straight ahead it leads to the subway station," he explains.

He strides to the center of the room and sits in the fancy chair. He presses a button and the exit route straight ahead begins to close. A thick brick wall descends from the opening of the cave. A large white board hangs from the brick wall and it is covered in news articles, pictures of people and crime scenes, and notes handwritten in print so sloppy it almost looks like hieroglyphics.

"Chloe calls this my spy zone," he says with a little chuckle. "This is where I spend my time when I'm not with the others."

My eyes wander to the camera feed. He watches everything and everyone. On the right wall there is camera feed from within the tunnels. My eyes zoom on one stream of video feed in particular. Emery has a picture of Max on the wall in what looks like a rec room with a pool table, couch, and flat screen television. He's pointing at it. It looks like he's fussing at it while a few other people laugh. He picks up a handful of darts and uses Max's picture for target practice. Chloe is in the gym by herself training on the exercise equipment. Then I see something very familiar. It's video feed from Stax. It shows me sitting at a table eating pizza wearing raggedy clothes with big bushy hair. It's the video feed from the night I first arrived at Max's underground compound. The video stops on an image of Geezer talking to me.

Max knows. I feel him watching me and his silence is painful. I force myself to meet his gaze and find he looks a little too calm for my comfort.

"If there was something Geezer wanted to know, all he had to do was ask."

He sounds convincing but it can't really be that simple with Max.

"All I've ever wanted was for me and every other Errant to be free to live without someone trying to kill us all the time. No one is invincible, not even the Posers. They have a weakness and I plan to use it to destroy them."

"Posers?"

"The Immortals go by a few names, but Poser stuck. They know how to manipulate the system, how to infiltrate the most powerful and influential places in society," he explains.

He's right. Santos pretended to be a psychiatrist and a police officer to get access to me. He's obviously got money and connections. How do you fight someone that can control everything?

"Then there's the way they move when we road-run. Normal people are at a standstill. We move too fast for them to see. Not them. Posers can't quite keep up with our movements but they're good at predicting our patterns and anticipating what we'll do. When the rest of the world freezes, they can make small movements that can catch us unaware. They've lived for centuries. They've had a lot of time to perfect their skills. We don't have that time. That's why I train everyone so hard."

I shake my head. "How do you kill someone that can't die? How can we win?"

Max leans forward in his seat. "Geezer and Ollie probably don't know this since they're too busy running. Our enemies are immortal because they're linked in some kind of cluster. As long as one of them lives, they all reset in perfect, peak condition every new day, one minute after midnight. But they're not exactly invincible."

"They sound pretty invincible to me," I say.

"It won't be easy, but it's possible to defeat them. We can either pick them off one by one and destroy their bodies so they can't reanimate. Or we could kill them all in less than 24 hours. If there's no one left alive from their cluster, they can't reset."

I blink, trying to take in even more startling news.

Max sighs. "All the stacks of papers you saw on my desk are research. I'm trying to figure out who they are. Anonymity keeps them safe. If I know who they are, we can find them and kill them. Picking them off will take some time, time that we may not have. I want to flush them out of hiding, get them all in one place, and end this for good."

Just like that, Max tells me everything I need to know. His plan is ambitious. It's dangerous and near impossible. If they really are as old as he thinks they are, there's no way we can outsmart them. With everything that we can do, I can't help feeling like our powers still aren't enough.

Max touches my hand. "Stakes are high, Red, and we might not make it. But we're already dying."

He presses another button and the video feed from the underground compound disappears replaced by horrific images that burn into my memory.

"These are the other footage we recovered from their prison. This is what's in store for all of us if we don't make a stand and fight. This could've been me. It could've been you. If we don't do something, this will be all of us in the end."

I stare at the images, all of corpses. As much as I want to, I can't look away until Max finally switches the cameras back to real-time footage. I'm terrified. I'm enraged.

"Tell Geezer everything I've told you. Tell him I've found a way to get rid of our Poser problem once and for all. He and the others, yourself included, are welcome to stop running and join the cause," Max says, "and have Doc take a look at you. Chloe did a number on you."

CHAPTER 33

$\mathcal{I}$ use Max's exit to the subway to visit Doc's clinic in Chinatown. The tunnel isn't as complex as the rest of the compound. It's a 20-minute stroll, enough time for me to digest everything Max told me. The more I think about what we're up against, the harder it is to breathe. Anxiety forges a path through every cell in my body, until it rests like a block of cement against my chest. When I walk through the doors of the clinic, Doc's eyes widen and he hugs me.

"Foolish girl, where have you been? We've all been worried sick."

He leads me to one of the rooms. Steadying me carefully by the shoulders, he helps me onto one of the medical beds. "What is the first rule of survival, Savannah?"

"We can't always run," I manage to say, my voice a trembling whisper.

Doc's dark eyes soften and his forehead creases.

"Tell me what happened. Where were you?"

"Call Geezer. Just Geezer. I need to see him now."

I must fall asleep or maybe I pass out. I'm exhausted. Who would blame me after everything that's been going on? I wake up with two sets of eyes studying me. Doc is upset with the state of my health. Among a few minor fractures, some sprains, tears, internal bleeding and bruising, I'm dehydrated and a little anemic. Geezer shushes the older man.

"You're not going to like it, but I'll explain everything later," Geezer tells him.

"No. You'll explain now."

I close my eyes, deciding to sleep while I can. I'm not in the mood to hear Geezer and Doc fuss about my safety or what's right or wrong about what I'm doing. They don't get that privilege anymore. No one does. After what I've been through and the things I've seen, I have a sudden clarity and conviction. I guess the old saying is true. The things that didn't kill me have made me much stronger than I could ever imagine. The scars are worth the strength I've gained.

The second time I wake up, things are tense between Doc and Geezer but they're not arguing anymore.

"Savannah, how are you feeling?" Doc asks.

I sit up. "How long have I been out?"

"About a day," Geezer says.

I really want to go back to sleep, which only adds to my frustration. I'm grateful for the accelerated healing, but I don't have time to sleep. Doc wants me to eat something and drink two gallons of water before we discuss anything.

"We're wasting time. I'm not eating until I've said what I need to say."

Doc gets quiet, but his disappointed daddy look speaks for him. I look away from him and focus on Geezer. His concern mirrors Doc's, but I can tell his curiosity trumps concern.

"What did they do to you?" Doc whispers.

"They told me the truth. All of it. Which is more than I can say for any of you. After I say what I have to say I hope you understand that running won't solve anything. You can't imagine, you didn't see ...the things they did–"

I didn't come here to cry but I do. Doc and Geezer don't seem to mind. They stand on either side of me, holding my hands until I can talk again. I tell them everything, starting with the night Santos posed as a police officer and abducted me from the custody of the real police. When I'm done telling them about Max's underground city, his camera system, and the video feed from the Immortal compound, their mood is just as somber as mine.

"You've got to find out more details on what he's planning," Geezer says, sounding much more urgent than the first time he asked me to spy on Max. Only this time I won't have to spy. All I have to do is ask.

Doc objects. "This is too dangerous! You know how Max is, how he uses people."

Geezer frowns. "But if we don't find out what he's doing, a lot of people could get hurt or worse."

"Even if you do figure out his plans in time, what will you do to stop him?" Doc demands.

I eat as promised, after I've told them my discoveries, while they argue about what I should and shouldn't do. I don't tell them that I already know what I'm going to do. When I'm done eating, I leave without word or warning. I run as fast as I can, determined that I won't be afraid to make my own decisions and my own mistakes.

I return to Max's compound using the subway trail. I stand outside knowing he's inside and probably watching me. Sure enough, the wall lifts and I find Max sitting in his leather chair studying the camera feed.

"Well?"

"Geezer wants to know exactly what you're planning. So do I."

Max looks up from the cameras. His eye twitches but he smiles.

"Not yet," he says.

"Not good enough," I say.

His jaw tightens. "I've got a plan to flush them all out. Anonymity gives them advantage. So do the fat bank accounts they've built over the centuries. They use their money and thousands of years of knowledge to connect to people in power and make the system work for them. They're masters at infiltration and manipulation. "

I can't help but smirk.

Max frowns, "What?"

"That's what some people say about you. The manipulation part, anyway."

He doesn't get upset or try to deny it. He just shrugs his shoulders like its old news. "If anonymity is their advantage, that's what we have to target. I'm learning who they are and where they come from. It's not easy but I'm persistent. We've got an inside man giving us the information we need to lure them into one place. If I threaten to expose them, they'll come out of hiding. We trap them, and we kill them all."

Max's plan sounds like it's literally us against the world. Still, something bothers me even more. I don't understand why there's a fight in the first place.

"They have everything. Why do they hate us so much? Why do they want to kill us?" I ask.

Max sighs, "My source told me something about a legend. They took a pledge to protect humans and save the world from any force that threatens the natural balance and order of existence. Apparently, vampires, werewolves, and other monsters were real at one time. Until they made them extinct. We're next."

I shake my head. "You've gotta be kidding me."

Max shrugs. "We're last on their list. If we don't act soon, they'll do the same to us."

"But they're not exactly normal either. Once they get rid of us- ."

"There won't be anyone to stop them," Max finishes.

CHAPTER 34

We spar like we're gladiators and work out more than celebrities. At the end of the day, if we aren't thirsty, hungry, bruised, sore, and exhausted, we haven't worked hard enough. When I'm not training, I'm gorging on Shax's pizza. I think of Rox and her lectures on food. So I force myself to give up the pizza afterwards, trading in dough, marinara, and seasoned cheese for salads and lean meats. Max lets me keep the bedroom since he spends most of his time in his spy zone. He attributes it to privileges associated with my rank, but I don't see anyone else sleeping in a private suite.

I remember Chloe and how she likes to sleep burrowed deep in her dorm tunnel near the escape exit. I can't sleep in a nice cozy bed knowing she's nestled up in some dirt tunnel. I invite her to stay with me in Max's suite. When we aren't exhausted from training, we talk through the night until one or both of us falls asleep. She gives me training tips and I listen.

"Max calls us The Fleet because we move so fast and because we're fighters," she says, "He says our lives are fleeting. Whatever that means."

There goes our super cool comic book name. It's cliché, but I like it.

"Max says that when we're injured or super tired from using our *extras*, our body pushes us to sleep so it can work double time to make us feel better faster," she tells me. "Our extras take a lot of time to recover from. That's why Max doesn't like us to use them unless we have to."

Extras is Chloe's way of describing all the special things we can do.

"Max says blackouts happen when someone is in denial and doesn't know how to accept their extras," she says.

"I have blackouts sometimes," I tell her.

She shrugs, "You haven't had any since I've known you. Guess you're not in denial anymore."

I smile, "I guess not."

Chloe talks a lot about Max and I learn early that she has a crush on him. She even confesses that she hopes to marry him when she grows up. She's already got plans for their wedding. "We'll have our wedding on an airplane and skydive to our reception in the Amazon rainforest."

I let her talk and laugh with her but silently pray her crush is just a faze. Still, the more time I spend with him, the more I understand his appeal. When he's not talking about killing the hunters, Max can be a charming guy. He's open, honest and confident and his smile almost makes me forget his flaws. Almost. He's so different from K.O, but thinking of K.O. makes my chest ache. It's been so long since I've seen him or the others. Even Geezer's been silent since I met him last at Doc's.

"I've been meaning to ask you something. What's with all the Houdini stuff?" I ask Max one day to distract myself from thinking about K.O.

His hand hovers over Machiavelli's *The Prince* to open his spy zone, but he stops and turns to look at me . His eyes are bright and excited. "I think Houdini was an Errant. I've been studying his tricks, trying to tweak them. It might come in handy one day."

He goes to his desk, opens a drawer, and pulls out a pile of thick ropes. "Maybe I could show you a thing or two?"

My cheeks heat up. As direct as Max can be, gauging his mood is the biggest challenge. I can't tell if he's joking, flirting, or genuinely serious.

"I don't think so."

He shrugs. "Too bad. I was hoping you'd help me scare Emery. I don't appreciate him using my face for target practice."

I almost change my mind, but I laugh and shake my head. Max tosses the rope on the desk and walks up to me. "It's nice hearing you laugh for a change."

"There hasn't been much to laugh about lately," I admit.

He smiles, stepping closer to close the space between us. "We'll have to change that."

He leans forward. I back up. "I thought I wasn't your type of girl."

His smile widens. "Says who?"

I step back again, tripping over my shoestrings. "It doesn't really matter. I just– don't make things awkward."

He grabs my hand to steady me. "You're right."

"Right about what?" I ask, pulling my hand out of his.

He steps away from me, turning down the charm. "You're more of Ollie's type. I just wanted to make sure you were good enough for my brother. After we kill Santos and his friends, you two should make things official."

My cheeks are on fire and the ache in my chest goes from sore to agonizing.

Max winks at me. "Don't worry. You passed the test."

He opens the entrance to his Cave and disappears down the stairs.

*****

I fall into a steady routine and the underground begins to feel like home, especially since my rank is good and I get so many perks and privileges. I get manager shifts at Stax and a nice salary, a salary I'm dedicating to pay for all the clothes and food I've stolen since I've been on the run. Max's system makes me feel like less of a fugitive and more like I'm part of a community. I almost forget why I'm here and that not everyone is as friendly as Chloe. Max helps me remember one day after training. He gathers everyone in the gymnasium for a big announcement.

Max stands in the center of the arena and monologues like a politician. "Some time ago I was captured by the hunters. I could've died but your bravery and your unity made the difference. There were many who were not as fortunate as Red and I."

I feel a few glances straying in my direction. The looks are curious but far from friendly. I ignore them and try to focus as Max continues to drone on.

"When you saved my life, you destroyed that horrible place, but we will not stop there. The hunters will not go unpunished for all the lives they've destroyed. We will end them."

Everyone cheers.

"We have an advantage over the hunters because we have one another. There's strength in our numbers, strength in our cause. They've hunted us for years. They tried to erase us. It's our turn now."

The cheers and excitement are deafening, but I feel like screaming. We're not going to a party. We're going to war.

"What's the plan?" Emery asks.

Max dismisses everyone but the top five ranked Fleet, so he can talk strategy. As number four in ranking, I'm included in the meeting. My position is a bit intimidating considering that most of the top ranked members are familiar faces I still don't get along with. Though Chloe's number five, she isn't expected to come to our meeting. Her rank is only so high to provide her with an extra level of privilege and safety.

I do my best to put on my game face and listen closely to their planning. I try to keep my mouth shut and my opinions to myself, but the more they talk, the more I realize Doc and Geezer were right to be worried. They have history with Max. They know him better than anyone here. They've seen him talk crowds up before. Because of him a lot of people died in Kansas. Though everyone's a little tightlipped about the particulars, I'm sure he's about to make the same mistakes.

When Emery and his team raided the hunter compound to rescue us, they recovered some vital information on the hunters and struck an unlikely alliance with someone who has access to the hunters. The informant is one of their major weapons against the enemy, but Max refuses to provide details on who that informant is. He's got this elaborate scheme that he and the informant put together. To pull it off will take nothing short of a miracle. If one thing goes wrong, we're going to lose a lot of lives.

"Our inside man will inform the hunters that we plan on exposing them with the information we have. Our man will tell them where to find us and when they come for us, we'll be waiting. They'll come in pairs but never all united together. It would be too risky for them. Kill who you can and burn the bodies. Lure those you can't to the abandoned charter school. This is the only time it will be acceptable for you to run," Max informs us, staring at me pointedly with his last few words.

My cheeks heat up as the others laugh at me.

He presents the pictures of the hunters we'll be facing. There are six men and one woman, all from diverse backgrounds, and all of them look lethal in their own right. He points at Santos.

"Our inside man says they call Santos 'Rey' in their circles, or 'King'. If he's the type of man I think he is, he won't be chasing after us. He'll send the others out while he remains at another one of their bases. Thankfully, we've got his coordinates. I'll need an elite team to infiltrate his place and take him down. If you can't, and if everything else fails, we've got another surprise for them."

"Why would we lead them to the charter school? It's connected to our underground network," I point out.

Max smiles, "As I said, we'll have a surprise waiting for them."

"What makes you think we can pull this off? You're putting a lot of people's lives at risk. And who is this informant? Can we really trust him or is he setting us up?" I ask.

Max's jaw ticks and he cuts me a sharp look, warning me to be quiet. Still, he answers. "Trust me. He's got some skin in the game. He hates them as much as we do. But the less you know about him, the better."

"What's the surprise we're leaving at the school?" I dare to ask.

Max clears his throat and looks past me to the other ranked members.

"You know, Red, I like your enthusiasm and your spunk but, before we continue this conversation, there's something else we need to discuss."

They form a circle around me.

"Jamie, come in," Max commands.

Mohawk walks into the room, striding forward until we're standing face to face. He looks me right in the eye.

"Challenge, girlie."

My mouth goes dry, and I glance at Max. "Guys, I know we don't get along, but I'm not our enemy. We don't have time for this."

"Fight! Fight!" the guys chant.

I look at Max again, but he shrugs, "I told you to watch your back."

This is really happening, and it only gets worse when his pal Tattoo steps up beside him. I've fought these two before and it wasn't pretty. I might not be stronger than them, but I've got to be smarter. There are no rules to this challenge.

I smile at the two guys who are too cowardly to fight me one on one. Two can play that game.

"I accept your challenge."

They both come charging at me, growling with fists swinging. I duck just in time to see Tattoo punch Mohawk in the jaw. I don't hesitate. I maneuver around them and make a run for the exit. Bursting into the halls I know where my secret weapon will be. I just need to get to my destination faster than my challengers. Sheer adrenaline kicks my speed into overdrive, and within a matter of seconds, I find myself at the dorms banging on the door to Max's room.

"Chloe!"

Mid-knock she opens the door.

"Help!"

She looks confused. I must've interrupted a good nap, but when she sees Mohawk and Tattoo barreling behind me, her eyes light up.

"I'm in."

They both dive at me but Chloe moves fast, grabbing Mohawk by the collar and shoving him against the nearest wall. Dust stirs up and his back makes a painful cracking noise under her strength. I duck as Tattoo tries to grab me by the shoulder. He stumbles into the doorway, hitting his head against the wood.

"You take the big boy. That one, challenged me," I tell Chloe, giving Mohawk my meanest glare. We switch opponents.

"Are you challenging me, Dawson?" Chloe asks.

Tattoo stumbles to a halt and stares at Chloe.

"I-I… Chloe, I can't!"

If there's anything I've learned, no one messes with Chloe. Messing with Chloe is like messing with Max and no one wants to do that. I guess Tattoo isn't a complete idiot.

Chloe groans, "No fun!"

She jumps up, swings her fist and delivers a knockout punch to Tattoo. She cracks her knuckles and sets her eyes on Mohawk.

I shake my head. "I've got this one."

Crowds form in the narrow hallway as people watch. Max stands in front of everyone else, surveying our fight with an unreadable expression. I'm not as fast or as confident as Chloe. Our fight lasts way too long but at least it's a fair fight. Or it is until Mohawk pulls out a switchblade. I don't see it in time to dodge the attack and he slices my abdomen. Thanks to practice with Chloe, I'm able to disarm him and get close enough to knee him hard in the groin. His eyes cross and he crumples to the ground. I pin him there and enforce the sleeper hold on him until he stops struggling and passes out. I roll off him, exhausted from the battle and the fresh wound. Max takes note of the unconscious boys.

"Congratulations. You keep your rank. Now let's get to work."

I move to follow him back to the gym. He stalks down the hall. I struggle to match his pace. Then I realize the wet stain coming from my shirt. I'm bleeding. A dark curtain falls over my line of vision and my head feels light. I fall but I don't feel the impact. I hear Chloe scream my name, but I can't make out much else. As bad as the stab wound hurts, it feels so good to finally get the best of those two bullies. I slip into unconsciousness with a smile on my face.

***

By the time I'm conscious again, I find myself in the all too familiar makeshift hospital room of sterile, silver medical tools and a stiff bed. I'm at Doc's again but I'm not alone. Chloe is half asleep, slumped in a chair by my bedside. When she notices I'm awake she brushes her own fatigue aside and leaps to her feet.

"I didn't know what to do. You were bleeding everywhere, and it wouldn't stop. Max told me you come here sometimes. I made him bring you."

I smile at her, thinking that not many people can make Max do anything.

"Hey Doc!" she screams at the top of her lungs.

A black and white blur speeds into the room. When the figure slows, I see Doc standing with windswept hair, breathing hard, and sweating. He looks close to panicking until he realizes I'm awake. He takes a deep breath and shakes his head.

"Savannah, we've got to stop meeting like this. When Chloe showed up with you at my doorstep you were hemorrhaging. You could've died."

I try to sit up, but my head gets light and the room spins. The wound in my abdomen burns. I carefully lay back down and close my eyes.

"Good to see you too, Doc. I hate to cut your lecture short, but we've got big problems. I need to see Geezer. I need his help."

CHAPTER 35

Chloe and I return to our underground base early the next morning, just in time to receive updates about Max's big plan. Both Chloe and I have been sidelined and neither of us are happy. We both descend into the spy zone to argue with Max.

"I want in," I demand.

"Yeah, me too!" Chloe says.

Max studies the video feed of the city. He doesn't look at us.

"Max!"

"I heard you the first time," he murmurs.

"Well?" Chloe whines.

"You're both staying here."

"I thought you don't discriminate," she fires back, "I know I'm only ten but I'm one of your best fighters."

Max ignores her.

"How's the stab wound?" he asks me.

"Not bleeding anymore. What can I do?"

"Watch Chloe."

"I thought you don't discriminate," I say, copying Chloe.

Max turns to look at me then. "I thought you didn't like the plan."

I don't but I definitely won't like sitting on my butt while everyone else risks their lives. Before I can respond again, he repeats, "Watch Chloe."

His eyes soften before he turns back to look at the cameras. He doesn't acknowledge us again. I know Max is protecting Chloe. He really seems to care about her. But what's his real reason for keeping me out of the fight? It can't just be because I'm injured.

Chloe runs back up the stairs vowing she'll never speak to Max again. His eyes flicker in her direction but he quickly resumes his work. I start to follow her when he calls me.

"I like you, Red, and I know you'll do right by Chloe. She looks up to you."

"Don't try to pacify me," I snap, still not buying his reasoning. I storm out of the room and up the stairs, but a strong hand covers my mouth and nose with a strange smelling cloth. Inhaling a whiff of the chemicals, my eyes begin to sting.

"Ollie would kill me if I let you die," Max says.

My body goes limp before my mind even registers that I'm losing consciousness, but I know what I hear.

I wake up swinging, but no one is holding a chemical laced rag to my face anymore.

"Max said you passed out again," comes Chloe's concerned voice.

"I'm fine," I tell her, not wanting to admit that Max drugged me and lied about it.

"You were out for a few hours. Mostly everyone's gone, everyone with rank anyway. Everyone else is stuck here guarding our base or the school, trying not to worry about what's going on."

"Where's Max?"

Chloe shrugs, "He came up from the spy zone and took off before I could ask any questions."

I glance at the alarm clock beside our bed on the nightstand. 8:08 PM.

"Come on," I say, getting a sudden idea.

I open the hidden door in the bookshelf and race down the stairs. We are almost to the bottom when we hear a big rumble and the ground starts shaking. Dust flies forming a smoky cloud around our heads. We both look at each other when the dust clears.

"What was that?" Chloe wonders.

I don't answer her but hurry as fast as my injury and my lifting chemical haze will allow. The lights and camera feed are automatic in the spy zone and there is no lock or code on any of the equipment. I look at the camera feed. Errants are running down the tunnels along every direction and in every camera. Some ceilings have caved in and walls are disheveled.

Chloe takes to the other cameras stationed around the city and no sooner does she lay eyes on it than she screams and starts crying. Alarmed, I turn to see what's going on, only I'm not prepared for what happens. Max's plan is falling apart just like I hoped it wouldn't. Dead bodies crowd the camera feed at just about every angle in almost every location and those who aren't dead are surrounded by men in black military gear and face masks. They've got guns in every hand and extra weapons strapped to their sides. Some Errants try to run. Others try to fight, but in the end, they are all littered with bullets.

A tremor rocks our underground headquarters. Tunnels collapse, smashing some victims before they even know what's going on. Whatever pathways aren't blocked are being overrun with men identical to the ones who attacked Errants within the city. I may not know all the details, but I know this isn't what Max had planned. Our compound isn't supposed to be in shambles. Our people aren't supposed to die.

"What're we supposed to do?" Chloe asks, "Where's Max?"

The better question is: how did this happen? I can't help but wonder if Max's inside man double crossed us, gave bad information then partnered with the hunters to get rid of us in one sweep.

"We've gotta get out of here," I say.

"And go where?" Chloe asks.

There are tears in her eyes, but she looks angrier than afraid.

I search the cameras for an open and clear path free of flying bullets and unstable tunnelways. I start to open the exit route that leads to the subway through spy zone, but an aggressive pounding from the other side of the door makes me look at the cameras again. More men with guns, all dressed in black military style clothing are on the other side. They're trying to block all exits. That leaves one route I'd rather not travel. But we have no other choice. I'm not exactly in shape to fight and Chloe's just a kid, a kid I've been left to protect. I can't let anything happen to her.

I grab her hand and we race up the stairs back to the room and to the nearest dorm hole. I push Chloe in just as we hear a round of gunshots. The air is hot with smoke and burning flesh. There are screams. I force myself into the hole after her, trying to ignore the burning pain in my abdomen. If I make one wrong move, the stitches could bust, and I could start bleeding again. I don't know if I'm going to be able to crawl down the long, dark, tight pathway. My body is tired. I can barely keep my eyes open. By the time I make it to the end of the tunnel, Chloe has to squeeze past me to pull me out.

"You're going to have to lead us out from here. I'm not sure where the exit is," I tell her.

Chloe takes my hand and leads me slowly to the exit.

"You're bleeding," she notes.

Before I can dismiss the pain or severity, she hefts me up on her shoulders and takes off running. She's not as fast as some Errants, probably because I'm twice her size, but we emerge quickly from the cave and the tunnels. I try to stay conscious and alert, but I can feel my eyes growing heavy.

My mind drifts as Chloe takes us out of a building I don't recognize. My eyes blur. I can barely see in front of me, but I don't really care. At least we're out of the compound, unlike many of the others.

"We've gotta find Max. He can keep us safe," Chloe murmurs.

Finding a doctor would probably be a better idea. All I want to do is sit down and close my eyes.

"Doc's. We need to go there."

Chloe pauses but she nods racing us to Chinatown. This time I do close my eyes and when I open them again, my bandage is fresh and clean. My stitches are resewn. I sit up slowly and ease my way out of bed.

"Get back to bed. You can't go out there," comes Doc's voice.

"Where's Chloe?" Doc doesn't answer. "Doc, where is she?"

"Central Park."

"Max is there," I guess.

"Max and some of the Fleet are fighting the hunters at Central Park. My clinic's full of people who don't look like they're going to make it through the night."

Tears roll down his face. "Each of the hunters led their own private team at all the underground Fleet locations. They caved in all the exits with small, hardwired explosives to flush everyone out and used tear gas to disorient them before they attacked. Santos used his connections to employ private soldiers to fight for him. Max and the others are fighting them. Geezer, K.O., Tristan and Rox are there too."

I wipe my tears away with the back of my hand. "What do you mean? Are they-"

He shakes his head. "Not yet, but it doesn't look good."

"And you let Chloe go?"

Chloe has no business being there. If my stab wound doesn't kill me, Max certainly will.

"I'm doing what I can, Savannah!"

As much as I want to blame Doc for letting her run into danger, I can't. Chloe's not his responsibility. She's mine. If anything happens to her, it's my fault. I force myself out of bed, my body protesting with each move.

Doc's eyes widen. "Savannah, you're not in any shape to-"

"I can't leave Chloe or any of my friends."

I'm not nearly as strong as they are, but I've come a long way, and after everything they've done for me, I'm not laying around while they fight for their lives. I may not be the best, most skilled Errant, but there's no more denying the power I do have.

Doc looks like he wants to argue, but he sets his lips firmly in a narrow line. "You do what you have to."

"I will."

I make my way to the door and Doc calls out to me one more time.

"I don't know your parents, but if they're good people, I'm sure they'd be proud of you. I know I am."

I offer him the best smile. "I hope so."

Walking out of the clinic, I steady myself like I did in my fight with Chloe. My anxiety builds. My nerves electrify. But I don't mistake it as a weakness anymore. I let it boil over and spread throughout my entire body, harnessing it into strength. Power replaces my pain, even if just for a small window in time. I breathe in deeply, and when I exhale, I take off.

CHAPTER 36

Central Park is a warzone. Bullet shells, weapons, and bodies cover the ground. Max's Fleet move like fireflies, flitting around at blurred, nearly insubstantial speed. There are dozens of fully armed soldiers that appear frozen, until I look closer. Compared to the Fleet, they move in slow motion. They're no match for the Fleet, who easily disarm and stun them. In the wide-open space, Errants have the advantage. The real trouble comes from the hunters. I recognize them almost immediately, even though they're dressed in the same military gear as the hired soldiers. The hunters are stony sentinels, strong, and unyielding, but fluid enough to anticipate our power. Posers. They remind me of cats waiting for the mice to get tired of running, and if the Fleet keep going at their current rate, they're sure to burn out soon.

So many of the Fleet are already down and so few are left. Rox, Tattoo, and Mohawk work against a graceful figure who eases out of attacks with languid precision. Tattoo is the first to crash with exhaustion, falling hard to the ground. His opponent strikes like a serpent.

"No!"

I run toward them. Fueled by desperation I dive forward, connecting successfully with my mark. I ran into the hunter as they slam their blade into Tattoo's hand. His scream echoes the hunter's, a woman from the sound of her voice, as she flies through the air and slams into the hired soldiers. I scramble to get back on my feet, my injuries burning, while desperately searching for a weapon. Rox tears the hunter's dagger out of Tattoo's hand and tosses it in my direction. It whizzes past my head and into the body of another hunter, right in the center of their forehead.

I try to shake away dark floaters, to clear my vision, but my head tingles, and the world around me spins at three different speeds. Cold sweat spreads across my face and down my limbs. The logical part of me wishes I had stayed back at Doc's. The other part of me, the part of myself I'm just now discovering, welcomes the pain and the chaos.

Then I see him, and I freeze. K.O. is as savage as he is beautiful. His movements are so graceful it's almost as if he's dancing. He's got a machete in one hand and a gun in the other. He shoots a stocky bald man in the forehead and moves to behead him with the blade, but then he looks up and our eyes meet. He stops mid-swing. That's all the distraction it takes for another man to attack. I dive at his attacker, a regular soldier, forcing him to the ground.

K.O.'s dark eyes shine, and he does the unthinkable. He smiles, a small quirk of his mouth that makes me forget we're in the fight of our lives. His smile drops almost as sudden as it appears, and he opens his mouth to speak. Whatever he would've said is interrupted when tear gas explodes and screams sound.

"Chloe."

I need to find Chloe. I promised Max I'd keep her safe. I break away from K.O., stumbling half blind through the chaos.

Smoke bursts in a thick cloud, burning my eyes. For a moment I'm disoriented.

I drop to the ground, feeling my way along the grass for a weapon, anything that can protect me. Just as my fingers wrap around a curved hunting knife, the smoke dissipates enough for me to regain some focus. I squint through the haze, ignoring the burning irritation in my eyes, just in time to see Chloe in the distance. Her face is covered in dirt and soot. She's coughing, and a soldier hovers over her while she struggles to recover. The soldier pulls on Chloe's arm, forcing a gun out of her small hands.

On instinct, I kick up my speed, knocking into her attacker. My head swims and my vision blurs but I press on. Chloe recovers and runs off. The soldier grabs my arm before I can chase after her. I swing before I think and the hunting knife slices through their tactical gear, the blade slicing into tender flesh. This isn't a hunter. A hunter wouldn't be caught off guard so easily. There's no way it would be so simple to kill one of them, not if they're anything like Santos. A strangled cry escapes a bloody mouth. The soldier collapses to the ground.

This isn't the real enemy. The soldiers are just pawns. I take a closer look at the soldier, a young woman. Her face mask is broken from the impact of my attack, and her golden hair spills out, mixing with the blood from the wound I've caused. The woman opens her mouth to speak but I can't make out her words. She reaches for me and I stumble backward, lips trembling. She tries to speak again, "Sa… Sa…"

Blood pours out of her mouth and she grips her throat. Guilt weighs down heavily, draining the adrenaline and fight out of me. Wounding and even killing a hunter is different.

There's a possibility their death isn't permanent. Whoever this woman is, there's no bringing her back to life, and that's something I'll have to live with, if I can make it out of here at all. I take the gun she took from Chloe before haunching over to vomit.

I look through the blood and chaos. My vision doubles but I don't care. Then I find Max, bent over and on his knees, covered in blood. He's holding someone in his arms, someone who isn't moving, and there are tears in his eyes. It's Chloe. I rush towards them, grateful to notice the rise and fall of her chest. She's breathing. She's alive but she has a nasty gash in her side.

A helicopter arrives, and a team of soldiers drop down to retrieve the bodies of the two fallen immortals, while the rest cover their retreat with an unrelenting line of bullets. It's time for a retreat of our own. Max shields me as I hold Chloe close to my chest and before I know it, he's lifting Chloe out of my arms. He grabs for me too, but Mohawk stops him. "I've got her."

He hoists me over his back and just as I lock eyes with K.O., Mohawk races after Max. I want to scream for them to leave me. I want to stay with K.O., but I don't have any more strength to fight.

We don't go back to the underground hideout. It's been destroyed. The only safe place left is Doc's. Mohawk stoops to the ground and helps me carefully off his back. I nod my thanks at him, not expecting the hug that follows.

"I'm sorry I stabbed you." he says.

I don't know how to respond, but thankfully, a heavy-handed tap on my shoulder saves me from rambling. It's

Tattoo. He waves his freshly wrapped, injured hand at me. "We treated you bad, but you saved my life tonight. Thank you, Sister."

"We won't challenge you again," Mohawk says, "And anyone who tries will have to answer to us."

They've gone from being my bullies to brothers. I guess that's what war does. We've suffered so much loss tonight. Our homes. Our friends. We almost lost our lives. Not one person who has survived tonight is without scars or injuries. It was a blood bath. But rather than admit his failure, Max stubbornly clings to the idea that we made big strides and that the sacrifices were worth the small victory we obtained.

"What victory? The Posers we killed are coming back. All we did was provoke them," Emery mutters to another member of the Fleet, "Max has done a lot for us, but he might not be the best leader when it comes to facing the hunters. He's got a lot to answer for."

I frown, listening as Emery hovers over other Errants. We don't need more division right now. We need to heal. I take a step in his direction, but a hand grips my shoulder. It's Max.

"Don't waste time on Emery. He's been trying to work up the nerve to challenge me for some months now."

His voice is light. He even chuckles. "Nice work, by the way."

I bite my lip to keep from crying. "How can you say that? You gave me one job, and I couldn't even do that right. Chloe–"

"– is tough and she'll make a full recovery," Max interrupts.

I wipe my eyes, hoping he doesn't see the tears that manage to break through, but Max is observant. "What's really going on, Red?"

A few more tears escape. I wipe at them again, and then at my runny nose. I've always been such an ugly mess when I cry.

"I–I killed someone. Not one of the hunters."

Saying the words out loud doesn't make me feel better. It makes the reality of what I did harder to ignore.

In that moment, K.O., Geezer, Tristan and Rox arrive at Doc's. They're all dirty and bloody like us, but they're alive. K.O.'s eyes meet mine. I turn my back to him.

Max leans into me, nudging my shoulder, and he whispers, "If anyone's at fault, it's the hunters. Blame them and blame me. No one here in this room has more blood on their hands than I do."

I don't try to convince him of anything different. He's right. A lot of people are dead because of his ambition, his arrogance and reckless behavior, but I can't blame him for something I've done. He wasn't holding the knife that killed that woman. I was.

"H–how do you deal with the guilt?"

He lets out a heavy sigh. "Sometimes survival isn't pretty. It leaves stains and scars that aren't visible on your skin. Some will never go away or heal completely but others can, if you let them."

Max takes me by the shoulders, turns me around and gives me a firm push forward. "Now, pull yourself together, Red. We've got company."

I look up, ready to deal with K.O., but I see Tristan and Rox rushing toward me instead. Rox pushes Tristan out of her way and grips me up in a hug so tight she lifts me off my feet.

"We were so worried about you."

I wince when she drops me on my feet.

Tristan looks at my arms. "Look at you. Look at those guns. You look good."

"Good as in alive," Rox clarifies, "Your roots are showing."

I wipe away the last of my tears and smile at her. "We just survived an epic beatdown and you're going to talk about my roots?"

She laughs and pulls me in for another hug. "I missed you too, Savannah."

"We're proud of you Scarlett," comes Geezer's voice, "Heard you were something out there."

He flashes me one of those quick, bright smiles, but I don't smile back. I don't remember seeing him at Central Park and it bothers me. "Where were you tonight?"

His face is colored in bruises and the way he holds his hands in his pockets and his shoulders hunched gives me the impression that he's in a lot of pain. "Santos. I'm sorry I couldn't- I thought that if I could just- that you could get out of all this and go back to your mom. I couldn't get to him. We're still not safe."

"You went after Santos for me?"

"For all of us, but it wasn't enough," he says.

"He almost got himself killed," Tristan tells me.

"Did not. I knew what I was doing," Geezer snaps back.

I throw my arms around him. "I'm just glad you're alive."

He stiffens and eases his way out of my hug. Tristan catches him in a headlock and ruffles his hair. "Same here."

Rox kisses Geezer's cheek and his face turns red as we round him up in a big group hug.

"Guys, that's enough. I get it. Stop it." he says, even as he returns the hug.

Doc steps in the middle of the room, announcing the food and sleeping arrangements. He requests we take a moment of silence for everyone who didn't make it out of the attack alive. Out of all the Errants we started with, only a rough handful are left. Our numbers are sobering. Even Emery stops campaigning long enough to comply, and like everyone else remains silent long after the moment has passed. Everyone retreats to the sleeping quarters. Those who are wounded the most get priority and take the hospital beds. Everyone else sleeps on worn gym mats a few Errants managed to scrounge from a nearby rec center's storage.

As wounded and exhausted as I am, I can't sleep. I need space. I need fresh air to help me wind down before I can even think about resting and healing. The night is silent for once. Tonight's attack has stained the entire city, something the media explains as an escalated drug and gang war. I wonder what they would think if they knew what was really going on.

As tired as my mind and body are, my thoughts keep straying to the only person I haven't talked to tonight. Standing in the streets of Chinatown I look into the dark as K.O. emerges. He approaches me cautiously. It almost looks painful for him to walk. His face, though bruised, is still handsome.

He searches my face and reaches out tentatively to touch my cheeks. His touch is so light I barely feel the heat of his fingers. Then he pulls me into a tight embrace. Tired numbness wears off quickly, and pain rushes to the forefront. Even though it hurts, I don't want him to let me go.

"You're alive. You're alright," he says.

"Barely. Kind of." I say, resting in his arms, as the pain, guilt, and exhaustion take a backseat to something I can't quite put my finger on. It's an uncomfortably wonderful feeling. It scares me as much as it excites me.

I breathe in the smell of his dirty leather jacket, gathering courage to say all the things I haven't had the chance to say until now. "K.O., I"

"I want you," he says, his confession cutting my own words short. I pull away from him, not sure I heard right. His eyes go wide and for moment he fishes helplessly for words. "I mean; I want you to stay."

He rushes on, not giving me the chance to speak. "You said you needed us, but that we didn't need you. I wanted you to stay, but I didn't think you wanted to or that you would once your training was over. So, I didn't tell you how I felt."

He quiets, and his eyes dart across my face searching for an answer to a question he hasn't asked. I search for words of my own, completely caught off guard. My nerves dance under my skin.

K.O. nods as if my silence is what he expected. He rubs his face and turns away from me. It's only then that I manage to find my voice. "Why would someone like you want someone like me around? I'm nothing but a problem for you."

His hair veils his face, so I can't read his expression, but he sighs and turns to me with a shrug. "I can't give you a single reason that makes sense."

He pushes his hair out of his face, and his gaze lightly touches mine. "I don't know. Maybe it's the way you danced all over my feet or the way you ran that sink water over your hair to make it curl."

My cheeks burn, but a small flicker of a smile touches his lips.

"It could be how fearless you looked ghosting through the train or how you ran with me right after falling off the Empire State Building. And the leather jacket. I liked the leather jacket."

I cover my face with my hands. "I'm far from fearless and I looked ridiculous in that leather jacket."

His hands touch mine, pulling them away from my face. "Not to me."

His hands are shaking. So are mine.

"Why'd you leave?" I ask.

"Max was missing. I thought finding him would be the perfect way to avoid you, but then you went missing too."

"When the Fleet rescued me and Max, I wanted it to be you."

"I looked for you," he said.

He closes the distance between us and we're so close I can feel his breath tickle my face. I know I should say something or do something, but I'm paralyzed. My mouth is dry from hanging open and I can hardly breathe, let alone think." You told me not to expect you to keep saving me."

"I wanted to. I tried," he says.

I bite my lip. "I know, but you were right. It wasn't fair to you. To any of you."

"Savannah, I know what I said, but when I realized Santos had you, none of that mattered. You have a place with us, if you want, but we understand if you want to be with your mom. It's not safe now, but we'll get you home. We can figure something out."

I find my voice again. "I can't go home, but I can't leave with you either."

K.O. frowns. "Geezer told me everything. You don't have to stay with Max."

"Red's free to go where she wants, Ollie." comes Max's voice from behind K.O. He walks slow and confident to stand beside me and drapes an arm around my shoulder. I shrug him off and he chuckles, amused by the discomfort between me and K.O. It doesn't make what I need to say any easier.

"I'm tired of running. I'm staying with the Fleet," I say.

Max is right about one thing. Running won't keep us alive forever. His methods are far from perfect, but something needs to be done.

K.O. nods. "You don't need us anymore. I get it."

He turns his back to me, and I reach for him. Max stops me and shakes his head as K.O. let's out a sharp whistle. Geezer, Rox, and Tristan appear at his side.

K.O. steps forward to meet Max head to head. "A lot of people died tonight because your plan failed. I'm not going to let Savannah or anyone else be another one of your casualties."

Max cocks his head to the side. "What's the plan, Ollie. Are you going to keep begging Savannah to run away with you? She's not a coward like you. "

"I'm not running anymore," K.O. says.

"None of us are," Geezer agrees. Tristan and Rox stand firm beside them.

Max pins his gaze on K.O. "So, what. You plan on challenging me now, Ollie?"

K.O. grits his teeth and Max's fists tighten. I hold my breath, wondering who will throw the first punch or who will win. They're equally fierce and equally stubborn. I can't see either one admitting defeat, and at a time like this, we can't afford two of our strongest fighters to be at each other's throats. I draw in a breath to stop them before they start, though I'm not sure either of them will hear me.

"We don't want to fight you. We're joining you," K.O. says.

For a long moment, Max keeps his guarded stance. His confidence wavers. I'm shocked myself. But then a smile creeps up on Max's face. "Well, well, brother. Welcome to the Fleet."

What's left of it. I think.

We've lost a lot tonight, but there's still so much more to lose. I have family. I have friends now. I finally know who I am and what I could be. I've finally found my place, my purpose, and my own power, and I'll do whatever it takes to keep it.

Tonight, is only the beginning. Tonight, we lost the battle, but tomorrow's war is brewing. We've all got to be ready. I don't know if we'll survive against the impossible odds we face, but I know that we're stronger together.

ACKNOWLEDGEMENTS

To everyone who made this work possible:

Readers, I hope you feel the love leaping off the pages. If you enjoyed reading Savannah's story, please spread the word. Your reviews and recommendations matter!

To my family, friends, and loved ones, thank you for all your support, prayers, and love. I couldn't have made it this far without you.

To everyone who read and loved this story long before it was ready to be shared, thank you.

Thank you to everyone who worked with me to turn this beastly work into a beauty.

To the Greatest Author & Creator. *With God, all things are possible.*

ABOUT THE AUTHOR

Montrez is a fantasy and science fiction author who lives in the moody Midwest with her husband and two sons. She loves writing about extraordinary worlds hidden in the folds of ordinary places and everyday life.

Don't be a stranger! Join the Novel Creature Community at authormontrez.com for all the latest updates and exciting giveaways.